THE DARK AT THE END OF THE TUNNEL

The giant night-preying rats had not been destroyed as most of humanity thought. They had been driven underground to breed and create their huge subterranean empire, and to await the time when their human enemy weakened his guard.

Now their time had come. The Bombs had exploded above ground. Survivors who poured into the tunnels and carefully prepared underground complexes thought they were ready for this emergency. Culver, Dealey and Kate searched frantically for the door that would lead them to the special shelter for the government elite, but all they could hear were sounds they couldn't identify. "It's getting closer," Dealey hissed in the darkness of the tunnel they were moving through. He sounded desperate, almost tearful.

Little did he or the others know that for the first time in earth's history, human beings had lost the upper hand. The rats were swarming in for the kill . . .

DOMAIN

Great Fiction From SIGNET

JAMES HERBERT
DOMAIN

A SIGNET BOOK

NEW AMERICAN LIBRARY

NAL BOOKS ARE AVAILABLE AT QUANTITITY DISCOUNTS WHEN USED TO PROMOTE PRODUCTS OR SERVICES. FOR INFORMATION PLEASE WRITE TO PREMIUM MARKETING DIVISION, NEW AMERICAN LIBRARY, 1633 BROADWAY, NEW YORK, NEW YORK 10019.

SIGNET TRADEMARK REG. U.S. PAT OFF. AND FOREIGN COUNTRIES
REGISTERED TRADEMARK—MARCA REGISTRADA
HECHO EN CHICAGO. U.S.A.

SIGNET, SIGNET CLASSIC, MENTOR, PLUME,
MERIDIAN and NAL BOOKS
are published by New American Library,
1633 Broadway, New York, New York 10019
First Printing, March, 1985

1 2 3 4 5 6 7 8 9

PRINTED IN THE UNITED STATES OF AMERICA

PLACE: LONDON

TIME: 12:37

DAY: TUESDAY

MONTH: JUNE

YEAR: THE NOT-TOO-DISTANT FUTURE . . .

DOMAIN

PART ONE

ADVENT

They scurried through the darkness, shadowy creatures living in permanent night.

They had learned to become still, to be the darkness, when the huge monsters roared above and filled the tunnels with thunder, assaulting the black refuge—their cold, damp sanctuary—with rushing lights and deadly crushing weight. They would cower as the ground beneath them shook, the walls around them trembled; and they would wait until the rushing thing had passed, not afraid but necessarily wary, for it was an inveterate invader, one that killed the careless.

They had learned to keep within the confines of their underworld, to venture out only when their own comforting darkness was sistered with the darkness above. For they had a distant race memory of an enemy, a being whose purpose was to destroy them. A being who existed in the upper regions where there was vast dazzling light, a place that could be explored safely only when the brilliance diminished and succumbed to concealing and pleasurable blackness.

They had learned to be timid in exploration, never moving far from their sanctum. They fed on night creatures like themselves, and often came upon food that was not warm, that did not struggle against the

11

stinging caress of the creatures' jaws. The taste was not as exciting as the moist and tepid moving flesh, but it filled their stomachs. It sustained them.

Yet in this, too, they were cautious, never taking too much, never returning to the same source, for they possessed an innate cunning, engendered by something more than fear of their natural enemy; it was an evolvement accelerated by something that had happened to their species many years before. An event that had changed their pattern of progression. And made them alien even to those of their own nature.

They had learned to keep to the depths. To kill other creatures, but never to leave remains. And when there was not enough food, they ate each other. For they were many—black, bristling beasts with huge, humped hindquarters and long, jagged incisors, their eyes pointed and yellow. They sniffed at the dank air, and a deep instinct within craved for a different scent, a scent that they did not yet know was the sweet odor of running blood. Human blood. They would know it soon.

The sound started as a low rumbling, quickly becoming a great roar, shaking their underworld, renting the darkness with its violence, tearing at the walls, the roof, causing the ground to rise up and throw the creatures into scrambling heaps. They lashed out at one another, clawing, gouging, snapping frenziedly with razor teeth.

Dust, fumes, sound, filled the air.

Rumbling, building, becoming a shrieking.

The world and its underworld shivering.

Screaming.

The creatures ran through the turbulence, black-furred bodies striving to reach their inner sanctum within the tunnel network. Fighting to exist, deafened by the noise, squealing their panic, desperate to return to the Mother Creature and her strange cohorts.

The man-made caverns shuddered but resisted the unleashed pressure from the world above. Sections collapsed, others were flooded, but the main body of tunnels withstood the impacts that pounded the city.

And after a while, the silence returned.

Save for the scurrying of many, many clawed feet.

The first bomb exploded just a few thousand feet above Hyde Park, its energy release, in the forms of radiation, light, heat, sound, and blast, the equivalent of one million tons of TNT. The sirens that had warned of the missile and its ensuing companions' approach were but a thin squeal to the giant roar of its arrival. .

Within two-thousandth of a second after the initial blinding flash of light, the explosion had become a small searing ball of vapor with a temperature of eighteen million degrees Fahrenheit, a newborn mini-sun of no material substance.

The fireball, ghostly luminous, immediately began to expand, the air around it heated by compression and quickly losing its power as a shield against the ultraviolet radiation. The rapidly growing fiery nucleus pushed at the torrid air, producing a spherical acoustic shock front that began to travel faster than its creator, masking the fireball's full fury.

As the shock front spread, its progenitor followed, quickly dispersing a third of its total energy. The fireball grew larger, almost half a mile in diameter, leaving behind a vacuum and beginning to lose its luminosity. It started to spin inward, rising at an incredible speed, forming a ring of smoke that carried debris and fission-produced radioactive isotopes.

Dust was sucked from the earth as the swirling vortex reached upward, dust that became contaminated by the deadly, man-activated rays, rising high into the skies, later to settle on the destroyed city as lethal fallout.

The angry cloud, with its stem of white heat, was more than six miles high and still rising, banishing the noonday sun, when the next missile detonated its warhead.

Four more megaton bombs were soon to follow. . . .

1

As the heat wave spread out from the rising fireball,
everything flammable and any lightweight material burst
into flame. The scorching heat tore through the streets,
melting solids, incinerating people or charring them to
black crisps, killing every exposed living thing within a ra-
dius of three miles. Within seconds, the blast wave, traveling at the speed of sound and accompanied by winds of up
to two hundred miles per hour, followed.

Buildings crumbled, the debris released as deadly missiles. Glass flowed with the winds in millions of slicing
shards. Vehicles—cars, buses, anything not secured to the
ground—were tossed into the air like windblown leaves,
falling to crush and maim. People were lifted from their
feet and thrown into the sides of collapsing buildings. Intense blast pressure ruptured lungs, eardrums, and internal organs. Lampposts became javelins of concrete or
metal. Broken electricity cables became dancing snakes of
death. Water mains burst and became fountains of

bubbling steam. Gas mains became part of the overall explosion. Everything became part of the unleashed fury.

Farther out, houses and buildings filled with high-pressure air, and as the blast passed on to be followed by a low-pressure wave, the structures exploded outward. Anyone caught in the open had their clothes burned off and received third-degree burns from which they could never recover. Others were buried beneath buildings, some to die instantly, many to lie beneath the rubble, slowly suffocating or suffering long, lingering deaths from their injuries.

One fire joined another to become a destructive conflagration.

Alex Dealey was running, his breathing labored, perspiration already staining the white shirt beneath his gray suit. He hung on to the briefcase almost unconsciously, as if it mattered anymore that ''sensitive'' government documents could be found lying in the street. Or among the rubble that would be all that was left. He should have taken a taxi, or a bus even; that way he would have arrived at his destination long ago. He would have been safe. But it had been a nice, warm June day, the kind of day when walking was preferable to riding in enclosed transport. It wasn't such a nice day any longer, even though the sun was still high and bright.

He resisted the temptation to duck into one of the many office buildings that flanked High Holborn, to scurry down into one of their cool, protective basements; there was still time to make it. He would be so much better off if he reached his proposed destination, so much safer. Also, it was his duty to be there at such a catastrophic and, of course, historic occasion. Oh, God, was he that far down the bureaucratic road that he could mentally refer to *this* as historic? Even though he was only a minion to the ruling powers, his mind, his outlook, had been tainted with their cold, logical—inhuman?—perceptions. And he had certainly enjoyed the privileges his office had brought him; perhaps the most important privilege of all lay just ahead. If only he had time to reach it . . .

Someone in front, a woman, tripped and fell, and Dealey tumbled over her. The pavement jarred his hands and knees and for a moment he could only lie there, protecting his face from the moving feet and legs around him. The noise was terrible: the shouts and screams of office ers caught out in the open, the constant belling of car s, their progress halted by other abandoned vehicles, ...e owners having fled leaving engines still running. The awful banshee sirens, their rising and falling a mind-freezing, heart-gripping ululation, full of precognitive mourning of what was soon . . .

They had stopped! The sirens had stopped!

For one brief, eerie moment there was almost complete silence as people halted and wondered if it had all been a false alarm, even a demented hoax. But there were those among the crowd who realized the true significance of the abrupt cessation of the alert; these people pushed their way through to the nearest doorways and disappeared inside. Panic broke out once more as others began to understand that the holocaust was but moments away.

A motorcycle mounted the pavement and cut a scything path through the crowds, scattering men and women, catching those not swift enough and tossing them aside like struck skittles. The rider failed to see the prostrate woman whom Dealey had fallen over. The front wheel hit her body and the machine rose into the air, the rider, with his sinister black visor muting his cry, rising even higher.

Dealey cowered low to the ground as the motorcycle flipped over, its owner now finding his own course of flight and breaking through the plate-glass window of a shopfront. Sparks and metal flew from the machine as it struck the solid base of the window frame. It came to rest half in, half out of the display window, smoke belching from the stuttering engine, its metal twisted and buckled.

The rider moaned as blood seeped down his neck from inside the cracked helmet.

Dealey was already on his feet and running, not caring about the woman left writhing on the pavement, not even mindful of the lost briefcase with its precious documents, only grateful that he had escaped injury and even more anxious to quickly reach his particular refuge.

The Underground station, Chancery Lane, was not too far away, and the sight gave him new hope. His destination was not far beyond.

Too soon the world was a blinding white flash, and fo ishly, for he, of all people, really should have known ter, Dealey turned to look at its source.

He stood there paralyzed, sightless, and screaming inwardly, waiting for the inevitable.

The thunderous, earsplitting roar came, but the inevitable did not. Instead, he felt rough hands grab him and his body being propelled backward. His shoulders crashed against something that gave way and he was being dragged along. He felt himself falling, something, perhaps someone, falling with him. The earth was shaking, the noise deafening, the walls collapsing.

And then there was no longer burning white pain in his eyes, just the cool darkness of unconsciousness.

The initial nuclear explosions lasted only a few minutes. The black mushroom clouds rose high above the devastated city, joining to form a thick layer of turbulent smoke that made the day seem as night.

It wasn't long before the gathered dust and fine debris began its leisurely descent back to earth. But now it was no longer just dust and powder. Now it was a further, more sinister harbinger of death.

2

He kicked out at the debris that had covered his legs, and was relieved to find nothing solid had pinned them down. He coughed, spitting dust from his lungs, then wiped a hand across his eyes to clear them. There was still some light filtering through into the basement corridor. Culver groaned when he saw smoke filtering through with the light.

He turned toward the man he had dragged in from the street, hoping he hadn't killed him in the fall down the stairway. The man was moving, his hands feebly reaching for his face; there was debris and a fine layer of dust over his body, but nothing too solid seemed to have landed on him. He began to splutter, choking on the fine powder he had swallowed.

Culver reached toward him, groaning at the sudden pain that touched his own body. He quickly checked himself, making sure nothing important was fractured or broken. No, everything felt okay, although he knew he would be stiff with bruises the next day . . . if there was a next day.

He tugged at the other man's shoulder. "You all right?" he asked, twice attempting the question because it had come out as a croak the first time.

A low moan was the only reply.

Culver looked toward the broken staircase and was puzzled by the sound he heard. As more dust and smoke swirled into the openings, he realized he could hear a wind.

He recalled reading somewhere that winds of up to two hundred miles an hour would follow a nuclear blast, creating an aftermath of more death and destruction. He felt the building shifting around him and curled himself into a tight ball when masonry began to fall once again.

Pieces struck his brown leather jacket, one large enough to cause his body to jerk in pain. A huge concrete slab that half-covered the staircase started to move, sliding farther down the wall its bulk leaned against. Culver grabbed the other man's shoulders, ready to pull him away from the advancing segments. Fortunately, the concrete settled once more with a grinding moan.

There was not much to see through the gaping holes of the ceiling above and Culver guessed that the upper floors of the building—he couldn't recall how many stories the office building had, but most of the buildings in that area were high—had collapsed. They had been lucky: he was sure they had fallen close to the central concrete service column, the strongest part of any modern structure, which had protected them from the worst of the demolition. How long it would hold was another matter. And the choking smoke meant another problem was on its way.

Culver tugged at the shoulder nearby. "Hey." He repeated his original question. "You okay?"

The man twisted his body and pushed himself up on one elbow. He mumbled something. Then he moaned long and loud, his body rocking to and fro. "Oh, no, the stupid idiots really did it. The stupid, stupid . . ."

"Yeah, they did it," Culver replied in a low voice, "but there are other things to worry about right now."

"Where are we? What is this place?" The man began to scrabble around, kicking at the rubble, trying to get to his feet.

"Take it easy." Culver placed a hand around the man's upper arm and gripped tightly. "Just listen."

Both men lay there in the gloom.

"I . . . I can't hear anything," the man said after a while.

"That's just it. The wind's stopped. It's passed by." Culver gingerly rose to his knees, examining the wreckage above and around them. It had seemed silent at first, then the rending of twisted metal, the grinding and crashing of concrete, came to their ears. It was followed by the whimpers and soon the screams of the injured or those who were in shock. Something metallic clattered down from above and Culver winced as it landed a few feet away.

"We've got to get out of here," he told his companion. "The whole lot's going to come down soon." He moved closer so that his face was only inches away from the other man. It was difficult to distinguish his features in the gloom.

"If only we could see a way out," the man said. "We could be buried alive down here."

Culver was puzzled. He stared into the other's eyes. "Can't you see anything?"

"It's too dark. Oh, no, not that!"

"When I grabbed you out on the street, you were looking straight into the flash. I thought you were just shocked. I didn't realize—"

The man was rubbing at his eyes with his fingers. "Oh, God, I'm blind!"

"It may be only temporary."

The injured man seemed to take little comfort in the words. His body was shaking uncontrollably.

The smell of burning was strong now and Culver could see a flickering glow from above.

He slumped back against the wall. "Either way we're beat," he said, almost to himself. "If we go outside, we'll be hit by fallout; if we stay here, we'll be fried or crushed to death. Great choice." The bottom of his clenched fist thumped the floor.

He felt hands scrabbling at the lapels of his jacket. "No, not yet. There's still a chance. If you could just get me there, there'd be a chance."

"Get you where?" Culver grabbed the man's wrists and pulled them from him. "The world's just a flat ruin up there. Don't you understand? There's nothing left! And the air will be thick with radioactive dust."

"Not yet. It will take at least twenty to thirty minutes for the fallout to settle to the ground. How long have we been down here?"

"I'm not sure. It could be ten minutes, it could be an hour—I may have blacked out. No, wait. We heard the winds caused by the blast; they would have followed soon after the explosion."

"Then there's a chance. If we hurry!"

"Where to? There's no place to go."

"I know somewhere where we'll be safe."

"You mean the Underground station? The tunnels?"

"Safer than that."

"What the hell are you talking about? Where?"

"I can direct you."

"Just tell me where."

The man was silent. Then he repeated. "I can direct you."

Culver sighed wearily. "Don't worry, I'm not going to leave you here. You sure about the fallout?"

"I'm certain. But we'll have to move fast." The man's

panic appeared to be over for the moment, although his movements were still agitated.

Something overhead began a rending shift. Both men tensed.

"I think the decision is about to be made for us."

Culver grabbed the other man below his shoulder and began to pull him toward the dimly lit staircase. The huge slab of concrete lying at an angle across the broken stairs began to move again.

"We haven't got much time!" Culver shouted. "The whole bloody building's about to cave in!"

As if to confirm his statement, a deep rumbling sound came from the floor above. The building itself began to shake.

"Move! It's coming down!"

The rumbling became a roaring and the roaring an explosion of crashing timber, bricks, and concrete. The wide basement corridor was a confusion of swirling dust and deafening noise.

Culver saw the right-angled gap between tilted slab and staircase narrowing. "Come on, up the stairs!" He pushed, shoved, heaved the stumbling man before him, lifting him when he tripped over rubble, almost carrying him up the first few steps. "Get down! Now crawl, crawl up those bloody stairs for your life! And keep your head low!"

Culver wondered if the man would have followed his instructions had he seen what was happening.

The side of the stairway was collapsing, its metal handrail already twisted and torn from its mounting; the blast-caused sloping roof over the stairs was slowly descending, slipping inch by inch down the supporting wall. Culver could just see the murky gray daylight creeping in from the streets faintly tingeing the top steps. He quickly ducked and followed the blind man's scrambling body, unceremoniously pushing at his ample buttocks. The man suddenly flattened as part of the concrete stairs fell inward.

"Keep going!" Culver shouted over the noise. "You're okay, just keep going!"

The descending ceiling was brushing against the top of his head now and Culver considered pulling out, going back. But the situation was even worse behind: the downfall had become an avalanche and he knew that most of the floors in the building had to be collapsing inward. He pushed on with renewed vigor, not bothering to shout encouragement, which could not be heard anyway, just heaving and shoving, forcing his way through the narrowing tunnel. He was soon flat out and beginning to give up hope; the edges of each step were scraping against his chest.

Then the obstruction in front was clear: the blind man had made it to the top and was rising to his knees and turning, realizing he was free, one hand waving in front of Culver's face to help him. Culver grabbed the hand and suddenly he was being yanked upward, the blind man shrieking with the effort, his mouth wide open, eyes shut tight. Culver's toe caps dug into the stairs, pushing, the elbow of his free arm used as a lever to heave himself up. The screeching, heard clearly over the background roar, was caused by the concrete slab tearing deep score marks in the supporting wall.

Culver's torso was out and he curled up his knees, bringing his feet clear as the coffin lid all but closed.

He scrambled to his feet, pulling his companion with him, hurrying on, making for the wide doorway that was the entrance to the office building. The big glass double doors they had thrown themselves through only minutes earlier had been completely shattered by the blast; walls on either side of the hallway were beginning to crack.

They staggered out into the shattered, devastated world. Culver did not take time to look around; he wanted to be as far away as possible from the collapsing building.

The blind man was limping, clinging to him, as though afraid he would be left behind.

Vehicles—buses, cars, trucks, taxis—lay scattered, disarranged in their path. Some were overturned, some just wildly angled; many rested on the roofs or hoods of others. Culver quickly found a path through the tangled metal, dragging his companion with him. They finally collapsed behind a black taxi, half the driver's still body thrusting through the shattered windshield.

They gulped in mouthfuls of dust and smoke-filled air, shoulders and chests heaving, bodies battered and bleeding, their clothes torn and grimed with dirt. They heard the crumpling falling sound of the building they had just left, and it mingled with the noise of other office buildings in similar death throes. The very ground seemed to vibrate as they tumbled, their structures no more than concrete playing cards.

As the two men began to recover from their ordeal, they became aware of the other, human, sounds all around them, a clamor that was the discordant outcry of the wounded and the dying.

The other man was looking around him as though he could see. Forcing himself to ignore anything else, Culver quickly appraised him. Although it was impossible to be sure, because of the white powdered dust that covered his clothes, he looked to be somewhere in his late forties or early fifties; his suit, disheveled and torn though it was, indicated he was perhaps a businessman or clerk of some kind—certainly an office worker.

"Thanks for the helping hand back there." Culver had to raise his voice to be heard.

The man turned toward him. "The thanks are mutual."

Culver could not manage a smile. "I guess we need each other." He spat dust from his throat. "Let's get to this safe place you mentioned. Time's running out."

The blind man grabbed his arm as Culver began to rise.

"You must understand: we cannot help anyone else. If we're going to survive, nothing can hinder us."

Culver leaned heavily against the side of the taxi, flinching when he saw the jumbled corpses of its occupants. There was a child in there, a little boy no more than five or six years old, his head resting against a shoulder at an impossible angle; a woman's arm, presumably his mother's, was flung protectively across his tiny chest. A fun day out shopping? A trip across town to the cinema, a show? Perhaps even to see Daddy in his great big office. Their day had ended when the cab had been picked up and thrown through the air like some kid's toy, its weight nothing to the forces that had lifted it.

For the first time Culver took in the devastation, and his eyes widened with the horror of it all.

The familiar London landscape, with its tall buildings, both old and new, its skyscraper towers, the ancient church steeples, its old, instantly recognizable landmarks, no longer existed. Many buildings still stood, but not in their entirety. As Culver looked west, he saw what could only be described as a shielding effect. Toward the center of the blast—he wasn't yet aware of just how many bombs had dropped—the area looked to be completely flattened, but as the shock had traveled outward, many buildings had been masked from the worst of the fireball and shock waves by other buildings in front. As far as he could make out, none had escaped damage totally, but a few were in better shape than the others. He guessed the missile had been detonated right in the heart of the West End, possibly Piccadilly, or Oxford Street.

Fires raged everywhere. Ironically, he realized, the whole city could have been one vast conflagration had not the blast itself extinguished many of the blazes caused by the heat wave and fireball. The skies overhead were black, a vast turbulent cloud hanging low over the city. A spiraling column, the hated symbol of the holocaust, climbed into the cloud, a white stem full of unnatural forces.

Culver looked around and for the first time understood that more than one bomb had fallen: two rising towers to the west—one well beyond the column he had been watching—one to the north, another to the northeast, and the last to the south. Five in all. Dear God, *five!*

He lowered his gaze from the horizons and slammed the flat of his hand against the taxi's roof. He had witnessed the stark face of ultimate evil, the carnage of man's own sickness! The destructive force that was centuries old and inherent in every man, woman, and child! God forgive us all.

People began to emerge from buildings, torn and bloody creatures, white from shock, the look of death already on their faces. They crawled, staggered, dragged themselves from their shattered refuges, some silent, some pleading, some in hysterics, but nearly all separate islands, numbed into withdrawal from others, their minds only able to cope with their own individual hurt, their own personal fate.

Culver closed his eyes and fought back the rage, the screaming despair. A hand tugged at his trouser leg and he looked down to see the grimy face of the sightless man.

"What . . . what can you see?"

Culver sank to a squatting position. "You really don't want to know," he said quietly.

"No, I mean the dust—is it settling?"

He silently studied the blind man for a few moments before replying. "There's dust everywhere. And smoke."

His companion rubbed at his eyelids as though they were causing him pain. "Is it falling from above?" he asked almost impatiently.

Culver looked up and frowned. "Yeah, it's coming. I can see darker patches where the air is thick with it. It's drifting slow, taking its time."

The other man scrambled to his feet. "No time to lose, then. We must get to the shelter."

Culver stood with him. "What is this shelter? And who the hell are you?"

"You'll see when—if—we get there. And my name is Alex Dealey, not that it's important at this particular point in time."

"How do you know about this place?"

"Not now, for God's sake, man! Don't you realize the danger we're in?"

Culver shook his head, almost laughing. "Okay. Which direction?"

"East. Toward the Daily Mirror Building."

Culver looked to the east. "The Mirror isn't there anymore. At least, not much of it is."

The announcement had no visible effect on Dealey. "Just go in that direction, past the Underground station, toward Holborn Circus. And we keep to the right-hand side. Are all the buildings down?"

"Not all. But most are badly damaged. All the roofs and top floors have been skimmed off. What are we looking for?"

"Let's just move; I'll tell you as we go."

Culver took his arm and guided him through the jungle of smashed metal. A red double-decker bus lay on its side, crushing the cars beneath it. Figures were emerging from the shattered windows, faces and hands smeared with blood. Culver tried not to hear their whimpered groans.

An elderly man staggered in front of them, his mouth and eyes wide with shock. As he fell, Culver saw the whole of his back was a pincushion of glass shards.

Bodies, mostly still, lay strewn everywhere. Many were charred black. He turned his eyes away from limbs that protruded from heaped rubble and beneath overturned vehicles. Shattered glass crunched under their feet; even in the false dusk, it glittered everywhere like spilled jewels. The two men skirted around a burning van, shielding their faces from the heat. Something fell no more than thirty yards away from them, and from the squelching thump they knew it had to be a body; whether the person had jumped or accidentally fallen from a high window of one of the more intact office buildings, they did not know, nor did they care to know. They had a goal to reach, something to aim for, and neither man wanted to be detracted from their purpose. It was their only defense against the horror.

An explosion nearby rocked the ground and they fell to their knees. Coughing, choking, Culver hauled Dealey to his feet once more and they stumbled on. Others were moving in their direction. Now many were helping the injured, leading them toward the only place they felt could be safe. Groups carried those unable to walk, while those who could crawl were left to make their own way.

"We're just passing Chancery Lane Underground station," Culver said close to Dealey's ear. "Everyone seems to be taking shelter down there. Everyone that's left, that is. I think we ought to do the same."

"No!" Dealey's expression was grim. "It will be too crowded to get through. We've more chance if you do as I say."

"Tell me what the hell we're looking for."

"An alleyway. A wide, covered alleyway that leads to a courtyard and offices. There's a big open iron gate at the entrance. It should be just a few hundred yards ahead."

"I just hope to God you know what you're doing." Culver took a last wistful look at the opening leading to the Underground tunnels, then shook his head once. "Okay, we'll do it your way."

The nightmare continued, a dream far worse than any Culver had ever experienced. Destruction to a degree he had never imagined possible. A mad, stumbling journey that tore at his mind and made him weep inwardly. Havoc. Madness. Hell exposed.

Culver wiped an arm across his eyes. "How much farther?" he shouted, irrationally beginning to hate the man.

"Not far. We should be nearly there. Cross a small side street, go on a bit more, and we're there."

Culver yanked him around and led the way, Dealey's grip on his arm hard, as if he would never let go again.

After a short distance, Culver said, "There's a break in the curb here. This must be the side street, only now it's just piled with rubble. The buildings on one side have collapsed into it!"

"Just ahead, then. Not far." A look of hope was on the blind man's face.

They had to move out into the vehicle-littered street to skirt debris and Culver suddenly caught sight of the alleyway's entrance. "I can see it. It looks as though it's still intact."

Their pace quickened, both men desperate for refuge. They plunged into the darkness of the entrance and tripped on rubble lying there. Culver pushed himself to hands and knees, then moaned aloud. "Oh, Jesus Christ, no."

Dealey looked toward the sound of his voice, eyes closed tight against their pain. "What is it? For God's sake, what is it now?"

Culver slumped against one wall and closed his own eyes. He drew his legs up, resting his hands over his knees. "It's no good," he said wearily. "The other end's blocked, piled high with debris. There's no way we're going to get through."

3

They were running again. Frightened, exhausted, wanting to wake up, to see the sun streaming through parted curtains, wanting the nightmare to end. But they were running. And around them the fires raged, the dead lay still, the injured writhed their agony. The nightmare refused to end.

The steps leading down to the Underground station were heaped with rubble; the round metal handrails were wet with blood. It wasn't as crowded as Culver imagined it would be below; he guessed that most of those who had reached the station had gone farther down, away from the ticket area, into the tunnels. As far away as from the crazy world above as possible. Even so, there were still many people scattered around the gloomy circular hall with its ticket booth, machines, and few shops.

"We may need light," Dealey told him, the irony not lost on him. If only his eyes did not hurt so much. If the stinging sensation would just go away. He forced his mind to concentrate. "We have to get into the eastbound tunnel."

"We should have tried this other entrance in the first place," Culver said, quickly looking around. Other figures were still staggering into the Underground station.

"No, only under extreme circumstances are secondary access points to be used."

"Extreme circumstances? You've got to be kidding!"

Dealey shook his head. "Only in an emergency. I knew the station, the tunnels, would be filled with people. It would have been too dangerous to use; now we have no choice."

"Are you saying this . . . shelter . . . is only available to certain people?"

"It's a government shelter. There isn't room for the public."

"Yeah, I get it. We're the cannon fodder."

"The government has to be practical. And so do we." Dealey's voice became tight, as though he were fighting to keep control. "We can stay here and debate the morality, or lack of it, in the government's survival plan while radiation quietly kills us, or we can try and make our way to safety. I'm giving you a chance to live through this; it's up to you whether or not you take it."

"You can't make it without me."

"Possibly not. It's your choice." For a few long, sightless moments, Dealey thought that the other man had walked away from him. He breathed a silent sigh of relief when he heard him speak.

"I doubt there's going to be much left to survive for after this, but, okay, we'll find the shelter. I'd still like to know how you know about this place, though. I take it you work for the government."

"Yes, I do, but that's not important right now. We must get into the tunnels."

"There are some doors on the other side of the hall. I

can just about make it out in the darkness; one could be the station master's office, so we're bound to find a flashlight or a lamp of some kind.''

''There's no light down here?''

''Nothing. Just daylight—what there is of it.''

''The emergency lighting may still be working in the tunnels, but a flashlight might be useful.''

Dealey felt a hand on his arm and allowed himself to be led across the hall. The cries of the injured had died down, but a low coalescent moaning had taken its place. Something clutched at his trouser leg and a voice begged for help. He felt his guide hesitate and Dealey quickly pulled the other man to him. ''You haven't told me your name yet,'' he said to distract him, walking on, keeping the other man going.

''Culver,'' came the reply.

''Let's concentrate on one thing at a time, Mr. Culver. First, let's find a flashlight; second, let's get to the tunnels; third, let's get into the shelter. Nothing else must sidetrack us, not if we want to live.''

Culver knew the blind man was right, yet it was difficult to disregard his own misgivings. Would it really be worthwhile to survive? Just what *was* left up there? Had most of the northern hemisphere been wiped out, or had the strikes concentrated only on major cities and strategic military bases? There was no way of knowing for the moment, so he closed the questions from his mind, just as he kept further, more emotional thoughts at bay. Only the mind-numbing shock would see him through, so long as it did not affect his actions; for now, nothing else but finding a flashlight mattered.

The ground trembled briefly and screaming broke out once more.

The two men stopped in their tracks. ''Another bomb?'' Culver asked.

Dealey shook his head. ''I doubt it. An explosion not

too far away, I think. It could just be a fractured gas main.''

They reached the first door and Culver twisted the handle. Locked. ''Shit!'' He took a pace back and kicked out. Once more, and it gave. Another, and it was open.

Culver went in, Dealey following close behind, a hand on his guide's shoulder. A voice came from the darkness. ''What d'you want? This is London Transport property, you're not allowed in here.''

Culver was not surprised at the irrationality. ''Take it easy, we just want a flashlight,'' he reassured the man, whom he could just see crouching behind a chair in one corner of the tiny room.

''I can't let you . . .'' His voice broke. ''What's happened out there? Is it all over?''

''It's done,'' Culver said, ''but it's not over. Is there a flashlight in here?''

''There's a flashlight on the shelf, to your right, by the door.''

Culver saw it. Reached for it.

The crouching man raised an arm to protect his eyes when Culver flicked the switch and shone the beam in his direction.

''My advice to you is to get into the tunnels,'' Dealey said. ''You'll be safer there.''

''I'm all right where I am. There's no need for me to leave here.''

''Very well, it's up to you.''

Culver turned the beam away, switching it off as he did so. The flashlight would be useful: its casing was made of heavy-duty rubber and the light reflector was wider than normal. ''We're wasting time,'' he said quietly.

They made their way through the ticket barrier toward the escalators. There were three, and none was working. Culver noticed that the ticket hall had filled with more people, most of whom appeared to be totally disoriented, their movements uncertain, their eyes blankly staring.

Concentrate. The stairs. Have to ease our way over to them. Ignore the old woman sitting on the floor rocking her blood-covered head back and forth. Forget about the kid clinging to his mother, yelling for her to take out the horrible pieces of glass from his hands. *Don't look* at the man leaning against the wall vomiting black blood. Help one, and you had to help another. Help another, and you had to help everybody. Help everybody, and you were finished. Just help yourself. And this man, Alex Dealey, who seemed to know so much.

They were soon at the top of the center escalator. Bodies were sprawled all the way down, sitting, lying, some just slumped against the handrails. He could just make out dim emergency lights below.

"We'll have to be careful going down," Culver said. "The stairs are packed with people and we'll have to work our way through them." He released the blind man's arm and clamped Dealey's hand around his own. "Hold tight and stick close." He pushed his way through to the stairs.

Men and women looked at them, but no one objected. Some even tried to move aside when they realized Dealey was blind. It was slow progress and Culver was careful not to trip, allowing his companion to lean on him, to use his strength for support; one slip and they would never stop rolling.

They were halfway down when people below came pouring from the platform entrances.

They clawed at those on the escalators, trying to get on to the stairways, calling out, screaming something that Culver and Dealey could make no sense of. The renewed panic was infectious: the confused mass on the stairs rose as one and began to beat their way back up, punching out at those who blocked their path, pushing their way over those who lay injured.

"What now?" Dealey asked in frustration as they were shoved aside by the group just below them. "What's happening down there, Culver?"

"I don't know, but maybe it's not such a good idea after all."

"We have to get into the tunnel, don't you understand? We can't go back up there."

"You know it and I know it; try telling them!" A fist struck him in the chest as a man struggled to get by. He staggered back, but resisted the urge to retaliate. Instead, he shouted above the din, "There's only one way down, and it's going to be dangerous for you!"

"It can't be more dangerous than what's behind us!"

Culver pushed him against the rubber handrail and lifted his legs onto the center section, jumping up himself, holding on to the rail with one hand, his arm crooked under Dealey's, the flashlight still grasped tightly. "Use your feet to control your slide and I'll try to keep hold of the rail!"

The descent began and both men soon found it impossible to maintain a regulated speed. The arm lock Culver had on Dealey became too difficult to maintain; his other hand slipped from the handrail and they plunged down, feet striking the climbers on the stairs, so that their bodies twisted, their descent becoming completely uncontrolled. It was a frightening, helter-skelter ride toward another, unknown terror, a heart-churning rush into fresh danger.

Their fall was cushioned by the desperate figures massing around the bottom of the escalators. They landed in a flurry of arms and legs, wind knocked from them, but striking nothing hard that could cause serious damage. Culver was only slightly dazed and the flashlight was still gripped firmly in his hand.

"Dealey, where the Christ are you?" he shouted. He pulled at a hand rising from the bodies beneath him and released it when he realized it wasn't the blind man. Dealey!"

"Here. I'm here. Help me."

He used the flashlight to pinpoint the voice's source, the emergency lighting very limited. Culver found Dealey and tugged him free.

"You okay?" Culver asked.

"I'll find out later," came the reply. "So long as we can both walk, that's all that matters for the moment. We must find the eastbound tunnel."

"It's over there." Culver pointed the beam in that direction, as though the other man could see. "Westbound is on a lower level than this." The flashlight was almost knocked from his hand as someone hurtled by. The congestion at the foot of the escalators was growing worse, and both men fought to resist the human tide. Culver helped up one of the men who had cushioned his fall moments earlier.

He pulled the man's face close to his. "Why is everyone running from the tunnels? It's the only safe place!"

The man tried to get away from him, but Culver held on. "What is it? What's in there?"

"Something . . . something in the tunnel. I couldn't see, but others did! They were cut, bleeding. They said they'd been attacked in there. Please, let me go!"

"Attacked by what?"

"I don't know!" the man screamed. "Just let me go!" He tore himself free and was instantly swallowed up by the crowd.

Culver turned to Dealey. "Did you hear that? Something else is in that tunnel."

"It's mass hysteria, that's all, and it's understandable, under the circumstances. Everyone's still in a state of shock."

"He said they were bleeding."

"I'd imagine there are not too many people who *haven't*

been injured in some way. Perhaps a rat or some other creature got trodden on in there and bit back. Whoever was bitten obviously panicked the others.''

Culver wasn't convinced, but he had no intention of returning to the world above, where the air would be laden with radiation-contaminated particles by now. "We'll have to fight our way through. Get behind me and hold tight. I'm going to push my way in. You can put your weight behind me. Keep pushing, no matter what.''

Culver shielded his face with his arms, the flashlight held before him as an extra guard, and together he and Dealey forced their way through the mob. It was hard going, like swimming against a strong current, and both men were soaked with sweat before they reached the outer fringes of the crowd. There they found others who had not joined the throng, those who were wary of what lay behind them, but who realized the danger from above. And then there were those who could not move, the injured, the dead.

"The platform's through here," Culver said as they reached one of the platform's entrances. And then he noticed there were more people pouring from the shorter staircase leading up from the westbound platform; they frantically joined the mass, their shouts mingling with those of the others. He was curious: why should the panic have spread to a totally different tunnel, the one *below* the eastbound?

"Take me to the tunnel entrance," Dealey said. "To the left, the east. We have to go back down the line.''

"Look, I'm not so sure. Those people seemed pretty scared of whatever was in there.''

"We have no choice but to find the shelter.''

"We could stay here. It's deep enough underground to be safe.''

"Not necessarily. It isn't sealed; there are openings, vents, all along the tunnels where radiation can penetrate.

Even if that were not the case, we'll need to stay under cover for at least two weeks while the contamination above us dissipates. We may survive without food—and that would leave us in a considerably weakened state to face the outside world—but we certainly couldn't live without water."

"There must be a supply down here."

"If the mains are ruptured, which they probably are, the water won't last long, even if there is sufficient pressure to pump it through."

"Are you always so pessimistic?"

"I'm sorry, but it's pointless to pretend optimism under these circumstances. From now on, we must look at the worst possibilities if we're to live."

"How far into the tunnel is this entrance?" Culver looked toward the round arch of the dark tunnel, his brow furrowed in anxious lines.

"Eight to nine hundred yards. It won't take us long."

"Let's get on with it, then."

The platform entrance was not far from the tunnel itself and the two men approached the black gaping hole cautiously. Culver stepped close to the platform's edge and shone the flashlight into the darkness.

"It looks clear," he called back over his shoulder to Dealey.

"If there was anything in there, the crowds probably scared it off long ago."

"Let's hope you're right."

Dealey had felt his way along the side wall and had caught up with Culver.

"Grab my shoulder and keep your left side against the wall; we're going down," Culver said.

The air was cool, clammy, in the tunnel, and they could see the emergency lights stretching singularly into the blackness, their dim glow barely making an impression. It felt to Culver as if they were descending into a void, an emptiness that was itself threatening. Perhaps it was just the unnatural stillness after the turmoil above, or that he felt an unseen presence, eyes watching him from the shadows. Perhaps his nerves were just stretched to breaking point. Perhaps.

The tunnel curved slightly, the single chain of lights ahead disappearing. The dim glow from the platform behind vanished as they rounded the curve, leaving them in total isolation. Their footsteps echoed hollowly around the arched walls.

Culver noticed there were gaps in the wall to his right; he shone the beam in that direction and light reflected back from another set of tracks.

"I can see another tunnel," he told Dealey, his voice strangely loud in the confines of the shaft.

"It must be the westbound. Keep your flashlight to the right—I'd hate to miss the shelter."

Dealey's weight dragged against Culver now and he knew the man was near exhaustion. His eyes must have hurt like hell and the mental agony of not knowing if he were permanently blinded couldn't have helped much. Again, he wondered who the man was and how he knew about the shelter. Obviously he . . .

Something had moved in the darkness ahead. He'd heard it. A scurrying sound.

"Why have you stopped?" Dealey was clenching his arm tightly.

"I thought I heard something."

"Can you see anything?"

He swung the flashlight around in a wide arc. "Nothing."

They went on, their pace quickened despite the tiredness that dragged at them, their senses acutely aware, a sudden, awful foreboding growing within. Culver frantically searched for the opening, the doorway that would lead them to safety. There were recesses in the wall, but none held the magic door.

Surely they must be near. They'd walked more than eight hundred yards. It felt like eight miles. They had to find it soon. Jesus, let them find it soon.

He fell. Something was lying across the line. Something that had tripped him.

"Culver!" Dealey shouted, suddenly alone. He stumbled forward, arms outstretched, sightless eyes wide, and he, too, fell over the something that lay across the line.

His hands touched metal and quickly recoiled. At least they were now certain of one thing: there was no power in the line. His hands scrabbled around in the darkness. Felt something. Soft. Sticky soft. A head, a face.

His groping fingers found the eyes. But there were no eyes. Just deep, viscous sockets that sucked at his fingers as he withdrew them. He fell back and his hand touched something else. It was warm, and it was abhorrent. It was something slippery and it belonged inside a body, not outside.

"Keep still!" Culver's voice commanded.

Dealey's throat was too constricted to allow speech.

Culver, lying sprawled across the outer track, shone the flashlight around them. Bodies littered the tunnel. Black shapes moved among them, feeding off them.

They crouched, eluding the beam. Or scuttled away, back into the shadows.

"Oh, no, I don't believe it." Culver's voice was a moan.

"What's there, Culver? Please tell me."

"Keep still. Just don't move for a moment."

Slowly, very slowly, he pushed himself into a sitting position. The light flashed across a bristle-haired humped back; the creature tensed, fled.

He half-rose, the flashlight held before him. Its beam fell upon a human foot, a leg, a torso, the wicked yellow eyes of the animal squatting on the man's open chest. The creature plunged its bloodied snout deep into the wound, pulling flesh free with huge incisor teeth.

It stopped eating. It watched the man with the flashlight.

"Dealey." He kept his voice low, but could not control the tremor. "Move toward me—*slowly*—just move slowly."

The other man did exactly as he was told, the fear in Culver's voice all the warning he needed.

Culver carefully reached for him, remaining crouched, avoiding any sudden movement. He drew the crawling man to him, then moved back so that they were both against the tunnel wall.

"What is it?" Dealey whispered.

Culver took a deep breath. "Rats," he said quietly. "But like I've never seen before. They're big." He wondered at his own understatement.

"Are they black-furred?"

"Everything's black down here."

"Oh, God, not again, not at a time like this."

Culver glanced at him curiously, but could not see his expression in the darkness. He did not want to take the beam away from the dead bodies or the shapes that moved among them. His eyes narrowed. "Wait a minute. There were a couple of outbreaks of killer black rats some years ago. Are you saying these are the same breed? We were told they'd been wiped out, for Christ's sake!"

"I can't see them, so I can't say. It's hardly the time to discuss the point, though."

"Yeah, I'm with you there. But what do you suggest—we shoo them away?"

"Can you see the shelter door? We must be close."

Reluctantly and very slowly, Culver swept the beam across the carnage. He winced when he saw the tangle of torn human forms and fought back nausea as the creatures steadily chewed at their victims. He had never before realized that blood had such a strong odor.

He froze when he saw one rat stealthily creeping toward them, its long body kept low, its haunches hunched and tensed. The flashlight beam reflected in its eyes and the creature stopped. It moved its head away from the glare, then moved back a few paces. It slid back in the darkness, unhurried and unconcerned.

"Have you found the doorway yet?" Dealey hissed urgently.

"No. I got distracted."

The light resumed its slow journey, revealing too much, each new horror chilling Culver to his core, causing the hand guiding the beam to tremble so that the very cavern seemed to quake. The poor bastards, he thought. They'd sought refuge from the holocaust above, only to be eaten alive in this other, equally deadly subterranean world. He shuddered. Of the two, this was the more ghastly way to oblivion.

His intention was to aim the light along the wall he and Dealey rested against; Dealey had said the doorway was on the right-hand side of the eastbound tunnel. He hated the idea of allowing darkness to conceal the gorging creatures once more, for he felt somehow it was only the light holding the black creatures back, as if it were a force field of sorts. Deep down, he knew he was wrong. They had not been attacked because the vermin were content with their kill for the moment; their hunger could be satiated without further effort.

But if they felt threatened, the slaughter would start again, and this time he and Dealey would be the victims.

Oh, Christ, where was that damn shelter?

The slow-swinging beam came to a halt. What was that?

He moved the light back a few feet.

It came to rest on a figure standing in one of the openings dividing the two tunnels.

She was perfectly still, eyes staring directly ahead into the brickwork of a column opposite the one she leaned against. Her clothes were torn, dirt-smeared, her hair matted, unkempt. She did not appear to be breathing, but she was alive. Alive and shocked rigid.

"Dealey," Culver said, keeping his voice low. "There's a girl on the other side of the track. Just standing there, too scared to move."

He tensed as a black shape appeared in the opening, at the girl's feet. Its pointed nose twitched in the air before it leapt off the small ledge to be among its gluttonous companions.

"Find the door, man, that's more important."

Culver grimaced, a smile without humor. "You're all heart," he said.

"If we find the shelter, then we may be able to help her."

"She could collapse at any moment, and if she does, she'll fall right into them. She'd have no chance."

"There isn't much we can do."

"Maybe not." Culver began to rise, his back scraping against the brick wall, the movement slow, easy. "But this time we're going to try."

"Culver!" A hand grabbed his sleeve, but he shook it off. He began to move away from the slaughter, backing off in the direction they had come.

When he felt he was at a safe distance—although a few hundred miles would have felt safer—Culver crossed the track. Then he began the cautious, deliberate walk back, keeping the beam low, not wanting to disturb the unholy feast. His footsteps light, Culver stepped through one of the openings onto the adjacent track, hoping none of the creatures was lurking there. Less intimidated by the bloodletting because now it was out of view, he made faster progress.

The girl scarcely blinked at the glare as he reached her from the other side of the opening. He stepped up on to the small ledge and faced her.

"Are you hurt?" he asked, raising his voice a little when there was no response. "Can you hear me? Are you hurt?"

A tiny flicker of life registered in her eyes, but still she gave no acknowledgment of his presence.

"Culver," came Dealey's hissed voice from the other side of the tunnel, twenty feet or so back from the opening Culver and the girl stood in. "I can hear them getting closer. You've got to help me. Please find the shelter." He sounded desperate, almost tearful, and Culver could understand why. The sucking guzzling of the vermin was nauseous as well as terrifying, and the cracking of small, brittle bones cruelly accentuated the horror.

Becoming impatient with his own caution, Culver quickly swung the wide beam along the opposite wall, starting at a point farther down the tunnel. There was more than one recess set in the brickwork, but none held a doorway, until . . . *There it was!* Almost opposite. A goddamn iron bloody door! Unmarked, but then it would be!

"Dealey! I've found it!" It was difficult to keep his voice low. "It's just a little ahead of me, about thirty yards from you. Can you make it on your own?"

The other man was already on his feet. He began to inch along the wall, feeling with his hands, his face almost pressed against the rough brickwork. Culver turned his attention back to the girl.

Her face was smeared with blood and dirt, although he could see no open cuts, and her eyes remained wide and staring. She may have been pretty, he couldn't tell, and her shoulder-length hair may have looked good with the sun reflecting highlights, but again, it was hard to tell and not the uppermost consideration in his mind. When his hand touched her shoulder, the air exploded with her scream.

He staggered back from her thrusting arms, his head striking the column behind. His eyes closed for just an instant, but when they opened, she had gone. He swung the flashlight and found her again. She had fallen among the half-eaten bodies, startling the black vermin so that they scurried away. And now he saw just how many of the creatures there were.

Hundreds! My God, more. Many more!

"Dealey, get to the shelter! Move as fast as you can!"

The girl was trying to rise, trying to crawl away from the glare, and the rats had stopped, were turning, were watching her, were no longer afraid.

4

Culver jumped, slipped, lay sprawled, the flashlight gone from his grasp. His hands were in a sticky mess and he quickly withdrew them, afraid to see what they had touched. The girl was just a few feet away and he lunged for her ankle to prevent her moving any farther, for the beasts were waiting for her just beyond the circle of light.

She screamed again when he gripped her leg and pulled her back. His other hand scrabbled around for the flashlight, ignoring the wet, mushy things he touched in the darkness. He grabbed the handle, but the girl was fighting against him, kicking, beating at him with her fists. The taste of blood was in his mouth and he turned his head aside to avoid the blows. A weight thudded against him and he felt something tear at his thigh.

He cried aloud and brought the heavy flashlight down hard on the rat's skull. It squealed, high-pitched, piercing, but its teeth would not release their grip. The flashlight came down again, harder, harder, again, and the creature's claws scrabbled at the dust beneath it. It released its hold, squealing, the sound of a baby in pain. Culver struck again and it staggered sideways. But it did not run.

Culver jumped to his feet, the fear overcoming his exhaustion; he stamped on the creature's skull, his boot crunching bones, squashing the substance beneath. The rat writhed, twitching spasmodically between the human bodies it had been feeding off, its screeches becoming a mewling sound, fading as it died.

He saw the other rat just before it leapt, and he brought the flashlight around in a crushing swing, striking the black, bristling body in midair, his whole weight behind the blow, losing balance as he followed through. He was on the ground again, among the corpses. Why didn't the creatures attack in force? What were they waiting for? The answer flashed into his mind as he scrambled to his feet: they were testing his strength! The first two were just the advance party; the rest would follow, now that they knew how weak their opponent was! There was no time to wonder at their cunning.

He pulled the girl up, holding her around the waist, and flashed the light around the tunnel.

They were waiting there, watching him. Dark, hunched monsters, with evil yellow eyes. Slanted eyes that somehow glinted an unusual intelligence. Their bodies quivered as one and he knew they were ready to strike. In the periphery of his vision he saw Dealey edging his way along the wall.

"It's just a few feet ahead of you," he said, fighting to keep down the hysteria. "For Christ's sake, Dealey, get that bloody door open."

Culver began to make for the recess himself, forcing the girl to go with him, moving inch by inch, careful not to stumble over a body, to slip in the blood. Fortunately, the girl seemed to realize what was happening. She was still tense, stiff, but she no longer fought against him. He eased his grip on her.

The rats had started to creep forward.

He risked a look at Dealey. The blind man had reached the door. But he was sagging against it. His face was turning in Culver's direction. His eyes were closed tight and his mouth was open in a silent moan of agony.

"Dealey?" Culver said, still moving toward him.

"The keys. The keys were in my briefcase!" His last words were screeched and his fists began to flail at the door's metal surface.

"Don't!" Culver warned, but it was too late. The screams and the banging had spurred the black creatures into attack.

Culver cried out as the leaping bodies slammed into him, his arms instinctively protecting his face. Both he and the girl went down under the weight and a million razor-sharp teeth seemed to sink into his skin. He kicked, thrashed out with his arms, shouted his pain and terror.

The tunnel shook. Dust and bricks fell from the ceiling. The explosion ricocheted around and around the curved walls, spiraling toward them, heaving the earth. Three hundred yards away, the tunnel collapsed, flames roaring through in a great ball that billowed outward.

The vermin screeched, their attack on the two humans forgotten. They cowered to the ground, a mass of dark quivering bodies, completely still, they themselves now rigid with fear.

Culver rose to his elbows and swiped at a rat nestled on his lap. It fell to one side with a snarling hiss, but did not retaliate.

Another explosion, louder than the first, and the fireball expanded, raced toward them along the tunnel, filling every inch, a swelling yellow that scorched the walls.

The creatures ran, scrabbling over the bodies, slithering past or leaping over Culver and the girl, squealing in alarm, they themselves the hunted now, the fast-approaching billowing flames the merciless hunter.

Culver was on his feet, lifting the girl, the vermin

forming a dark-flowing river around his legs. He ran with her, just a few feet, praying that the recess in which Dealey knelt would offer some protection, the wall of fire hurrying to meet them, eager to incinerate them in its fiery embrace.

It was too near, they could never make it! He jumped the last few feet, the dead weight of the girl unnoticed in his panic.

They crashed into the metal doorway as the flames reached them and Culver felt the searing heat against his skin, licking at his clothes.

It was hopeless. The narrow refuge could offer little protection as the fire swept by. They would all be burned to a crisp.

And then he was tumbling forward with the others, falling into a different light, the metal door giving way, the scorching flames at his back, dropping, tumbling, over and over and over, never wishing to stop, the world just light and pain and sound . . .

And then blackness.

5

"Oh, Jes—"

A gentle hand forced him back down onto the narrow bunk bed.

"It's all right," a voice equally as gentle said. "You've got a nasty wound in your leg; we're dealing with it."

Culver looked up into the white face that seemed to hover above him. The woman was frightened—he could just detect the glimmer of alarm hiding behind her outwardly calm gaze—but she worked steadily, professionally, swabbing away the blood from the gash in his thigh.

"You were lucky," she told him. "Whatever did this just missed the artery."

He closed his eyes, but the memory of his attacker became even sharper.

A silence fell between them, one that Culver eventually broke.

"There were rats in the tunnels," he said. "But like no goddamn rats I've ever seen before."

She looked at him curiously.

"They were big, some as big as dogs. They . . . they were feeding on people who'd fled into the tunnel."

"They attacked you?"

He nodded. "They attacked. It's hard to think . . . I don't know how . . ."

"Some of the technicians heard you pounding on the emergency door. You literally fell in among us."

He tried to look around him. "Just who . . . What is this place?"

"Officially it's the Kingsway telephone exchange. Equally officially, but not for public knowledge, it's a government nuclear shelter. You happen to be in the sick bay at the moment."

Over her shoulder, Culver could see other two tiered bunk beds. It was a small room with gray walls and ceiling; strip lighting glared overhead. There were other figures around a bed farther down.

The woman followed his gaze. "The girl you brought in with you is being treated for shock. I took a look at her first —she doesn't appear to have sustained any serious injuries, just minor cuts and bruises. Her hair is a little singed, but you must have protected her from the fire out there."

"Fire?"

"Don't you remember? The technicians said the tunnel was ablaze for a few seconds, a fireball of some kind. You'd have all roasted if the door hadn't opened at the crucial moment. As it was, you were lucky you were wearing a thick leather jacket or your back would have peeled."

"Where's Dealey?"

"The skin on your hands and the back of your neck is scorched."

"He didn't make it?" Culver sat up.

A hand splayed against his chest and eased him back down again. "He made it. He's talking with the CDO."

"The what?"

"Civil Defense officer. Dealey wanted me to take care of you and the girl first."

"You know he's been blinded?"

"Of course. With luck, it may only be short-term; it depends on how long he looked into the flash. I assume that's how it happened?"

"Yeah. And it was only for a split second."

"He may be fortunate, then. It'll be a long wait for him, though."

She busied herself tending his wound and for the first time he was aware of his naked legs.

"If it was a rat bite I think we'll need to disinfect, perhaps with Lysol," she muttered. "Feeling strong?"

"Not particularly. Who are you?"

"Dr. Clare Reynolds." Still no smile. "I'm only here for a meeting with Alex Dealey and several others; it has been scheduled for this afternoon."

"You work for the government?"

This time a brief, tight smile flashed. "I was drafted when the situation reached crisis point. Normal precautions, nobody thought it would escalate to this. Nobody."

She turned to a small cart by her side and poured fluid onto a small pad. Wisps of premature gray mingled with the dark auburn of her hair, which was cut short in a practical rather than glamorous style. Her features were pinched taut—not surprising in the circumstances—and her pale skin seemed almost anemic, although that could have been due to the harsh lights above. He noticed she was wearing a wedding ring.

She turned back to him. "This is going to sting," she warned, brushing the soaked pad into the gash.

"Shhhhh"—Culver gripped the sides of the bunk—"iiiiit!"

"No masochist you. Okay, it's done. I want to put you out for a short time; you've been through a lot."

"I'd rather you didn't."

"Sure you would. Just think yourself lucky to be out of this for a while. What's your name, by the way?"

"Steve Culver."

"Pleased to know you, Mr. Culver. I think we'll be seeing a lot of each other."

"What happened, Doctor? Why did they *let* it happen?"

"It all comes down to greed in the end." Some of the forced stiffness went out of her. "And envy. Let's not forget our old friend envy."

She finished dressing the wound, then reached back into the trolley for a diazepam-filled syringe.

He awoke to find a different pair of eyes staring down at him. Her blond hair fell around her face, a face that was still marked and grimy from the ordeal in the tunnel. Her eyes were wide and, unlike the doctor's, cried out her fear. A hand clutched at his shoulder.

"Where am I?" she asked, almost in a whisper. "Please tell me."

He struggled to sit up and his head rode a roller coaster. Her hands tightened on his shoulder, digging into the flesh.

"Take it easy," he begged. "Just give me a minute." He slowly eased his back against the wall behind and waited for the spinning to stop. His head began to clear, making way for jumbled thoughts to rush in. His senses sharpened rapidly as he remembered. The dread drifted down into the lower regions of his stomach like a ship sinking to the seabed. He looked at the girl, then pushed a hand between her hair and cheek.

"You're safe now," he told her softly. He wanted to hold her, to hug her to his chest, to tell her it was all a bad dream that had ended. But he knew it was just beginning. "We're in a government shelter," he told her. "The entrance was in the tunnel near where we found you." He watched her shudder.

"I remember." Her voice, her gaze, was distant. "W•
heard the sirens. No one could believe it was really hap
pening, but we ran, we hid. We thought the tunnels woul•
protect us. Those things—" She broke and he pulled he
to him.

Her sobs were muffled against his chest and he felt hi
own emotional barrier, a shield that was tissue-thin, be
ginning to tear. There was a closeness between them—h•
was sure it was shared—an intimacy imposed by wha
they had both been through, a desperate touching of spir
its. Culver held on to the girl and fought against his ow•
despair.

After what seemed a long while, her shudderin•
stopped, although she continued to tremble slightly. Sh•
pulled away from him.

"Were . . . were you the one who helped me? Ou
there, when those . . . Oh, God, what were they?"

"Vermin," he answered, keeping his voice calm
"Rats that must have been breeding underground fo
years."

"But their size! How could they get to that size?"

"Mutants," he told her. "Monsters that should hav•
been wiped out years ago when they first appeared. W•
were told that they had been, but it looks like we were mis
informed. Or deceived."

"How could they survive, how could they breed, ho•
could they go unnoticed?" Her voice was rising and Cu
ver could see she was beginning to lose control again.

"Maybe we'll find the answers later," he answere•
soothingly. "The main thing is that we're safe no•
Whatever's above, whatever's in the tunnels, can't touc•
us here."

He would never forget the haunting shadow tha•
touched her face at that moment. "Is . . . is there any
thing left . . . above?"

He could not answer. To have done so, to have had •
think of it, would have broken him. Push it away, Culve•

save it for later. It was too much to take right now, too much to envisage. Keep away thoughts of black-charred children, torn bodies, crushed, bewildered children, a devastated, ravaged city, country—world?—contaminated, shrieking children, children, children!

He cried out then, not loudly, not frenziedly—a piteous sound that was faint, but nevertheless, an outpouring of anguish. And now it was the girl who comforted him.

The doctor came for them a little later. She stopped for a moment in the doorway of the small sick bay, briefly wishing that she, too, had a pair of arms to fall into, someone who would hold her, tell her things would be all right. If only she knew if Simon . . . Mustn't think about it, mustn't even consider her husband's death.

"How are you both feeling?" she asked, professionalism stifling rising emotion.

They looked at her as if she were some weird alien, perhaps the creator of the havoc above; but the man, Culver, recovered quickly.

"How long were we out for?" he asked as they separated.

"About six hours." She glanced at her wristwatch. "It's now just after seven. Evening." Dr. Clare Reynolds approached them. "Now tell me how you're feeling. Any aches, pains, you think I should know about? You?" She looked at the girl.

"I'm just numb."

The doctor now looked even paler to Culver, if that were possible, but she managed a sad smile. "We all are, mentally. How do you feel physically? Do you hurt anywhere?"

The girl shook her head.

"Good. Do you want to tell us your name?"

The girl sat upright on the edge of the bed and wiped a hand across her eyes. "Kate Garner," she said.

"Welcome to the survivors' club, Kate Garner." The icy tone hardly sounded welcoming. "How does your leg feel, Mr. Culver?"

"Like it was bitten by a rat." Culver raised his knees beneath the single blanket and rested his wrists over them. "What's been going on while we were asleep?"

"That's why I'm here. A meeting is about to start in the shelter's dining room. You'll find out all you want to know there. Are you fit enough to get dressed?"

Culver nodded and realized that, for the moment at least, he had put something behind him. The pain, the tormenting images, could be kept in cold storage for a while. They would never leave him, of that he was sure, but for the time being they could be suppressed. A cold fury was taking hold inside and he knew it would help sustain him throughout whatever was yet to come. For a while.

The doctor reached up to the bunk bed above, then tossed his clothes into his lap. "Jacket's a little burned and your jeans and shirt are somewhat torn, but no need to worry—the meeting won't be formal. Kate, could you come over to another bed? I just want to have another look at you."

Culver dressed quickly, wincing at the pain sudden movement caused. He must have been more bruised than he realized, and the whole of his thigh had stiffened. He found his tan boots beneath the bed and grunted as he bent to lace them up; it felt as though someone had slammed a medicine ball into his stomach. He stood, using the upper bunk as support until he felt steady, then joined the doctor and the girl.

"Everything okay?" he asked, looking from one to the other.

"No serious damage." The doctor stood. "Let's join the others."

"How many 'others' are there?" Culver said. "And who are they?"

"Technicians permanently based here to operate the telephone equipment. The rest are ROCs—members of the Royal Observer Corps—and one of two Civil Defense people. More should have joined us at the first warning of attack, but"—she shrugged—"such clinically devised plans don't always work out in practice. Especially when a whole city is in a state of panic. There are about thirty of us in all."

She led them from the sick bay, and both Culver and the girl gasped at the size of the area they had entered.

"Impressive, isn't it?" Dr. Reynolds said, noticing their astonished looks. "It would take well over an hour to walk around the whole complex. I won't bore you with a list of technical equipment housed down here—mainly because I don't understand most of it myself—but we have our own power plant *and* two standby plants. We also have our own artesian well, so water won't be a problem. That's the switching unit area to the left and the power plant is just ahead of us. Farther on is the kitchen, the dining room, and the rec room; that's where we're headed."

The harsh glare from the overhead neon lights added to the atmosphere of mechanical sterility, no warmth reflected from the gray-green walls. A quiet hum of power indicated electronic life in the nonhuman world, but Culver noticed that no individual machinery appeared to be functioning. He briefly wondered if there was anyone else left to communicate with.

Eventually, after what seemed like a long journey through confusing corridors, a different kind of humming reached his ears, but this was distinctly human: it was the sound of many voices in low-pitched conversation. The three of them entered the dining room and heads swung around in their direction, all conversation coming to a halt.

6

Dealey sat at one end of the room, white pads held by a bandage covering his eyes. At the same table, positioned at a right angle to the three rows of dining tables, were two blue-uniformed figures, one female, and two other men in civilian clothes. One of the latter whispered something to Dealey, who stood.

"Please come forward, Mr. Culver," Dealey said. "And the young lady, too. Dr. Reynolds, if you would join us at this table."

Many of the people in the room were wearing white overalls and all looked pale and tired. They watched Culver and Kate curiously, almost as though they were interlopers gate-crashing an exclusive club. Two seats were offered them and they took their places close to the top table. The doctor sat next to Dealey.

Two mugs and a coffeepot were pushed toward Culver. He nodded his thanks, pouring for himself and the girl. No sugar or milk was offered. The buzz of conversation had started again, and as he raised the mug to his lips, he was aware of the barely suppressed stridency that prevailed. He glanced at Kate; she was gazing into the darkbrown liquid as if it would somehow reveal some insane reasoning for all that had happened, some crazy logic as to why man should choose to shutter the very earth he lived upon. He wondered what she had lost personally—husband, family, lover? No wedding or engagement ring, so perhaps lover . . . or even lovers. Parents, brothers and sisters. The memory of them all had to be bombarding her emotions, a relentless tormentor that only oblivion itself could vanquish.

Culver sipped his coffee, realizing he was probably more fortunate than those around him: his losses back there in the past, the worst of his suffering carefully stored away, the lid shut tight. And though he had fought to survive that day, he wasn't sure it really mattered that much to him.

Dealey was conferring with the doctor and the civilians on either side, all keeping their voices low, conspiratorial. The blind man looked weary, the unhealthy pallor of his skin heightened by the harsh overhead lighting. Culver had to admire his stamina, wondering if he had taken any time at all to rest after their arduous and gut-wrenching ordeal. He had to be in pain from the injury to his eyes, and the mental anguish of not knowing whether or not the damage was permanent must in itself have been draining. He seemed different from the frightened, disoriented man that Culver had dragged through the wreckage, almost as if his badge of office had reasserted the outward shell, officialdom his retrieved armor. Dealey looked up at those assembled, his head moving from right to left, as if picking up threads of conversation.

The man next to him stood. "Can I please have your attention?" he said, his words calm, measured, a rebuttal of the pernicious hysteria that skitted around the room from person to person like some quick-darting gadfly.

Conversation stopped.

"To the few who don't already know me my name is Howard Farraday, and I'm the first line manager or senior technician of the Kingsway Telephone Exchange. At the moment, because there is no one of senior position here, that makes me the boss." He attempted a smile that was barely successful. He cleared his throat. "Since further excavation work, begun in the 1950s, the exchange has had a dual role: that of automatic exchange, carrying some five hundred lines, and as a government deep shelter. Most of you will be aware that the first NATO transatlantic cable terminates here."

He paused again, a tall man whose normal stature would have been described as robust, had not the events of that day dragged at his shoulders and hued shadows of weariness settled around his eyes. His voice was quieter when he continued, as if incipient confidence was fast draining from him. "I think you'll also have been aware of the increased activity regarding Kingsway over the past few weeks—standard procedure, I might add, in times of international crisis. Although the situation was regarded as serious, no one imagined this . . . this . . . that events would escalate to such disastrous proportions."

Culver shook his head at the simplistic description of the genocide. The coffee was bitter in his mouth and the wound in his thigh throbbed dully. His rancor, his deepfelt hate for those who had instigated the devastation, was frozen within for the moment with the rest of his emotions.

"Because of the increasing hostilities in the Middle East, and Russia's invasion of Iran, all such government establishments have been receiving similar attention . . ."

The man droned on and what he said meant little to Culver. Words, just words. Nothing could adequately convey the horror, the dreadful loss, the ravages of what was yet to come.

Farraday was pointing at the seated man on his left.

". . . Senior Civil Defense Officer Alistair Bryce. Next to me here, on my right, is Mr. Alex Dealey, who is from the Ministry of Defense, and next to him, Dr. Clare Reynolds, who has been associated with this particular establishment for some time now, so many of you will already know her. Then we have two Royal Observer Corps officers, Bob McEwen and Sheila Kennedy. There should have been several other, er, officials, with us today—a meeting had been planned for this afternoon. Regrettably, they did not reach the shelter." He swept back a lock of hair that dangled over his forehead, his upper body tilting backward as if to assist the maneuver. "Perhaps, Alex, you would like to continue." The tall man slumped rather than sat, his hands clenched tight on the table before him, his shoulders hunched. Culver had the impression that Farraday's address had not ended a moment too soon; the man was ready to crack.

Dealey did not rise. And there was something chilling about listening to a man whose expression was hidden behind a white mask.

"Let me start," he said, his voice surprisingly filling the green-walled dining room without raising itself beyond conversational level, "by saying I know how each and every one of you must be feeling. You're afraid for your families, your loved ones, wondering if they have survived the nuclear explosion. Afraid, too, for yourselves: Is this shelter safe from fallout? Is there enough food, water? What will be left of the world we know?

"Two things I can reassure you of immediately: we are all well-protected here, and there are provisions to last for six weeks, probably longer. As for water, those of you who are employed here will know that the complex has its own artesian well, so there will be no risk of contamination. I think it's important to stress these factors to relieve your minds of just some of the terrible burden they are bearing."

There was still an uncomfortable, unnatural silence around the room.

"Mr. Farraday has already mentioned that I'm from the Ministry of Defense. Actually, I belong to the Inspector of Establishments division. I suppose you could call me a government shelter liaison officer, one of the chaps who sees that our underground defense units are in running order and in a permanent state of readiness."

He leaned forward on the desk as if taking the whole room into his confidence. "It's because of that specific role that I have full knowledge of every underground shelter and deep shelter, both public and governmental, in London and the surrounding counties, and that I can assure you that we are neither *alone* nor isolated."

At last there were murmurs among the gathering, at last a reaction.

Dealey raised a hand to bring the room to order. "Before I give you general details of these shelters and operations centers, I think it best we appraise our present position. I'm sure the questions uppermost in your minds must be, what exactly has happened and what is the extent of the damage to our country?" He placed both hands flat on the table. "Unfortunately, we have no way of knowing the answers."

This time the murmuring was stronger, and angry voices could be heard over the general buzz. Farraday quickly cut in.

"Communications with other stations have temporarily been lost. For the moment we cannot even make contact with the underground telecommunications center near St. Paul's, which is less than a mile away."

"But the tunnel network should have protected the system," a technician sitting close to Culver said sharply.

"Yes, you're quite right: the cable tunnels and deep tube tunnels should have afforded ample protection for the communications system. It would appear that the amount of damage nuclear bombs could cause has been badly underestimated and that vital sections in the network have been penetrated.''

Dealey spoke up. ''From information gathered before communications failed, we believe at least five nuclear warheads were directed at London and the surrounding suburbs.'' He licked his lips, betraying the first signs of nervousness since the meeting had begun, and his next words came quickly, as though he were anxious to impart the information. ''We're not absolutely sure, but we think those targets were Hyde Park, Brentford, Heathrow, Croydon, and the last somewhere northeast of the city. The nuclear weapons themselves would have been a mixture of one and two megatons, ground bursts and air bursts.''

Culver was confused. ''Wait a minute,'' he said, raising a hand like a child in a classroom. ''You're talking about a cable system being knocked out, right?''

Although their recent conversations had been fraught, mainly shouted, Dealey recognized the voice. ''That's correct,'' he replied.

''Then why can't we communicate by radio?''

Farraday gave the answer. ''One of the effects of a nuclear blast is something we call EMP—electromagnetic pulse. It's an intense burst of radio waves that can destroy electrical networks and communication systems over an area of hundreds of miles. Any circuits with sensitive components such as radios, televisions, radar, computers, and any systems attached to long lengths of cable—telephones, the electricity power grid—are subjected to incredible surges of current which overload and so destroy. Much of the military equipment has been EMP-hardened by placing sensitive circuits inside conductive boxes and, of course, laying cables deep underground, but it appears that even these precautions haven't been as effective as they might have been.''

''Jesus, what a fuck-up,'' Culver said quietly, and those near him who heard nodded their agreement.

Dealey attempted to still the disquiet that was rumbling around the room like muted thunder. "I must emphasize that these conditions are only temporary. I'm sure contact with other shelters will be made very soon. Mr. Farraday himself has assured me of that."

Farraday looked at him in surprise, but quickly recovered. "I think we can safely assume that other such shelters have been left intact and all efforts to link up are already under way."

Culver wondered if Farraday's statement was as dissatisfying to others as it was to him. He was startled when the girl next to him, her voice dulled but clear to everyone in the room, suddenly said, "Why was there no warning?"

"But there was a warning, Miss, er"—Dr. Reynolds leaned toward him and whispered the name—"Garner. Surely you heard the sir—"

"Why didn't anybody know it was going to happen?" This time there was an icy shrillness to the question.

There was a short, embarrassed silence at the top table before Dealey answered. "Nobody, not one person in his right mind, could imagine another country would be foolish enough—no, insane enough!—to begin a third world war with nuclear arms. It defies all sensibilities, all logic. Our government cannot be blamed for the lunatic suicidal tendencies of another nation. When the USSR land forces invaded Iran with a view to overrunning *all* the oil states, they were warned that retaliatory steps would be taken by the Combined World Forces—"

"They should have been stopped when they took total control of Afghanistan and then Pakistan!" someone shouted from the back.

"This is not the time for such a discussion," Farraday interrupted, fearing the meeting could so easily get out of hand. Hysteria was thick in the air; the smallest upset now could turn it into outrage, perhaps even violence.

"It may not have even been the Russians who fired the

first missile, so until we know more, let's not argue among ourselves.'' He instantly regretted his words, realizing he had just implanted a fresh seed of thought.

Dealey quickly tried to cover the mistake. ''The point is that nobody imagined the situation had reached such a critical state. Our own government was making provisions for war, just in case, against all odds, it did break out.''

''Then, why weren't we, the public, told that it was so imminent?'' Culver's cold anger was directed solely at Dealey, as though he, the representative figure of government authority, was personally responsible.

''And create nationwide panic? What good would that have done? And besides, nothing was certain; the world has had more than its share of false crises in the past.''

And the world had cried wolf too many times before, Culver thought sourly. The girl was shaking her head, a slight, mournful movement that bespoke bewilderment as well as despair.

''Now perhaps our CDO can advise us on what will happen over the next few weeks.'' Dealey sat back in his chair, his masked face inscrutable, only the quick darting of his tongue across already moist lips again betraying an inner nervousness.

Alistair Bryce, the senior Civil Defense officer, decided he would carry more authority if he stood. He was a small, balding man whose jowls hung in flaps on either side of his round face; heavy pouches under his eyes completed the impression of a face made up of thick, spilled-over liquid. His eyes were sharp, however, and never still, bouncing quickly from left to right like blue pinballs.

''A few words, first, about what's likely to have occurred above us. What I'm going to say will frighten you, will distress you, but the time for lies is long gone. If we are to survive, we have to work together as a unit, and we've got to trust one another.'' His eyes took a more leisurely sweep around the room. ''I promise you this: our chances for survival are good; only our own fear can defeat us.''

He drew in a deep breath, as though he were about to plunge into deep water. ''Anywhere between sixteen and thirty percent of people in the Greater London Council area will have been killed outright. I know official figures lean toward the lower estimate, but as I said, it's time for honesty. My opinion is that the number of dead will be at *least* twenty-eight percent, and that's on the conservative side.''

He allowed a little time for the unsettling information to sink in. ''Another thirty to thirty-six percent will have been injured by the blast alone. Many will have been crushed or trapped in buildings, or cut by flying glass. The list of various types of injury would be endless, so it's pointless to itemize. It's enough to say that burns, shock, and mutilation will be widespread, and many will have received permanent or temporary eye damage caused by retinal burns from the initial flash.

''Blast pressure from each of the bombs will have damaged approximately seventy-five percent of the GLC area: most tall buildings and many bridges will have collapsed and the majority of roads will have been blocked by rubble, fallen telegraph poles and lampposts, and overturned vehicles. About thirty percent of the houses in Greater London will have been reduced to rubble and over forty percent too badly damaged to be repaired in the immediate future. I hardly need to say there probably won't be an unbroken window left in the capital.''

Bryce's face looked drained of blood, his overhanging jowls resembling empty money pouches. ''Fire damage will be extensive and I'm afraid our fire services will be little more than useless. It may be that most of London above us is in flames.''

The cries, the sighing moans of despair, could no longer be contained. Several men and women were weeping openly while others merely sat grim-faced, staring straight ahead as if seeing something beyond the room, beyond the shelter. Perhaps the suffering that was out there.

Bryce raised both hands to quiet them and said reluctantly, "There is still a consequence of the attack that must be dealt with. I know it's difficult for every man and woman in this room, but the reality of what has happened and what is going to happen must be faced now. If we are all aware of the worst effects of nuclear war, then nothing will be unexpected, nothing more will further demoralize us. Hopefully," he added ominously.

"The next problem for every survivor of the blast is fallout. Most of the city's population would have had less than half an hour to get under cover before radioactive dust fell. Those still unprotected within six hours of the attack will have received a lethal dose of radiation and will die within a matter of days or weeks, depending on the individual dosage. And, of course, anyone injured by the blast or its effects will be even more susceptible to radiation. Unofficial figures indicate that around four million people within the Greater London boundaries will be dead or dying within two weeks of the attack from a lethal dose of more than six thousand rads."

Farraday's voice was shaky when he spoke and Culver had the impression that he asked the next question for the benefit of his staff rather than his own curiosity.

"Can you tell us how many will be left alive after all this?"

Eyes riveted on the Civil Defense officer. He was thoughtful for a moment or two, as though silently counting bodies.

"I would say—and this is purely a rough judgment on my part—that barely a million Londoners will survive."

He paused again, his eyes cast down, as though expecting uproar; but the hushed silence that briefly filled the room was even more daunting.

"We've got families out there!" It was a wild shout, and Culver turned to see a small man at a center table who had risen to his feet, his fists clenched, a moistness to the anger in his eyes. "We've got to get to them! We can't leave them out there on their own."

"No!" There was a brutal coldness to Dealey. "We can't leave this shelter to help anyone. It would be fatal."

"Do you think we care about that?" This time a woman was on her feet, her tears unrestrained. "Do you think there's anything left for us here? Any life for us to live?"

Other voices joined hers.

"Please!" Dealey's arms were raised once more. "We must not lose control! It's only if we survive—and other units like ours—that we can help the people outside. If we panic, then the survivors of the blast will have no chance at all. You must understand that!"

Farraday leapt to his feet. "He's right. If we leave this shelter too soon, we'll be subjected to lethal doses of radiation poisoning. How will killing ourselves save those on the outside?"

They understood the logic of his argument, but such high emotion was not subservient to hard fact. There were more shouts, some of it abusive and particularly directed toward Dealey, who, as a Ministry of Defense employee, was held in some way responsible for the disaster.

It was Dr. Reynolds who calmly brought the room to order. "If any of you go out from this shelter now, you'll be dead within a matter of weeks, possibly days." Her voice was raised just enough to be heard over the clamor. She, too, was standing, her hands tucked into the pockets of her open white coat, and it was probably the uniform of her profession that gave her some credence. She represented the physical antithesis of Dealey, a man who was the puppet of a government that had brought their country to war.

"I can tell you this," she said, the noise beginning to subside. "It won't be a pleasant death. First, you'll feel nauseous and your skin will turn red, your mouth and throat inflamed. You won't have much strength. Vomiting will follow and you'll suffer pretty excruciating diarrhea for a few days. You may start to feel a little better after this, but, I promise you, it won't last.

"All those symptoms are going to return with a vengeance, and you'll sweat, your skin will blister, and your hair will fall out.

"You women will find your menstruation cycle will ignore the usual rules—you'll bleed a lot, and badly. You men will have pain in your genitals. If you do survive, which I doubt, you'll be sterile, or worse: the chances are that any offspring will be abnormal. Leukemia will be a disease you'll know all about—from a personal point of view.

"Toward the end, your intestines will be blocked. You might find that the worst discomfort of all. Finally, and perhaps mercifully, convulsions will hit you, and after that, you won't care very much. You'll sink into a brief coma, then you'll be dead."

The eyes behind the large glasses were expressionless.

Jesus, thought Culver, she didn't pull her punches.

"And if that isn't enough, you'll have the pleasure of watching others around you dying in the same way, watching the agonies of those in the more advanced stages, *witnessing* what you yourself will soon be going through.

"So if you want to leave, if you want to expose yourself to all that, knowing you'll be too ill to help others, I don't see why we should stop you. In fact, I'll plead on your behalf to allow you out, because you'll only cause dissension in this shelter. Any takers?"

She sat down when she was sure there wouldn't be.

"Thank you, Dr. Reynolds," said Dealey, "for explaining the reality of the situation."

She did not look at Dealey, but Culver could see there was no appreciation of his thanks.

"Perhaps now that you've heard everything at its pessimistic worst, we can continue on a more constructive note.'' Dealey briefly touched the bandages over his eyes, as though they were causing discomfort. ''I said earlier that we were not isolated here in this shelter. I know our lines of communication have been temporarily cut, but at least we're secure in the knowledge that there are many others who will have survived the blast in shelters such as this. And all these shelters are connected by either the post-office tube network or the London Transport Underground system.''

''It stands to reason that if our radio and telephone connections have been knocked out, then these tunnels will have been destroyed too,'' someone called out.

''True enough. I'm sure a few of the tunnels have been damaged, perhaps even destroyed completely, but there are too many for the whole system to have been wrecked. And also, certain buildings have been constructed to withstand nuclear explosions, buildings such as the Montague House 'Fortress' and the Admiralty in Pall Mall. I won't give details of all the bunkers and what are called 'citadels' that have been built since the last world war, but I can tell you that there are at least six shelters on the Northern Line tunnel system alone, below stations such as Clapham South and Stockwell . . .''

Culver had the feeling that however candid Dealey was appearing to be as he listed other sites in and around London, he was still holding back, still not telling all. He mentally shrugged; it would be hard to trust any government man from now on.

''Dealey!''

Heads turned to look at Culver. Dealey stopped speaking, and the telltale tongue flicked across his lips.

''Have you told anybody about the creatures out there?'' Culver's voice was level, but there was a tightness to it. The girl beside him stiffened.

''I hardly think it need wor—''

''It's got to worry us, Dealey, because sooner or later

we've got to go out there into those tunnels. The main entrance is blocked, remember? The tunnels are our only way out.''

''I doubt they'll stay underground. They'll scavenge for food . . . on the surface. And in that case, they'll die from radiation poisoning.''

Culver smiled grimly. ''I don't think you've been doing your homework.''

Farraday broke in. ''What's he talking about? What are these creatures?''

This time it was Dr. Reynolds who spoke. She removed her glasses and polished them with a small handkerchief. ''Dealey, Culver and Miss Garner were attacked by rats outside this shelter. It appears they were particularly large and, to say the least, unusually ferocious. They had attacked and were devouring survivors who had taken shelter in the tunnels.''

''They will be no threat to us,'' Dealey insisted. ''By the time we leave this shelter, most of these vermin will be dead.''

Culver shook his head and Dr. Reynolds answered. ''You really should have known this, Mr. Dealey. Or perhaps you wanted to forget. You see, certain forms of life are highly resistant to radiation. Insects are, for instance. And so, too, are rats. And if these creatures are descendants of the black rats that terrorized London just a few years ago—and from their size, I'd say they were—then not only will they be resistant to radiation, but they'll thrive on it.''

7

A noise.

He listened intently.

A scratching sound.

He waited.

Nothing. Gone now.

Klimpton tried to stretch his body, but there wasn't room even to straighten his legs. He flexed his back muscles and twisted his neck from side to side, refraining from groaning, not wanting to wake the others.

What time was it?

The digital figures of his watch glowed green on his wrist. 11:40 P.M. Night.

There was no other way of telling night from day, not there, not in their small dusty prison.

How long? Dear God, how long had they been down there? Two days? Three? A week? No, it couldn't be that long. Could it? Time didn't count for much when shadows failed to move.

But what had woken him? Had Kevin cried out in his

sleep once more? What did the boy think of the grown-up world now?

Klimpton reached for the small penlight he carried in his shirt pocket and flicked it on, sheltering the small beam with his hand. The urge to switch on the larger lamp hanging from a peg just above his head was strong, but he had to conserve the batteries; no telling how long they would have to stay down there. The candles, too, had to be saved.

He shone the light toward his son, the pinpoint of light barely touching the boy's eyes. His sleeping hours had been erratic and restless enough without spoiling what now appeared to be a deep slumber. Kevin's face was peaceful, his lips slightly parted, only a dust smear on one cheek giving evidence that all was not quite normal. A slight movement of the wrist and another face was revealed close to the boy's, but this was old, the skin gray, like dry, wrinkled paper. Gran's mouth was open too, but it held none of the sensuous innocence of his son's. The opening—hardly any lips anymore—was too round, the cavern too black and deep. It seemed every breath exhaled let slip a little more of her life. And, face turned toward her, his son drew in that escaping life in short, shallow intakes, as though quietly stealing his grandmother's existence.

"Ian?" Klimpton's wife's voice was distant, full of sleep. He turned the light toward her and she closed her barely opened eyes against it.

"It's all right," he whispered. "Thought I heard something outside."

She turned from him, snuggling farther down into the sleeping bag. "It was probably Cassie," she mumbled. "Poor dog." Sian had already returned to her dream before he switched the penlight off, and he was hardly surprised; like him, she had slept only fitfully and not for very long since they had been ensconced in the improvised shelter.

Thanks to him, his family had been saved. Sian had scoffed when he had studiously read the Home Office's survival booklet, and he himself had felt embarrassed by his own attention to it. Nevertheless, he had taken it seriously. Not at first, of course. His initial inclination when the booklet had fallen through the slot onto the doormat was to glance through, then toss it into the wastepaper basket; but something had made him keep it, hide it between books in his study. A rational fear that someday the instructions might come in useful. And later, tension around the Gulf States had caused him to retrieve it and study the directions more thoughtfully.

The booklet had advised householders to find a protected refuge in their own houses, a cellar or closet beneath the stairs. Klimpton's house had both: the steps leading down to the basement area had a closet beneath them. To go to such lengths as whitewashing all the windows of his house would have made him the laughingstock of the neighborhood, even when the world crisis was reaching breaking point, but internal measures could be easily taken without public knowledge. Things like collecting one or two plastic buckets, for sanitation purposes as well as storing water, and stocking canned food, not upstairs in the pantry, where it would just disappear through daily use, but down in the basement itself, on a shelf where it would be forgotten, until it was needed. Keeping sleeping bags and bedding somewhere handy, somewhere it could be conveniently grabbed should the emergency arise. Having more than one flashlight—and a lamp—plus a supply of batteries. Candles. Containers. Portable stove. First-aid kit. Other items like magazines, books, comics for Kevin. Toilet paper. Essentials, really.

Of course, the clutter under the stairs had to be cleared. And a tattered mattress brought down from the loft to lean against the outside of the closet door. He hadn't blocked up the small basement window whose top half was at street level, and there had been no time to do so when the sirens had alarmed the district. But he had done the best for his family, and they had survived the worst. And most of all, he had been with his family when the bombs were dropped.

The scratching sound again.

Somewhere outside, in the basement itself.

Was it the dog? Had Cassie found a way into the cellar?

Impossible. Klimpton had had to lock their pet out, much to the distress of Kevin, for there was no way they could have an animal living with them. It would have been too unhygienic.

Klimpton shifted his legs, groaning as bones wearily protested. The only way he could sleep was in an upright position; there just wasn't room for them all to lie down.

They were supposed to stay inside the refuge for at least forty-eight hours, and inside the house, preferably the basement, for much longer, two weeks at least, maybe more. The sirens would sound again when it was safe to come out.

He could risk leaving the closet now, he was sure. They *had* to have been inside for at least a week. And the stink from the plastic bucket, dosed with disinfectant and covered with a plastic bag though it was, would make them all ill before much longer.

Klimpton shrugged himself loose from the covering blanket and groped for the larger flashlight he kept by his side. His hand closed around Gran's bony ankle, but she did not stir. Her flesh was cold even though the atmosphere inside the closet was warm and clammy.

He found the flashlight, then groped for the plastic bucket with its full contents. The bucket was easy to find in the dark—practically everything was within reach—and he lifted it by its wire handle. His nose wrinkled in disgust.

Half-turning, Klimpton pushed against the small door to his right, only the pressure from the mattress outside giving some resistance. He leaned his shoulder more firmly into the wood and the gap widened.

Once he had wriggled himself outside, he switched on the flashlight, waiting for the dazzle in his eyes to fade before venturing farther. He swallowed hard. The sooner he was out in the comparative openness of the cellar, the better.

He wondered if there would be any cellar left. Perhaps the whole house had fallen in, leaving the basement open to the skies. To the fallout. Stupid. They would surely have known if that had been the case. It had been quiet down there. And the air was heavy, stale.

Fearfully, Klimpton raised the flashlight, dreading what he might find. The ceiling, though large chunks of plaster were missing, had withstood the impact. He quickly swept the beam around the basement and stopped when it fell upon the small window. Rubble had poured through, smashing both glass and frame, creating a slope of debris. At least the opening was completely filled, leaving no room for fallout dust to sneak in.

Using elbows and knees, he pushed himself clear of the tunnel and stood, his chest heaving with the exertion, surprised that such a small effort had left him so breathless. All the hours of cramped inactivity, combined with the stale air they had been forced to breathe, had taken their toll.

The scratching sound again.

His chest stopped its swelling, his breath only half drawn in. He swung the beam into a far corner. Nothing there. Then along the base of one wall. Another corner. The next wall, leading back toward the stairs. Nothing. No junk, no discarded furniture, just . . . just . . . something that shouldn't be there.

A shadow.

He steadied the flashlight, peered closer, and—

Scrabbling sounds from above!

Frantic. Claws against wood.

The stairs. It came from the top of the stairs.

And then a whimper. A mewling, begging whimper.

Klimpton let the half-breath go, then drew in a full slow breath. Cassie had heard him down there. The poor old bitch was trying to get to him. He shone the flashlight up the stairs and the scratching became more frenzied. She could probably see the light beneath the door. He'd better calm her down before she woke the others.

Quietly as possible, Klimpton climbed the wooden steps, at once relieved and disappointed that Cassie was still alive. Alive, she posed a problem.

A small, excited yelp as he approached. The clawing increased. As his head drew level with the foot of the door, he leaned forward, one hand resting against the top step, his mouth moving close to the gap under the wood.

Below him, something moved from the unusual shadow in the wall.

"Cassie," he said quietly.

A small, tired bark came back.

"I know, Cassie; I know, girl. You're scared, you want to be with us. But I can't let you in, not just yet. Understand, I want to, but I can't."

Another shape was born from the shadow. It lingered for a moment, a dark form concealed by the surrounding blackness. It moved, stealthily, joining its companion.

Klimpton wondered if he should open the door a little, just enough to reassure Cassie, perhaps calm her. The dog was losing control, becoming too frenzied.

The man on the stairs had not noticed a rent in the wall and floor, a fissure caused by the shifting of earth, the movement of concrete. He was unaware of the skulking, bristle-furred beasts, as they filed swiftly from the opening like smooth black fluid.

One of the night creatures stood poised at the foot of the stairs, its yellow eyes glinting, a reflection from the flashlight beam. Two long clawed feet rested against the bottom step; the vermin's back was hunched, giving it an arched appearance. It studied the man for long moments, until its snout twitched, sniffing the air. It moved away from the step and sniffed its way around the plastic bucket, attracted by the aroma of excrement and urine. The sounds of movement close by diverted its attention. And instinctively it was aware that the animals who made the sounds were weak. Its jaws opened to reveal long, sharp teeth that dripped with wetness.

The rat entered the tunnel, its body, with its wide powerful haunches and hunched back, fitting comfortably. One of its companions followed. Then another.

The scaly pink tail of the last rat slithered snakelike through the dust of the cellar floor before disappearing into the inner blackness.

Above, Cassie was barking frantically, running away from the door, then returning with a crashing thump, throwing herself so hard at the wood that Klimpton felt sure she would burst through. He was frightened by her actions, fearing that if she did break into the cellar, she would run amok. Her screeching bark was near-demented, and Klimpton shuddered to think of the effects of a bite from a mad dog.

He staggered back at the force of the next throw, grabbing the handrail to keep his balance. How the hell could he pacify her, how could he soothe her? How could he make her damn well stop? Wasn't their nightmare enough?

A scream. From below.

Sian!

Kevin!

He turned on the stairs and the flashlight beam swung down.

Klimpton almost collapsed. And if he had, he would have fallen among them.

For the cellar was alive with thick, furry bodies, a black carpet of moving shapes, squirming, leaping over one another's backs, never still, long pointed noses raised here and there to sniff the air, eyes caught in the glare of the flashlight, glinting yellow, like those of cats, a terrible mass of writhing vermin, so big, so huge, like nothing he'd ever seen before, monsters, hideous . . .

"Nooooo!" he cried when his family's screams broke through his shock. Looking over the handrail, he saw the creatures disappearing into the mattress tunnel to the shelter. His family was screaming beneath his feet.

Klimpton ran down the steps, leaping the last few, landing among the rats, stumbling, falling to his knees. He lashed out with the flashlight, and the creatures scurried away. He was up, kicking out, screaming at them, tearing at the chest of drawers, pulling it aside, ignoring the teeth that sank into his calf muscles. He pulled at the mattress and the closet door swung away with it.

A weight thudded against his back, but he did not feel the razor teeth slash his skin, tearing flesh away with his shirt material in a large, loose flap. He did not feel the mouth that tightened around his thigh, the long incisors seeking the warm liquid within. He did not feel the claws that raked the back of his legs, nor the snapping jaws that gained purchase between them.

He only felt the pain of his wife, his son, his mother.

As the screams eventually faded, so the dog's blows against the door became weaker. And when the sounds in the cellar were only feeding noises, Cassie's barks became a wailing moan. And when the blows stopped and the door was still, all that could be heard was a whimpering, muffling sound.

And, from below, a rapacious gnawing.

8

"How is he?"

Dr. Reynolds, whose eyes had been cast down in thought as she closed the sick-bay door behind her, looked up in surprise. She smiled at the girl, and Kate saw the tiredness behind the smile. And the anxiety.

Clare Reynolds leaned back against the door, hands tucked into her coat pockets, a familiar gesture. "He'll pull through," she answered, and Kate realized the anxiety was for more than just Culver; it was for all of them.

"The radiation penetration was minor—less than a hundred rads, I'd say." The doctor took out a cigarette pack and offered it to Kate. "Do you smoke? I haven't noticed."

Kate shook her head.

"Sensible." Dr. Reynolds lit her cigarette with a slim lighter. She drew in a deep breath and closed her eyes, face toward the concrete ceiling. The gesture of removing the cigarette and exhaling a thin stream of blue smoke was almost elegant. Her eyes opened once more.

"Thanks for helping out over the past few days."

"It kept me busy, and that helped me."

"That seems to be a problem in this place: very little to do for most of the staff. For some it induces apathy; for others, discontent. They need something other than death and destruction to keep their minds occupied."

"Farraday's tried to keep them busy."

"Any luck with communications?"

"Not as far as I know. It could be that we're all that's left."

Dr. Reynolds studied the girl thoughtfully. She looked better than when she had first arrived, but the fear was still there, that barely disguised brittleness, a reed that could snap at any moment rather than bend. Her hair was clean, a lively yellow, her eyes softer now, but still uneasy. The torn blouse had been replaced by a man's shirt, hanging loose over her skirt. On one side, high on her chest, a film badge was pinned, a dosimeter that everyone in the shelter had been instructed to wear; at the end of each week, these were to be analyzed by the small radiology department housed in the underground complex. Dr. Reynolds could not quite understand the need, for there were enough ionization instruments strategically placed around the shelter to give full warning of any radiation leakage, but she assumed they were used for psychological effect, a reassurance to the wearer. What reassurance, should they begin to become cloudy?

"Would you like a coffee?" she asked. "I'm desperate for one. It'd give us a chance to talk."

Kate nodded and Dr. Reynolds pushed herself away from the door. They headed toward the dining area.

"Will Steve be all right?" Kate asked again, not satisfied with the doctor's previous answer.

A technician stood aside to allow them room to pass along the narrow corridor. Dr. Reynolds nodded her thanks, smiling briefly. "Oh, yes, I think he'll be fine. Although the radiation dose was comparitively minor—the worst physical effect, apart from the nausea and dizziness, was to render him sterile for a day or two, and I'm sure that didn't bother him in his condition—I'm afraid it considerably lowered his resistance to infection from the rat bite. Fortunately, the powers-that-be thoughtfully provided an antidote to the disease this particular beast—"

Kate had stopped. "Disease?"

The doctor took her arm and kept her walking.

"Some years ago, this breed of rodent—a mutation, as I understand it—inflicted an extreme form of leptospirosis into anyone it bit. A cure was found soon enough, and it was thought that the vermin had eventually lost this extra weapon in their nasty little arsenal. It seems the medical authorities were never quite sure, though, so they decided to play it safe, should the worst ever happen. I found our lifesaver among the medical supplies."

"Then why wasn't I infected? And Alex Dealey?"

Dr. Reynolds shrugged. "You weren't bitten—at least not deeply. You suffered scratches, mostly. And Dealey wasn't touched by them."

The thrum of the power generator reached their ears and was somehow comforting, an indication that technological civilization had not broken down totally.

"In Culver's case, the radiation weakened his system enough to leave him susceptible to the disease. Luckily, I injected both of you after I put you out the other day. You yourself probably didn't need it, but I wasn't taking any chances."

They passed the ventilation plant and Dr. Reynolds gave a small wave to a group of technicians. Only one, a stocky blond man, returned the wave.

"Hope they're not planning a revolution," the doctor commented, drawing on the cigarette.

The two women entered the kitchen area and Dr. Reynolds poured two coffees from the unattended machine on the small counter. One or two groups were scattered around the dining area talking in lowered voices. Kate poured cream into her coffee; Dr. Reynolds took hers black. They found a table by a gray-green wall and the doctor gratefully sank into a chair, flicking ash into the scrupulously clean ashtray. Kate sat opposite and looked intently into the big spectacles windowing her companion's eyes.

She looked back at the girl. "Who did you lose?"

Kate's eyes lowered. "Parents. Two brothers. I assume they're gone."

The doctor leaned forward and touched her wrist. "That may not be so, Kate. There's still a chance they survived."

The girl shook her head, and there was a sad, tearful smile on her lips. "No, it's better this way. I don't want to live in hope for them. And I wouldn't want them to have suffered. Better to believe they went instantly and with as little pain as possible."

Dr. Reynolds stubbed out her cigarette in the ashtray. "Maybe that's the best way. At least you can't be disappointed. Did you have a lover, a boyfriend?"

"I did." She didn't elaborate. "But that ended months ago." The familiar pain was there, familiar to Dr. Reynolds because she had observed it in the faces of so many in the shelter. She had seen it in her own reflected image each time she looked into a mirror.

"You know, Culver had nobody."

Kate's attention returned, not swiftly, because memories sought to overwhelm.

"He told you that?"

"Not directly." Clare reached for another cigarette. "Couple of nights ago, when his fever was at his worst, Culver was crying in his sleep calling out something, perhaps a name—I couldn't catch it."

"It could have been someone who died in the attack."

"No, I got the feeling it was long before. He said over and over again: "I can't save her, the water's got her. She's gone, gone . . ." My guess is that this woman—

girlfriend or wife—was drowned, and in some way he feels responsible.''

"Why do you say that?''

"Just a feeling. I suppose his dreams reveal classic guilt symptoms. Perhaps they had a tiff and he wasn't around to drag her out of the water. Who knows? Whatever, he's still bothered by it. Maybe that's why he went for you out there in the tunnel.''

"Because of guilt?'' Kate's eyes widened in surprise.

"No, no, not exactly. But it must have been very tempting to leave you there and sneak into the shelter. Let's face it, the odds were against all three of you surviving an attack from those monsters. Did you know he also pulled Dealey into safety when the first bomb hit? Maybe he's trying to make amends for something he didn't do in the past, or maybe he just doesn't care about himself. Maybe both reasons.''

"It could be he's just a very brave man.''

"Uh-huh. Could be. I haven't met many of those, though.'' She flicked ash. "Culver should be up and around in a day or two. He's sleeping now, but why don't you go down and see him later. I think you'd be welcome. In fact, I think you'd be good for each other.''

"It's too soon for that. Too much has happened.''

"I didn't mean it that way. I meant you could give each other some comfort, some moral support, if you like. God knows, all of us need it. But as you implied, if it comes to sleeping together, it's precisely because so much has happened that from here on in, *nothing* will be too soon. Kate, have you any idea what we've got to face when we get out of this shelter? I'll rephrase that: *if* we get out of this shelter.''

"I don't want to think about it.''

"You're going to have to. We all are. Because we may be all that's left.''

"Dr. Reynolds—''

"Forget the formality. Call me Clare.''

"Clare, I'm not a fool. I've got some idea of what's happened outside this shelter and I know it's going to be grim—no, not grim, awful, God bloody awful—and I know that nothing will ever be the same again. I didn't care at first, but now I want to live through this; I want to survive, no matter what the world has become. For now, though, just for a little while, I need to adjust. Give me that time and I'll help you in anything you want. I can't promise I'll make a good nurse—I hate the sight of blood—but I'll do my best to help in any way I can."

Clare smiled, patted Kate's hand. "You'll do," she said.

They drank their coffee in silence for a while and the doctor wondered how any of them would really cope once they were outside. The prospects were daunting, not least for members of her own profession, for she knew that at least half, if not more, of the city's hospitals would have been demolished by the blasts, and many doctors, nurses, and medical staff would have been killed or injured. The demand on the services of those who survived would be too enormous to contemplate.

She tried to close her mind to all the possibilities crowding in, but they were ruthless harpies who refused to give her peace.

In the days, weeks, that would follow, other environmental hazards would arise. There would be millions of decomposing corpses, both human and animal, lying in the streets or under rubble, food for insects . . . and vermin. God, supposedly there were a hundred million rats, double the human population, living in England alone, only strict measures controlling their constant growth in numbers. Those measures would not exist anymore . . .

"Are you all right?" Kate was leaning forward anxiously. "You suddenly went deathly pale."

"Uh? Oh, just thinking. Just considering the mess we've got ourselves into." She stubbed out the half-smoked cigarette, then lit another. "Shit, I should stop doing that. Cigarettes might not be so easy to come by from now on.''

"Do you want to share your thoughts?"

"Not particularly, but since you ask . . .'' She rubbed her neck and twisted it in a circular movement, easing the stiffness. "I was just mulling over the diseases that are likely to be rife when we eventually get out. Without proper sanitation, and with everything rotting up there, enteric infections—"

Kate looked puzzled.

"Sorry—intestinal infections could soon reach epidemic proportions. Some of the illnesses will be respiratory—pneumonia, bronchitis, that kind of thing— while others will be disorders such as hepatitis, dysentery, tuberculosis. I think typhoid and cholera will spread. Any sickness, you see, any debilitation, will be exaggerated, and will lead to worse illnesses. Simple measles could become an epidemic. Any childhood infectious disease could wipe out thousands, maybe millions. Meningitis, encephalitis—that's inflammation of the brain—even veneral diseases. The list is endless, Kate, just damn well endless, and I don't think any of us—the government, the medical profession—can do anything about it! They'll kill us all, maybe not tomorrow or the next day, but eventually. We don't have a hope in hell.''

It was all said in a flat monotone. An underlying hysteria in the doctor's voice would have been less frightening to Kate. Others in the room were looking in their direction and she wondered if they had heard, soft-spoken though Dr. Reynolds' words had been.

"Clare, there must be some chance for us. If we can get to another part of the country . . .''

The other woman sighed deeply. "I wonder just how much of the country is left. We've no way of knowing how many missiles were used against us. And whatever parts haven't been destroyed will be subjected to fallout drifting on air currents. Oh, Kate, I'd like to have hope, and I know that, as a doctor, I shouldn't be talking like this; but all I feel is a despairing numbness inside, a huge dull-gray blankness. It won't allow room for anything else.''

Kate searched in the older woman's eyes for some sign of inner conflict, a softness, an indication of hidden tears perhaps, or even anger. But the eyes were expressionless. Not cold, not dead. Just void of all emotion.

Kate shuddered inwardly, and a chill touched her with the knowledge that the nightmare was not over. It had only just begun.

9

Culver looked around the sick bay, hoping he might find one of the other "patients" awake, eager to talk. He was bored, annoyed at his confinement. The others were all asleep, as he guessed they would be, for they had been heavily sedated. Three technicians and one ROC officer had given way under the pressure so far. One of the technicians, a young man in his late twenties, had sliced his wrists with a razor blade. Only blood spilling beneath the toilet door had saved him. The woman, whom Culver had seen wearing the Royal Observer Corps uniform on the first day inside the shelter, had tried pills stolen from the medical store. The sound of her retching as they forced a rubber tube into her throat had roused him from a deep sleep the night before.

He sank back onto the pillow, an arm going behind his head to prop himself up. Five days he'd been out, according to the doctor, the radiation sickness hitting him first, then reaction from the rat bite jumping in like some eager bully who wouldn't be left out of the fun. Well, he'd been lucky. The dose was minor although weakening, and Dr. Reynolds had found something to counteract the infection. She had explained about the disease the vermin carried and, as a precaution, had inoculated everyone in the shelter against it. They were safe inside, she had said, but eventually they would have to surface and it was just as well to be prepared for *any* dangers that might be out there. Rats would be the least of their problems, Culver had thought.

He lifted the sheet to examine the bite. The wound, no longer dressed, looked an angry red. It felt sore, but not too painful. He'd live.

Letting the sheet drop back over his naked body, he stared up at the bunk bed above. As with the aftermath of any debilitating illness, everything seemed fresh, even the turgid colors of the sick-bay walls. The neon lights shone cleaner, brighter, the wires beneath the bed overhead sharp, their pattern precise. Even the filtered air smelled fresher. He could hardly recall the agonies he had gone through—save for the acute stomach cramps—but Dr. Reynolds had told him he had become yellow as a Chinese at one stage. Sudden spasms of muscular pains, constant vomiting, and delirium had been the results of the fever— all, she assumed, heightened by the radiation his body had absorbed. Fortunately, the antidote had worked quickly and much of the badness had been flushed from him through open pores and other orifices within the first couple of days. After that, total exhaustion held him in its smothering embrace, and complete rest was the only cure for that.

Culver felt fit enough. Maybe just a little weak, but he was sure his strength would soon return when he was up on his feet. If only he knew where they'd put his clothes.

He pulled the sheets back and swung his legs onto the floor, then rapidly swung them back and covered his lower body as the door opened. The girl entered and smiled when she saw him half-sitting in the bunk bed.

"You look good," she said, walking toward him.

He nodded. "I feel, uh, okay."

She sat at the end of the bed, leaning forward a little to avoid the top bunk. "We were worried for a while. I never realized the human body could lose so much waste in such a short period of time."

"Yeah. Well, I'd rather forget about that. Did you take care of me?" He seemed surprised.

"Dr. Reynolds and I took it in turns. Don't you remember? She was with you *all* the time when your fever was at its peak, though."

He rubbed the stubble of his chin. "Sudden images flash into my mind." He was silent for a few moments, then said, "I remember you watching me. I remember your face looking down. You were weeping."

She avoided his eyes. "I didn't know how serious it was, whether you'd survive. You looked so awful." She moved closer and ran her fingers through his tousled sandy hair, using them as a rough comb. "There's a brightness to your eyes."

"I guess it's all the vitamins our lady doctor is pumping into me."

"She says that in a strange way you've been luckier than the rest of us."

He gave a short laugh. "This I gotta hear. Just how does she figure that?"

"You've been away from it. Your mind's been concerned with just one thing over the past few days: self-preservation. Even through your delirium it's been fighting, refusing to let go. And Clare—Dr. Reynolds—says your mind's been doing something else too."

Culver gently caught her wrist to stop her fingers moving through his hair. "What would that be?"

"The brain is a remarkable machine, it can do several things at once. While it was helping you pull through, it was also adjusting."

"Adjusting?"

"To everything that's happened. Oh, you've had your nightmares—some beauties, by the sounds of them—but all the time, your mind was accepting, going through everything that's happened, and, well . . . digesting it, if you like. We've had to go through the same stages, but consciously. We've had to live through it over and over again, and as you can see, some of us didn't make it. There are others who still won't."

He let go of her wrist and her hand dropped into her lap. "Will you?" he asked.

"I'm not sure. At first I thought it would be impossible. Now I don't know. It's incredible what you can learn to accept. I don't mean that this nuclear war will ever be acceptable to any of us, but eventually I think our circumstances will. We'll live with what we have."

Culver was startled by the change in her. But then, she had still been in a state of profound shock in their first few hours inside the refuge. There had never been the chance for him to see what lay beyond that state. He brushed her cheek with the back of his hand.

She blinked, and he guessed it was to clear the moistness in her vision. "We're both wanted elsewhere," she told him.

He raised her eyebrows.

"Alex Dealey wants to see you in the operations room."

"So he's already set up a company command."

"This place is more surprising than you think. Even the technicians who worked here on a day-to-day basis had no idea what the shelter comprised exactly. Apparently, much of the complex was out of bounds even to them."

"Yeah, that makes sense. The authorities wouldn't want the word to get around that such underground bunkers existed. People might have read something into it and become frightened." He grinned. "You mean I can get out of this goddamn bed without the doc slapping my bottom?"

"She won't condone any more malingering."

He shook his head once, still grinning. "She's changed her tune. One problem: do I go naked or do I make a toga out of this sheet?"

"I'll get your things."

Kate quickly walked to a small door at the other end of the sick bay, glancing at the prone figures lying in the other bunk beds as she did so. She disappeared through the door and Culver heard the sound of what must have been a locker opening then closing. She returned with some familiar items of clothing.

"Cleaned, but not pressed," she announced, dumping them in his lap. "Oh, and I did my best with the hole in your jeans. It doesn't look too good, but at least it's stitched."

"You've been busy."

"There hasn't been much else to do."

He separated the clothing. "Er, do you want to wait outside?"

She surprised him again by laughing, for there was genuine humor in the sound. "Mr. Culver, I've washed you and wiped you and seen anything you've got to offer. It's too late to be coy."

His feet touched the floor, but the sheet remained over his nakedness. He flushed red. "This is different."

Kate turned away, still smiling. "Okay, I promise not to peek, but I won't step outside. You may not be quite as strong as you think."

When he stood, Culver understood what she meant. Dizziness hit him and he grabbed the top bunk. She was at his side instantly.

"Easy, Steve," she said. "It'll take a little while."

He waited for his vision to clear, one hand on her shoulder, locks of her hair brushing against his fingers. He was conscious of her body's natural scent, its freshness, and the arm she had around him, the warmth of the hand on his hip.

"Thanks," he mumbled. "I should have listened. I'm coming together, though. If you could just hang on to me for a minute."

She did, and was glad to.

"You could easily get lost in this place," Culver remarked as Kate led him through the gray corridors. His legs still felt weak, his head still light, but there was a swift-returning vitality to his senses that made Culver wonder just *what* Dr. Reynolds had been dosing him with.

"It's quite a complex," said Kate. "I don't pretend to understand any of their machinery, but apparently this place is a repeater station, according to the technician who gave me a guided tour. I'm afraid intermediate distribution frames and motor-driven uniselectors don't do much for me." Kate glanced at him. "It's eerie seeing all this electronic equipment that isn't actually *doing* anything. I mean, you can feel it's alive, the current's still running through, but it's like some slumbering dinosaur, just waiting for something to rouse it."

"Maybe it's already become extinct. This kind of technology may not play much part in our immediate future."

"I don't think I could survive winter without my electric blanket."

"Try a hot-water bottle. Or another warm body."

She avoided his eyes and he suddenly felt foolish. Stupid remark, he scolded himself. He quickly went on. "I take it they haven't managed to contact anybody yet?"

"No. They've even used a continuous punched tape on a telex machine, but nothing's come back. We've no way of knowing what's going on out there."

"That could be for the best right now."

The corridor opened out and they almost bumped into a small but broad-shouldered figure emerging from behind a ceiling-high row of apparatus. Unlike many of the men inside the complex, he was clean-shaven and his light-yellow hair neatly combed.

"Hiya," the man said almost cheerfully. "How you doing? Feeling better?"

"Yeah, okay."

"Good. Catch you later."

He passed them and strolled down the corridor, hands tucked into overall pockets and whistling tunelessly.

"He seems cheerful enough," Culver said, watching the man's back.

"His name is Fairbank. He's one of the happier souls down here. Nothing appears to bother him. He's either supremely well-adjusted or crazy."

"How about the others? From what I saw last time they didn't look too good."

"Moods change all the time. It's contagious. One day the atmosphere's charged with an unnatural optimism; the next day you can feel the deep depression hanging in the air like a black thug. You've seen how disturbed some are in the sick bay. One or two others have been treated in there that you wouldn't know about—you were having your own problems."

They finally reached a closed metal door.

"HQ," she said, pushing through.

The people gathered in the room were facing away from Culver, studying a wall-mounted map. He noticed other maps around the room, mostly of the U.K., colored pins decorating each one. One was marked with a gridwork of thick black lines.

Dealey was pointing at something on the chart before them, stubbing a chubby finger against the plastic-coated paper as if emphasizing a point. Culver couldn't quite understand what was different about the man until Dealey turned to face him.

"No bandages," Culver said. "You can see?"

"As well as ever." He pointed to a chair. "Cleared up after the first day. No permanent damage, thank God."

Culver thought the man still looked drawn, weary, and who could wonder at it? It was obvious that Dealey had taken leadership on his own shoulders, a responsibility Culver didn't envy. He looked around the room and saw the same fatigue on the faces of the others. Perhaps the doctor had been right: he, Culver, had been well out of it for the past few days.

"We don't know much about you, Culver, except that you can take care of yourself pretty well." Dealey was frowning, as if the compliment wasn't easy. "May we ask what your occupation was before the attack?"

"Is it relevant?"

"I can't say until we know. We are a small group, and any variant skill could be useful for our survival. There will undoubtedly be other groups—whole communities, in fact—and I would hope eventually all our resources will be pooled. For now, though, we have only ourselves to rely on."

Culver smiled. "I don't think my, er, particular occupation will help in those circumstances." He added, almost apologetically, but still smiling, "I fly helicopters. Had my own outfit, nothing big. Just me with a partner to run the business side of things. Another pilot and a small ground crew. Nothing fancy."

"What did you carry?" Farraday asked.

"Freight mostly, passengers now and then. We operated out of Redhill, convenient for London and the south, but I wouldn't say we were a threat to Bristow, the big helicopter company based in the same area." He was smiling wryly. He found Dealey gazing at him in a peculiar way and realized the man was literally seeing him for the first time. Whatever physical attributes Dealey had associated with Culver's voice were now being confirmed or denied.

"Just as a matter of interest," Farraday said, "what brought you up to London last Tuesday?"

"I've been trying to raise money for a new chopper, an old Bell Two-twelve Bristow was selling off. They weren't interested in leasing, so I had to scrape up the cash. My bank was finally convinced the company was good for it."

"You were asking for a loan from your bank wearing a leather jacket and jeans?" Dealey asked incredulously.

Culver grinned. "Harry, my business partner, was the man who wore the suits. Besides, most of the begging had been done; the idea of the meeting was to clinch the deal." The grin disappeared. "I was running late, something Harry couldn't stand too well. He must have been there, at the bank, waiting for me. Probably apologizing to the manager."

"He may have been safe inside the building," Dealey said, realizing what was going through Culver's mind.

Culver shook his head. "The bank was close to the Daily Mirror Building. When we were out there I saw there wasn't much left of the Mirror, nor the buildings around it."

A silence hung in the air, a silence that Culver himself broke. "So what happens now? I assume the reason for this meeting is to discuss our future."

Farraday moved away from the wall and sat on a corner of Dealey's desk, his arms still folded. "That's correct, Mr. Culver. We need to formulate a plan of action to cover not just the weeks we'll have to stay inside this shelter, but also when we leave."

Culver looked around the room. "Shouldn't everybody be involved in this? It concerns us all."

Bryce, the CDO, shifted uncomfortably in his seat. "I'm afraid a situation is developing between us, if you like, the 'officers,' and the exchange staff. It's quite uncanny, but it's almost a minuscule encapsulation of how governments, since the last world war, have foreseen civil insurrection in the aftermath of a nuclear war."

"You may have noticed," Dealey said, "how many latter-day government buildings resemble fortresses."

"I can't say that I have."

Dealey smiled. "The fact that you, and the public in general, haven't is an achievement in itself for the various governments who commissioned such buildings. They were built, of course, as strongholds against civil uprising or attempted coup d'état, and not just in the event of revolution following a nuclear war. Several even have moats around them—Mondial House in the City is a good example, and the American Embassy—or they may have recessed lower floors to make entry difficult. The most obvious is the guards barracks at Kensington with its gun slits built into its outer walls.''

"Hold it." Culver had lifted a hand. "You're telling me there's a revolution going on down here?"

"Not yet," Clare Reynolds broke in. "But there is growing resentment among the technicians and staff of the telephone exchange. They've lost so much, you see, and we, the 'authorities,' are to blame. It doesn't matter that we've lost everything too, and that we, personally, are not responsible for this war; in their eyes, we represent the instigators."

"Meetings like this, where they're shut out, can't be helping matters," Culver said.

"We've no choice," Dealey said brusquely. "We can't possibly include everybody in policy decisions. It wouldn't be practical."

"They might feel that's how the world got into this sorry mess in the first place."

Dealey and Bryce glanced at each other, and the former said, "Perhaps we were wrong about you. We thought as an outsider—a 'neutral' if you like—you would be useful in bridging this unproductive division that's presented itself. If you feel you can't cooperate . . ."

"Don't get me wrong. I'm not against you. I'm not against anyone. What's happened has happened; nothing's going to make it different. I'd just hate everything to continue the way it has in the past; in a way that's led us to just this point. Can't you see that?"

"Yes, Mr. Culver," Farraday replied, "we understand your intent. Unfortunately, it isn't as simple as that."

Dealey interjected, "On your first day inside this shelter you witnessed for yourself the dissension among them. You saw how many wanted to leave, only Dr. Reynolds' good sense dissuading them. We cannot shirk our responsibilities toward everybody, including ourselves, by allowing mob rule."

"I wasn't talking about mob rule. What I'm referring to is group decision."

"There'll be time enough for that when the crisis has passed."

"This is a crisis that isn't going to pass." Culver could feel his anger growing, and he remembered Dealey urging him to leave Kate to the mercy of the rats in the tunnel. Throughout their ordeal, his priority had been one of self-preservation. "We've all got a stake in this, Dealey, me, you, and those poor bastards outside that door. It's not for us to decide their future."

"You misunderstand us," Bryce said placatingly. "We merely intend to plan, not decide. Our ideas will then be presented to everyone in this complex for discussion. Only after that will any decisions be made."

Culver forced himself to relax. "Okay, maybe I'm reading too much into this. It could be that yours is the only way, that we shall need some kind of order. But let me just say this: the time for power games is over." With these last words, he stared at Dealey, whose face was expressionless.

"We can take it, then," Dealey said, "that you will support us."

"I'll do what I can to help everyone in the shelter."

Dealey decided it would be pointless not to accept the rather ambiguous statement. He had hoped to find an ally in Culver, for any addition to their small nucleus of authority would help in the imbalance of numbers. If events had worked out as intended, many other outsiders would have reached the shelter, and this particular problem would never have arisen. He was disappointed, imagining that perhaps earlier circumstances might have created a bond between himself and Culver, but he could see that the pilot distrusted him. Culver was no fool.

"Very well," he said, as if to dismiss the dispute. "Before you arrived we were pinpointing the city's shelters and their linking tunnels. The other maps around the walls locate the country's thirteen sites for regional seats of government and various bunkers, most of which will have been immune from nuclear attack, provided there were no direct hits. The grids indicate the communications lines between RSGs and sub-RSGs." Dealey pointed to a particular chart showing the southwest of England. "Over there you can see the position of HQ U.K. land forces, operating from a vast bunker at Wilton, near Salisbury."

"Is that where the government will operate from?" Culver was already beginning to be intrigued.

"Er, no. There are several locations for the national seat of government, Bath and Cheltenham, just to name two." He appeared hesitant, and Culver saw Bryce give a slight nod of his head. Dealey acknowledged and went on. "Although the facts have been carefully kept from public attention, several more-than-educated guesses have been made concerning the whereabouts of the government's secret emergency bunker. Most have been correct, but none has understood the magnitude or the complexity of such a shelter."

Culver's voice was low. "Where is it?"

"Under Victoria Embankment," Dealey said mildly. "Close to Parliament and within easy reach by tunnel from the Palace, Downing Street, and *all* the government buildings packed into that rather small area of the city. The shelter itself stretches almost from the Parliament buildings to Charing Cross, where another tunnel, one that runs parallel to the Charing Cross–Waterloo tube tunnel, crosses the Thames."

"There are *two* tunnels?"

"Yes. The second, secret tunnel, a bunker in itself, provides a quick and safe means of crossing the river should the nearby bridges be destroyed or blocked.''

"How could such a place be kept quiet? How could it be built without people knowing?''

"Have you ever wondered why most of our cable tunnels and new Underground lines inevitably run over budget and invariably take longer to build than planned? The Victoria and Jubilee lines are prime examples of excavations that have far exceeded their financial allocation and completion dates.''

"You mean they were used to cover up work on secret sites?''

"Let's just say that room for more than just Underground lines was made. And all the construction workers—at least those employed on the more sensitive sites—were sworn to secrecy under the Official Secrets Act before they were assigned.''

"Even so, there must have been leaks.''

"Quite so, but the D Notice prevented any media exploitation.''

Culver released a short, sharp sigh. "So the elite got themselves saved.''

"Not the elite, Culver," Dealey said icily. "Key personnel and certain ministers who are necessary to pick the country up off its knees after such a catastrophe. And members of the royal family, naturally.''

"Would they have had time to reach the shelter?''

"Such provisions are always made possible for cabinet ministers and royal family in times of foreign aggression, no matter what particular location they happen to be in. From the headquarters itself is an escape route that stretches for miles underground. It emerges beneath Heathrow Airport. From there, one can escape to any part of the world.''

"Unless the airport has been destroyed," said Clare Reynolds, cigarette smoke streaming from tight lips.

"In which case, transport can be provided to another

part of the country," Dealey replied. He tapped unconsciously on the desktop with his fingers. "As yet, we have not been able to communicate with the Embankment headquarters, and it's vital we make contact soon. We intend to send out a small reconnaissance party to explore the conditions above us when the fallout level permits. We also need to evaluate the state of the tunnels, which may provide a safer route to the main government shelter."

He stared directly at Culver. "We hope you'll agree to be part of that reconnaissance group."

"Are you hungry, Steve?"

"Since you mention it, yes, I am." He grinned at Clare Reynolds, who had asked the question. "In fact, I'm starving."

"Good, that's how it should be. You'll be good as new in a day or two." She nodded in the general direction of the canteen. "Let's get you something to eat, then I want you to rest for a while. No sense in overdoing things."

She led the way, Kate and Culver following close behind. "I could use a stiff drink after that long meeting," she said, looking back at them over her shoulder. "It's a pity the hard stuff is being rationed so frugally."

"I could use a drink myself," Culver agreed. "I guess they didn't store much away down here, right?"

"Wrong," said Kate. "There's plenty, but Dealey thinks it wise to keep it under lock and key. Too much firewater no good for natives."

"He may have a point," the doctor said. "The natives are restless enough."

"It's really that bad?"

"Not that bad, Steve, but it's not good. Dealey may be suffering from a slight persecution complex because most of the resentment is directed toward him as the token government man. But as large as this complex is, there's a certain amount of claustrophobia prevailing; and that, coupled with a general feeling of melancholia, even repressed hysteria, could lead to an explosive situation. Too much alcohol wouldn't help."

Culver silently had to agree. The atmosphere in the shelter did somehow feel charged and he could understand Dealey's nervousness. He felt tired once more, the meeting draining much of the buoyancy he had felt earlier. Culver had been surprised at the elaborate contingency plans that were regularly scrutinized, amended, modified, and put into action throughout the decades of the cold war and détente eras, a festering, unspoken conflict, insidious in its durability. Now it had ended, mass destruction the terminator.

Culver shuddered to contemplate the New Order that must have already taken over. Unless, of course, the damage had been far greater than anyone had ever anticipated, the world itself dying and unable to respond to any kind of organization.

The doctor had come to a halt as a technician—later Culver was to find out his name was Ellison—approached her and said something in a low agitated voice. He turned without waiting for a reply and quickly strode back the way he had come.

"What's wrong?" Culver asked.

"I'm not sure," Dr. Reynolds replied, "but there seems to be something interesting going on. He wants me to hear something."

They followed the retreating figure and came to the ventilation plant room.

A group of men, some wearing white overalls, others in ordinary clothes, were gathered around a large air duct, the shaft of which, Culver assumed, rose to the surface. He guessed filters removed any radioactive dust from the air intake. Fairbank was among the group.

"Something we should know about?" Dr. Reynolds asked of no one in particular, and it was Fairbank who replied. There was a brightness to his eyes, but also an uncertainty.

"Listen," he said, and turned back to the air duct.

Above the hum of the generator they could hear another, more insistent sound. A drumming, a constant pattered beating.

"What is it?" Kate asked, looking at Culver.

He knew, and so did the doctor, but it was Fairbank who answered.

"Rain," he said. "It's raining up there like never before."

PART TWO

AFTERMATH

Their time had come.

They sensed it; they knew.

Something had happened in the world above them, a holocaust the creatures could not comprehend; yet they were instinctively aware that those they feared were no longer the same, that they had been damaged, weakened. The creatures had learned from those who had hidden in the tunnels, killing and feeding upon the humans, satisfying a lust that had lain dormant for many years, repressed because survival depended on that repression. The blood lust had been revived and set loose.

And the tunnels, the sewers, the conduits, the dark holes they had skulked in, never knowing or craving for a different existence, had broken, allowing the world of light to intrude upon their own dismal kingdom.

They crept up, steathily, sniffing the air, puzzled at the relentless drumming sound, emerging into the rain that drenched their bristle-furred bodies. The brightness dazzled their sharp eyes at first, even though it was muted an unnatural gray, and they were timid, fearful, *in their movements, still hiding from human eyes, still apprehensive of their age-old adversary.*

They moved out from the dark places and stole among the ruins of the city, rain-streaked black beasts, many in number, eager for sustenance. Hunting soft flesh. Seeking warm blood.

10

Sharon Cole thought her bladder might easily burst if she didn't do something about it soon. Unfortunately, the dark frightened her and she knew that beyond the Pit, the darkness was absolute. All the others appeared to be sleeping, their breathing, their snores, and their murmured whimpers filling the small steep-sloped auditorium with their sounds. If you couldn't sleep, the horror was ever-present; yet sleep and the nightmares allowed no peace.

They knew it was night only because their watches told them so, and dutifully, by agreement made between them all in the first days, they endeavored to maintain a natural order, as if adherence to ritual would bring a semblance of normalcy to abnormal circumstances.

Only three precious candles kept complete darkness at bay, the men deciding the flashlight batteries were more precious and not to be wasted in hours of inactivity. One or two had suggested a *total* blackout at night, but the majority, as many men as women, had insisted on keeping some light through the sleeping hours, perhaps believing, like their Neanderthal forefathers, that light held back any oppressive spirits. Most rationalized that there should always be some light source in case of emergencies; it made sense, but they knew they drew comfort from those small flickering flames strategically placed around the underground cinema.

Sharon shifted uncomfortably in the three seats she was sprawled across, the movement only causing the uneasy weight inside to press more insistently. She groaned. Oh, God, she'd have to go.

"Margaret?" Sharon whispered.

The woman who lay in the same row as her and whose head almost touched Sharon's did not stir.

"Margaret?" she said, a little louder this time, but there was still no response.

Sharon bit into her lower lip. She and the older woman had formed an unspoken alliance over the past few weeks, a bond of mutual protection against the embarrassments as well as the hazards of their predicament. They were among a group of survivors, less than fifty in number now that several had recently died. Sharon was just nineteen, a trainee makeup artist from the theater on the upper level, pretty, slim, and a pseudo-devotee to the arts; Margaret, fiftyish, round, once jolly, and a member of the brown-smocked corps of cleaners to the huge concrete cultural and business complex. Both had offered reciprocal comfort when the stresses of their existence had become too much, their frequent breakdowns managed as if on cue, relying on each other to be strong while one was temporarily weak. Both assumed their families—Margaret, a husband and three grown-up children; Sharon, parents, a younger sister, as well as several boyfriends—were lost to the bombs, and both now needed a support, someone to cling to, to rely on. They had become almost like mother and daughter.

But Margaret was sleeping deeply, perhaps for the first

time in so many weeks, and Sharon did not have the heart to wake her.

She sat and looked down at the dim rows, each one filled with restless bodies. One candle glowed in the center of the small stage, its poor light barely reflected from the gray screen behind. To one side lay the hastily gathered and meager provisions from the destroyed cafeteria two levels above the tiny, plush cinema known as the Pit. The food had cost dearly.

A security guard had led six others, all men, on a forage after one week's confinement, driven out by hunger. They had brought back as much unspoiled food as they could carry, as well as flashlights, candles, buckets, a first-aid kit, disinfectant, and curtains for blankets. They had also brought back with them the cancer that was the nuclear bombs' deadly afterthought.

It was two days before they would talk about the destruction they had witnessed above—no living person had been found, but there had been an abundance of mutilated bodies in the rubble—and three days before the first of them went down with the sickness. Shortly, four were dead, and within days the last two were gone. Their corpses were now lying in one corner of the foyer outside, the curtains they had brought back their shrouds.

And the toilets were also in the black tomb of the foyer.

For heaven's sake, Margaret, how could you be sleeping when I need you?

The lobby outside the theater was regarded almost as an airlock between the survivors and the dust-diseased world above, only to be entered when necessary, the cinema doors kept permanently closed, to be opened briefly for access and then just enough for a body to squeeze through. The danger from radiation out there seemed minimal, for the main staircase, a narrow-enough spiral, was blocked by debris. In the foyer were the telephone booths, long, curved seats around small fixed coffee tables, a bar, the elevator shafts, and the invaluable rest rooms—invaluable because they provided a source of water and they meant sanitary hygiene could be maintained. In an effort to preserve the supply, flushing was allowed only at the end of every two days, and the possibility that the drinking water could itself be radiation-contaminated was disregarded on the grounds that if they didn't drink, they would die anyway.

So, Sharon knew she would have to go out there into the high-ceilinged tomb where the dead men lay and walk by candlelight to the toilet. Alone.

Unless another female among the slumbering audience was awake and also needed to pee.

Sharon stood and hopefully scanned the rows of seats, peering through the gloom in search of another upright body. She coughed lightly to gain attention, but nobody acknowledged. It was strange how many hours most of them slept, albeit fitfully, despite the long days' inactivity. She supposed it had some psychological basis, an escape from the real, shattered world into another of dreams. Pity the dreams were usually so bloody awful.

Her bladder insisted time was running short.

"Hell," she whispered, and carefully edged her way toward the aisle, avoiding contact with the recumbents on the mauve and green seats. The material of her tight jeans stretched against her knees and thighs as she cautiously mounted the steps, one hand using the wall on her left for guidance and support. She reached the candle burning by the door and dutifully lit another beside it from the flame, ignoring the flashlight placed alongside for emergencies.

Sharon opened the door a fraction, just enough for her slim body to slide through, the tips of her breasts brushing against the edge. The door closed behind her and she raised the candle high to look around the cold mausoleum.

Back inside the theater, a figure quietly rose from the darkness.

Fortunately for Sharon, the feeble light did not reach the draped corpses in the far corner, but the smell of their corruption was strong. Heading for the closest toilet, she quickly crossed the thick-carpeted floor, her steps leaving unseen footprints in the dust that had settled into the pile.

Pushing briskly through the toilet door, relieved to be separated from the corpses, Sharon passed by the urinals and washbasins, making for the two cubicles at the far end. The mirrors above the basins reflected the candle-light and ghosted her presence.

Both cubicle doors were ajar and she was glad that to-night had been flushing night: the stench wasn't too bad. She entered one and, decorum unaffected by circum-stances, pushed the bolt to behind her. Retracting her stomach muscles, Sharon released the top button of her jeans, unzipped, and gratefully settled onto the toilet. She sighed deeply at the relief. She gazed at the candle glow by the gap beneath the cubicle door for several long mo-ments after the flow had stopped. The flame held faces, images, the pattern of her own life, all swimming incandescently before her in that small fire. People and memories, now consumed by a greater fire. Her eyes misted, the glow becoming softer, its edges even less de-fined, and she forced herself to stop thinking, to stem the spilling tears. There had been too much of that.

The candle flame leaned toward her, flickering wildly. Disturbed by a draft. She thought she heard the swish of the main door as it closed automatically.

Sharon stood, pulling the jeans over naked hips. She zipped up and listened.

A footstep?

"Hello?" Sharon listened again. "Hello? Is someone out there?"

Imagination?

Her own nervousness?

Maybe.

She stopped to pick up the candle, then unbolted the cu-bicle door. Her arm was outstretched, pushing the light into the darkness as she stepped through the door.

Sharon paused, listening once more. The blackness around her was more oppressive; the feeling of confinement, the sensing of millions of tons of concrete bearing down on the underground theater, was almost unbearable. She suddenly felt that the air itself had become thick, somehow sluggish in her lungs, but sensibly told herself it was all nerves, that distress was the instigator and her own imagination was gullible to its suggestions.

But someone was in there with her.

She could hear breathing.

A harsh, short breath and the candle was out. Acrid smoke from the expired flame. A scuffing sound against floor tiles. A quavery sucking in of air. The stale smell of another body.

A hand touching her face.

Her scream was cut short as strong fingers covered her mouth. Another arm reached around her, enclosing her ribs. The expired candle fell to the floor as a head pressed against her own.

"Don't struggle," came the urgent whisper. "I'll hurt you if you do."

It was then she knew the intent.

She panicked, her legs kicking empty air as her body was lifted. She tried to scream again, but the grip over her lips was too tight. She bit down hard and tasted blood.

The man who had followed her from the cinema, the man who had covertly watched her through the trauma of their forced internment, who knew that civilization was at an end, that there was only death awaiting them all, who knew there was no law to punish him, nothing left to prevent him taking what he wanted, cried out in pain, but did not relax his hold.

Their two bodies were half-slumped against the toilet wall, the back of Sharon's head against her assailant's chest. Her heels pressed hard against the floor, sending her body upward and back in a violent motion, the top of her head cracking against the man's jaw, sending his head snapping back to hit the wall tiles. He howled and his grip loosened.

Sharon slid away, slithering along on her back, brushing off his clutching hands. Her fingers curled around the edge of a urinal and she pulled herself forward, making for where she knew the main door had to be.

She screamed loudly as his weight bore down on her.

He had landed on her legs and was slowly crawling up the length of her body, using his weight to pin her against the floor. She felt his hands on her back, on her shoulders, fingers now curling in her hair, smashing her face against the hard floor tiles.

He pulled her around to face him, and her nails tore at his eyes. He slapped away her hands and pulled at her sweater, exposing her body. She screamed again, and a fist squelched against her already bloodied nose. Sharon groaned as invisible hands groped at her clothing.

Neither of them heard the scratching at the door.

The man was tearing at his own clothing, ripping off buttons, shoving underpants and trousers down over his hips in one movement, the total darkness stimulating him to an even greater frenzy.

Sharon's eyes were closed, though it made no difference in the absence of light, and blood flowed into her mouth. She heard his movements above her, his grunts, the murmured animal sounds. And part of her was aware of the draught that tickled at her scalp.

The man began to lower himself, and she felt his warm penis settle against her stomach. She moaned and turned her head away from his foul breath, her cheek scraping against his rough beard.

As the tip of his penis pushed against the tender opening between her thighs, one hand grabbed at his hair and yanked, twisting his head around; the stiffened finger of her other hand jabbed wildly for his eyes. She felt sickened when the untrimmed nail of her index finger sank into something soft and movable.

He lurched away, his turn to scream, his pulped eye popping from its socket and hanging by a thread as the girl's finger withdrew. He fell into the space beneath the washbasins, hands reaching for the dangling eyeball.

But the rat reached it first.

The muscles were severed by a clamping of jaws and a rapid shaking of the vermin's head, and the eye was swallowed virtually unscathed. The creature, whose natural habitat was darkness and shadows, lunged with barely a pause for the opening from which bloody juices streamed. It buried its pointed snout deep into the empty socket.

Sharon thought the man's screams and thrashings were because of the injury she had caused him. She kicked out at his body, not realizing she was striking other, scuttling forms. Sobbing, she pulled at her jeans, tugging them back over her hips, her back against the smooth floor. Something sharp snapped at a leg and she thought he had bitten her again. Her other foot struck out and connected with something solid. Her leg was released.

She staggered to her feet and hurled herself toward the door, praying she was moving in the right direction. The man's screams filled the small toilet, bouncing off the walls and ceiling, amplified in the tiled chamber, and she felt no remorse for the injury she had dealt him. Through her own sobs and his screams she failed to hear the squealing.

She tripped against something low to the ground, imagining it was one of his flaying limbs, and her head struck the edge of the half-open door. Only momentarily did she wonder why the door was still open, for her main thoughts were on reaching the safety of the cinema, where the other survivors would protect her, where Margaret would comfort her, would rock her soothingly to and fro just as her own mother had done when she was little and helpless.

But her mind could no longer ignore the squirming wriggling creatures beneath her feet, the high-pitched squealing, the sharp, tearing pain as daggers ripped at her legs.

She saw light, for the cinema doors had been opened by those inside who had heard the terrible screams, who were now screaming themselves as a thick, black-running river poured into the small theater.

Sharon staggered over the flowing bodies, running with the rats, all control completely gone, not knowing what else to do, just flowing with the stream.

And when she toppled over the top stair of the steeply tiered theater, the jaws of one creature clamped around an arm, another clinging to her back, teeth and claws entwined in her hair, it was like cresting and plunging with a small but forceful waterfall.

A black, consuming waterfall.

11

The weight of the .38 Smith & Wesson Model 64 strapped inside its holster was uncomfortable against the side of his chest, but then Culver was not used to carrying such a weapon. Dealey had informed him it carried six bullets rather than the five its predecessor, the Model 36, had carried. Culver saw no reason for his having to fire off even one bullet: the war had already been fought and there could be no enemy and surely no victor. Dealey had agreed but had added that the dangers would be from within. Culver felt disinclined to pursue the point.

He shone the flashlight ahead, its beam reflecting goldly off the water-dripping tunnel walls. The others—Bryce, Fairbank, and the ROC officer, McEwen—waded behind him through the knee-deep water, wary eyes constantly seeking out cracks or niches in the curved brickwork where dark creatures could lurk.

Mercifully, the murky water covering the Underground tracks also hid the rotten remains of those who had been slaughtered near the shelter's secret doorway. It had been

unfortunate that Fairbank had accidentally kicked something loose beneath the surface, for white bones had risen
like ghosts from a liquid grave. The four men's steps had
been more careful after that, each one pushing from their
minds the thought of skeletal hands reaching for them
from the dirty, flowing water.

Despite their trepidation, however, it was a relief to be
beyond the confines of the shelter. In the four weeks they
had been trapped inside, morale had sunk even lower and
attitudes had varied between deep despair and sluggish
apathy . . . until the past few days, when a bitter tension
had replaced both moods.

Many of the engineers and exchange staff resented
Dealey's refusal to allow them to leave, particularly when
Bryce, the Civil Defense officer, had admitted that the extraordinary heavy rainfall, which had not ceased for a moment since it had begun weeks before, should have all but
washed away the worst of the fallout.

Yet Alex Dealey had insisted that everyone should re-
main where they were and wait for the all-clear sirens. If
the unremitting downpour could be heard by means of the
air shafts, then so would the sirens. But Culver sensed
there was more to the ministry man's objections, almost
as though giving sway to the mob meant relinquishing not
just his own self-given authority, but the power of government rule itself. And only chaos would take its place.

As of yet, that retention of command had not quite become an obsession with Dealey, but it had certainly developed into a capricious objective. Perhaps, too, it was a
way of saving himself from complete despair, this pursuit
of a familiar and orderly regime, for it seemed that each
survivor, prisoner to the holocaust, strived to find some
semblance of their old existence in this new world.

Culver did not think too much of the past. But even he
did not change into other clothes provided for in the shelter's stores; he kept his torn jeans and worn leather jacket.

The idea of the reconnoiter was to boost morale a little,

possibly to dissipate some of the tension, and more than just an attempt to make contact with the outside world. Culver realized it was too soon for the latter, that if there were survivors above, they would still be in a state of shock. And many would still be in a state of dying. Yet he was glad to go. Before, when the idea had first been brought up, he had been reluctant and may have even refused if a decision had had to be made there and then; but now the exchange, huge though it was, was like a prison to him. It was the same for many others, for there had been no shortage of volunteers for the mission. Dealey had been selective, using Bryce as representative of authority, McEwen almost in a military role, Fairbank as worker delegate, and Culver as a neutral, perhaps even an intermediary. It was a nonsense to Culver, but he was prepared to go along with Dealey's little games if it meant breaking free of the shelter for a short while. In fact, the group's time limit was two hours, and if the ionization instrument carried by McEwen registered an unhealthy amount of radiation still around, then their return to the exchange was to be immediate.

Yet their depature had not raised the spirits of the other survivors as much as Dealey and his closer associates had hoped: Culver had felt uneasy as he prepared to leave and had studied the faces of the technicians and work force as they gathered around to wish the departing team good luck. They showed interest but little excitement. Perhaps there was some dread in their gaze.

In Kate's eyes there had been fear, and the fear had been for him alone.

"I think I can see the station!"

It was Fairbank who had called out, jerking Culver from his thoughts. All four men shone their flashlights straight ahead.

"You're right," Culver said, his voice low, not reflecting Fairbank's excitement. "I can make out the platform. Let's get out of this water."

Their pace quickened and the tunnel echoed with splashing sounds. Culver moved to the side when the platform was close. He paused, climbed up, and shone his light along the platform while the others waited. The station appeared to be empty.

He turned to the others and found he had nothing to say. It was Bryce who suggested they move on.

Culver helped each one onto the platform and they did not stop again until they had reached the opening leading to the escalators. The only sound was that of flowing water, a disturbed hollow gushing that echoed eerily around the tiled walls. They turned their lights on posters announcing new films, the finest whiskey, the prettiest panty hose, and felt acutely saddened for things past. An Away Day was now a journey beyond existence, not a trip to another town, another county.

Culver remembered the screams, the panic cries, of just a few weeks before, and his chest ached as though there was pressure from within. He had half-expected the platform to be filled with bodies, perhaps even one or two survivors among them; the emptiness was somehow more frightening. The sudden thought that possibly there had been survivors who had returned to the surface, who had already begun to adapt, had even begun to rebuild some kind of life, cut into his fear—not decisively, but enough to raise his hopes just a little. That barely formed optimism lasted but a few fleeting moments.

"Oh, my good God!"

They turned to see McEwen standing by the corner of the small exit archway. He was aiming his flashlight toward the escalators beyond. The three men approached McEwen slowly as his hand began to rise, the beam traveling up the stairway. Fairbank moaned aloud, Bryce sagged against a wall, Culver closed his eyes.

Bodies were sprawled on the stairways as far as the light would reach. There were more, many more, piled up at the bottom of the three stairways, disheveled bundles, decomposing, stains of dark blood, dry and crusted, spilling like frozen lava from the heaped forms. And even from where the four survivors stood they could see that the corpses were not intact and that their mutilation had little to do with rotting flesh.

Limbs did not decompose before the rest of the body. Surface organs—noses, ears, and eyes—did not just fade away. Stomachs did not split as though intestines had broken free from dying hosts.

Bryce had begun to vomit.

"What happened to them?" Fairbank asked incredulously. "There's no bomb damage down here, nothing to cause those inj—" He broke off abruptly, realizing what the others already knew. "No, it couldn't be! Rats wouldn't attack this many people." He stared wildly at Culver. "Not unless they were already dead. That has to be it! The radiation killed the people first and the rats fed off them."

Culver shook his head. "There's dried blood everywhere. Corpses don't bleed."

"Sweet Mother of—" Fairbank's knees began to sag and he, too, leaned against a wall. "We'd better get back to the shelter," he quickly said. "They may be still around."

McEwen was already backing away toward the platform. "He's right; we've got to get back."

"Hold it." Culver grabbed his arm. "I'm no expert, but by the look of them, these people were attacked some time ago. If the rats were still around I think there'd be a lot less left of the corpses. They'd be"—he fought down his own nausea—"a regular food supply for the vermin. My guess is that they've moved on, maybe searching for fresher food."

"You mean they can afford to be choosy." Fairbank's voice was too weak to sound scornful.

"I think we should go on. If the bastards are anywhere, they'll be behind us in the tunnels."

"Oh, great. That'll give us something to look forward to." The technician shone his flashlight back in the direction they had come from.

Bryce, wiping his mouth with a handkerchief and still using the wall for support, said, "Culver is right: we should go on. These vermin have existed in the darkness for so long the world above will be alien to them. They'll hide where they feel safe and attack only the weak and defenseless. These poor unfortunates may have already been dying before they were set upon." He managed to straighten and his face looked haunted in the beam of light. "Besides, two of you have guns; we can defend ourselves."

Culver could have smiled at the thought of two handguns fighting off hordes of monster vermin, but the effort would have been too much. "We've come so far, almost to the point of no return, if you like. If we go back now, we'll have achieved nothing. If we get to the top of those stairs, then at least we'll have some idea of what the world has left to offer. Who knows, it may be teaming with human life again. Perhaps they're even creating some order out of the mess."

"But we'd have to climb through those dead bodies." McEwen looked at the other three as though they were insane.

Culver was already walking away. "You've got a choice: come with us or walk back on your own."

Bryce and Fairbank pushed themselves away from the wall and followed. After a brief moment of hesitation, a moment when his face pinched tight and his bowels considerably loosened, McEwen went after them.

Culver could not keep his gaze from the first few bodies; they held a peculiarly morbid fascination for him, a compulsion to see how much damage could be inflicted upon the human frame. It was the things that crawled between the openings, the gashes, the empty eye sockets, that made revulsion the catharsis of his curiosity rather than the mutilated flesh. He tried not to breathe in too deeply.

They climbed the stairs, forcing themselves to step between the stiffened corpses, deliberately keeping their eyes unfocused, their flashlights beams never lingering too long on one particular spot.

Culver wondered how long the generators operating the emergency lighting had continued to run. Had these people died in total darkness, feeling only the slashing jaws and talons, or had they witnessed the full terror of their assailants? He slipped and his knee thudded against the hardened chest of a man whose face was just a gaping hole.

Culver recoiled, almost backing into Bryce, who was just below him on the stairs. Bryce grabbed the handrail for support, preventing them both from toppling back down the escalator. Recovering, Culver continued to climb, but an abhorrent question could not be pushed from his mind: why would the creatures burrow so deeply into a man's head when softer flesh and organs were more accessible?

He stopped and surveyed the pileup of bodies before him. They would have to be lifted clear, and the idea of touching them did not appeal.

"Help me," he said to Fairbank, who was next in line behind the Civil Defense officer. Bryce moved aside to let the technician pass.

The first body they lifted was that of a woman, and with nothing much left inside her open chest, she was as light as a feather. They carefully avoided looking at the featureless face.

"Put her onto the section between escalators—she'll slide down."

Fairbank did as instructed and watched the body swiftly descend into the darkness below. "There's a ride she couldn't enjoy," he said, and froze as Culver looked at him sharply. He cast his eyes downward, avoiding Culver's icy gaze. "Sorry," he mumbled. "It's . . . it's bravado, you know? I'm scared shitless."

The other man turned away, reaching for the next corpse. It was another woman, but this one had some substance to her and was not as easy to lift, even though her breasts were gone, her stomach hollowed. Both men grunted with the effort, and when an arm fell around Culver's shoulder in a lover's casual embrace, he had to bite into his lower lip to prevent himself from screaming. All her fingers were missing.

When her body had careered off into the blackness, twisting sideways as it sped down, they reached for the next. For a few seconds they could only look at the tiny child, her curled body untouched, perfect, but her skin the white alabaster of death. The heavy woman had protected the little girl from scything teeth, but her weight and the weight of others had been suffocating.

Culver knelt and cupped a gentle hand around the child's face. Her mouth was slightly open, her eyes closed. He brushed a lock of pale yellow, almost white hair from her cheek and pulled her toward him, snuggling her against his chest. The others watched, not knowing quite what to do. Fairbank looked at Bryce, who gave a slight shake of his head.

Finally, Culver lifted the girl and placed her on a clear, lower step, laying her on her side and arranging her unmarked limbs so that her body was at rest. Perhaps the others expected to see tears in his eyes when he rose, perhaps remorse, his face crushed with grief; they were not prepared for the tight-lipped grimness, the anger that exuded a frightening coldness. For the first time Bryce saw something more in this somewhat laconic stranger who had arrived in their midsts so dramatically just a few weeks before, something he realized Dealey had appreciated from the beginning.

Culver was pulling at another body, this time a man whose eye socket was enlarged as though something had bored straight through. Fairbank moved forward and helped the pilot lift the body onto the makeshift slide. As he did so, he glanced up toward the top of the escalators, a movement catching his eye.

"What's that?"

The others followed the direction of his gaze. A black shape was moving toward them, sliding down in the same manner of the corpses they were disposing of. It gathered momentum as it drew nearer.

Fairbank drew away from the handrail, fearing the worst. McEwen drew his revolver.

Culver raised a hand as if to stop the ROC officer firing. "It's okay; it's a body."

Fairbank gave a quick sigh of relief and stepped toward the handrail again, hands outstretched to catch the sliding figure.

"Let it go," Culver said quietly but urgently.

The technician raised his eyebrows in surprise and withdrew his hands. As the sliding figure went by, he understood Culver's command. The corpse was headless.

This time he staggered back from the handrail. They all followed the descending body with their flashlight beams.

"What could have done that?" Fairbank asked breathlessly.

"The same that did all this," Culver said, waving his flashlight at the carnage above and below them. "Come on, there's room to get through now." He stepped over two corpses, using a handrail for balance.

"Wait a minute," Bryce said. "They could still be up there. Something caused that body to move."

Culver went on, his pace quickening. "Maybe we disturbed it," he called back over his shoulder. "It could have been resting on the handrail and movement down here made it shift. Or maybe it just rotted itself free."

The three men left behind glanced anxiously at one another, then moved as one after Culver. McEwen kept the .38 clear of its holster.

There were two more human blockages before they reached the top, and these were cleared quickly and with little thought.

At last they were at the turnstiles leading to the escalators. They shone the lights around the circular ticket hall and their spirits sank still further as the nightmare was reinforced.

The round chamber, sunk just below the city streets, was nothing more than a huge open grave. Culver rejected the idea: it was more like a slaughterhouse.

A steady torrent of rain poured through the two entrances, diffusing the grayish light of day. The tangled shapes before them could have been hewn from rock, so still, so colorless were they.

Many of the blast survivors had obviously staggered or dragged themselves down into the station, seeking refuge from the killer dust they knew would soon fall. Culver remembered those whom he and Dealey had met fleeing from the tunnels. Had they thought that it would be safe to linger here in the ticket hall, that their very numbers would keep the vermin away? It would have been packed with the injured, the dying. The smell of fresh-flowing blood would have been overpowering, attracting the creatures below.

Fairbank had walked over to the ticket office, a long isolated booth near the center of the round hall, careful to step over husklike corpses and brushing away flies that buzzed greedily over them.

The office door was open, a man's body sprawled half out as though he had tried to flee from something inside. Fairbank pushed at the door until it nudged against something solid on the other side. The gap allowed him to see all he wanted to.

"Jes—Hey, over here!"

The others, preoccupied with their own disturbing observations, turned toward the booth. He waved them over.

They crowded into the doorway, their combined lights showing every detail of the carnage inside the ticket office. They soon spotted what had taken Fairbank's breath away.

The black rat was huge, almost two feet in length. Its scaly curved tail offered at least another eighteen inches. Its fur was stiffened, dull and dry with death, its massive haunches still hunched as though the rodent was ready to leap. But there was no life in the evil yellow eyes, no dampness to the mouth and incisors. Even though its neck was twisted at an awkward angle, its skull indented unnaturally, still it emanated a deadliness, a lethal malevolence that made three of the men shudder and back away.

Only Culver moved forward.

He stooped and examined the dead beast closely. Someone had fought back, had battered the rat to death. That person was probably also dead, killed by the creature's companions, but at least he or she had not given in easily. Possibly there were other dead vermin out there, lying among the bodies of the humans they had attacked, corpses of both species decaying together.

There seemed to be little weakness in the creature, even in its present state. Yet the skull was caved in. How hard had it been struck? He touched the outer rim of the dent, and the bone beneath his fingers moved inward. It was brittle and thin. And there was no sign of blood. The blow had not even broken the skin; yet it had presumably caused the rodent's death. Culver turned the body over and found no other wounds. So possibly the vermin had paper-thin skulls—at least, this one had. Where did it leave him? Nowhere. It might be feasible to win a battle with one or two of these creatures by crushing their heads, but they moved around in packs . . . large packs.

He straightened and coldly kicked the bristle-furred corpse before leaving the booth.

His companions were watching the booth warily as Culver carefully picked his way toward them. He slapped

away flies and other insects, averting his eyes as they
landed in the open wounds of the dead and laid their eggs.
How fast would these insidious insects multiply now they
had no opponents? And what epidemics would they carry
and spread among those who survived? Once the rain had
stopped, this tiny-sized menace would take to the air to
breed, develop, and devour. Only winter would stem their
tide, and then only temporarily.

Culver faced Bryce. "How many of these vermin have
been living in the sewers and tunnels? And for how long?"

The Civil Defense officer had to look away; once again
the glint of Culver's eyes was intimidating. The voice was
low, controlled, but the anger was barely suppressed.

"I don't know," Bryce answered, frightened by everything around him and especially by Culver's tone.
"There were no reports of them that I know of."

"You're lying. They're too big and too many to have
stayed concealed for this long." His face was only inches
away from Bryce's. The other two men looked on, interested in the answers themselves.

"I swear I know nothing of them. There were some rumors, of course—"

"Rumors? I want to know, Bryce."

"Nothing more than that! Just hearsay. Stories of large
animals, perhaps dogs roaming the sewers. Nobody gave
the stories any credibility. In fact, the reports were that
rats were becoming scarcer down there in recent years."

"Yeah, ordinary rats. Didn't anybody stop to wonder
why?"

"You . . . you mean these creatures drove the others
out?"

"It's possible. Come on, Bryce, you're a government
man—you must know more."

"I'm telling you the truth! I work for Civil Defense,
nothing more! If anyone knows something, it'll be
Dealey."

Culver stared at the older man for a few more moments

before the tenseness left his body. "Dealey," he said, almost as a sigh. He suddenly remembered the flight into the tunnel again, just after the nuclear bombs had detonated, when he had told Dealey, then blind, that there were huge rats around them. Dealey had asked if they were black-furred, and had said something like, "No, not now," as if he knew of them. He may just have been referring to the previous times when the mutants had rampaged, or he may have already known they were still in existence.

"Maybe he'll do some explaining when we get back," Culver said, and turned away from Bryce. "Let's see what's left upstairs."

Together they clambered over the dead, watching warily for any black moving shapes among them. They saw one or two rat carcasses lying among their victims, but Culver noticed something more. He looked around at Bryce and their eyes locked. Something passed between them, a sensory acknowledgment, and neither one mentioned their observation to the other two, who were more interested in the opening ahead.

The rain bounced hard off the metal-edged steps and fallen masonry, sending up a low splattering spray. The sound was intense, almost violent.

"They've destroyed the skies, too."

It was a strange and poignant thing for Fairbank to say, and it sent a shiver through each of them. They stood by the opening, becoming damp with rain, even though not exposed to its full force.

Bryce spoke to the ROC man. "Check the Geiger. In here first, then outside."

McEwen switched on the machine hanging over one shoulder by a strap, realizing he should have checked the atmosphere for radiation at each stage of their exploratory journey. Too many shocks had overwhelmed such a precaution.

Brief, separate clicks came from the ionization instrument's amplifier, and McEwen quickly reassured Culver and Fairbank. "It's normal. It's just picking up very high energy particles natural to the atmosphere. See—it's irregular, weak, nothing to worry about."

"Care to take a shower?" Fairbank pointed with his thumb at the pouring rain.

McEwen looked less sure of himself. He took the Geiger counter from his shoulder and pushed it out into the downpour. "It's warm, the rain's warm!" He quickly withdrew his arms and brushed off droplets as though they were acid.

"It's all right," Bryce quickly said. "Nothing's registering on the counter."

Fairbank nodded toward the rain-soaked stairway. "I'd like to take a look up top."

Culver's smile was slow in coming. "Yeah," he said. "I think we'd all like to see what's left." He stepped out into the rain.

It felt good, so good. A cleanser, a purifier. He turned his face up, closing his eyes, and the heavy raindrops pelted his face. McEwen was right: it was warm, unnaturally so. But it was alive and it was wonderful. He climbed the steps, the others close behind.

Culver reached the top and stopped until the others caught up with him. They looked around, their faces white with shock, the warm rain battering their bodies, its sound the only sound.

It was Bryce who fell to his knees and cried, "No, no, *no . . .*"

12

Many years before, when Culver had been no more than a boy, someone had shown him a sepia print of Beaumont Hamel, a small town in a sector of the Somme front. The old photograph had been dated November 1916—the time of World War I—and the image had stayed frozen in his mind ever since.

The battle long over, just thin trees remained, bare and stunted, without branches, their tops jagged charcoal. No grass, not one solitary blade poking from the solid mud. No buildings, just rubble. No birds. No growth. No life. Only desolation, total, unremitting. And unforgiving.

He had just stepped through that frame and found the tangible equivalent to the sepia waste.

The ruined city lay humiliated and crumbled around them, nothing moving except the relentless rain. Not every building had been completely demolished, although none had escaped anything less than extensive damage; those remaining stood like broken monoliths amid the mountains of rubble, misshapen parodies of man's construction powers. Some rose up with innards exposed, gigantic doll houses with one wall removed so that furniture and decor could be viewed; all that was missing were the tiny dolls themselves. Of others, only skeletal frames were left, the steel girders twisted, buckled, yet still proclaiming their resistance to whatever forces their makers could thrust upon them. There appeared to be no definite order by which one building had collapsed completely while another had remained partially erect, although the damage seemed worse in the distance, as if the power of the shock waves had reduced as they swept outward, each preceding office building or dwelling absorbing a fraction of the force, dissipating the fury, affording a small protection to its neighbor.

Among the rubble, like tossed-away toys, lay cars, buses, other vehicles, some merely black-stained husks, completely burned out, others smashed into irregular shapes. The roads—what could still be discerned as roads—were metal graveyards, full of silent, defunct machines. Most lampposts were bent, many doubled up like matchstick men with stomach pains; some, torn from concrete roots, lay stiffly across other wreckage, defeated but unbowed. Office equipment, furniture, television sets, tumbled from the debris, shattered and somehow incongruous in their exposure.

Also shattered, but far less incongruous because the search party had almost become used to them, were the misshapen bundles that had once been living, moving humans. They lay everywhere: in cars, in overturned buses, among the debris, in the roads. Many were huddled in doorways—whatever doorways were left—as if they had crawled there to await the poisoned air's descent.

The four survivors were relieved that the insects were held at bay by the rain torrent.

Shock upon shock hit them, sweeping through them in waves, their numbed minds mercifully restraining the rapid, horrifying visions. Yet the full impact of one sight could not be defused, for it was literally a panoramic state-ment of what had come to pass, a cruel affirmation of the devastation's magnitude.

It was awesome and it was intimidating. And each man experienced a terrible loneliness, a longing for the world they had lost, for the people who had died.

Above them the sky was black and low, the new horizon silver. The warm rain drenched them and could not wash away their fears, nor their deep-felt misery.

Bryce was on his knees, his bowed head against the litter-strewn pavement.

McEwen's tears mingled with the rain on his cheeks.

Fainbank's eyes were closed, his head tilted slightly up-ward, his body stiff.

Culver looked around, his feelings locked inside.

To the east he could see the round structure of St. Paul's, its dome gone, the walls cracked and broken, huge sections missing. He was puzzled, for although there had been little time for observation when he and Dealey had fled after the first explosion, the damage had not seemed this bad. Then he remembered that other bombs had been dropped—five or six had been estimated—and was then surprised the city had not been totally flattened.

In the distance he could just distinguish red glows where some parts still burned, or where fresh fires had broken out. As if to confirm his thoughts, light flared from the north as though an explosion had occurred. The heavy rain was fortunate, not just because it helped clear the ra-diation dust, but because it had also kept the fires under reasonable control. What was left of the city could have easily become one raging inferno.

He walked over to McEwen and prodded his arm. "Try the Geiger; see if anything's registering."

The ROC officer seemed glad to have something else to think about. A surge of clicking erupted from the machine and the needle flickered wildly for a second or two. "It's okay," McEwen quickly reassured him. "Look, it's settled down. There's a certain amount of radiation around, but it's below danger level.'' He wiped his face to clear its wetness, the tears and rain.

''What now?'' Fairbank asked.

''Let's get Bryce to his feet, then have a quick look round. I don't want to stay out here any longer than necessary.''

Together they lifted the Civil Defense officer, who leaned against them for several moments for support. His strength returned slowly, but his spirit would take much longer.

''Any suggestions,'' Culver said, ''as to where we should look?''

Bryce shook his head. ''There's nothing left to see. There's no hope for any of us.''

''This is just one city,'' Culver replied sharply, ''not the whole bloody country. There's still a chance.''

Bryce merely continued to shake his head.

''There's a store over there,'' Fairbank said, his voice loud so that it could be heard over the downpour. ''It's a Woolworth's—I used to pass it every day. There'll be food, clothing, other things that might be useful.''

''We don't need anything for the shelter yet, but it might be worthwhile taking a look,'' Culver agreed.

''Leave me here,'' said Bryce. ''I've no stomach for rummaging among the dead.''

''No chance. We're sticking together.''

''I won't be able to make it. I'm . . . I'm sorry, but I must rest. My legs seem to have gone. The stress—''

Culver looked at Fairbank, who shrugged and said, ''He'll only slow us down. Leave him.''

''Stay here, then. But don't wander off. We're going straight back into the tunnel when we return. Remember, the idea was to get back within two hours; we won't have time to start looking for you.''

''Yes, I understand. I won't move from this spot, I can promise you that.''

"You might be better off out of the rain. Try one of the cars over there, but keep a lookout for our return."

Bryce nodded, relieved to be left alone. He watched the others making their way through the ruins of what once had been one of London's busiest thoroughfares. Clambering over rubble, weaving between inanimate traffic, their figures soon blurred by the rainfall. Then they were gone and the acute loneliness they had all felt only moments earlier pressed harder on him, almost crushing in its ferocity.

The feeling of being the last person alive on the chastised planet was overwhelming, even though he knew his companions were not far away. His whole being cried out, in pity, in anguish; but mostly in despair.

Bryce pulled his coat collar up, clutching the lapels to his chest, a symbolic gesture; the downpour was tepid, but it chilled his inner core.

There were many vehicles to take shelter in; he walked over to a car nearby, its door hanging open as if the owner cared little for security as he fled the havoc. Bryce almost smiled at the thought of someone meticulously locking his vehicle while the city crumbled around him. The windshield was shattered and he brushed glass fragments from the front passenger seat, relieved to find no bloodstains among them. He climbed in and the rain rattled its steady drumbeat on the metal over his head, splatters still reaching him through the opening, but adding no discomfort to his already soaked person.

A folded newspaper lay at his feet, sodden pages merged into one soft, mildewy lump. He glanced down, then bent to retrieve it, perhaps wistful for a remnant of natural order, a memento of yesterday's comfortable existence. All crispness long vanished from its malty-gray leaves, the midday *Standard* flopped like an important organ into his lap, threatening to disintegrate should its handling be too rough.

At first he frowned at the headline that said: PM URGES: STAY CALM.

Then he began to laugh.

And he laughed so much that tears flooded his eyes, and they were tears of mirth and bitterness, neither emotion giving way to the other.

And his shoulders jerked with the effort.

One leg stamping at the floorboard.

Making the car vibrate.

Causing something in the backseat to stir.

13

Fairbank was the first to slip through the opening that lead down to the shop. Mounds of debris, a hazardous mixture of masonry, powdered concrete, and glass, had all but covered the wide display windows and swing doors, but heedless of the danger, the three men had clambered up toward the dark opening. Fairbank's enthusiasm to taste once again the confectionery delights denied to them among the shelter's plentiful but unexciting rations, to don a clean shirt, put on fresh underwear, was too keen for him to be discouraged by his two more cautious companions. And Culver himself had to admit the prospect appealed after their weeks of austere confinement.

He warned, however, that everything could be spoiled by now, and that clothing and other items might well have been ruined by fire.

"Just one way to find out, Culver," the technician had replied, grinning, the earlier emotional shock apparently overcome for the moment. Culver surmised that the man was either completely insensitive or a natural survivor, his durability perhaps a strong quality in such times. He had followed Fairbank's scampering figure up the incline.

At the top, Culver turned to McEwen. "We'll need the Geiger counter in here; the place could be full of radiation."

Somewhat reluctantly, the ROC officer climbed the slope. They watched Fairbank slither down the other, much steeper side, using their flashlights to guide him.

He settled at the bottom, waving his own flashlight around. "Christ," he exclaimed, "the stink in here!"

"We can smell it from here," Culver told him before sliding into the gap. McEwen quickly followed and all three squatted in the disturbed dust, peering into the gloom, their lights penetrating the darkest corners.

"Ceiling's caved in at the far end," McEwen observed.

"Everything looks safe otherwise," said Fairbank. His voice took on a lighter tone. "Hey, d'you see what I see?" His beam had caught multicolor wrappers in its glare. He was up and at the candy counter before the other two had a chance to rise.

"Don't scoff them all, Bunter, you'll make yourself sick," Culver advised, unable to stop himself from smiling.

"Crunchie bars, Fruit and Nut, Walnut Whips— Christ, I'm dead and this is heaven." They heard him chuckle and began to laugh themselves.

"Bournville Plain, Dairy Milk, Pacers, Glacier Min—" His voice broke off.

By then, Culver and McEwen had joined him and they, too, were examining the array of bright wrappers that a fine layer of dust only faintly subdued. They soon discovered what had brought his exultation to a sudden halt.

"Someone else has been at 'em," McEwen commented.

"Someone or something." Culver picked up a loose wrapper, a vision of black-furred creatures snuffling their way through the chocolate bars and candy sending a prickly coolness along his spine.

"Rats?" Fairbank regarded him with wide eyes.

"They'd have done more damage, made a bigger mess," said McEwen.

"He's right," Fairbank agreed, but there was still a nervousness to him. "Let's grab as much as we can carry and get out."

"Wait a minute." Culver stayed Fairbank's hand midway between counter and trouser pocket. "If it's not vermin, it may be something more important."

"People?"

Culver shone his flashlight along the litter-filled aisles. The store's interior stretched a long way back, opening out halfway down in an L shape. No light came through the collapsed ceiling in the far corner, off to his left. The smell that assailed them had become all too familiar over the past hour or so, and Culver had no real desire to investigate further. Unfortunately, conscience told him he had to. Maybe a morbid curiosity added its weight, too.

His footsteps sounded unnaturally loud in the store that had now become a vast cavern.

Fairbank shrugged and went after him, snatching goodies from the counter as he passed and squeezing them into his pockets. He espied a set of shelves containing handbags, shopping bags, and even better, suitcases, and made a mental note to grab one on their way back.

McEwen found the idea of being left along in the shadowy consumer grotto unacceptable and swiftly caught up with the other two.

Culver in the lead, they drew near the corner where the store widened. An electrical department came into view, plastic-coated wires hanging loosely from their spools like oversized cotton thread, light sockets, switches, and lamps lying scattered as if swept from their displays by angry hands. Beyond that, the record and hi-fi department looked as if the choices had not been appreciated: album sleeves littered the floor, stereo equipment lay scattered. Bodies, some still moving, lolled in the mess.

Damp fingers, disembodied by the darkness, curled around Culver's wrist.

He recoiled by instinct, the others by design, for they had seen the hideous figure just before it had touched him.

Culver wrenched his arm free and staggered back against a nearby counter, but the figure went with him, unbalanced, clawlike hands clutching at Culver's clothes. The man fell to his knees, preventing himself from sinking farther by hanging weakly on to the pilot's leather jacket.

The man's voice was a thin, rasping sound. "Help . . . us . . ."

Culver stared down at the emaciated face with its wide, bulging eyes, the torn lips, cracks filled with dry blood, gums exposed and teeth decayed brown. A few sparse tufts of hair clung to the man's scalp. His skin was puckered with fresh sores and there was a thin line of dried blood trickling from both ears. Fright gave little room for pity in Culver.

The man groaned, although it was more of a throat-singed croak. He seemed to shrivel before them.

Overcoming his revulsion, Culver caught the collapsing figure and gently lowered him to the floor. The man's clothes were torn and bedraggled; they smelled of excrement.

"Please . . ." The voice was weaker this time, as though the effort of seizing Culver's wrist had taken most of his remaining strength. "Help . . . us."

"How many are left alive here?" Culver said, his mouth close to the dying man's ear.

"I . . . don't . . ." His head lolled to one side. "Don't . . ."

Culver looked up at his two companions. "Radiation

sickness,'' he said unnecessarily. "He won't last much longer. Try the Geiger, see how bad it is in here.''

McEwen switched on the machine and they jumped when its amplifier discharged urgent, burring clicks. The needle jumped wildly before settling just beneath the quarter-way mark.

"Too many rems,'' McEwen told them hastily. "It's dangerous; we've got to leave immediately.''

"I'm on my way,'' Fairbank said, beginning to turn.

"Wait!'' Culver snapped. "Take a look at the others. See if we can save any of them.''

"You gotta be kidding. Oh, shit, look . . .''

They followed Fairbank's gaze and saw the shuffling shapes emerging from the shadows, most of them crawling, some stooped and bent, stumbling as if with age, a whining coming from them that was more frightening than piteous. In that moment of abject fear, it was hard to think of these unsteady, shambling figures as fellow humans, wretches that had had no time to properly shelter from the disaster and its disease-carrying aftermath, for they came at the three survivors like lepers escaping their colony, like hunched demons rising from unhallowed earth, like the undead reaching out to embrace and initiate the living . . .

It was too much for Fairbank and McEwen, one trauma too many in that day of traumas. They backed away.

The ravaged faces, fully revealed in the flashlights' combined glare, pleaded for pity, for compassion, for relief from their suffering.

"It's no good, Culver,'' Fairbank said wearily. "We can't help them. There's too many.'' He turned and broke into a stumbling run toward the front of the store, chocolate bars and sweets tumbling from his overloaded pockets.

A hand scraped against Culver's cheek. He flinched,

but did not pull away from the feverish man he knelt beside.

"Don't . . . leave us," the man whispered.

Culver took the hot trembling fingers from his face and held them. "There's nothing we can do for you. I'm sorry!" he shouted, and then he was running, staggering after the others, his only thought to be away from this dark limbo and away from these poor wretches whose best hope was to die sooner rather than later.

He heard their wailing cries, and he thought he heard footsteps coming after him, but he did not stop to look around until he was at the foot of the slope. His two companions were already through the narrow opening at the top, Fairbank reaching back to help him, his face a confused mask of fear and shame.

Culver leapt at the slope, Fairbank grabbing his hand and yanking him upward. He was through the opening, warm rain and gray light enveloping him as he rolled down the other side, not stopping until he had reached the bottom, and even then rolling to a crouched position, facing the store as if expecting the dream to follow. Only Fairbank came sliding down to join him. McEwen stood a few yards away, poised to run.

Fairbank wiped rain from his forehead and nose. He spat into the muddied dirt at his feet. "We'd better get to the shelter."

He walked away, leaving Culver staring up at the few visible letters of the store name and the narrow gap beneath. The mausoleum's name was WORT.

Culver caught up with the others as they squeezed between a bus, all its windows smashed, red paint in the front blistered and flaky, and a sky-blue van, the bottom of its side panels already showing rust. He tried to avert his eyes from the rotted corpse of the bus driver, thrown back in his cab, hands still on the steering wheel as though he had insisted upon carrying his passengers right up to the very doors of eternity. Culver tried not to look, but eyes can be skittishly curious. Glass shards embedded the figure, gleaming from the body like diamonds in an underground rock face, the largest segment neatly dividing the man's face in half.

Something low in Culver's stomach did a mushy backflip and he forced himself to concentrate on the two men in front. McEwen was walking unsteadily, using the hoods and roofs of cars for support, Geiger counter slapping against one hip, rain-soaked shoulders hunched forward. Fairbank, who had turned to see if Culver was following, was white-faced, deep creases stretching from cheekbones to jawline making his normally broad countenance seem suddenly thin, almost gaunt.

The urge to return as quickly as possible to their sanctuary was strong within them, for more than ever it represented a form of survival. They hoped.

Skirting a five-car collision that resembled an artist's metal sculpture, they climbed another hill of debris and were relieved to see the Chancery Lane Underground sign once more, a section of its blue and red symbol missing.

"It ain't much, but it's home," Fairbank said weakly in an effort to shake off his own despondency.

"Can you see Bryce?" Culver peered at the cars below, rain bouncing off their roofs forming misty halos.

Fairbank shook his head. "He can't be far—he looked pretty done in when we left him."

Culver noticed that McEwen was visibly trembling. "You going to make it?" he asked.

"I just want to get away from here, that's all. It's like .̇ . . like one massive graveyard."

"Pity some of the dead won't lie down," added Fairbank in unappreciated black humor.

Culver ignored the remark. They all had different ways of coping; Fairbank needed to make jokes, no matter how lame or how tasteless.

"There he is." Fairbank pointed, then frowned. "At least I think it's Bryce."

They descended warily, not risking a fall on the unstable slope.

"Over here," the technician said, leading the way through the tangle of machinery. Culver spotted the Civil Defense officer on the entrance platform of an empty double-decker bus. His feet were in the road, his body hunched forward over his lap, oblivious to the pounding rain. He appeared to have stomach cramps, but as they drew nearer, they realized he was clutching something.

McEwen caught sight of a familiar form sheltering in a doorway not far from the Underground entrance. For the first time that day he managed to smile. There wasn't much left of the building above the doorway, for the blast had sheered off the roof and upper floor, but although wrecked, the shops below remained, and it was here, in an open doorway, that the dog shivered over a scrap of food lying at its feet.

The mongrel—McEwen was no expert, but it resembled a German shepherd mostly—looked forlorn and weak, its fur bedraggled, almost colorless with grime, ribs showing like struts through stretched canvas. Saliva streamed from its mouth, soaking the meager rations it had managed to salvage from somewhere, and McEwen's heart went out to the disheveled animal. After witnessing so much human suffering, the dog's plight stirred deep emotions in him for, unlike its masters, this creature was inculpable, having no say in its own destiny, innocent of all blame for the destructively sick world it inhabited. McEwen squeezed between two cars and made toward the animal.

The dog's head was bent low, too concerned for the raw meat at its feet to notice the man's approach.

Poor little bastard, the ROC officer thought. Half-starved and probably still bewildered by everything that had happened.

He watched it wolf down one of the sausagelike scraps between its front paws. The food was red, bloodied, and McEwen wondered where it had found such fresh meat.

"Good boy," he said, moving forward cautiously, not wishing to frighten the animal. "Good old boy," he repeated soothingly.

The dog looked up.

14

Bryce was in pain. He moaned and his body rocked quickly backward and forward in swift rhythm that sought to ease the hurt.

Culver and Fairbank saw there were scratch marks on his neck, blood flowing from the wounds with the rain. They rushed to him, Culver kneeling and grasping the CDO's shoulder.

"What's happened to you?" Culver said, using pressure to get the man to straighten. "Did you fall?"

Fairbank looked around uneasily, then bent closer, hands resting on his knees.

Bryce looked at them as if they were strangers, a terrified, glazed expression in his eyes. Recognition slowly filtered through.

"Thank God, thank God," he moaned.

They were shocked when they saw his face. The neck wounds stretched around to his cheeks, where they became large gashes from which blood flowed freely. A thin line of blood dotted with small bubbles of drying blood stretched across the bridge of his nose as if he had been slashed with wire. One eyelid was torn, blood clouding the eyeball beneath red. "Get me back to the shelter. Get me back as quickly as possible!"

"What in hell did this?" Culver asked, reaching for a handkerchief to stem the seeping tide from the man's neck.

"Back, just get me back! I need help."

"Culver, there's something wrong with his hand." Fairbank had moved closer and was reaching for Bryce's arm. He tried to ease the injured man's hands from his lap, but met with surprising resistance.

"Bryce, were you attacked by rats?" Culver asked. "Did they do this to you?"

"No, no!" It was a shout born out of acute pain. "Please take me back to the shelter."

"Show me your hands. Let me see them."

Culver and Fairbank pulled at the arms together.

Bryce had been clutching one hand with the other, and when they were withdrawn from between his blood-drenched lap, they came apart. The other two men flinched when they saw the fingerless right hand.

Fairbank turned away from the bloodied stumps, pushing his forehead against the coolness of the bus. Culver held the wrist of Bryce's injured hand. He folded the handkerchief, now rain-sodden, over the finger stumps, pressing them against the protruding bones.

"Hold the handkerchief against them," he told Bryce. "It'll stop the bleeding a little." He guided the hand toward the man's chest and placed the uninjured hand over it. "Keep it there. Keep your elbow bent and your hand pointed upward. Try not to move it." He quickly ran his eyes over Bryce, checking for further wounds. He found them, but none was as bad. "Where were they, where did they attack you from?"

"No, not rats." It was an effort for Bryce to speak. "It

was a dog. A mad dog in the car. Rabid. It was rabid. That's why you've got to get me back.''

Culver understood, and it was almost a relief. Bryce had come across a wandering dog and it had attacked him. Not rats. Not bloody mutant rats, but a lost, probably starving dog! But if it had rabies, then Bryce was in even more serious trouble. No wonder he wanted to get back to the shelter. Dr. Reynolds would have an antiserum, something that might save his life. If she didn't—Culver tried to push the thought away—then Bryce would be dead within four to ten days.

"Can you stand?" He asked.

"I . . . I think so. Just help me up.''

Fairbank forgot his nausea and helped Culver lift the injured man to his feet.

"Okay," Culver assured Bryce. "We'll get you back. There's bound to be an antirabies vaccine in the medical supplies, so don't worry. The sooner we get you there, the better."

"It's essential that I'm treated before the symptoms begin to show. Do you understand that?''

"Sure, I understand. Try to keep calm.''

Through his pain, Bryce remembered the bitter irony of the newspaper headline he had read in the car just before the rabid dog had snapped its jaws into his neck. Keep calm, that was only annihilation knocking on the door. Keep calm, that was only death tapping you on the shoulder. He began to weep and it was not just because of the throbbing pain.

They half-carried him toward the Underground entrance, keeping a wary eye out for the animal that had caused the injury, avoiding open car doors where possible, kicking them shut first if there was no option but to pass by.

The rain pounded ceaselessly, and even though it was warm, Culver felt a chill creeping into his bones. The outside world was as bad as they feared it would be; the city was not just crippled, it was crushed.

Culver and Fairbank both saw McEwen at the same time. He was leaning forward, one hand extended, reaching for something crouched in a doorway. Something that was partly obscured by his own body.

McEwen smiled at the dog as he tried to coax it from the doorway. "Come on, boy, no one's gonna hurt you. You just finish your food and then we'll see what to do about you. We could do with a rat catcher."

A low, warning growl came from the dog. Its head was still bent close to the food, and its eyes looked up at him with distrust. McEwen noticed there was a moroseness in those large brown eyes.

"Yeah, I know you're starving. I'm not going to take your food away from you. You just gobble it down, there's a good boy."

Before the final scraps disappeared into the dog's jaws—snapped up and swallowed whole, as if it feared they would be taken away—the ROC officer noticed something odd. One of the two slivers of meat had what appeared to be a fingernail attached to it.

He hesitated, his hand poised in midair, suddenly not so sure that the animal should be patted. It looked a little wild-eyed now. And it was trembling, and its snarl was not encouraging.

There were red blood specks in the foamy white substance drooling from its mouth.

"McEwen!"

His head whirled around and he saw Culver running toward him through the rain, reaching for the gun in its shoulder holster. Everything became slow motion, the running figure, the turning back to the dog, the animal quivering, moving forward, its back legs stiff, as though semiparalyzed, the hunching of its shoulders, the bristling of its damp fur, the wide gaping jaws and blood- and saliva-filled mouth . . .

Culver stopped and aimed the gun, praying he wouldn't miss from that range. The dog was tensing itself to leap, but something was wrong with its haunches. Its own madness carried it through. It was in the air, yellow teeth exposed, ready to clamp down on the man's outstretched hand only inches away.

Culver fired and the shock wave jerked his arm back.

The mad dog spun in the air and landed writhing at McEwen's feet, jaws snapping, yelping, screeching.

McEwen stepped back, his feet moving rapidly over the wet pavement. He tripped over rubble, sprawling backward.

The animal, mortally wounded, tried to reach him, crawling forward, its howls diminishing to a low snarling.

Culver moved in for the kill.

He aimed at the dog's head. Fired.

Then again, into the jerking body.

Again, and the body went rigid.

Again, and the body went limp.

He let his breath go and holstered the weapon.

McEwen was slowly rising to his feet and wearing a stunned, disbelieving expression when Culver reached him.

"Did it bite you?" Culver asked.

McEwen stared at him before answering. "No, no, it didn't touch me. I didn't realize—"

"It attacked Bryce."

"Oh shit."

"Help us get him back." Culver had already turned away and was walking over to Fairbank and Bryce.

McEwen studied the still canine body and bit into his lower lip. He had been so close, so fucking close. The realization dawned on him that nothing could be taken for granted anymore, that the ordinary could never again be trusted. That was a legacy that had been left them. Just one of the many.

As with Culver, the chill was now inside McEwen. He

hurried after the three figures as they disappeared down the steps leading into the station's ticket hall.

The sweet, putrid smell hit them before they had even reached the bottom step. Eagerness to get back into the shelter's cocoon safety, the same feeling a rabbit had for its burrow when a fox was on the prowl, battled with their reluctance to enter the gloomy interior with its infestation of glutted insects and rotting human cadavers. Bryce's moaning urged them on.

The awkward descent down the corpse-crowded escalator was almost surreal now that their initial horror had been muted by an excess of shocks. They had the feeling of creeping into the pit of Hades and that the dead littering their path were those who had tried to flee but had not managed to reach the sunlight. Paradoxically, the four men realized that the hell was above them.

They heard the peculiar rushing noise long before they reached the bottom, looking at one another quizzically before resuming the descent. The sound was emanating from the archway leading to the eastbound platform, and as they drew nearer, the four men began to understand its source. McEwen anxiously hurried ahead, the others hampered by the injured man.

The sound became a roar as they rounded the corner into the archway. McEwen's lone figure was standing at the edge of the platform, his flashlight held low. They reached him and they too shone their lights down into the raging torrent, its sound amplifed by the circular walls and ceiling of the station platform.

"The sewers must have flooded!" McEwen shouted above the roar. "All this rainfall must have been too much."

"Too many cave-ins, caused by the explosions," Fairbank agreed. "The water's had nowhere to run."

"We must get back!" There was panic in Bryce's voice.

"Don't worry, we'll make it." Culver shone his flashlight into the eastbound tunnel, from which direction the water was pouring. "It's not too deep, not waist-high yet. We can use the struts and cables inside the tunnel to pull ourselves along."

"What about Bryce?" said Fairbank. "He won't be able to use his hand. I doubt if he's strong enough to fight the current anyway."

"We'll keep him between us, help him along. One in front, two behind. He'll be okay."

Fairbank shrugged. "If you say so."

"McEwen, you get behind Fairbank, help him support Bryce as much as you can." Adrenaline flowing through him once more, reviving his beleaguered body, Culver prepared himself for the ordeal ahead. "We'll use just my flashlight—that'll leave your hands free. You set?"

Fairbank and McEwen nodded, tucking their flashlights into their clothing. Bryce's had long since disappeared.

They walked to the end of the platform and Culver dropped down into the tunnel.

The water was icy cold and took his breath away for a moment. The current tugged at his lower body and it was an effort to move against it, much more so than he had expected. He grabbed one of the metal struts that ribbed the arched tunnel and pulled himself along, struggling to maintain his balance, hindered by the flashlight in his right hand. He stopped when the other three had dropped into the water. Bracing his back against the wall, he turned to them.

"Put your left arm through my right," he told Bryce, crooking his elbow, still holding the flashlight in that arm. Bryce did so, and Culver gripped tight so that their arms were linked. That way he could keep the light shining ahead while still supporting the injured man, and use his other hand to grab any holds along the tunnel wall that he could find. Providing both he and Bryce kept their backs against the wall, they would be all right.

They moved off once more, a bedraggled procession, the force against their legs becoming greater as they waded deeper into the tunnel. It was soon evident that Culver would not be able to use the flashlight and support Bryce at the same time; the weight on his arm was too great.

He brought them to a halt. "You'll have to use your flashlight, McEwen," he shouted. "Try to shine it ahead of us, against the wall on this side."

McEwen's light flickered on and Culver tucked his own flashlight into the waistband of his jeans. He linked Bryce's arm again, this time keeping his fist tucked tight against his own chest.

But Bryce began to slip from his grasp.

"Hold him!" he shouted back to Fairbank as the injured man started to sink.

Fairbank grabbed Bryce beneath his shoulders and heaved him up. He held him against the wall, Bryce's mouth wide open against the dirt-grimed brickwork, gasping for breath. He tried to speak, but they could not hear his words.

Culver slid one arm from his jacket and slipped off the shoulder holster. Pulling the jacket sleeve back on, he tossed the flashlight into the swirling water, knowing there would not be room enough for both flashlights and revolver. He took the gun from its holster and tucked it securely into his jeans. Somehow it was more important to him than the flashlight. He reached for Bryce's uninjured arm once more and tied the leather straps of the holster around his own arm and the Civil Defense officer's.

"You've got to help me, Bryce!" he yelled. "I can't do it on my own. Lean into me and don't let the current pull you away! Fairbank, keep close! Keep bloody close!"

"I'm up your arse," Fairbank assured him, even managing a grin.

Culver moved away from the brickwork, a foot brushing against a rail beneath the swirling dark waters. He stepped over it, nudging Bryce ahead of him, his body angled against the current. He stretched his arm forward for balance. The pressure was tremendous and he noticed that the water was up to his waist.

Fairbank pulled and Culver pushed, and they might have made it had not something rammed into McEwen's midriff. The object spun around so that its length jammed against all three men midstream.

When McEwen looked down and saw the wide rictal grin of the dead man, the lifeless eyes somehow conveying the agony of drowning, something snapped inside. He screamed and both hands lost their grip.

The merciless water snatched him away before he could regain his balance.

The sudden total burden of Bryce's weight was too much for Culver's own precarious balance. Both he and Bryce plunged backward.

Fairbank, shoved against the wall, could only watch in dismay as the three men hurtled back along the tunnel, only heads and occasionally shoulders bobbing above the surface. McEwen's screams could be heard over the roar.

The technician pressed himself back against the shiny brickwork and closed his eyes. "Oh, Jesus," he said. "Oh Jesus."

Culver went under, his body spinning beneath the churning surface. Something was pulling him down, a weight that hardly struggled against the force that tore at them. Whether Bryce was unconscious or merely shocked into immobility, there was no way of knowing, but regret that he was tied to the injured man stabbed at Culver's disordered thoughts like a taunting barb. He choked on the water that filled his throat, his lungs, forcing his way back above the foaming surface, spluttering, coughing, wheezing for breath.

Culver felt the straps around their arms loosening, Bryce's body beginning to slip away. It would have been a relief to have let the burden go, to use all his unencumbered strength to reach safety, but old, unrelenting memories stirred inside, rising through the panic like dark shadowy ghosts.

He reached beneath Bryce's shoulder and struck out for the side of the tunnel, digging his heels into the firm ground below. Carried along by the momentum of the water and his own efforts, he crashed into the wall. Culver clung there, holding Bryce to his chest with his other arm, gasping in air and praying that the surge would not grow any stronger.

When he had regained his breath, he called out for Mc-Ewen, but there was no answer. Maybe he couldn't hear above the noise. He may have found a hold somewhere and was hanging on for dear life just out of earshot. Culver doubted his own hopes, for inside the station itself the walls were smooth, with nothing to cling to. Unless Mc-Ewen had managed to scramble onto the platform, he had no chance of preventing himself from being swept through into the next tunnel. Light suddenly skimmed along the surface of the broiling water from the other direction, the glare dazzling him.

Fairbank! Fairbank was still back there! This time he called out to the technician, but again doubted his voice could be heard.

Bryce began to stir and Culver drew him upward, so that their faces were level.

Holding the Civil Defense officer's arm tightly, Culver began to edge his way forward once more.

The light moved closer and Culver realized that Fairbank was coming back for them. He renewed his efforts, fighting against exhaustion as well as the tide. Fortunately, Bryce had revived enough to help himself a little.

The journey was easier for Fairbank, who was traveling with the flow, and soon he was next to them, shining the light directly into their faces.

"Thank God you're all right," he yelled. "I thought that was the last I'd see of you." He shone the beam past them. "Where's McEwen?"

Culver could only shake his head.

Fairbank stared into the distance, hoping to see the lost man. He soon gave up the search. "You ready to try again?" he asked Culver.

"I'm ready." He eased Bryce around him so that the injured man was sandwiched between Fairbank and Culver as they made their way forward again.

It was a long, painstaking crawl, but mercifully the force against them did not increase. They were aware of bodies floating by, but by now corpses had become nothing new and nothing to spend thought on.

It couldn't have been hours—it only felt like it—when they reached the recessed door. They collapsed into the opening, careful to keep their feet and relieved that some of the pressure decreased slightly.

Fairbank began pounding on the metal surface with the end of his flashlight. "Open up, you bastard! Open this fucking door, you shitheads!" He pounded harder, rage giving him the energy.

Culver forced himself to stay erect by sheer willpower and it was only when that instinct had decided to desert him that he felt the metal behind him giving way.

The door opened and he, Bryce, and Fairbank were washed through with the torrent.

Hands reached for them as they tumbled over the floor. Culver came to rest between a large locker and a concrete wall; he lay there, resting his back in the corner, watching the figures struggling to close the metal door against the floodwater. It was a hard-fought battle, the water cascading in and threatening to flood the whole complex.

More figures rushed forward to help and he saw Dealey standing nearby, watching anxiously, water already lapping around his ankles.

Culver's tired mind could not understand why the man standing next to Dealey was holding a gun on him. Nor why the technician called Ellison was also pointing a gun, this one directed toward Culver himself.

15

"Would someone tell me what the hell is going on?"

Kate passed a steaming hot mug of coffee to Culver. He accepted it gratefully and sipped, the liquid burning his lips but tasting good, warming. He was still soaking wet and had not yet been allowed to change into drier clothes. The faces surrounding him in the operations room were neither hostile nor friendly; they were curious.

"What happened to McEwen?" one of the technicians Culver knew as Strachan asked, ignoring the pilot's own question. Strachan was sitting in the seat behind the room's only desk, the one usually occupied by Alex Dealey. Culver noted that there were no longer any guns in evidence, but the shift in power was obvious even without them.

"We lost him," Culver answered. His hair was damp and flat over his forehead, his eyes heavy-lidded, an indication of his exhaustion.

"How?" Strachan's tone was cold.

"In the tunnel. He was swept away with the floodwater." He tasted more coffee before adding, "There's a chance he's still alive out there. Now, would you mind telling me what this is all about?"

"It's about democracy," Strachan replied, his expression serious.

"Lunacy, more like it." Dealey was sitting on one side of the room, agitated and looking as if ready to erupt.

Farraday, leaning back against a wall map behind the desk, shirt sleeves rolled to the elbows and hands tucked into his trouser pockets, said, "Perhaps not, Alex. Their attitude could be the correct one."

"That's nonsense," Dealey retorted. "There has to be some kind of order, some voice of authority—"

"Some ruling power?" Strachan smiled, and Culver thought the smile didn't look good on him.

"Wait a minute," the pilot interrupted. "Are you saying *you're* taking control, Strachan?"

"No, not at all. I'm saying there'll be a majority decision from now on. We've seen what bloody power-mad individuals can do, and that all ended with the first bomb."

Dealey's tone was acid. "Government by consensus, if I understand you correctly. Well, we had a little example of that just a short time ago, didn't we?" He turned to Culver, who did not enjoy *his* smile either. "Do you know they had to take a vote on whether or not to let you back into the shelter? They were worried it would be flooded once they opened that door. You were lucky they wanted any information you had gathered."

Culver looked at Strachan, then around at the others who had managed to cram into the room. He said nothing, just sipped the coffee. The revolver had disappeared from his waistband and he wondered if he had lost it in the tunnel or if it had been taken from him while he lay exhausted on the floor near the tunnel doorway.

Strachan betrayed only a hit of anger.

"From here on, everything's to be decided for the common good. If that sounds like Marxist or Troskyist phraseology, then it's your own blinkered thinking that's telling you so. There aren't enough of us left anymore for hierarchy or government by a few fools. Your kind of politics are over, Dealey, and the sooner you realize it, the better it will be for you.''

Culver turned to Strachan. ''I want to know what you plan to do about the situation we're in.''

Ellison spoke. ''We're going to abandon this shelter, for a start.''

Culver leaned back in his seat and sighed. ''That may not be a good idea.''

''Would you tell us why you think that?'' asked Farraday.

This time it was Fairbank who answered.

''Because there's hardly anything left up there, you silly bastards.''

There was a stunned silence before Strachan said, ''Tell us exactly what you found. We've already decided on our course of action, but it would be helpful to know what we've got to face.''

''You've decided?'' Fairbank shook his head in mock dismay. ''I thought this was a democracy. What happened to our vote?'' He pointed at Culver and himself.

''It's a majority decision.''

''Without proper consultation and, more importantly, without all the facts,'' said Dealey.

''The most important fact is that most of us want to leave.''

''It's not safe, not yet,'' said Culver, then began to tell them of their expedition, the sheer horror of their discoveries. They listened in wretched silence, each man and woman lost in his own personal despair. There were no questions when he had finished, only a heavy quietness hanging in the room like an invisible, oppressive cloud.

Finally, Strachan broke the silence. ''It changes nothing. Most of us have families we have to get to. I accept that not many may have survived in London itself, but not all of us had homes in the city. We can get out to the suburbs, find them."

Culver leaned forward, wrists on his knees. "It's up to you," he said calmly, "but just remember: there are rabid animals out there, people who are dying, too many to help, and buildings—those left standing in some form—are collapsing all the time. Nothing's solid above us, and the rain is making it worse."

He drained the last of the coffee and gave the cup to Kate to be refilled.

"Disease is bound to spread," he continued, "typhus, cholera—Dr. Reynolds has already listed them for you. If that isn't enough, you've got vermin roaming the tunnels, maybe even aboveground by now. We saw one or two dead rodents in the station and we saw the damage they'd inflicted. If you come up against a pack of them, you'd have no chance."

"Listen to him, he's right," Dealey said almost triumphantly. "It's what I've been telling you all along!"

"Dealey," Culver warned, well aware that the man's attempt to dominate, to run things to his order, had led to this confrontation. Law and order did not exist anymore, and Dealey had no force behind him to back up his command. As far as Culver could tell, those who had been aligned with him had soon defected; Farraday was a prime example. "Just keep your mouth shut."

Dealey's mouth closed, more in surprise than in obeyance. Culver stared at him directly, trying to convey that the situation was more threatening than it appeared; he sensed the mounting tension, despite his own tiredness, a hysteria that had steadily risen during the weeks of their incarceration. The fact that these men had used arms as an aid to their coup was an indication of just how high emotions were running. And there was a gleam in Strachan's eye that was an unwelcome as his grin.

"Well, isn't this cosy?" Clare Reynolds pushed her

way through the cluster of bodies around the doorway. She cradled a brandy bottle in one arm. "Thought you two could use some of this," she said, making her way over to Culver and Fairbank. She uncorked the bottle and poured stiff measures into their coffee mugs. "You ought to get out of those wet clothes right away. I've treated Bryce's wounds and given him his first rabies shot, but it looks like he's in for a rough ride over the next few weeks. Unfortunately, for him, his incubation period could last from anything to ten days, a month—maybe even two years, if he's really unlucky."

The doctor turned toward the men seated around the desk. "So how's the revolution going?"

"Take it easy, Clare," Strachan told her. "You were just as disgusted with Dealey's imposed regime as any of us."

"I didn't like his high-handed ways, sure, but his objectives made some sense. One thing that disgusts me above all else, though—and particularly after all that's happened—is the use of force."

"We didn't use force," Ellison snapped.

"You used weapons, and in my book, that's force! Haven't you learned anything?"

"We've learned not to listen to bastards like him!" Ellison pointed at Dealey.

She sighed wearily, knowing it was pointless to continue the argument; she had tried that just before and after the takeover. "Bryce was able to tell me a little of what it's like up there. Can you fill in the details?"

Culver repeated his story, giving an even more graphic account of the radiation victims' condition; when he had finished, faces around him looked even more distraught.

"That settles it, then," the doctor said. "There's no way you can leave the safety of this shelter. If all the other factors don't destroy you—including the flooding in the tunnels—then the vermin will."

"The water will subside once the rain stops," Strachan said quickly. "And it may even have done us a favor."

All eyes turned toward him.

"It will have flushed out the rats, destroyed their nests," he told them. "They won't be a threat anymore."

"Don't be so sure," said Dr. Reynolds. She lit a cigarette. "These creatures can swim." She exhaled smoke into the tightly packed room. "I think it's time we learned a little more about these black rats. Did you come across any 'live' vermin, Steve?"

Culver shook his head and Fairbank added a thank-God.

Clare regarded Alex Dealey coldly. "And what does—did—the government know about them? You see, I found poisons in the supply store that could be used only against rats, as well as the antitoxin I administered to yourself and Steve when you first arrived at the shelter. That antitoxin was specifically for the disease carried by this particular strain of mutant black rat, so I figure their threat was still known and still feared. Was the government aware that the problem hadn't been completely eradicated, that these creatures still existed in our sewers?"

"I was just a civil servant, Dr. Reynolds, and not one to be taken into ministerial confidence," Dealey said uneasily.

"Your office was the Inspectorate of Public Buildings and you yourself admitted a large part of your duties involved fallout shelters. You *must* have had some knowledge of it! Look, Dealey, try to understand that we're all in this together; the time for 'official secrecy' is long past. Just tell us what you bloody well know, even if it's only to prevent people leaving this shelter."

Dealey looked more irritated than intimidated. "Very well, I'll tell you what I know, but believe me, it isn't much. As I implied, my position was not very high in the civil servant echelon—far from it."

He shifted uncomfortably in his chair. "I'm sure most

of you know that during the first London Outbreak—that was what the black-rat infestation of the capital became known as—it was discovered that a certain zoologist, by the name of Schiller, interbred normal black rats with a mutant, or possibly several mutants, he had brought back from the radiation-affected islands around New Guinea. The new breed soon proliferated and spread throughout London, a stronger and much more intelligent animal than the ordinary rat with, unfortunately, an insatiable taste for human flesh.

"Most were exterminated quickly enough, although the havoc they caused was severe—"

"You mean they killed a lot of people," Strachan interrupted bitterly.

Dealey went on. "It was thought at the time that all the vermin had been eliminated, but several must have escaped. In fact, the new outbreak several years later occurred just northeast of the city, in Epping Forest."

"I seem to remember we were told the problem was solved permanently at that time," said Dr. Reynolds.

"Yes, it was believed to be so."

"Then how d'you account for those bloody things out there?" Fairbank's eyes were narrowed, anger boiling in his usually genial face.

"Obviously some escaped the net, or had never left the city in the first place."

"Then why wasn't the public informed of the danger?" asked Strachan.

"Because, by God, nobody knew!"

"Then, why the antitoxin, the poisons?" Dr. Reynolds asked calmly. "There's even an ultrasonic machine in the supplies store."

"They were provided as a precaution."

Ellison's fist thumped against the desktop. "You must have known! D'you think we're really that simple?"

Some of Dealey's composure had gone. "There have

been rumors over the years, that's all. Perhaps one or two sightings, nothing—"

"Perhaps?" Strachan was furious, and so were others in the room.

"Nothing definite," Dealey continued, "certainly no attacks on anyone working in the tunnels or sewers."

"Any disappearances?" Culver sipped his coffee-mixed with brandy as he awaited the answer to his quietly put question.

Dealey hesitated. "I have heard of one or two workmen going missing," he replied eventually. "But that wasn't unusual. Sewers flood from time to time after heavy rainfall, tunnels collapse—"

"Were their bodies ever recovered?" persisted Culver.

"Not all, but, yes, some were."

"Intact?"

Dealey shook his head in frustration. "If they weren't found until weeks, perhaps months later, then of course you'd expect the bodies to be decomposed."

"Eaten?"

A snort of annoyance. "I'm not denying there are rats living beneath the streets, but not of the mutant kind. We've never had evidence of that."

"You said earlier there'd been sightings."

"They could have been anything—cats, even lost dogs. And, yes, I admit, large rats. Not monsters, though, as you're suggesting."

Clare Reynolds' cigarette was almost singeing the filter, but still she did not extinguish it, conscious of just how low the supply was running. "Autopsies must have been carried out on the remains that were found, so I'd imagine existence of the mutant black would easily have been determined."

"That may be so, but I was never privy to such knowledge."

Dr. Reynolds quickly strode to the desk and regretfully stubbed the meager remains of her cigarette into an ashtray lying there. "The real point is that if we're to deal with these overblown rodents, we need to know as much about them as possible, and what poisons are most effective."

"I promise you," Dealey said, "I know no more than I've already told you."

The doctor's words were measured, each one a single capsule, as though she were speaking to someone whose own retardation demanded uncomplicated syllables. "Have you any idea of how many mutant rats are living in the sewers?"

"There can't be a great number; otherwise there would have been much more evidence of them."

"How d'you explain the slaughter we saw outside?" said Fairbank. "Just a handful couldn't have done that."

Dr. Reynolds looked around the room. "Does anyone here know the breeding habits of rodents?"

A small man, unshaved and skin almost as pale as the white smock coat he wore, nervously raised a hand, almost as if the sudden limelight would shrivel him up completely. Clare Reynolds knew him as one of the shelter's caretakers-cum-maintenance men. "It's—it *was*—my job to keep this place free of the buggers, being belowground 'n all, with the tunnels nearby, and the drains."

"Have you seen any indications of these larger-sized rats over the years?" Dr. Reynolds asked.

The small man shook his head. "Can't say that I have. I've killed off a few of the other kind, but I couldn't say this place has been plagued with 'em." Scratching his nose reflectively, he added, "Surprisin' really, considerin' the amount of outlets—pipes and cable tubes and things. Poisons have kept 'em down, I suppose."

"I don't see where this is getting us," Ellison said. "If we're going to leave the shelter, we won't have to bother with putting down poisons. When we get outside, we'll have guns to protect us."

Dr. Reynolds whirled on him. "Do you really think

that kind of weapon would save you if a pack of rats—or even a pack of rabid dogs—attacked you? It's about time you faced up to the truth of the situation, you idiot."

Ellison pushed back his chair, but did not rise. "Look, just because you're a doc—"

Culver did rise, but it was a tired movement. "You figure out what you're all going to do. I don't give a shit one way or the other. I've told you what it's like out there, so you can make your own choice. As for me, I'm beat."

Fairbank stood as if in agreement.

Both men made their way toward the door and Culver turned before pushing his way through the throng. "One thing I remembered when you were discussing the bodies that had been recovered from the sewers over the years." He ran a hand around the back of his neck, twisting his head to relieve a creeping stiffness. "I don't know what it means, or even if it's particularly relevant, but I noticed something odd about many of the bodies we found on the escalators and in the station itself."

Kate Garner, already shocked by his revelations, felt a fresh shiver of anticipated dread rush through her. Could there really be anything worse to hear, more suffering to contemplate? Perhaps not, but what he told them added a touch of the macabre to an already horrific account.

"The heads of many of the corpses were missing," Culver said before leaving the room.

16

Something, someone, was pounding him. His name was being called from a long way off, drawing closer, insistent, piercing the sleepy folds of exhaustion he had drawn around himself.

"Steve, wake up for God's sake, wake up!"

Culver tried to push the tugging hands away, unwilling to relinquish the soft respite, but other parts of his consciousness were aroused, alerted, already instigating the waking process. He stirred in the narrow bunk bed and protested at the unrelenting prodding. Still fully clothed, too exhausted to remove them hours before when he and Fairbank had slumped onto the beds—stacked three high in the men's cramped dormitory—he forced his eyes open.

Kate's face hovered above him, its edges blurred by his own sleepiness. He blinked his eyes several times and the face finally focused.

"Steve, get up, right now," she said, and her urgency quickly dismissed the remaining vestiges of tiredness.

He raised himself on one elbow, his head almost touching the bunk above. "What is it?"

Noises intruded from the open doorway—shouts, even screams, and an all-too-familiar rushing sound. Fairbank was awake, too, on the opposite bunk bed, staring confusedly across. Culver recognized the background noise before Kate told him.

"The shelter's being flooded!"

His stocking feet were over the side almost before she had time to give him room. Cold water swirling around his ankles completed his revival.

"Where the hell's it coming from?" he shouted, grabbing his boots, the only items he'd bothered to remove before lying down, and pushing his soaked feet into them. Opposite, Fairbank was following suit.

"The well!" Kate told him. "The artesian well has flooded. The water's pouring through."

Culver stood, Kate rising with him, and stepped out into the corridor, water dragging at his feet.

"Wait!" Kate grabbed his shoulder. "There's worse—"

But he had already seen with his own eyes.

Water gushed toward him from the opening farther down the corridor, the switching unit area, figures thrashing around in the bubbling torrent, fighting against the flow. There were other shapes in that churning mess, though: sleek black projectiles that torpedoed through the water seeking targets.

"How did they get in?" yelled Fairbank.

"Maybe from the well, maybe from the pipe inlets!" Culver was pushed aside as two figures, a man helping a panic-striken woman, splashed their way down the corridor. Something black followed in their wake.

Culver, Kate, and Fairbank shrank back into the dormitory and watched another of the water-sleek rats skim by. They heard distant gunshots.

"I thought these shelters were supposed to be impregnable," Culver said to Fairbank.

"This is a communications center as well as a shelter. I suppose it was never completely sealed off."

The girl tugged at Culver's sleeve. "The water level's rising. We have to get out!"

"If the generator floods, we're really in trouble. We won't even have emergency lighting." Fairbank cursed.

Culver pulled Kate closer to him. "Where were Dealey and the others when you last saw them?"

"Back in the operations room, still fighting it out between them."

"Okay, that's where we'll head for."

"Why there, for fuck's sake?" Fairbank demanded. "Let's just get outa here."

"We need weapons, that's why. We won't stand much chance without them. We can cut through the Carrier section, then back to the operations room."

Fairbank shrugged. "Okay, lead on."

He waded over to a metal locker and reached for a heavy-duty lamp perched on its top—flashlights and lamps were kept all around the shelter for lighting emergencies. "We may need it," he said, and all three hoped they wouldn't.

Culver fought for balance as he stepped back into the corridor. One hand stretched for the far wall as the water, now past his knees, endeavored to unbalance him. Kate held on to his other arm and Fairbank kept close behind, constantly looking over his shoulder to make sure no dark creatures were swimming toward them. Something nudged the back of his leg and he was relieved to see it was only an empty shoe. Ownerless, it swept by.

Sparks suddenly sprouted from machinery just ahead. "Christ!" Fairbank shouted. "If it goes, we'll all be electroluted!"

The other two heard him, but no reply was necessary. Culver just hoped that someone had the sense to shut down all the unnecessary machinery. He pushed between two towering racks of telecommunications equipment, pulling Kate in with him. Fairbank, still busy looking over his shoulder, would have passed the opening had not Culver reached out and yanked him in. Figures raced by at the other end of the narrow alleyway they had taken refuge in.

"Looks like they're making for the door to the Underground tunnel!" Fairbank shouted over the noise.

"That might make matters worse," Culver replied, and Fairbank understood what he meant. The flooding in the tunnel could be even greater than before. A deeper sense of dread surged through them, for they realized *that* was their only way out.

Culver pushed on, setting himself only one objective at a time, the acquisition of firearms being the first. Guns would give them some protection against the rats, though they would be useless against too many. Then perhaps they could find high ground—on top of machinery, possibly—where they could be above the water level and in a position to hold off any clambering vermin. Culver knew that the exchange had two other entrances, but both had been sealed by fallen buildings; how the government planners had been so stupid not to have foreseen such an event, he could not fathom—perhaps they felt the tunnel exit was safeguard enough.

He stepped from the narrow, machine-created passage out into a wider area where the crushing water had become a torrent. On the opposite side was a metal catwalk, just seven or eight feet above floor level, which enabled the technicians to reach the upper parts of communications equipment built into the wall there. If they could get to the catwalk ladder just a few yards ahead of them, then the narrow platform would provide an easy passage for some considerable distance. Culver pointed to the ladder and the others nodded vigorously, failing to see the black vermin that raced toward the pilot.

Suddenly, one bit into the hem of his short leather jacket as he pitched forward into the water.

Kate screamed, involuntarily shrinking back into the slightly calmer current of the passageway they had just passed through. Culver's body thrashed around in the water, one scrabbling black shape clinging to him.

Almost without thinking, Culver slipped an arm from the jacket, turned, and used the tough material to smother the thrashing rat. He bore down, water cascading over his back and shoulders, using his weight to keep the lethal-clawed creature below the surface, unaware that Fairbank was undergoing a similar encounter.

Culver clenched his hands tightly around the wriggling bundle underneath, resisting the gray, swirling claustrophobia. Huge, single bubbles of air fought their way from beneath the jacket, becoming a frothy stream of effervescence, finally exploding into a gush of larger bubbles as the struggles beneath him grew weaker, began to fade, became almost still. Ceased.

He rose up, his own lungs spurting their protest, falling backward, rising again, trying to gain his feet. Arms reached for him, and he gratefully used Kate's support to draw himself up. Before he had fully risen, he saw Fairbank's head just above water, resting against a bank of machinery, hands desperately holding away the snapping jaws of a mutant rat. He plunged for the animal, rage burning inside, loathing for these grotesque creatures overcoming the fear.

He pulled at its body, gripping it beneath the shoulders, heaving and taking the weight from Fairbank's bloodied chest. The technician twisted free, keeping his hands around the rat's throat. Air rose to the surface and it was fetid, an evil smell befitting the monster it escaped from. Soon the creature no longer struggled, no longer twitched. They released it and the body drifted away with the current.

Culver and Fairbank rose, breathless and shivering,

both leaning back against the machinery. Kate allowed them no respite.

"It's getting deeper!" she cried. "We have to get away from here!"

Culver blinked water from his eyes and looked back along the wide corridor in the direction of the operations room. It was not just the rising water that alerted him further, for where the corridor opened out to accommodate the Repeater power plant, there was total chaos. Figures attempted to run through the water, fleeing from the vermin that skimmed toward them.

The light abruptly faded, returned, faded again, then remained a dim twilight for terrifyingly long seconds. Something shattered in the complex machinery, an explosion of glaring light and blue smoke. They saw the flame licks and looked aghast at each other.

"This place is finished, Culver!" Fairbank shouted. "We've got to get out—*now!*"

The lights revived, then flickered before they resumed their normal brightness. Culver saw the dark shapes gliding from the narrow passageway they had themselves used only minutes before.

"Onto the catwalk, quick!" He grabbed Kate and pushed her ahead of him, wading through what had now become a wild bubbling waterway.

Kate reached the metal ladder leading up to the catwalk and Culver, with a brusque push, urged her to climb. He looked to see if Fairbank was with them, and drew in a breath when he saw the closely packed group of rats bearing down on the technician.

Clinging to a lower rung of the ladder, Culver stretched out his other arm toward Fairbank. "Hurry!" he yelled.

The technician must have seen the warning in Culver's eyes, for he made the mistake of turning his head to look behind. He staggered when he caught sight of his pursuers.

A deluge of water surging from the opposite direction saved him.

Culver realized that someone, in an effort to escape the flooding shelter, had opened the door to the railway tunnel, allowing more floodwater to pour in. Now they did battle with the counterflow, a fresh sweeping tide that met and pushed back at an opposing force, creating a violent meshing, a rolling turbulence.

He just managed to grab Fairbank's outstretched hand before the tidal wave submerged him. The vermin were swept back, twisting and squealing in the foam, kicking out frantically with useless paws as they were smashed into machinery and tossed back along the wide corridor like flotsam.

"You first!" Culver yelled, and Fairbank did not argue.

Kate, already on the catwalk, helped him up the last few rungs. He lay there, gasping for breath, like a floundering fish just hooked from the river.

Culver watched as other bodies were swept past, their impetus too great for him to reach out and pull them in. The floodwater wasn't too deep yet—perhaps just below chest level—so they would have a chance, provided they were not knocked unconscious by unyielding objects.

The catwalk was narrow, just wide enough to take one person at a time, the railing on the outside single and frail-looking. The grilled walkway beneath them trembled with their weight.

Fairbank was already up, but still gasping. He squeezed past Kate and began to make his way along the catwalk, heading in the direction of the operations room. Culver wiped strands of hair away from the girl's frightened eyes, then nodded after Fairbank. She moved, clutching at the railing with one hand, her fingers never losing contact with it. Culver followed, gently urging her along, his eyes constantly alert. He shouted a warning when he saw the creeping thing on the conduits above Fairbank's head.

The rat dropped, but Fairbank was ready. He caught he creature in midair, its weight sending him back against the wall of instruments, slashing teeth just inches away from his face. He heaved the abomination from him, his strength gained from sheer fright, and the rat hurtled over the railing into the waters below.

There were more dark shapes crawling through the pipe network and wires in the ceiling, and the three bedraggled survivors wasted no more time in moving along the thin, precarious platform. Ahead, they heard the sound of machine-gun fire.

Dr. Clare Reynolds had just finished her third cup of coffee and fourth cigarette when the water had poured through the swing doors of the canteen. Sick and tired of reasoning with the rebel technicians, who were now adamant about leaving the refuge, despite the dire warnings, dismayed at the continuing duplicity of Dealey, Clare had forsaken the rigid rule of cigarette rationing for the moment. What the hell? If the shelter was abandoned, there would be a glut of tobacco among the ruins upstairs, and never enough people to smoke it all. She supposed it wasn't much of an example for someone in her profession to be setting, but that had never bothered her in the past, so why now? She stubbed out half of her cigarette and lit another.

The powdery ash in the small dish before her seemed symbolic of all that was left. She stirred it with the glowing tip of her cigarette and it was insubstantial, a miniature pulverulent waste. Like her own shattered life.

It was funny how people seemed to dismiss the personal emotions of certain professions—an airline pilot was supposed to think only of his passengers' lives in a crisis, never his own; a priest wasn't allowed to brood on personal problems, only on those of his parishoners—and the medical profession evoked a similiar regard. A doctor was not a machine but functioned on a level higher than nor-

mal human emotion. He was supposed to be immune
Physically and mentally, doctors were meant to be a rac
apart. But people failed to see beyond the robes of office
the professional facade. Few cared to—they had their owr
problems. Only one person in the shelter had concernec
herself with Clare's personal loss, and that was Kate Gar
ner. In fact, more than once they had cried on each other'
shoulder. No one else had even asked.

She breathed on her spectacles and wiped them with a
piece of tissue. There were others in the canteen, but ar
empty coffeecup and a half-filled ashtray on the yellov
Formica tabletop were Clare's only companions. Still
that was of her own choosing. Although there was a higl
degree of casualness in her medical manner, she retainec
a studied measure of aloofness, a mild authority that for
bade disintegration either on her part or of those arounc
her. It was a role she played to the hilt, but one that wa
slowly, ever so slowly beginning to crumble, her dream
the sly and guileful wrecker. For the dreams sent Simon t
her, presenting him as whole, complete, approaching ii
his own easy, restful way, brushing aside each gossame
veil that was somehow not of material but of hazy smok
layers, with casual waves of his hand, speaking her name
softly, lovingly, and sometimes reproachful that they hac
been apart for so long; and he would draw nearer, yet sh
could not move toward him, could only reach out with he
arms, her hands trembling and eager, tingling with antici
pation, fingertips sending forth invisible beams of energy
that only the Kirlian process could register, strands of lov
ing magnetic energy drawing him inescapably closer t
her, until just a few veils drifted between them.

Clare's glasses fell with a clatter onto the yellov
tabletop. Others in the canteen looked around in surpris
and resumed their own conversations when she quickl
donned the spectacles and tapped her cigarette into th
ashtray.

Her eyes blurred behind the lenses and the gesture o

fiercely inhaling cigarette smoke enabled her to keep some control. Simon, her husband, her constant friend and never-failing lover, was dead. Simon, who was—*had been*—a surgeon, a saver of lives, a giver of hope, a cutter-away of malignancy, had been on duty at St. Thomas' the day of the bombs, and she knew, she *positively* knew, he would have had no chance. The initial shock wave would have demolished the building totally. God rest you, Simon, my love; I pray it was instant.

When she had awakened screaming from the first nightmare, Kate had been there to hold her, to rock her in her arms until the shaking had calmed. Others had stirred in the small dormitory the few woman survivors shared, but nightmares and screams in the night were commonplace; they turned on their sides and went back to sleep. She and Kate had shuffled their way down to the canteen, where lights were always kept burning and coffee was always available. They had talked for hours, Clare allaying her particular ghost for that night, not then knowing it was to return on other occasions. Kate's sympathy and her understanding were something to be cherished, their role reversal a switch that Clare needed and appreciated. Tomorrow she could be stolid, unbreakable, Dr. Reynolds once more; that night she was a frightened, lonely woman who required a shoulder to cry on, a friend to listen.

She stubbed out the cigarette, breaking it at the filter. Enough of this, Dr. Reynolds. Others needed your professional services. Time to close tight the self-scrutiny bottle; you can take a few snorts later, in private.

That was the moment Clare heard the shouts of alarm. Motion and conversation froze in the canteen as the few insomniacs and those still on duty listened and wondered. The floodwater announced itself by bursting through the swing doors.

Pandemonium greeted the announcement.

Tables and chairs were swept back with the tide, cups

dancing on the water like floating plastic ducks waiting to be hooked. The wave hit Clare, throwing her backward onto the next table. She fell to the floor when this, too, was tipped over. She suddenly found herself fighting for air, her head crashing into something, stunning her. Other objects, other flailing arms and legs, were all around, unable to resist the deluge, tossed in its fierce tide.

Clare Reynolds rose unsteadily, the choppy floodwater reaching a point just above her knees. Her spectacles were gone and blinking water from her eyes only improved her vision to a degree. A floating table bumped against her and she grabbed one of its upturned legs for support. It afforded little stability and she soon let the table drift away.

She began to wade toward the exit. Others followed, keeping to the right-hand wall for support, pushing away floating chairs and tables, helping the injured.

The lights dimmed and a woman screamed. Everybody became still for a few heart-stopping moments before the power regenerated itself.

Clare breathed a sigh of relief and edged her way forward, keeping her back to the wall, legs stiff against the fast-flowing current. There was no one behind the wall-length kitchen window that acted as a service counter, and she could not remember if any staff had been on duty there when she had helped herself from the chrome coffee machine. Probably not, not at that time of night. Would it be easier to escape from that exit? The floodwater was rushing down the corridor so that its full force pushed against the canteen's swing doors; the kitchen door was farther back and to the side—the pressure would not be as great. It might just be the best bet, even though it meant crossing the worst of the current to get to the open counter.

She turned to the man directly behind her and shouted her intentions over the roar. He wiped water from his face and nodded, agreeing that it might be their best chance. She heaved herself away from the wall, splashing wildly as she struggled to keep her balance. The current was swilling around her thighs, tugging, pushing, a relentless bully. She almost slipped, went under, but strong hands held her. Clare looked up into the face of the man whom she had spoken to only a few moments before.

"Thanks, Tom," she shouted, and added, "We've got to get the others to follow. I'm sure we'll have more chance going through the kitchen."

Others were already following, though, realizing what the doctor had in mind. Those too injured for rational thought were helped by colleagues, and a human chain was soon formed across the room. The rising water had begun to swirl around the canteen in a whirlpool effect and the battered group had to avoid dangerous objects rushing at them.

It seemed an eternity, an inch-by-inch stagger through a foaming maelstrom, clinging to those who fell, preventing them from being swept away, but still losing one, then two, then more.

Finally they were only a few feet away from the counter, and Clare gratefully clutched at the shiny rail that served as a queue barrier. She hoisted herself over the barrier and reached for the counter. But stopped. And sagged back against the rail. And stared at the black creature as it scurried onto the yellow-topped counter.

Squatting there, sleek and black.

Watching her with deadly, slanted eyes.

Wet fur rising like sharp needles.

Claws splayed into talons.

To be joined on the yellow surface by another of its kind. And another. Another.

Clare screamed as the lights danced their crazy, tormenting flutter.

17

Ellison had never held a gun, let alone used one, before that day. It was a new feeling to him and, he discovered, a pleasurable one. Many hours earlier, when they had taken the keys to the armory from Dealey and had surveyed the range of weapons thoughtfully provided and updated by successive governments that obviously had been nervous of insurrection in the ultimate crisis, he had viewed the weapons with both fear and growing excitement, the dull shine in his eyes matching that of the black weapons themselves, a peculiar affinity in their muted glow.

Farraday, who had spent several youthful years in army service and who had maintained a keen interest in military hardware since, had given names to the various guns and somewhat reluctant instructions on how they worked.

The guns had hardly been necessary for their minor coup, but Ellison and several others had been worried about the reconnaissance party's return and their attitude toward the takeover, particularly Culver's, who, in the weeks of confinement, had remained an unknown quantity. He was friendly enough, but seemed indifferent to their arguments, their complaints. And there was something faintly daunting about the pilot, even though he seldom showed aggression. Perhaps he appeared too self-contained when the rest of them desperately needed collective support. It had been a relief that he had offered no resistance on his return to the shelter, for Ellison was by no means sure he could have pulled the trigger on the man, even though he enjoyed the power that went with the weapon.

Now, as water swirled around his waist, he had found a target. In fact, many creeping, darting, swimming targets.

He concentrated his fire on the rats that were above, crawling through the pipe and wire network or over the tops of machinery, the bullets thudding into soft bodies, screeching off metal, embedding themselves in the concrete ceiling. The vermin he hit were knocked squealing from their perches, plummeting down to thrash around in the fast-flowing water, red bloodstains billowing around them like octopus fluid.

There were more dropping onto the catwalk over Ellison's head and he waded into the corridor, breaking a path through the still-rising torrent, quickly reaching out for machinery on the other side to support him before he was swept away. He leaned back against a rack, legs braced firmly against the current, and began firing toward the shapes scuttling along the catwalk, only aware of the three people running up there with them as he pulled the trigger.

Culver pulled Kate down as bullets spat into the ceiling just a few feet over their heads. Fairbank had seen the figure below pointing the gun at them as the lights had begun to flicker, and he had ducked low, shouting a warning to his companions. He cursed loudly as something tore through the metal gridwork just a few inches from his left leg.

Kate was shaking as she clung to Culver, but when he lifted her chin to look at her face, he saw no hysteria, just fear and perhaps despair. There was no time for comfort, no time for encouragement. The floodwater was still rising and the lights were liable to fail completely at any moment. He pulled her into a sitting position and spoke close to her ear. "We've got to go back down into the water."

"Why?" Now there was panic in her expression. "There's nowhere to go, we can't get out!"

"If we're going to stay above water level, we'll have to find weapons to fight off the rats. And we'll have to do that before the water rises too high!" He failed to mention the black shapes he could see continuing to climb through the pipe network and wiring.

"Let me stay here," she cried. "I can't go back down there!"

Culver began to lift her. "Afraid I can't do that."

As Kate stood she realized why. She shrank away from Culver, her eyes searching out the black shapes creeping overhead, backing into Fairbank, who was preparing to climb down a ladder close by. He glanced around, up, lips forming a single-syllable word, and swifly lowered himself onto the first few rungs of the ladder. He looked up once more just before his head and shoulders disappeared from view, his gaze catching Culver's and a knowing look passing between them. The understanding was of cold desperation.

Kate slid into the opening after Fairbank and froze when she saw the foaming water beneath her feet. A less-than-gentle shove from Culver set her moving again. Icy wetness gripped her, closing around her thighs, her stomach, stealing her breath, pulling and tugging in an effort to dislodge her from the ladder. Yet she felt the current was not as strong as before; the waters flowing from separate sources were now fusing with less force. However, she still needed Fairbank's strength to keep her steady once she had stepped onto the floor.

Culver joined them in time to see Ellison take aim at the ceiling again. The technician released a short spurt of bullets and Culver was surprised when a grimace that could have only been a smile appeared on Ellison's face.

"Where're Dealey and the others?" he called across to Ellison, who lowered the sub-machine gun toward him before indicating the operations room with the barrel.

There were figures already emerging from the doorway of the operations room, struggling through the current and staring at the chaos that confronted them with disbelief. Dealey was among them, and he had that same frightened look he had worn when Culver had first laid eyes on him just, it seemed, a few centuries ago. Culver let go of the steadying ladder and made his way toward the group, Fairbank and Kate following close behind, the girl clinging to the technician for support. Debris floated by— pieces of equipment, paper, books, chairs—spinning with the converging currents. The body of a dead rat, its belly exposed and ripped where bullets had torn through, bumped against Culver's hip; he hastily pushed it away. He reached Dealey as more gunfire opened up, but this some distance away, in another part of the complex. As if encouraged, Ellison resumed shooting.

Culver almost knocked Dealey over as a sudden surge carried him forward into the group; Farraday, close behind the ministry man, was able to hold them both.

"Can the shelter take it?" Culver shouted, bracing himself against the flow. "Will it be completely flooded?"

"I'm not su— God, yes, if the flood doors in the tunnels haven't been closed—"

"They won't have been!"

"Then it depends on how heavy the deluge is."

"Are we above the sewers?"

Dealey shook his head.

"Okay, our best chance is up on the machinery and the

catwalks. We'll have to turn the power off, though, before
everything blows. And we need guns to protect ourselves
from the rats.''

"No, we can't stay here, we must leave.'' Dealey tried
to move away from Culver, but the pilot held him.

"There's no way. Water's coming through the tunnel
exit. We'd never get through!''

"There's another place, another way out we can use!''

Culver moved his grip to the other man's jacket lapels,
angrily pulling him close. "What? You crazy bastard, did
you say there's another way out?''

Dealey tried to disengage himself. "There might be! At
least it will get us above ground level!''

"Where is—''

"Oh, my God, look!'' Farraday was pointing toward
the corridor leading to the dining area and kitchen.

For the moment, Culver forgot Dealey and drew in a
sharp breath when he saw Clare Reynolds pushing
through the water, sliding against the smooth wall for support, leaving a smeared trail of blood in her wake. Her
mouth was wide as if in a silent scream, and her eyes,
spectacles gone, were staring wildly ahead. Her body was
slightly arched, head drawn back; a black creature clung
to her back and chewed into her neck.

More torpedolike forms appeared, coming from the
switching unit area beyond which lay the artesian well.
That had to be the shelter's weak point, Culver surmised,
both the floodwater and the vermin must have gained entry from there. Even as these thoughts were rushing
through his head, Culver was rushing forward to reach
Clare Reynolds, treading high and brushing a path
through the water with his hands as if pushing through a
wheatfield.

Tiny water gushers exploded before him, beating their
own splattering trail toward the swimming rodents, and
Culver turned to roar at Ellison, to warn him off, for
Clare was too near, too exposed.

But the bullets continued to create a field of miniature eruptions between Culver and the doctor, who was feebly trying to reach behind and pull the gorging rat from her neck.

Culver moved forward again, wary of the gunfire and praying that Ellison would keep his aim as far away from him as possible. Meanwhile, Fairbank had seen the danger and was trying to reach Ellison.

But Culver was still five yards from Clare when her body jolted rigid and holes punctured her chest, rapidly moving upward, the last appearing in her turned-away cheek before continuing a splattering pattern in the painted plaster behind her. She turned her head, the rat and the searing pain forgotten in the all-encompassing white shock. Although dying's full agony would take a few moments to touch her, red stains swiftly spreading outward from the deep wounds, Clare was fully aware of what had happened, could see the gunman some distance away, the ugly, lethal machine he held now quiet, Ellison's staring eyes filled with their own shock. She was even aware of the teeth locked into her neck, immobile now, for the rat had been shot, too, although not mortally. Fear had gone as though released by the killing wounds, exorcised by the oncoming of death itself. All that remained was recognition, a fleeting insight to what was, what is, what *always* is—the acceptance before closedown. This, coupled with the knowledge that nothing was final.

The intense pain came, but it was brief.

Clare's eyelids covered the already fading scene as she slid down the wall into the water. Only the clinging thing, trapped by its own frozen grip, struggled feebly to rise to the surface once more.

Culver watched in dismay as the doctor disappeared, her white face devoid of expression, the hole in her cheek pumping dark-red blood the only blemish.

He dived full-stretch, the impetus carrying him through the meshing currents, and reached her limp, sunken body before it had time to drift. Gathering her in his arms, he heaved himself up, bursting through the rough surface to gasp in air, hugging her to him, his back against the wall. With horror he saw the rat still clinging to her neck, back legs kicking, raking her, and he reached for it with one hand, trying to tear it loose, incensed by its tenacity. The rat would not, or could not, release her.

In sheer rage, and in the knowledge that Clare was already dead, Culver gripped the giant rodent around the throat with both hands, squeezing as he did so, allowing the woman's body to slip back into the water, using her own weight and his strength to pull the rat from her. Flesh ripped as the creature came away, and a dripping sliver of skin dangled from its jaws. Culver spun wildly, swinging the rat's scrabbling body through the air, smashing it into the wall, feeling rather than hearing small bones break, swinging again and again until the animal hung soft and unmoving in his hands. He threw it away from him with a cry of disgust, then bent down, feeling for Clare's body, clutching at her hair, a shoulder, pulling her to the surface again. He cradled her in his arms and examined her face, gently lifting one eyelid, just to make sure, just to confirm, just to assure himself that she really was dead. The familiar coldness crept through him and he let her slip away.

He waited several moments, eyes closed, head resting against the wall, before wading back to the others, soon aware that the water had risen to a point only inches below his chest.

Culver knew that he and the others had no choice but to leave the shelter: either the water or the vermin would soon overwhelm them if they remained. He headed for Dealey.

Dealey tried to back away when he saw the look on Culver's face, but there was nowhere to go apart from the operations room, which was awash with dangerous floating furniture. He made a sudden break for the ladder leading up to the catwalk and stopped when he noticed the dark moving shapes through the grillwork. A rough hand spun him around.

"Where is it, Dealey?" the pilot yelled. "Where's the other way out?"

"The main ventilation shaft," the older man screeched. "There's a ladder inside, rungs set in the wall!"

"Why the hell didn't you tell us before?" Culver raised an angry fist as if to strike him, but checked himself. Maybe later—if they got out. "Why did you make us go through the tunnel? You knew the bloody danger!"

"We needed to know the state of the tunnels. That was our link with the other shelters."

"You used us, you bastard!"

"No, no. There's no way down from the shaft, you see, not on the outside! It rises to a tower above ground level and the top is sealed!"

"Christ, we could have . . ." Culver stopped. There was no sense in arguing, not now. Not with the complex flooding, the water still rising, the rats gathering overhead. "Let's get to it. We'll round up as many people as we can, grab anything that might come in useful on the outside. You take a couple of men and make for the sick bay, get anyone in there to the main vent shaft. Check the dormitories, the rest rooms, anywhere you can—but don't take long."

"What about the dining area and the rec room? There's bound to be people in there."

"You saw what happened to Dr. Reynolds, the rats swimming in that direction. I don't think we can help them."

Culver glanced upward. Several black shapes were directly over their heads. "Fairbank!" he shouted, but the technician could not hear over the general noise and was too busy venting his fury on Ellison to notice what was happening. Culver released Dealey and pushed his way over to them. He wrenched the machine gun from Ellison's grasp, knowing little about the weapon but hoping it still had more ammunition in it. Fairbank, Ellison, and Strachan watched in surprise as he raised the gun and pulled the trigger.

The effect was explosive. A hail of bullets whined off metal surfaces, smashed into the banks of machinery, scattering the black mutants, hitting many, propelling them into the air, wounding and destroying, but mainly causing panic. And a newfound respect in the vermin for the human aggressor.

Culver stopped firing, his eyes ever watchful, and quickly told the others of Dealey's disclosure. If their circumstances had not been so critical, he thought the three men would have grabbed Dealey and held him under water until he drowned. And he, Culver, might well have helped.

"Collect anything you can, to use as weapons," he told them. "The armory must be flooded by now, not that we have time to reach it anyway. Anyone you can find still carrying a gun will be an asset, so go look. *Now!* Get to the main shaft as quickly as you can, but try to find as many others as possible."

"We can't go looking for them!" Strachan was visibly shaking. "We must get to the vent right away."

Culver lowered the gun so that it was aimed at a point between Strachan's eyes. "I'm just telling you to take the long way around." He didn't shout, but his words were heard plainly enough.

Strachan and Ellison saw something in the pilot's eyes that was as frightening as the danger around them; they pushed themselves back in the water, watching Culver all the time, then disappeared into a channel between equipment racks.

Fairbank regarded Culver with raised eyebrows. "I'm with you, remember?"

Culver relaxed as much as circumstances would allow. "Yeah, and it's good to have you. Let's move."

He pushed himself away from that side of the aisle, allowing the current to carry him at a slight angle toward Dealey, Kate, and a small group of others who had gathered in the vicinity of the operations room. Fairbank followed.

"Dealey!" Culver shouted. "We need flashlights."

Dealey pointed into the doorway. "In there, on the shelves!"

At a flick of the head from Culver, Fairbank dived through, pushing away floating furniture and scanning the shelves lining the walls for lamps, flashlights, and anything else that might be useful as a weapon.

Outside, Culver moved the group of huddled survivors toward the passageway that would lead them to the main ventilation shaft. There were five others apart from Dealey, Kate, and himself: four technicians and the caretaker. They had formed a chain across the corridor leading to the dining area and kitchen, the currents there particularly fierce as floodwater from separate sources converged.

Culver was leading, his hand gripped tightly around Kate's wrist. Behind her came a black maintenance man named Jackson, then Dealey. The other three technicians were spread across the open corridor, struggling to keep upright in the current, the caretaker, backed against a wall on the other side, acting as anchorman.

The main ventilation shaft was not far away, just along the passageway, then left toward the switching units, but he wondered if they could make it, whether it would be rising water or the vermin that would defeat their purpose.

He breathed in acrid fumes and began to choke. Smoke spread rapidly across the ceiling and swirled downward, creating a thick, churning fog. *Oh, shiiiiit!* There were other alternatives. They could also be suffocated or burned to death.

The explosion seemed to rock the very foundations of the complex. Water either jumped above his head or he slipped down into it—Culver couldn't be sure which.

When his head and chest came clear again, the shelter was almost in total darkness. The red flickering glow from another part of the exchange, a glow that moved and spread, drawing closer by the second, dimmed only by swelling smoke, reminded him that the worst could always get worse.

18

For Bryce, the reality was more horrendous than any nightmare he had ever known. He had come to after his sedation with the full knowledge that the disease had him. It was too soon for the full symptoms to be evident, but the dryness in his throat, the feeling of burning up inside, and the fierce headache were the indications and the forerunners of the agony to follow. In a few days time there would be agitation, confusion, and hallucinations; then muscle spasms, stiffness of the neck and back, convulsions, and perhaps even paralysis. He would not be able to drink, and the inability to swallow properly would cause him to foam at the mouth, to be mortally afraid of liquids, to be terrified of his own saliva. The fits, the madness, would eventually lead him into a coma, a pain-filled exhaustion and, mercifully, death would come soon after.

His hand was numb at the moment, but the memory of Dr. Reynolds' quickly administered treatment sent fresh nausea sweeping through him. Then he heard the screams and shouts beyond the closed door, the strange rushing

sound, the lapping of water around the cots inside the
medical room itself. Sharp sounds that sounded like . . .
sounded like gunfire.

Bryce sat upright, and others around him, those whose
sedation allowed, did the same, all of them confused and
more than just frightened. A woman shrieked as water
dampened the mattress she lay upon.

Bryce pushed himself back against the wall when tiny
waves lapped over onto his blanket. He was still groggy,
and for a moment the cot-filled room swung in a crazy
pendulum movement. Someone splashed by his bed and
he flinched as ice-cold water slapped his cheek. Other figures followed, and Bryce drew in his legs, crouching there
in the gloom between his own cot and the one above,
shying away from the splashes as if they were droplets of
acid.

The patients were clamoring around the closed door,
pushing against one another to be first out.

Bryce sensed what was about to happen but could not
form the words to warn them. He raised his mutilated
hand, his eyes imploring them to stop, his mouth open
with just a rasping cry, a sound too weak to be heard.

The door burst open and those clustered around it were
thrown back as floodwater avalanched in. Within seconds
Bryce's shoulders were covered and he was forced to
scramble from the lower bed onto the one above, while
around him figures floundered and fought against the torrent. The iron-framed bunks began to shift, slowly at first,
like reluctant, ponderous animals; but soon the pressure
became too much and they began to tip, to scatter, to roll
toward the end of the room.

A double bunk toppled onto him and he was beneath
the water, choking on its brackish taste, the iron frame
heavy against his chest.

At first he fought against the weight, but as he struggled, a notion sifted through the terror, nudging him in a

quiet, stealthy manner. Why bother to fight? An inner voice asked, Why resist when death was inevitable?

The last of Bryce's air escaped in a huge, convulsive bubble, and although he was screamingly afraid and although his arms and his head thrashed the water, the pain was not for long.

Soft layers of unconsciousness began to fold over his eyes, like silky gossamer; the discomfort of not breathing relaxed and spiraled away, the anguish tapering with it. The feeling of helplessness was not so disagreeable and the suffering was beginning to subside, to torment less and less and less . . .

Peacefully, softly drifting. The weight from his chest gone. Floating. Upward. Rising. Upward. Something pulling? Hurting him? Hands on him? No, not that, not now! It was settled! It was accepted! Leave meeeeeee . . .

He burst through the bubbling surface, water jetting from his lungs, and tried to free himself of the hands that had yanked him from the restful peace. The choking muffled his protests as the two men held him; the pain returned, racking his muscles.

"Punch his back," Farraday yelled. "He's choking!"

Dazzling light blinded Bryce as he felt someone move around him. A sudden hard blow arched his back and he spluttered water and sickness over the two men. Another blow and he was retching, desperate to suck in air, involuntarily fighting for breath where just a moment ago it had been a relief to find it blissfully unnecessary.

Webber, one of the two technicians who had accompanied Farraday to the sick bay and who was now standing behind Bryce, slapped the Civil Defense officer between his shoulder blades, using the flat of his hand this time and not his fist. Bryce's own body reaction was clearing his throat and lungs, making outside force no longer necessary.

"Looks like we got to him just in time," Webber shouted to Farraday.

"Let's get out," Farraday shouted. "We can't help anymore!" He called for the others to follow, hoping they would hear, averting his eyes from the rear section of the sick bay, afraid of seeing something that would compel him to wade down there and help.

They began moving toward the door, fighting the undertow, careful not to trip over unseen loose objects.

Bryce allowed himself to be carried along, neither helping nor hindering. His mind was in a peculiar turmoil, a jumbled mixture of regret and elation. He knew what it was to die and it wasn't so frightening.

He stared into the face of Farraday, barely recognizing the senior engineer. He tried to speak but did not know what to say.

"It's all right," Farraday told him. "There's another way out of the shelter. We can make it. Just try to help us, try to walk."

Through the open doorway, the light seemed less bright, and Farraday supposed the power was fluctuating again until he noticed and smelled the rolling smoke. Thomas, another technician, was standing just outside the doorway, gaping down the corridor, his damp face a mask of dread, unsteady as water surged around his chest.

By the time they themselves reached the door, Thomas was rapidly heading for the switching units, seeming to swim and wade at the same time. Farraday peered toward the source of Thomas' obvious distress, the thick billowing smoke stinging his eyes, forcing him to squint. He just had time to observe flames licking from the test-room area when the complex rocked with thunder and searing white light rushed toward him, melting the protective film over his eyes, stripping the skin from his face. He fell back, carried by the blast, and water smothered his flaming hair, steam rising in a brief cloud from his burned face. He shrieked, and black water eagerly raced in, reducing the sound to a bubbling gurgle.

The others had fared no better, and to Bryce, it was just

the continuation of the long nightmare. He had been partly protected by the technician who stood directly in front of him and who had taken the full brunt of the explosion. Farraday's weight had been thrown against him, forcing him down, away from the flames, extinguishing the burning bandages of his mutilated hand, instantly soothing the scorching white heat that had exposed all the nerves on one side of his face, vaporizing the fire that had gristled his right ear. The water welcomed him back.

The tidal wave that followed, tightly packed into the narrow corridor, picked up the burned survivors and hurtled them along in a boiling stream, catching Thomas as it went, scraping their bodies along the walls, smashing into the machinery that finally blocked the tidal wave's path.

His neck was broken and other bones had snapped; Bryce could feel himself spinning, another bone crunching somewhere in his arm as it hit something solid, and although he turned and twisted, he was not giddy or confused, just tired.

He relaxed and let himself drift lazily into a strange, deep void, a total absence that was all encompassing.

Their bodies were churned and broken as they found their own, separate deaths, each one different, individual.

Water gushed through the complex, and the fire followed at a slower, yet no less lethal pace.

19

Culver searched for Kate, the red glow emanating from the fire in another part of the complex his only source of light. A huge wave had just passed over them, tossing their bodies like corks on an ocean, but now the level had settled to its former roughness once again. Smoke descended as if to join forces with the floodwater in absolute destruction. He glimpsed Dealey braced against the wall, his face red but eyes white. A technician, Jackson, was next to him; the others were gone, presumably swept back along the corridor their human chain had straddled.

"Kate!" Culver cried, afraid for her. She emerged from the black water a few feet away from him, sweeping her head to one side to free her face and hair from the wetness. She sucked in air and immediately began to cough as acrid smoke rushed in. He plunged toward her, a hand encircling her waist, and pulled her back against the wall for support. He held her steady until the coughing had subsided, relieved that the smoke had begun to drift upward, no longer disturbed by other forces. It was a brief respite, for he knew that the shelter would soon fill with the choking fumes, just as it might soon fill completely with floodwater.

There seemed to be hardly any energy left in Kate as she slumped against him. Her forehead nuzzled against his cheek, and she said, "It's no use, is it, Steve? We haven't a chance."

He was tempted to drag her over to the catwalk and climb up, to lie there and pray that the flames and smoke would die away, that the floodwater would gradually subside. That the mutant vermin would choose to ignore them.

"We've got one last shot," he told her, "and we're going to take it."

The shaft was their *only* chance.

A small ray of hope came literally from Fairbank, who shone the flashlight at them from the operations-room doorway.

"I'm coming over," he shouted, his voice barely audible over the confusion of sounds.

"Wait a minute!" Culver called back. "There's a bad pull there; we'll help you across!"

"Okay! I've got a lamp as well as a waterproof flashlight. I'm going to toss it over."

He switched on the second light and reached across the corridor as far as he could without getting caught in the treacherous currents. Culver had moved closer on the other side of the opening and caught the lamp deftly as Fairbank gently lobbed it over. He passed it back to Dealey.

"Keep it on us! Jackson, grab my arm and don't let go!"

Once he felt his upper arm gripped, Culver moved away from the relative protection of the wall. The current tugged at his legs immediately and he leaned into it, his other arm stretched toward Fairbank. The technician, clutching the rubber-insulated flashlight and something else in his left hand, reached out to Culver with his right.

He had to make his own way for at least a foot, then their fingers curled around each other's wrists and Culver pulled as Jackson drew him in.

They caught their breath on the other side and eventually Fairbank gasped, "This bloody water's getting higher."

Culver felt the choppy surface just below his armpits. "We haven't got much long—"

A scream from Kate and they turned to see the dark shapes, lit clearly by the lamp Dealey held, streaming toward her. There were three of them, yellow eyes, just above the waterline, perhaps sensing the most vulnerable in the group, the easy prey.

Fairbank's speed was remarkable. He leapt forward, the water barely slowing his movement, flashlight in his left hand, the other object now transferred to his right, raised high. He brought the blade down hard and swiftly, decapitating the lead rat, pulling the weapon clear and striking again, catching the second rat across its back, severing the spine.

The rat squealed, the cry eerily infantile, and blood gushed from the wound in a dark fountain. The cutter was more difficult to pull free this time, but the third rat veered away as its companions sank. It found the shadows and hid itself, keening for others who had been scattered by the thundering noise and who now crouched in other places, squealing and afraid of the smoke and approaching flames. They regrouped in the dark, massing together, for their combined force was their strength.

"We've no time to lose, Culver," Dealey said agitatedly, his head close to the pilot's, the lamp beam constantly moving, searching the area around them.

Curious, Culver ignored him. "What the hell did you use there?" he said to Fairbank.

The technician grinned and held his prize aloft, shining the beam onto it. "Guillotine blade," he announced. "The guillotine was kept close to the photocopier in the ops room. I managed to break off the blade.'' He swished it in the air like a straight, thick-backed cutlass.

"Come on, we've no time for this," Dealey urged.

"Link arms, like before," Culver ordered. They moved off, aware that the smoke was becoming more dense, the water level higher, but unaware that the rats were regrouping above them.

It wasn't long before Culver and the others found themselves inside the ventilation plant, spurred on by the threat all around, the red glow becoming a brighter orange, shadows dancing on the walls and ceiling, fiery highlights bouncing off the water's black surface. There was less smoke inside the plant room itself and the floodwater was calmer. It was quieter in there, too.

"Over there!" Dealey pointed. "That's the central air duct."

Culver shone the lamp and was reminded of the time he had seen the technician standing by the shaft, listening to the rain. He wished he had known then there was a way up, an easier passage into the world above. For his own devious reasons, Dealey had made the expeditionary group take the hard way, resulting in the probable deaths of two men—McEwen assumed drowned, Bryce with rabies—not to mention taking a few years off his, Culver's, own life. The ministry man was due for a reckoning, but that would have to come later.

"Is the grille screwed into the shaft, or is there a lock?" Culver asked Dealey.

The reply was despairing. "There's a lock to give the maintenance people easy access. I don't have that particular key."

Culver exchanged the lamp for Fairbank's insulated flashlight and plunged it down, hoping it really was waterproof. The beam glowed beneath the surface, diffused but strong enough to see by. His head and shoulders followed and he found the metal gridwork before him. He searched for the edges, his fingers running along the rim. He soon found the lock and examined it closely, the flashlight and his head only inches away. He rose to the surface, releasing the last of his air and gasping in another deep breath.

"We're lucky the opening isn't screwed into the wall. I think I can break it open," he told the others, who were watching anxiously. Holding a hand out toward Fairbank, he said, "Let me have the blade."

The technician handed him the makeshift weapon, realizing what he was about to do.

Noises came from outside, shouts, splashing, a frenzy of movement. They shone the lamp and the flashlight toward the door just as Strachan appeared; Ellison was close behind, and there were other figures jostling one another to get into the ventilation room. Strachan beamed his own flashlight in their direction and shouted with relief when he saw them.

A scream from outside changed his expression.

"Take a deep breath and come down with me," Culver instructed Jackson. "Hold the beam on the lock while I prise the grid open."

He disappeared and felt the long crack between door and frame with his fingers. The light appeared almost immediately and he guided Jackson's hand toward the lock. Using both his own hands, Culver slid the blade fractionally into the slit, just above the lock, then worked it in further, using only slight pressure to open the gap wider, pushing the metal blade in further as he did so.

A sudden greater use of force, without regard to breaking metal, and the door sprang open, its release quickly cushioned by water so that it stood ajar just six inches or so.

Culver pulled it wide, snatched the flashlight from Jackson, and swam through, rising up on the other side gasping for air.

He stood inside the shaft, pointing the beam upward. A metal ladder was set in the wall, not with separately mounted rungs as Dealey had supposed. The ladder went straight to the top, a height of some sixty or seventy feet, perhaps more; there were openings on either side, smaller shafts, metal arteries from a major vein.

Another grille obscured the top and he noticed that the ladder led to a small trapdoor set in it.

He dropped back down into the water and slid through the opening, emerging among a ring of expectant faces on the other side.

"It's okay," he told them. "We can make it." He handed the blade back to Fairbank and pulled Kate closer to the shaft. "Take a deep breath and go straight through the opening. You'll find a ladder to your right. Start climbing straightaway!"

He turned to Jackson, who still held the flashlight. "You go with her and keep the light on the opening inside the shaft."

Activity near the doorway caught his attention.

The water's surface was a churning pink foam and he realized that several of Strachan's party had been caught there, the rats dragging them down, tearing them to pieces beneath the water.

"Move," he yelled at Kate.

She vanished and Jackson quickly followed. The others in the group clustered around Culver.

As the next man went through, Culver saw that there were no more than a dozen left in the ventilation plant. There was no way of knowing how many others were still alive but trapped in other parts of the complex, and no time to reflect upon it. There was nothing more that he and the others could do; to attempt to rescue any more would probably prove fatal for them all.

The men were bunched together, forming a rough semicircle, their backs to the shaft. Culver found himself next to Ellison, who, like Strachan, held a flashlight.

"You two—together!" Culver snapped at two technicians between Ellison and Strachan.

"I can't swim," one of them said pleadingly.

"Move, you silly fucker!" Culver roared.

His companion pulled him down and their shapes disappeared through the opening.

"Give me the flashlight," Culver said to Ellison, who looked at him suspiciously before doing so. "Go through," Culver told him. "You too, Strachan. You can keep your flashlight."

The two men wasted no time in arguing. Bubbles rose where they had been standing.

Now only Culver and Fairbank remained outside the shaft. Just beyond the foaming patch where the unfortunate victims were under attack, the surface was covered almost totally, scarcely a break between them, by gliding dark humps, an army of vermin, now unhindered, streaming through the doorway like a thick black oil slick, spreading outward.

No words were necessary: both men swallowed air and dived.

Fairbank went through first and turned to help Culver. The pilot was almost inside when something dragged at his ankle. He whirled beneath the water as excruciating pain shot up his leg. His hands found the bottom of the frame and he pulled himself into the shaft, his right leg held back by the rat that had sunk its teeth almost to the bone of his ankle.

Fairbank pulled at one leg, slicing down with the blade at the same time. The lamp, its light gone as soon as it was below the surface, had been discarded, but Culver had the presence of mind to keep his light on the creature. The blade sank into the animal's shoulder, but not deep enough to shake its grip. Fairbank tugged the leg through and drove the cutter down again into the rat's back. Inky fluid almost blinded him.

The rat squirmed for several seconds before becoming rigid, then limp. In desperate need for air, Fairbank helped Culver prise the teeth from his ankle. The pilot kicked the corpse back through the opening and both men pulled the grille shut, feeling the tremors as their attackers darted forward and struck the other side. They pulled their fingers free before they could be bitten off, then rose to the surface together.

"We're not out of it yet," Culver told them, the words unusually loud in the confines of the tower, noises from the shelter itself completely cut off. "There's no way we can keep the grille closed, so start climbing that ladder—*fast!*"

They began moving upward, those below crowding around the foot of the ladder, anxious to be clear of the water.

"Those rats are going to be in here at any second," Fairbank muttered to Culver as they watched the others climb.

"If we just had something to keep the door tight against its frame . . ."

"A belt? We could thread a thin belt through the grille, hold it closed from this side. We wouldn't need much pressure to keep it shut."

"You want to put your hand outside to push the belt back in?"

Strachan's light went out and Culver shone his own flashlight on the technician. The tight-fitting bottom section of Strachan's flashlight came away and he held it in the palm of his, exposing the tough length of curled wire inside. He dropped the main section into the water.

"We can shape this so it'll fit around the grille," he said. "It isn't strong, but maybe we can keep the grille shut long enough for all of us to climb out."

"It's an idea," Culver agreed. "If we push it through near the top, one of us can stand and still hold on to it. Let me have it."

"No, you come down with me and hold the light." Strachan pulled the spring out, then bent it into a curve.

They took deep breaths and allowed themselves to sink. The rats outside were thumping their bodies against the grille, aware that their prey was just beyond the thin barrier. Teeth gnashed at the wire as it was threaded through.

Strachan gave the loop a testing tug, then straightened, his fingers still holding on.

Culver checked the improvised lock before rising himself. "It looks good," he said after taking a breath.

"Yeah," Fairbank commented. "The only question is, who hangs on to it while the rest of us get clear?"

"You two go," Strachan said. "I'll hold it for as long as I can."

Culver and Fairbank glanced at each other and the latter shrugged. "Who's arguing?" he said. He offered the blade to Strachan. "You want this?"

"No. When I climb that ladder, I want to get up fast. That thing's going to get in the way."

Culver briefly clutched the technician's shoulder as he pushed by him. "Okay. See you up top."

Strachan strained to keep a grip on the wire loop beneath the water, twisting his head every so often to suck in a breath, the level now well past his chin. The rats outside were frantically scrabbling at the grille and several had managed to widen the gap at the lock side and were pushing their claws through, excited by the blood tinging the water around them.

Strachan tensed even more when he felt something catch the wire loop on the other side. The loop jerked as razor-sharp teeth bit into it. It snapped.

Strachan wasted no time. He lunged for the ladder as the door began to swing away from him.

On the ladder, just ahead of Ellison, who was above Fairbank and Culver, the technician who had earlier announced that he couldn't swim moved his lips in silent prayer, eyes gazing through the rungs at the rough concrete directly in front of him, refusing to look either up or down; he wondered if he should have mentioned that he couldn't stand heights as well. Brilliant light suddenly filled the upper regions of the tower, followed closely by deep, rumbling thunder that seemed to shake the very ladder he rested on. He pressed closer to the wall. The thunder faded and a new noise caught his attention. A scraping sound.

Set in the wall beside him was a rectangular air duct, covered, as the one now below water, with a metal grid. Beyond the grid he assumed were the filters to purify the air that was sucked through. The scraping seemed to be coming from inside.

He peered closer, nervous of looking, but too nervous not to. He thought he heard movement inside. Thankful that the metal grid covered the opening, he looked even closer, squinting his eyes to see into the small, regular-patterned holes.

Lightning from outside invaded the upper regions of the tower again, not quite penetrating its depths but creating enough reflected light for him to see.

It seemed like a hundred yellow-gleaming eyes were staring out at him, black, hump-shaped bodies crammed into the tiny space behind them. As one, they leapt forward, crashing into the grid and rattling the metal in its mounting.

The man howled in fright, reflexively backing away. His foot slipped from the rung, his hands lost their grip. He fell outward, his cry continuing to a higher pitch, ending only when he plunged into the murky waters below.

Strachan felt rather than saw the descending body. He squeezed against the ladder, shoulders hunched and body tensed. A foot caught him a heavy blow on his scalp and he went down, only his tight hold on a rung saving him from falling to his knees.

He felt movement around his legs, smooth bodies bumping against them. The small, confined chamber abruptly exploded into a violent, thrashing caldron of motion and sounds. The fallen technician's gurgled shrieks merged with the high-pitched squealing of rats.

Strachan tried to heave himself up, but something held his leg. Sharp teeth punctured his thigh. He moaned at the men above to help.

Fairbank had tried to grab at the man who had fallen from just above him, and in the process he had lost the precious blade. He studied the seething foam below with consternation, blood spurting from the froth like scarlet geysers.

Culver looked down into Strachan's wide, pleading eyes, the pupils completely surrounded by whiteness. The technician was screaming, the sound too soft to be heard over the clamor. One hand gripped a rung while the other reached toward Culver, fingers outstretched and twitching, a gesture of imploration.

Culver started to descend, ignoring Fairbank's warning not to.

Strachan sank lower, forcing Culver to climb down farther. He crouched on the ladder, legs bent, clinging with one hand and reaching for Strachan with the other.

Their fingertips touched and slipped into each other's palms. They gripped.

A rat, seeming to grin as it emerged from the water behind the technician's shoulder, sped up Strachan's arm and onto Culver's as though their joined hands were nothing more than a ship's mooring chain. It was on Culver's shoulder before he had a chance to react.

By instinct alone, he had turned his head away as the mutant reached him. Teeth sliced through his ear and cut into his temple. He cried out as he let go of Strachan, pushing against the rat's underbelly, lifting it clear and throwing the animal away from him in one swift movement.

The rat twisted in the air, emitting its strange infant cry before it splashed back into the disturbed water.

Culver felt faint when he saw the mass of black, feeding shapes covering Strachan's back, torso, and lower limbs. The water was red beneath him.

It seemed that Strachan was almost smiling as he dragged himself up, but the smile became frozen, the eyes resumed their fearful stare as he realized there was no hope for him. He began to slide down again, the weight of the vermin dragging him back into the glutinous, heaving throng.

His shoulders went under. His chin. His face turned upward just before he sunk. His eyes remained open as water covered them. His mouth did not close as water rushed into it. His face became a white blur beneath the surface, a pale, screaming ghost. It faded in a cloud of deep vermilion.

A hand clutched Culver's shoulder and his head jerked around.

"There was nothing you could do," Fairbank said. "Now let's go before they come after us."

Thunder boomed as Culver crawled to the narrow opening in the tower where Fairbank waited. He looked out into the driving rain, seeing nothing else because of it, only the lights shining from below.

Lightning flashed and he was able to see that the buildings had collapsed all around the ventilation shaft, and their bulk had protected the tower from the blast. The tower itself was contained in some kind of stockade, the walls mostly broken now and covered in debris. The rubble was just twelve or thirteen feet below, an easy drop.

He nodded to Fairbank to go first, the night shuddering with thunder. Fairbank grinned, the expression just visible in the shining beams from outside, and clung to the sill for a moment before releasing his grip.

Culver watched as lightning forked the sky, lightning like he had never before seen, for it streaked the blackness in five different places simultaneously. Electricity charged the air, yet it was vibrant, infinitely preferable to the dank decay beneath him.

He slid from the edge and dropped out into the dark, rain-filled night.

PART THREE

DOMAIN

The black creatures moved easily through the ruins, seeking human prey, a keen, feverish excitement running through them in the knowledge that food was abundant and easily obtained. They sensed their victims' helplessness and showed no mercy, man, woman, and child falling to their slashing teeth and claws, weakened bodies finding little strength against the vermins' vicious might. Even the new-formed survivor communities afforded little protection against the sudden and overwhelming attacks, for the rats were instinctively aware of the shift in power, the balance so abruptly and unexpectedly in their favor.

They had found a huge source of food near the Mother Creature's nest, a warm, living supply that had sustained them for many days and nights; but as that flesh had putrified, the vermin had sought fresher nourishment, meat that was still moist, succulent with juices, filled with blood that had not dried solid, and inside the skulls, the palatable organ that had not yet been liquefied to slimy pulp by death's decay. The vermin grew bolder in their seeking, more daring in their gluttonous fervor, still preferring the night, but less timid of the daylight hours. They ruled the lesser rodents, their cunning and strength so much greater than that of their inferior kin; and they in turn were ruled by

211

others, strange, obscene creatures that skulked in the darkness below, that slithered on gross, misshapen bodies among bones and rotted corpses, communicating in high-pitched mewling, protected and fed by the giant black rats, mutants among mutants, the grotesque among the hideous. Weaker than their sleek black army, yet dominating them, feared and favored, obeyed and exalted as though they held some procreant secret within their ill-formed shapes, these monsters quivered with a new excitement, an expectancy.

They waited and received the thoughts of the Mother Creature, sensing its anguish, feeling its pain. They waited and, in their way, they rejoiced.

20

They thought they would be safe in the vast sunken chamber that had once been the banqueting hall of the hotel close to the river. They could almost feel the pressure of thousands of tons of concrete and rubble above them, bearing down, threatening to break through the high ceiling and crush them. By rights, that should have happened when the first bomb had dropped, but because of some quirk in the building's structure, or perhaps because of the way the mighty building had toppled, the ceiling had held. The great chandeliers had fallen, impregnating those early diners seated below with a million shards of fine glass; and most of the huge mirrors had tumbled or cracked. Part of the ceiling had collapsed, rubble descending in grinding, crushing avalanches, the openings formed soon sealed by more debris from above. Most of the hall's stout pillars had withstood the pressure.

Darkness followed within seconds and the rumbling, the shifting of the earth itself, continued. Those in the banqueting hall who had survived the eruption, or who had not been knocked senseless by falling masonry and glass, nor rendered immobile by shock, cowered on the floor, many beneath tables and chairs, others against pillars. A strange calmness befell them, a still numbness not uncommon in times of massive disaster; those who could crawled toward the helpless injured, drawn by whimpers and pleading. Lighters and matches were lit. A waiter found candles and placed them around the devastated dining hall; there was no romance in their glow, just a dim appraisal of human and material damage.

It did not take long to discover there was no apparent escape route from the hall: all exits had been blocked by rubble and there were no outside windows.

For some the hall came to represent an impregnable shelter where they could wait until rescue came, sustained by a carefully rationed food supply from the kitchens, heartened by the ample stock of alcohol from the bar; for others, more pessimistic, it represented a vast inescapable prison.

When nobody came to rescue the survivors after three weeks, anxiety mounted. At the end of the fourth, it was decided an attempt on their own part to reach the outside had to be made. A tunnel was to be dug.

The stronger of the men collected any tools they could find to dig with—broken table legs, long carving knives, even heavy soup ladles—and selected a point where the water appeared to flow more forcefully than at others. They cleared what they could with bare hands, then struck at the more resisting blockages with their implements. They found a fissure where a section of ceiling had caved in. The gap was swiftly widened, and although the earth was damp, no water ran from it. The first man squeezed through, pushing a candle before him. He pressed on, digging at the rubble with a short-bladed butcher's cleaver scavenged from the kitchen.

He stopped when he heard something ahead of him. He listened, sure it was not from behind, the sound of others following his path. Perhaps he had been wrong, for now he heard nothing. He began to dig again. Then he was certain he heard noises from ahead.

He called out. There was no reply except a scratching sound. He frowned. Now it sounded like . . . like . . . gnawing.

His scream escaped as a rat suddenly attacked. The light vanished as the candle fell, and he could only feel the creature eating into his face, his hands useless against the thick, hairy body.

The vermin had known there were humans close by, their keen sense of smell, their acute instincts, attracted by the distinct aroma of living flesh and human excrement. The digging noises had alerted them and given direction.

They poured into the tunnel, some eating their way through the body of the first man, others digging their way around him, finding more humans, aroused to an intense frenzy by their own blood lust. They swept along the tunnel, killing and feeding until they reached the huge cavern where the people waited.

21

She scratched at the itch on her cheek, her eyes still closed,
her other senses still captive of sleep. The insect moved on
in search of less resisting prey. Kate's full awakening was
sudden, eyelids snapping open like released blinds,
sprung by returning fear. The white blanketing mist did
not disappear with the blinking of her eyes.

It was several minutes before she was aware that the
rain had stopped and the sun had turned the earth's wetness to rising vapor. Her fear quietened.

They had escaped the underground refuge and its unnatural vermin. Flight through the rubbled city had been
a continuation of the nightmare, terror of being pursued
driving them on through the rain, each jagged streak of
lightning making them flinch, the ensuing thunder causing them to cringe. They had stopped only when they
found a clearing, each of them dropping to the ground,
drenched, exhausted, with little will left to carry on. She
had crawled into Culver's arms, and some time in the

night the rain itself had wearied and finally, after so many weeks, relented.

Kate glanced at her watch: nearly eleven-twenty. They had slept the morning away.

Culver lay like a dead man next to her, one arm thrown across his face as if to shield his eyes from the sun's nebulous presence—or perhaps to cover them against further horror. Without disturbing him, she raised herself on one elbow and looked around.

The mist was almost impenetrable beyond thirty yards or so, although occasionally warm air currents disturbed the swirling veils to reveal glimpses of the destroyed landscape beyond. Kate shivered, even though her body was soaked in perspiration.

The area they sheltered in had once been a park, a green, path-patterned oasis, surrounded by tall, once-gracious buildings. To one side had been the older law offices of Lincoln's Inn, a complex composed of buildings dating as far back as the sixteenth and seventeenth centuries, a high wall separating it from the park. The wall no longer stood, nor did the legal ghetto, for she knew they had climbed through its ruins the night before. She was sure, although she could not see them, that the other buildings that bounded the park would be gone, too, and that the nearby scrubbed stonework of the Law Courts—the huge Gothic Royal Courts of Justice—would be nothing but crushed rubble.

The grass and leafless trees—those still standing—were scorched black, and the only bustle was that of milling insects, their constant droning replacing the sound of voices, of laughter.

And she noticed that the peculiarity was not just in the number of insects, but in the unusually large size of many of them. Like the mutant vermin, they had thrived on the disaster. Maybe they were the meek who would inherit the earth.

Culver stirred, groaning a little as he wakened. Kate turned to him.

His eyes flickered open and she saw alertness spring into them. There was something more, too: the specter of deep dread was visible for just an instant as he looked into the drifting mists.

Kate quickly touched his face. "It's all right, we're safe," she said softly.

He relaxed only slightly and stared up at the white sky. "It's hot."

"Humid, almost tropical. The sun must be fierce beyond the mists."

"Any idea of where we are?"

"I'm pretty sure it's Lincoln's Inn Fields."

"Did we all make it?"

"I don't know—I think so. Wait—Strachan didn't get out."

Memories rushed in and his eyes narrowed as if from pain. "A technician fell. Two others went down before we even got into the shaft. And Farraday, the others, Bryce . . ."

"I don't think they had a chance. There were explosions before we got to the ventilation plant. And fire . . ." Kate shrugged.

She felt Culver appraising her and was conscious of the bedraggled mess she presented, with her torn clothes, tangled, matted hair, and grime-smeared skin.

Culver saw the softness of her features, the sadness in her brown eyes. The torn man's shirt she wore was too large and made her look small, vulnerable, and younger than her years. As yet, the ordeal had not etched irreparable lines in her skin, and the dirt on her face combined with the ripped clothing to give her a waiflike appearance. He pulled her to him and for a little while they rested in each other's arms.

Eventually, she asked him, "What happens now? Where do we go?"

"I think Dealey may have the answer to that," Culver replied. Despite the long heavy rainfall, he could still smell the acridity of the scorched grass. Nearby, a blackened tree rested its length along the ground like some discarded giant charcoal stick. Vapor rising from the ground added to the haunting desolation of the scene.

"He seems to be a man who likes secrets."

Culver's attention was drawn back to the girl. "It's ingrained in him."

"Do we have a chance?"

"While we've got him, we do. He was the only reason I got into the Kingsway exchange, remember?"

"He needed you then."

"Devious as he is, I don't think he'll desert us. Besides, I don't think he'll want to travel alone through what's left of this city. The dangers are too great. Which reminds me, my ankle's hurting like hell."

She moved down to examine the injured limb and winced when she saw the ragged holes in his blood-soaked sock. Even the top of his boot had blood-smeared puncture marks. Untying the lace, she eased the boot off, then began to gently roll down the torn sock; she was relieved to find no swelling.

"We need to clean the wound."

She reached into a pocket and pulled out a crumpled but unused handkerchief. "I'll wrap this around it for now and pull the sock back up to keep it in place. We'll have to find somewhere to bathe it, and we'll need antiseptic.

"Thank God Clare kept us regularly dosed against their disease." A shadow passed over Kate's face as she thought of the doctor's terrible death. She busied herself with the handkerchief, folding it carefully to make a rough dressing. "Your ear's been cut through too, Steve," she informed him, "and there's a nasty gash in your temple. They'll need looking at."

Culver touched the wounds, then closed his eyes, quickly opening them again when his thoughts became even more vivid. He stared into the surrounding fog and Kate became aware that he was trembling. She assumed it was a reaction to the previous night's events and quickly changed position to put an arm around his shoulder.

"You did what you could for all of them, Steve. Don't let it prey on your mind. You can't be responsible for all our lives."

His voice was sharp as he pulled away. "I know that!"

Kate did not allow the rejection; she moved with him. "What is it, Steve? There's something more that you won't tell me. Clare mentioned something to me back there in the shelter, when you were sick. You were delirious, talking, calling out for someone. Clare thought it was a woman, a girl, someone who meant a great deal to you and who drowned. You've never told me, Steve, not in all the time we were inside the shelter. Can't you tell me now?"

Kate was surprised to see a smile appear, albeit a bitter one.

"Clare got it wrong. It wasn't someone close and it wasn't a girl. It was a machine."

She stared at him in confusion.

"A goddamn helicopter, Kate. Not a person, not a wife or lover; a Sikorsky S-Sixty-one helicopter." His short laugh expressed the bitterness of his smile. "I crashed the bloody thing because of my own stupid carelessness."

She was relieved, but could not understand why the memory still haunted him.

As if reading her mind, he added, "I crashed her into the sea, and eighteen men went down with her."

It made sense to her now: his frequent remoteness, the aloofness toward the happenings around them and the decisions that had had to be made, yet the reckless bravery to save others, the risks he took. For some reason he blamed himself for the deaths of these eighteen men, and a natural survivor, he disdained his own survival. He had no death wish, of that she was sure, but his "life" wish was not so strong either. So far, it seemed to be the survival of others that drove him on, starting at the very beginning with Alex Dealey. She hesitated for a moment, but she had to dare to ask, had to know how justified his guilt feelings were.

"What happened?" she asked.

At first, coldness crept into his blue-gray eyes; then his gaze swept past her, staring intently into the mist as if seeing the destruction beyond. Whatever inner battle was taking place, it was soon resolved. Perhaps his own guilt feelings paled into insignificance against this vast obscene backdrop, itself a devastating indictment of mankind's culpability; or perhaps he had just wearied of his self-inflicted penance and felt that admission—confession?— would expel its demons. Whatever the motive, he lay back against the scorched grass and began to tell her.

"Years ago, when the North Sea oil boom really took off, the big charter companies found themselves desperately short of helicopter pilots to ferry oil-rig crews back and forth. Bristow's could take an experienced single-wing pilot and turn him into an experienced chopper pilot in three months, with no charge for the training; an agreement to work for them for at least two years was the only stipulation. I signed on, went through their training, but unfortunately didn't quite manage to fulfill the contract."

He avoided her eyes and flicked at a fly that was buzzing close to his head.

"The money and conditions were great," Culver went on, "so was the company. There wasn't much risk involved because flying wasn't permitted under extreme weather conditions; occasionally an emergency would take us out at such times, and now and again bad weather caught us without warning. The morning my chopper went down into the sea started perfectly: sun shining, calm waters, little breeze. I guess if it hadn't been like that, none of us would have survived."

He fell into silence once more and looked at her as if

asking for her trust. By lying close beside him, head resting against his shoulder, she gave it.

"I had a full load," he finally went on. "Twenty-six passengers—engineers, riggers, a relief medical team—and everyone seemed cheered by the fine weather. I remember the sun dazzling off the water as if it were no more than a huge placid lake. We took off and flew at a height of fifteen hundred feet toward our designated oil rig. We were soon over it and flying past, gradually descending. Everything was normal, no problems at all. I was still on the outbound course, leveling off, when we ran smack into a thick sea mist."

He shivered, his body becoming tense, and Kate held him tight.

"It was sudden, but no cause for alarm. I turned the machine and headed back in the direction of the rig, flying even lower to keep visual contact with the sea. I should have risen above the fog bank, but I figured we were close to the rig and would soon be clear of the mist. But you see, the fog was shifting and moving in the same direction—that's why it had come up on us so swiftly when we were outbound. Then, without any warning, I had nothing at all to focus on.

"I should have switched to instrument-flying, but I was confident I could rely on my own instincts to take us clear; all I had to do was maintain a constant altitude. But we hit the sea and bounced off. We hit again and the floor was ripped out. One of the flotation tanks must have been damaged, too, because next time we hit, the copter flipped over and sank.

"I found myself outside, lungs full of freezing water. Don't ask me how I got out, I don't remember—maybe through an escape hatch, or maybe I just floated through the ripped floor. I was semiconscious, but I could see the helicopter below, sinking fast, disappearing into that deep, never-ending gloom. I broke surface, coughing water, half-drowned, that murky vision already working its own special torture. I tried to get rid of my lifejacket, tried to tear it off so I could go back down, help those still trapped inside the helicopter, anything to relieve me of my guilt there and then, even if it meant my own death; but other hands grabbed me, held me there. My junior captain had escaped, too, and was clinging to me, one of the surviving riggers helping him. They stopped me diving and sometimes I curse them for it.

"Only eight of us made it. Other bodies were recovered later, but most went down with the Sikorsky. We were lucky that another helicopter was preparing for takeoff on another rig close to the one we were headed for; when we lost radio contact and disappeared from the radar scanner, it was sent out to search for us. By the time it reached our last point of contact, the fog bank had drifted on and we were visible. They winched us aboard just in time; any longer and the cold would have finished us, even though the weather itself was mild."

Culver sighed deep and long, as though some of the pain had been released with the telling. His voice became flat, unemotional. "The wreckage was never recovered, so the investigators couldn't be sure if instrument failure had been involved; but from my own account and my co-pilot's, "pilot disorientation" was assumed—an overwhelming compulsion for a pilot to believe in his own senses rather than what his instruments tell him. They say it's a common phenomenon, even among the most experienced aircrew. The CAA rarely classes it as a sign of incompetence or negligence, so no action was taken against me. But it was my fault, even though I was not officially blamed and no one voiced any accusations."

"And yet you blamed yourself," said Kate.

"If I'd followed the book, those people would still be alive."

"I can't answer that, Steve. It seems trite to say that accidents will always happen, even to the most careful. The fact that you weren't accused, not even in private, surely absolves you from any responsibility."

"The company didn't ask me to complete my contract."

"Do you really wonder at that? My God, they wouldn't be so heartless."

"It may have been the best thing for me, to fly that same route, to try to carry on as normal."

"How could your employers know that? It could have been the worst thing to have done. I can't believe you've been so foolish as to allow guilt to shadow your life for so long."

"It hasn't, Kate. Oh, it was bad for a long, long time, but gradually the thoughts found their own little hideway at the back of my mind. I wasn't too well-received at other companies after the crash, despite the inquiry's findings, and I was desperate to get back in the air. I needed to find my own peace."

The perspiration that trickled from his forehead was due to something more than just humidity. "Thank God an old friend came along just at the right time. Harry McKay and I learned to fly together and we'd kept in loose contact over the years. He suggested our own charter company; he'd handle the business side, I'd do the flying. Harry had a little money of his own and knew where he could find more. We'd be up to our ears in debt for a few years, but it would be our own company and eventually all the profits would be ours. Debt or no debt, profit or no profit, I jumped at the chance. From that moment on, we were so busy that I was able to keep those bad memories suppressed, even though I was always aware they were lurking on that shelf, ready to slip down."

She relaxed against him. "Have you spoken about the accident to anyone before?"

"Couple of people. Harry, for one. Usually in drinking sessions."

"Was the other person a woman?"

"No. As a matter of fact, it was a doctor. Not a shrink. Just an ordinary GP. About a year after the accident I developed sore testicles—at least, that was what it felt like to me. You can smile, but when that happens to a man, he fears the worst. I let it ride for a while, but it got no better. Finally, I went to see my doctor and he diagnosed an inflamed prostate, said it was due to stress. I offered that flying was a stressful occupation, but he was smarter than that. He explained that after the helicopter went down and all those lives had been lost, I had kept my emotions in check, had never allowed the breakdown that should have naturally followed—not necessarily a huge, hysterical breakdown, you understand, but perhaps a brief nervous collapse. I hadn't allowed it and the body won't be fooled. The inflamed prostate was a physical manifestation substituting for a mental one. The damage wasn't permanent, just a little uncomfortable for a while, and eventually it passed."

"But the anguish didn't."

"No, I told you: it found its little place to rest on. I guess the point I'm trying to make is that my only penalty for a stupid mistake was sore balls, when it was death for all those others, misery for their families. Doesn't that strike you as hilarious?"

"You suffered more than that. And it's never stopped for you, no matter how much you kept the hurt inside. You talk of penalties without realizing that life itself doesn't punish us; it's something we confer on ourselves. We create our own atonement. We manufacture our own crucifix and nail ourselves to it."

Culver was momentarily too surprised to answer. Whether or not he agreed with Kate's philosophy, he knew he had misjudged her. He should have realized there was more to her by the way she had adapted inside the shelter, how she had helped Clare Reynolds nurse the sick, himself included, how quickly she had accepted—no, adjusted to—the hideous and traumatic change in all their lives. And she had proved she was no fluttering, fainting damsel in their escape from the shelter.

He kissed her forehead. "Looks like the others are stirring."

"Steve . . ." She pulled at him as he began to rise.

He looked down at her quizzically and she returned his kiss.

A frightened voice called out. "Oh, God, where is everybody?"

Culver answered. "Take it easy, Ellison. You're safe enough." He pulled on his boots and reluctantly got to his feet, gazing down at Kate as he rose. He gently touched her hair before walking over to the technician, limping slightly as he went. Kate followed.

The others were waking, disturbed by Ellison's shout. They stared around them, startled by the mist. Culver did a quick check as he approached: Ellison, Dealey, Fairbank, stretched out beneath a fallen tree. Jackson and one other technician, a man he knew as Dene. Five of them, he and Kate, making seven. Had they lost others in their flight through the ruins? He didn't think so; the rest had probably drowned or been torn to pieces by the vermin back inside the shelter. Or maybe even burned to death: the choice of death was varied.

Ellison looked relieved to see him. "What is this place?" he asked, rising.

"As far as we can make out, it's what used to be Lincoln's Inn Fields," Culver replied. "What's left of it."

Ellison tried to penetrate the mist. "The rats . . . ?"

"Stay calm. We left them back in the shelter. We're safe for now."

Dealey had risen only to his knees as if the world were still unsteady. "This fog—is it a dust cloud?"

"Use your head." Culver grabbed his arm and hauled him up. "Can't you feel the heat, the humidity? After all that rain and with the sun beating down, the place has become a steam bath. And if that makes you uncomfortable, just wait until the insects start biting.'' He turned toward the fallen tree. ''How're things, Fairbank?''

The small, stocky technician yawned, then grinned back at him. ''Things is hungry.''

''That sounds healthy enough. Jackson, Dene?''

The two men looked less happy. They rose and joined the others, eyes warily watching their surroundings.

''Any injuries?'' Culver asked of them all.

''Do bruises and grazes count?'' said Fairbank, reaching the group.

''Only rat bites and broken limbs are eligible.''

''Then I'm not even in the race.''

''Check yourself anyway. You never know what you did to yourself back there.''

Each man examined his clothing for tears and his skin for abrasions. There were cuts and plenty of bruises, but no bites—except for Culver's.

''We were lucky,'' Fairbank said.

''Luckier than those poor bastards we left behind,'' Jackson remarked angrily, and a silence fell over them.

It seemed natural that Dealey should break that silence. ''We must get away from here. I believe it's still not safe to be out here in the open.''

Each man, soul-weary and afraid of what lay ahead for him, studied the disheveled ministry man with quiet, brooding disdain, as though now holding him solely responsible for the deaths of their colleagues and friends left behind in the exchange. Kate sensed and shared their contempt, yet oddly felt a tinge of pity for Dealey. She knew it was wrong of them to attribute so much blame to him. The grand folly was universal.

She broke the tension, anxious to avoid the confrontation that was looming; it would be so pointless. ''Will it be possible to get out of London?'' she asked, not just of Dealey, but of all of them.

Dealey, no fool and aware of their resentment, was grateful for her question. ''Yes, yes, of course. But there is an easier way than going overland. And there is still a safe place for us here in the city—"

"What city, you—" Jackson took a step toward Dealey, but Culver held his arm.

"Easy," he said. "I think I know where Dealey means. First, though, we've got a few minor things to take care of. I could do with some food, for one, and I think we need to rest up a little more before making plans. Besides, I've got to have my rat bite treated before I do any more walking."

"We can't stay here," Dealey insisted. "This very mist may be thick with radiation."

"I doubt it. The most critical time is over, and besides, the long rainfall must have flushed most, if not all, the radiation away. Anyway, we've spent a whole night in the open; if we were going to be poisoned, it'll have happened by now."

"But there's been no all-clear."

"Christ, get it into your head, Dealey: there's never going to be an all-clear. There's no one left to give such a signal."

"That's not true. There are other shelters, many of them; the main government shelter under the Embankment will still be intact, I'm sure."

"Then why no communication from them?"

"A breakdown somewhere. EMP, collapse of the cable tunnels—any number of things could have broken our communications with other stations."

"Let's cut out the crap," Ellison interrupted. "Right now we need food and maybe something for self-protection, if we can find anything. I don't like the idea of traveling unarmed."

Jackson agreed. "This looks like as good a place as any to rest up in. At least it's open ground and, man, I'm sick of confined spaces." He turned to Dene, who nodded in agreement.

Fairbank just grinned approval and Kate said, "You

need something on that wound, Steve. It looks clean enough and there's no puffiness around the bite, but you never can tell.''

Culver frowned at Dealey. ''I'd rather we all stayed together, but if you want, you can go your own way. It's up to you.''

After a moment's hesitation, Dealey said, ''I'll stay.''

Culver hid his relief: the civil servant had too much valuable inside knowledge for them to have let him leave. ''Okay, let's decide on who our scavengers are going to be.''

''I'll be one,'' Fairbank promptly volunteered. ''And you won't be the other,'' he told Culver. ''We'll try and find antiseptics, medicines, and analgesics along with some food; you rest that leg. I know the area and where to head for; let's hope we can burrow our way into some of the shops.'' He wiped sweat from his face and neck with his hands, then glanced at Jackson and Dene. ''You two game?''

''Sure, we know the area too,'' Jackson said for them both. Dene, a thin, sallow-complexioned man in his early twenties, appeared less certain, but did not feel inclined to argue. However, he thought of something that the others seemed to have overlooked. ''How we gonna find our way back in this fog? I mean, the streets won't exactly be the same, will they?''

''Is your wristwatch working?'' Culver asked. The technician checked it and nodded. ''You can just see the haze of the sun. Hold the watch flat and aim the hour hand toward the sun. Got it? Okay, south is midway between the hour hand and twelve o'clock. It'll give you a rough bearing on where the park is; once you locate it, you'll soon find us. Try and get back within the hour and save us some worry.''

''If you can find anything left to burn, a fire might help us,'' Jackson suggested.

"We'll manage something. Just be careful and don't take any chances."

Fairbank clicked his tongue against his teeth and pointed. The three men set off together, backs to the sun, heading toward the area that had once been High Holborn.

Culver and the others watched the mist swallow them up. It was an eerie and foreboding sight, and the immense emptiness they left behind had little to do with unoccupied space.

Culver shook off the feeling, concentrating on the task at hand. "Kate, will you help Ellison collect wood—branches, fencing, anything that hasn't burned to charcoal—and bring it here? Any paper would help too. Search the trash cans. And keep within shouting distance."

Ellison appeared ready to object, but evidently thought better of it. He walked away, a hand brushing flies from the air before him, and Kate went after him.

Culver slowly turned to face the last man left with him. "Just me and you now, Dealey. I've got one or two questions and you're going to give me straight answers. If not, I'll break your bloody neck."

22

Alex Dealey shifted uncomfortably against the tree stump, its blackened, jagged shape rising above him like an accusing finger pointed at the night sky. Not far away, the fire that had been kindled earlier in the day and constantly fed with anything that would burn, hued the mist orange. The blaze was welcome not just because of its warmth against the sudden chillness of the night air, but because it held the all-prevailing darkness at bay and, with it, its terrors. The others, except Culver and the girl, who seemed to have found warmth and comfort in each other, stayed close to the protective glow, gazing into the brightness, conversing in low voices. Occasionally laughter broke the quiet tones, although never raucous, always subdued, as if the men were afraid the sound might carry to hostile ears. Dealey stayed apart from the group, his hunched shoulders covered by one of the blankets the three technicians had brought back with them from their forage into the ruins, for their resentment of him was obvious, unequivocal, and discomforting. Fools. Ungrateful bloody fools.

He pulled the blanket over his head, holding the sides tight under his chin so that he resembled a huddled monk, only his nose and the tip of his chin caught in the fire glow.

The three men had been gone longer than expected, causing concern among those who had stayed. There had been no need to worry, though, for their delay had been caused by the amount of useful items they had managed to scavenge. Two café/restaurants, a hardware store, and a drugstore had been unearthed, and Jackson had remembered a bedding center, from where they had retrieved sheets and blankets in which they could carry their prizes. The men were ashen-faced when they returned, not even the accumulation of dirt disguising their skin's paleness, and had refused to speak of the harrowing sights they had witnessed, only Fairbank mentioning that piles of bodies had been blasted into corners or against rubble mounds like so much litter by fierce winds. They had come across no living person.

The fire, lit by a lighter taken from a corpse by Ellison, had been a beacon to them in the humid mists once they had found their way back to the desolated square where the blackened park was situated, and they had proudly, if quickly, displayed their spoils. Four short-handled axes, honed to a lethal sharpness, two hammers, and six long knives had been brought back as utensils or weapons, whichever purpose they lent themselves to at any time. Flashlights, already battery-loaded, thin rope, spoons, scissors, two can-openers, paper cups, a miniature camping stove along with a gas cylinder, had been retrieved from the hardware store. From the drugstore came bandages, Band-Aids, cotton wool, antiseptic cream, insect repellent, bicarbonate of soda, glucose tablets and vitamin pills, water-purifying Sterotabs, and, considered extremely important, three rolls of toilet tissue.

As for food, they had taken whatever canned items they

could find, but not too much, for it would prove too cumbersome, and once they traveled on, finding further supplies should not present too great a problem. The three technicians expressed surprise at how much canned food was kept by the café/restaurants as they produced their canned harvest of beans, soup, chicken breast in jelly, ham, sausages, tongue, peas, asparagus, carrots, peaches, pineapple chunks, condensed milk, and coffee. Cans of Coke and lemonade were also brought along in case they could not find an adequate source of water. They had all laughed when Culver had admitted he was glad they had decided not to bring back a *lot* of food.

Fairbank received loud commendations when he produced two bottles of Black Label Johnnie Walker. But Jackson almost upstaged Fairbank by producing four packs of cigarettes from his trouser pockets like a magician manifesting cute rabbits from thin air.

Dusk fell swiftly, more swiftly than was natural for that time of year, and the steam, slowly dissipating throughout the long afternoon, fell low, as if humbled by the incredible fiery sunset that followed. They stood as one and gazed into the southwest sky, their upturned faces bathed in the reflected flare.

As they watched, spellbound, the red boiling anger gradually subsided, for the sun was sinking farther into the horizon, turning the dusk into a softer, less frenzied vision, a warm richness subduing the violent-tossed clouds so that their hurried drifting became graceful, flowing rather than rushing.

The sun disappeared; darkness encroached, a definite curve, vignetted only slightly, moving steadily but warily forward, as if afraid of being scorched.

Dealey moved away from the others, tired of their attitude toward him, resenting their scorn. They didn't— *couldn't*—understand his importance to them, how he and he alone had seen them through the worst of the disaster, guided them through those early days, organizing, adminstering—*taking on the damned responsibility!* The events of the day, the alcohol, and the relief from the violence of the preceding night had obviously enhanced their drunkenness, for they treated him as though he personally had pressed the button that had precipitated this third and final world war. It was a mood that classified government circulars dealing with what was termed the "ultimate confrontation" had warned against. Civil unrest, aggression against the authoritative body. Subversion, anarchy, revolution. Events inside the Kingsway shelter had proved the correctness of the government view. And even now, when he had led this miserable few to safety, in that his knowledge had provided the escape route, they treated him with disrespect.

He shivered, glad of the blanket, for the warm clamminess of the evening had finally given way to the night's chill. He had watched Culver and the girl leave the fireside, they, too, taking a blanket with them. It was obvious why they wanted to be alone. Wonderful aphrodisiac was death.

He shook his head, the movement lost beneath the blanket. Culver could have been a useful ally, yet he chose to side with the . . . the—Dealey refused to allow the word to form in his mind, but the thought was there anyway—the rabble. The pilot's interrogation earlier in the day had been discourteous to say the least. Harsh, even brutal, might be more appropriate.

Dealey had answered his questions, calmly at first, but eventually becoming outraged by Culver's anger. He, Dealey, was only a minion, he didn't run the bloody show, he wasn't privy to every government document or decision. If he had been, he would have been inside the headquarters his bloody self! He just wished they would all get it into their thick skulls that he was nothing more than a glorified bloody building inspector!

His outburst had meant nothing to Culver, for the pilot was still curious about the rats.

Unlike before, when Dealey had been questioned inside the shelter on this special breed of vermin, he finally admitted that he knew they had not been entirely eliminated—nor could they be, unless the whole of London's Underground network, the sewers, the canals, the railway tunnels, and all basement areas were filled with poison gases or compounds, and even then there would have been no guarantee of total eradication. The task would be too dangerous and too immense. And the vermin could always flee into the surrounding surburbs.

Culver had not been satisfied. Dealey knew more—or at least, suspected more—than he was saying. The time for secrecy had long passed and, Culver warned, the others might not be as tolerant as he if they suspected Dealey was still withholding information. The older man had protested that there really was nothing more to tell. Except . . . except . . . Yes, there was a certain rumor circulating in various ministerial departments, a rumor that did not rouse much curiosity and, therefore, had died as swiftly as it had begun.

Dealey had been vague about the story, for he honestly did not recall the details, but the pilot had pressed him further, his eyes keen and searching. Something about a certain kind of rat—several, in fact, of this mutant species—in captivity. It was said that they were under observation in a government research laboratory, possibly—no, probably—being allowed to breed. The only interesting part of this rumor was that the creatures were apparently undergoing some extraordinary genetic transformation. The mutation had started in the radioactive atmosphere of the islands around New Guinea where atomic tests had been carried out years before, and the changing process was still ongoing. There were two types of mutant vermin, he had explained, the kind resembling the normal black rat, and another, which was a grotesque. It was the grotesque that the scientists were particularly interested in.

He had been afraid the younger man would strike him then. Why hadn't he told them all this before? Why had the government been so secretive about the mutants? What was there to fear? Culver had actually drawn his fist back and Dealey had stepped away, his own arm raised for protection. That movement may have saved him from the other man's wrath, for the rage disappeared from Culver's eyes and his fist dropped limply to his side. The anger was replaced by disgust.

There had been no further questions. Culver had walked away to sit by a blackened, branchless tree and had not spoken another word until Ellison and the girl returned with firewood. Dealey was relieved the pilot had not mentioned their conversation to the others.

The fire still burned brightly, for the men around it kept the flames fed with more scavenged wood, but the heat did not reach Dealey at his huddled position against the mutilated tree. Beneath his blanket, his eyelids began to close, his chin began to drop to his chest.

Sleep took him in slow stages, for trepidation did battle with fatigue: the night and darkness were something to fear, as were his haunting nightmares—dreams so violently graphic that he fought desperately to regain consciousness, for in these unspeakable visions he was transformed into a monstrous half-man, half-rat beast, plagued by a pack of grinning, yellow-eyed rodents that, in their frenzy for blood, slowly devoured him, piece by piece . . .

23

They stood like gray specters in the mist, unmoving yet somehow tenuous, like shadows cast on shallow water. They were silently watching the sleeping forms spread around the still-glowing embers of the fire.

Dealey suddenly awoke and nervously rose to a sitting position, careful not to make a sound, at first wondering if this was merely a continuance of his dream. He tried to count the spectral figures, but could not be sure if some were only stunted tree trunks, the morning mist—although not as dense as the previous day's—contriving to deceive. He was tempted to call out, to greet them, or at least to alert the others of his own group, but the cry stayed in his throat: there was something menacing in the vaporous silhouettes' unmoving, silent stance. Dealey pressed his back against the charcoaled tree stump.

One of the figures was moving, drawing nearer to the recumbents, becoming more visible. Dealey held his breath as the tall black man leaned over a heaped blanket, studying the sleeper beneath. The man wore a shapeless see-through plastic mac, buttoned at the neck like a cape, and in one hand he carried a rifle, in the other, a rusty butcher's knife. He stood erect once more, then moved on to another sleeping form. This time he used the blade to draw back the blanket.

The other figures were emerging from the mist, becoming more distinct. One of them picked up the whiskey bottle lying close to the embers and drained the last few dregs. The bottle was dropped back onto the blackened earth. The sleepers were beginning to stir.

Dealey counted ten . . . twelve . . . fifteen, at least fifteen figures approaching the makeshift campsite, and there were two, no three, small, crouched shapes moving among them. Dogs! Oh, God, they had dogs with them! Weren't these people aware of rabies?

He opened his mouth to shout—in part a warning, in part a greeting—and something smooth and hard slid along his throat. He choked as pressure was exerted, the iron bar pinning his neck against the tree stump behind. In the corners of his eyes he could see filthy, white-knuckled hands on either side of the metal bar, and he knew his captor was behind the stump, arms stretched around it. Dealey felt his tongue begin to fill his mouth from the pressure.

His companions were sitting up and looking around in surprise. Dealey watched, pinned to the tree, as one still, sleeping man was kicked. Ellison awoke with a shout and tried to rise; a foot against his chest flattened him. Jackson saw and protested, but the big black man pressed the discolored butcher's knife into his cheek. Fairbank reached for the short-handled ax lying close by, but a boot pinned his wrist against the grass stubble and another kicked the tool away. Dealey began to gurgle, his eyes staring like a ventriloquist dummy's in a garish pink painted face, his tongue pressing between his teeth. His heels began to kick at the ground and he tried to slide beneath the bar, but the aggressor was too strong.

The tall black man looked his way and waved the rifle. With a last spiteful jerk, the pressure against Dealey's neck was released. He slumped over, hands trying to soothe his bruised throat. A less-than-gentle nudge with the iron bar sent him scrambling to join the others.

They were a strange group, their presence made more sinister by their apparel and the assortment of weapons they carried. Much of their clothing was tattered and stained with filth, although several wore shirts and jackets that still bore sharp creases of newness. Like the tall black man, some wore unbuttoned raincoats, as if expecting the rains to return at any moment. One or two wore floppy-brimmed women's hats. Ripped T-shirts, sweaters, and jeans were the main dress, and shawls were draped around the shoulders of a few. There appeared to be more blacks than whites among the group, and all carried shoulder bags or cases of some kind.

There were three women with them, two West Indian girls who could only have been teenagers, and an older white woman with bedraggled yellow hair and an expression that was as stony hard as any of the men's.

Dealey saw now that the rifle the tall man held was, in fact, only an air rifle, although in his grip it looked lethal. A telescopic sight was even mounted on its top. As Dealey glanced around, he saw that others had similar weapons, while some had handguns tucked into the waistbands or pointed at the figures on the ground. By the look of them, these, too, were only air pistols. The rest of their armory consisted of knives and long stout sticks—pickax handles, he assumed. A frightening, unruly-looking bunch, he thought, and flinched as a dog trotted up and sniffed his feet. The animal looked as mangy as the rest of them, but at least no foam speckled its jaws and no madness glinted in its eyes. It appeared to be reasonably well-fed, too; but when the animal turned away, he noticed the sores and scabs on its sides and belly; parts of its body were also free of any hair.

Dealey turned his attention back to the people and realized they too were in a poor condition. One side of the tall black man's face was covered in sores and an eyelid was half-closed with an angry swelling; yellow, pus-filled spots flecked his lips. Others of his group bore the same marks. The youngest of the girls clutched her stomach is if it pained her, and several of the men looked equally as uncomfortable. Roughly tied bandages decorated several arms and wrists; dressings could be seen on legs through torn trousers. One, a youth of no more than nineteen, rested on crutches, favoring a foot swaddled in discolored bandages so that it was swollen to three times its normal size.

Unlike the creatures of Dealey's dream, none of them was grinning. But the threat they exuded was the same.

It was Jackson who spoke first. "You gonna take this blade outa my face, brother?" He used soft tones, as if gentling a wild beast.

There was no change of expression as the other man flicked the knife across Jackson's cheek with a swift, easy movement, drawing blood. The prone technician swore and touched his face; he drew the hand away and stared at his bloody fingers in disbelief.

"I ain't your brother, pigshit," the other man said quietly.

Someone sniggered.

Dealey began to rise, still clasping his throat, and two of the intruders moved close. "Who are you?" he asked, hoping the authority in his voice would carry some weight.

"Keep your mouth shut," he was told. "We askin' the questions, you givin' the answers." The tall black man raised the rifle, pointing it at Dealey's head. "This is a twenty-two, almost as powerful as the real thing. It hits target, it can kill."

"There's no need for this, I can assure—"

A pickax handle struck Dealey on the back of the legs and he tumbled to the ground, crying out sharply.

"I tol' you to shuddup," the black man warned. The man who had hit Dealey stepped back and allowed the end of the thick stick to rest on the ground. There was an unhealthy pallor to his face and a redness to his eyes.

"I wanna know how you escaped the bombs," the black man said. "How come you weren't blown to pieces?"

"We were belowground in a shelter before the bombs dropped," Jackson explained. He eased the end of the barrel away from his body, afraid the gun might go off. The other man allowed the movement.

"What fuckin' shelter? You govmint men or somethin'?"

Jackson realized his mistake. "Are you kiddin', me? I'm a fuckin' maintenance technician worked in a telephone exchange under the streets, that's all. We're all Telecom technicians 'cept for—" He avoided looking toward Dealey. "Come on, what's this about, man? We're all in the same trouble."

"I figure different. You look kinda healthy, nigger. You all look kinda healthy. All lil dirty, maybe, but in pretty good condition, considerin'. We ain't seen many like you."

He squatted beside Dealey, the wrinkled plastic mac opening out and spreading around him, and said confidentially, "Take a look at us, man. We got scabs an' coughs an' cuts that won't heal. We got the shits and some of our brothers have died jus' from bad colds. Know what I mean? See that lil sister over there? She got runnin' sores all down her body. See the guy on crutches? His foot stinks so bad we can't go near him." His voice became almost a whisper. "Half of 'em is dyin' an' they don't know it."

"Are there no hospitals, no medical centers?"

Royston, the tall black, allowed himself a short laugh and Dealey winced at the stale breath. "Nothin'. There's nothin' left anywhere, not in the whole fuckin' world. We come from th'other side of the river thinkin' somethin' had to be left over here, but all we foun' was the dead and the walkin' dead. Sure, a few other groups like us, survivin' on what they can, killin' to get it if necessary. Jus' law of the jungle, what you might think is right for me, huh? So here am I gassin' an' you ain't answered one question yet.'' He touched the top of the knife against Dealey's nose, and his voice became harsh. "How many of you aroun' here an' where do we find this shelter?"

"Look what I caught!" The interruption came from some distance away, and all heads turned to locate its source. Two figures came through the mist and one of them was Kate. Of course, Dealey remembered, she had drifted off with Culver the night before to find their own sleeping space. The other figure, a white man wearing trousers several times too large for him and an equally baggy jacket with just a vest beneath, was propelling her forward with one hand entwined in her hair. In the other hand he carried a curved meat hook.

"Found her sleepin' just a little way off,'' her captor announced with a grin. A red handkerchief was tied around his forehead to keep straggly hair away from his eyes. Like the others, he hadn't shaved for quite some time and there were blemishes on his skin that may have been healing burns.

"She on her own?" the man called Royston asked.

"Reckon so. She was sound asleep when I crept up on her."

Dealey looked off into the mist. Culver, where was Culver?

The big black man stood in front of Kate. "Not bad," he appraised, running the back of his fingers down her cheek. Not great, but not bad." He allowed his hand to stray beneath her chin, touching her neck, sliding into the open shirt collar. He felt her breast and squeezed hard.

Kate recoiled from his touch, hitting out with clenched

fists. The man still gripping her hair forced Kate to her knees, while the others, wary of the men they guarded, chuckled in anticipation. Over the past few weeks, they had learned that everything, anything, they could find, was for the taking. There was no control anymore, just survival.

Royston carefully laid the air rifle on the ground, but kept the knife blade pointing upward, and approached Kate once more. She glared angrily at him, but fear was in the expression too. Royston laid the blade flat against her cheek and the cold steel was as repugnant as his touch.

"You need a lesson, white lady. You ain't got the say no more." He twisted the blade so that the sharp edge was pressing into her cheek.

Kate tried to pull away as blood seeped onto the discolored metal, but the hand in her hair held her firm.

"What the fuck you doing?" Jackson screamed, outraged by the reflection on his own race as much as the assault on the girl. He sprang forward and kicked at the other black man, sending him reeling and following through by grabbing the knife-wielding hand. Baggy Trousers let go of Kate and caught Jackson from behind, using the meat hook to snag his shoulder, and pulled back. Jackson screamed as the curved point sank into a muscle. He was hauled off and he curled up into a tight ball as they attacked him with vicious kicks.

The two young blacks watching over Fairbank, one of them wearing a floppy-brimmed woman's hat, dared the stocky technician with their stares to make a move. Another, a white man of considerable girth but of tender years, held a thick arm around Dene's neck and pressed the barrel of an air pistol into his temple. Ellison was similarly guarded and Dealey remained immobile on hands and knees.

"Stop it, you're killing him," Kate pleaded.

"Hold it!" The big black man was on his feet once

more, and Kate sobbed with relief when the beating ceased. Her relief was premature.

The man stopped to pick up the rifle and said, "This mother's goin' to learn the hard way. An' maybe we'll git some questions answered at the same time. Bring him over here!"

He strode over to the remains of the fire and kicked at the ashes with his boot. Beneath the white dust, embers still glowed fiercely. "C'mon, git him over."

Baggy Trousers and another man caught Jackson by the elbows and dragged him toward the wide circle of smoldering ashes.

"Okay, shove his face in there." Royston pointed at shimmering embers.

"No!" Kate screamed, rushing forward.

Royston barely looked as he slapped her to the ground. He nodded to his men and stood behind the half-conscious Jackson, legs apart and gun butt resting against a hip, barrel pointing skyward.

The faces of Baggy Trousers and his accomplice were grim as they drew the kneeling technician closer to the fire. At its edge, they leaned him over so that he was off balance. They began to force his head downward.

Culver crept forward, crouching low, using the gradually thinning mist as cover. In one hand he held the small ax he had taken with him the night before. He and Kate had left the others chatting around the fireside, both wanting privacy, a chance to talk together. They had found a fallen tree and snuggled down beside it, Culver spreading the blanket they had brought with them and wrapping it around them when they had settled. The ax was in case any unwelcome visitors of the kind that had black fur and sharp teeth should come upon them during the night. Although it would have afforded little protection, the weapon gave him some comfort.

They had kissed, touched, a mild making of love, for

both found themselves still exhausted, that fatigue preventing emotions reaching any peak; but they were content within each other's arms, happy to talk in murmured voices, to explore and to confide. Sleep had not taken too long to overcome them.

Culver had been the first to awake the following morning, and he had gently untangled himself from Kate's arms. He had walked off to relieve himself, carrying the ax as a precaution; now that it was daylight, he was more cautious of rabid animals than of rats.

Near the center of the park he had found a partly demolished shelter. Ridiculously modest, he had stepped inside and was unzipping his jeans when the stench hit him. He took a step back in disgust and his foot slipped on something wet. His stomach heaved when he searched the human carnage beneath him.

He fled from the shelter, holding his mouth as though unwilling to further defile the mausoleum with his own vomit. The sickness poured from him in gut-wrenching spurts. And even when his stomach was empty, the muscles there still contracted painfully, expelling empty air as if purging more than just bile from his body. It was a long time before he was able to stagger away and find another place to relieve himself.

He was surprised to find her gone and assumed she had made her way back to the others around the campfire, thinking he had done the same. Following her and pondering over their plan for the day, Culver heard the voices before catching sight of the intruders. Something in their tone warned him that they were not friendly.

Culver crouched low, the mist still thick enough to conceal him until he got too close. He saw them and tension filled him.

The black stranger shouted something and Jackson was dragged toward the ashes of the fire. The girl had been knocked down and her assailant had turned his back toward him before Culver realized what was about to happen.

Jackson's face was only inches away from the smoldering embers when anger—more than just anger: it was a ferocity that filled every extremity of his body and sent seething pulses through his head—spilled from Culver in a silent scream, making his whole body tremble, his lips baring to reveal clenched teeth, a grimace of sheer hatred. Hadn't they been through enough without their own kind, survivors like themselves, subjecting them to this perverse treatment? Hadn't the destruction taught them anything? Had the madness only bred fresh madness? He restrained the cry and silently ran forward.

Culver was among them before they were even aware of his approach; the tall black man still had his back to him.

At last releasing the cry, Culver swung the ax in a sideways arc and the metal head cut deep into the raincoated man's spine, severing it completely. Culver had to tug hard to pull the ax free.

Royston screamed, a high animal sound, his arms splaying outward, throwing the weapons. He collapsed immediately and lay prone on the ground, unable to move, able only to die. His hands and feet twitched convulsively and a whining came from his scabbed lips.

Culver did not linger; his next target was one of the men holding Jackson over the ashes, a man who wore a red handkerchief around his forehead. The edge of the ax caught him beneath the chin, snapping his head, toppling him onto the hot embers. Culver felt something *thwack* against his leather jacket and saw the other man pointing a gun at him. It occurred to him in an instant that he had been shot, yet there had been no gunfire and no pain. He swung the ax again and the gun fell as the intruder clutched a fractured wrist.

Jackson fell face forward into the ashes and rolled over screaming, embers glowing in his dark skin.

Culver could not help him: there were too many of the

enemy to contend with. He ducked as a rifle was aimed at
him, feeling a stinging along his cheek. The man with the
rifle rushed him, using the weapon as a club.

Fairbank took advantage of the distraction. He grabbed
the ax still lying nearby, bringing the blunt end up into
the stomach of one of his guards. The other received the
sharp end across the bridge of his nose.

The fat man holding Dene released the pellet from the
air pistol into the technician's temple. Dene sank to his
knees, hands clasping at the wound. He slumped face forward to the ground and lay there silent and still.

Ellison attempted to run from the three men coming toward him. They easily caught him and he lashed out with
fists and feet, but quickly succumbed to their concerted
assault.

Catching sight of the man rushing toward Culver,
Dealey threw his arms around the passing legs. The
would-be assailant fell heavily and Culver stepped forward and brought a foot down hard against the back of his
head. Something crunched and he hoped it was the man's
nose; better still, his neck. He quickly scanned the chaos,
the ax poised before him to ward off further attack.

Kate was dragging Jackson out of the fire, slapping
burning embers from his face. Three other men and the
women stared with uncertain looks; the attack on them
had been so swift and so devastating that they were perplexed. And now, they, too, were afraid.

Culver turned to Fairbank and said quietly, "We'd better get away from here while we can."

"That's a fact," Fairbank replied.

They quickly observed the plight of their companions;
Ellison appeared to be in the worst trouble.

"Dealey, help Kate," Culver ordered. "Start running,
toward the river. You know where to go."

Dealey rose and stumbled toward Kate, who was
kneeling beside Jackson, still brushing ash from his face.
The three men beating Ellison were caught unawares as

Culver and Fairbank laid into them. Two went down immediately, although not seriously hurt; the third staggered back as Fairbank struck him with his left hand. Culver and Fairbank scooped up Ellison and dragged him after their retreating companions.

"Dene!" Fairbank shouted.

Culver glanced around and found the prostrate body of the young technician. "Keep going, I'll check him out."

Fairbank, ax raised in his right hand, his left supporting Ellison, staggered away while the pilot hurried over to Dene's limp form. He knelt and turned the technician over on his side. Death was now familiar enough to be easily recognized.

Culver was up and running again, racing through the ravaged park and wishing the mist had not thinned out so much; its cover would have been welcome. He caught up with the others and relieved Kate of the severely burned maintenance technician, who was groaning aloud. Dealey was supporting Jackson on the other side. They moved as quickly as possible, a stumbling, awkward run, passing the maggot-filled tomb Culver had come upon earlier, skirting around empty tennis courts, the wire fencing surrounding it strangely untouched by the blasts.

Jackson tripped, went down, almost dragged Culver and Dealey with him.

"Keep going!" Culver yelled at the others, waving Kate away. "They'll be coming after us!"

Rubble spilled down from varying heights to meet the edge of the park and they found themselves climbing, choosing the lower valleys, uneven passes in the debris. Culver noticed that one of Jackson's eyes was completely closed and a large part of his face had been burned raw; there were darker lumps enmeshed in his skin, pieces of charcoal that had seared their way through to the flesh beneath and become affixed there. His left shoulder was covered in blood.

At the top of a rise, Culver turned to see if they really

were being followed. Running figures were just visible in the swirling mist. He dropped into the ravine below, helping Jackson, aware that he had been seen: one of the figures had stopped and pointed at him.

Kate cried out when she missed her footing, but hobbled on, too afraid even to look back.

The valley ahead widened out and Culver knew they must be in what was once a broad thoroughfare leading to the Aldwych; beyond that was Waterloo Bridge and the Thames. Fairly close to that was the only place he felt they could be safe.

But at this rate, he knew they were not going to make it.

24

"In here!"

Culver pointed at the opening, a hole created by a large concrete slab leaning crazily against a shop front. Much of the building above the shop had slid down the chunk of concrete and around its sides; the gap was formed between the slab and a landslide of rubble. Culver and Dealey helped Jackson, who was still moaning with pain, while Fairbank held on to Ellison, whose steps were still unsteady after the beating he had taken.

They made for the opening as Culver quickly scanned the landscape behind. He couldn't see their pursuers, but he could hear them: a pack of screaming banshees, howling for blood. Revenge was all they had, their only motivation—that, and survival.

Dealey hesitated at the entrance. "It isn't safe in here. The whole structure is loose, unstable."

Culver gave him a shove. "Take Jackson, follow the others. Waste one second longer and the mob'll see us."

Dealey reluctantly did as instructed, bearing the whole

of the black man's weight, both of them crouching to get through the gap. The pilot backed his way in, eyes on the route behind them. He ducked from view when the first head came into sight over a small crest of debris, praying he hadn't been observed.

Dust sifted down, blinding him for a moment. He brushed it away, blinking rapidly. Something creaked above him, then concrete ground against concrete. Dealey was right: the whole place was ready to collapse.

He moved further in, the figures of his companions barely visible in the dim light.

Voices from outside. Culver and the others froze, listening. Shouts, angry and something more. Excited. Eager for the chase. A new sport born out of the chaos. The human hunt.

"Keep still!" Culver hissed, and they, the hunted, did not move.

Dealey breathed in dust and putridity and wondered what lay about them in the darkness. He squinted, peering into the gloom, knowing they were inside a shop, for, beyond the opening, they had stepped over a short sill, the edge of which must have been a display window. In the distance, far at the back of the shop, he could see a glimmer of light. Another opening, a means of escape, at least. He could just make out broken display racks and the littered floor beneath them. Ah, a bookshop. He knew the one, had broused through it in . . . in better times. What value the written word now?

Jackson groaned beside him and Dealey could feel a new wetness sinking into his own clothing, a sticky flowing that had nothing to do with his own body damp. The engineer was bleeding over him. He shifted, repulsed by the seepage, and Jackson groaned aloud. Frightened the sounds could be heard outside, Dealey clamped a hand to the injured man's mouth. Jackson's semiclosed eyes opened wide with the sudden sharp increase of pain in his charred lips; he screamed against the darkness and pushed against whoever was trying to stifle him. He was free and terribly afraid. There were moving shadows all around, hands reaching for him, fingers touching his burned skin. He screamed again and tried to escape. There was a light, an opening. He had to get through it. There were rats down in the shelter! Large black rats! Rats that could tear a man to pieces! He had to get out!

Culver lunged at the distraught man, knowing it was already too late, that those outside could not have failed to have heard. Mad with pain and panic, Jackson threw the pilot to one side, intent only on reaching the source of light, desperate to escape the dark hole in the ground where he could smell the burning of his own flesh and hear the screeching and scuffling of night creatures. He staggered toward the triangle of light, slipping on objects scattered on the floor, almost falling over more bulky shapes lying in the dust.

He was nearly there and already the air seemed cleaner. He sobbed with relief. But he could see shapes coming through, figures filling the opening, blocking the light, taking away the clean air. There were shouts and they reminded him of earlier sounds, the jeering as his face had been lowered into the heat, the sneering curses of men and women who had become worse than rabid animals, who had become like the vermin that roamed the underground world, mutilating not just to live, but for the pleasure it gave them. He roared, plunging toward the figures in the opening, pushing at fallen beams to get to them, wanting to feel *their* flesh open beneath *his* fingers.

The others heard the grinding sound and sensed the shift in weight over their heads.

"It's giving way!" Dealey screeched.

There was no need for further words. They moved as one away from the tearing, grinding noise above them, slowly at first, almost cautious, as if haste would precipitate the avalanche; but as the renting and cracking became a coordinated rumble and the walls creaked outward, they began to run blindly toward the rear of the building.

Kate fell, was up, not knowing if unseen hands had helped her, running, sliding, but never stopping, constantly moving ahead of the enormous surge, prodded by its cloudy draft. Toward light ahead, a sliver of light, a thin fraction of yellow-white. A door, still upright, slightly ajar, the building's lower portions protected by other buildings on the opposite side of the road, they themselves shorn of their upper floors.

Someone was pulling at the door from the inside, opening it wide, sweeping aside the clutter at its base; Fairbank was ushering her through, telling her to keep running. And then she was outside, others crowding behind her, all of them running away from the crashing building, climbing the long slope of rubble opposite, not stopping until there was no breath left, no more energy to carry them on, until clouds of dust covered and choked them, making them fall and cover their faces, desperately praying that they were far enough away, that they could not be reached by crushing rubble. Waiting for the rumbling to diminish, to fade away, to stop.

And eventually, the tremors did stop.

Kate raised her head and wiped dust away from her face and eyes. Someone groaned nearby and she twisted to see a slumped figure coated in pulverized masonry, just beginning to move. It was Ellison.

Kate sat up. Below her was Dealey—he, too, barely recognizable under the dust layers. Much farther down, Fairbank was beginning to rise, wiping his face with one hand, the other still clutching his ax, and turning to survey the demolition, much of the building's outer shell still standing—at least on their side. There was no sign of Jackson and no sign of—

"Steve?" It was a mild question asked of the dust clouds. "Steve!" This time Kate screamed the name.

The three men with her on the incline jerked to attention and looked at the rubble below with dismay. No, not Culver; they needed him! The sudden loss made it clear in all their minds just how *much* they needed him. Dealey sat down on the slope and ran a hand through his thin, now powdery hair, his brow knotted in exasperation. Ellison shook his head in despair; he hadn't liked Culver, yet had to admit there was something very reassuring about his presence. So much so, he wondered if they could survive without him. Fairbank's usual cheerful countenance was a mixture of grimness and incredulity, his eyes disbelieving, his mouth set straight, held rigid; Culver had come through too much to be killed in this stupid way. Kate was in shock, her senses numbed for the moment.

The dust clouds slowly dispersed, taking with them the humid mist, until the scene was only thinly veiled by floating particles.

Kate's emotions broke when Culver appeared from behind a mound that had once been a car, now half-buried in debris. Brushing powder from his head, shoulders, and arms, he strode up the incline toward them.

"Thought you'd lost me, huh?" he said.

It seemed that Kate's tears would never stop. The others sat some distance away, uncomfortable and anxious to move on, while Culver cradled her in his arms and did his best to stem the outpourings of her misery.

"I thought you were dead, Steve," she managed to say between sobs. "After everything else, I couldn't stand that."

"It's nearly finished, Kate. We're nearly clear of all this."

"But that can't ever be so. There's nothing left for any of us."

"We're alive. That's all that matters. You may think it's impossible, right now, but you've got to put everything else out of your mind. Just think of living and getting through this mess; think beyond that and you'll go mad."

"I'm close to it, Steve, I know I'm close to madness. I don't think I can take any more."

He kissed the top of her head. "You're the sanest one among us."

Her trembling was gradually subsiding. "But what's left for any of us? Where can we go? What can we do? What kind of world's been left to us?"

"It might just be a peaceful one."

"You can say that after what we've been through this morning? And last night?"

"Let's just say we've been knocked back a few thousand years to a time when other tribes are the enemy and certain breeds of animal are dangerous. We got through it then, we'll do it again."

"You're hardly convincing." Some of the color was returning to her cheeks.

"I know. I don't believe it myself. But our ancestors may have had the right idea about one thing: they spent most of their time considering how to live, not why they were living. They were too busy finding food and building shelters to concern themselves with despair."

"Thank God I found the oracle to take care of me," she sniffed.

Culver smiled. "All I'm saying is concentrate your mind here and now, and nothing else. The rest is too big to contemplate. Use Fairbank as an example: it's as if he's on autopilot. Maybe he'll crack up eventually, but it won't be until he's got time to, when he's in safer and more stable surroundings. As far as I understand him, he's not interested in yesterday, nor tomorrow. Only now, this moment, today."

"But we have to think ahead if we're to live." Her crying had stopped, and he wiped away the wetness, smearing the dirt on her cheeks.

"We think as far as a destination." He kissed her then,

and there was more than consolation in the touch. They broke away by mutual consent, neither one prolonging the sweet torment. A little breathless, Culver beckoned to the others.

"Ready to move on?" he asked of them.

"Waiting for you, pal," Fairbank answered, his teeth white against the blackness of his face.

"Move on to where? I've been beaten almost to a pulp, dragged through the ruins, and nearly crushed to death." Ellison spat dust from his mouth in disgust. "How much more do you think I can take?"

"None of us can handle much more, that's pretty obvious," Culver told him, "so you just be your usual charming self and we'll see what we can figure out."

He looked out over the hazy ruins and wished he could see the full extent of the damage. The mist was clearing, but it was still impossible to see the small hills surrounding the rubbled city. He wondered what lay beyond.

"All right," he said finally. "We can try to make it out of what's left of the city on foot, finding food and shelter as we go. It doesn't look as if we're going to get any help from official sources and I doubt we'll find any Red Cross soup kitchens set up along the way."

"But where *is* the government help?" Ellison snarled. "Just what the fuck are they doing about all this?"

"The devastation has been beyond all expectation," Dealey began to say. "It was all underestimated. No one foresaw—"

"No jargon, Dealey, no bloody officialese excuses!" Ellison's hand hovered threateningly over a brick by his side.

Fairbank stirred. "Cut it out, Ellison. You're getting too much to stomach." His words were all the more ominous for their quietness. He turned to Culver. "What about the main government headquarters, Steve? Wouldn't we be better off there?"

"That's what I was coming to next. Our friend from

the ministry here and I had a quiet chat yesterday, and he disclosed some interesting details about the place. It seems it's impregnable. Bombproof, radiationproof, and famineproof.''

''Yeah, but is it floodproof?'' Fairbank rumbled darkly.

''Each section can be sealed by airtight doors,'' Dealey said.

''You can get us in?'' Ellison asked eagerly.

''He knows the entrances,'' said Culver. ''We'll worry about getting inside when the time comes.''

''Then you think we should make for the shelter,'' Kate said.

''Yep. Literally go to ground. It's our best bet.''

''I agree.'' Dealey looked at them all individually. ''It's what I've advocated all along. Wait until the radiation has passed, then link up with main base.''

''It's a feasible choice,'' said Culver. ''Agreed?''

The others nodded.

''Jackson?'' said Kate.

Culver held her arm. ''He's dead, you know that. He had no chance in there.''

''It seems so cruel, after all he'd . . .'' She let the words trail off, aware that they all sensed the futility.

Without further words, Culver helped her up and they all began to clamber over the ruins. They concentrated their efforts on not stumbling over treacherous masonry and avoiding fragile-looking structures, steering well clear of any open pits and fissures.

Climbing, sliding, and brushing away swarms of oversized insects, they steadily made their way toward the Thames. A walk that would have taken no more than five or ten minutes in normal times took them the best part of an hour. They became almost immune to the unpleasant sights they came upon, their minds learning to regard the image of mutilated, swollen, and rotted corpses as part of the debris and nothing to do with human life itself. Vehicles, overturned, burned out, or simply askew in the roadway, had to be skirted around or climbed over, their ghoulish occupants ignored. Nowhere did they find walking, moving people; nowhere was there anyone like themselves.

"How much farther?" Ellison whined. He was panting and one hand was clutched tight against his side, as though ribs had been damaged in the beating.

"The bridge," Culver said, his own chest heaving with the effort. His cheek was caked with darkish blood and he had realized earlier that a pellet from an intruder's air rifle must have scythed a path across it. The wound throbbed, as did the rat-inflicted cuts in his ear and temple, but no longer stung. The pain in his ankle was sharp, but did not hinder him too much.

"If we can get to Waterloo Bridge, there's a staircase leading down to the Embankment. We can get to one of the shelter's entrances from there."

They journeyed on and were shocked when they reached Lancaster Place, the wide thoroughfare leading up to Waterloo Bridge itself. They should have expected it, but somehow hadn't. And one more defilement to their city should not really have surprised them. The bridge was gone, collapsed into the river.

They looked toward its broken structure with new bitterness. The open space from bank to bank looked insanely empty. On the other side, the National Theater was a mound of rubble.

"Please, let's not stop now," Dealey implored, fighting his own inexplicable sense of loss. "The steps may still be intact. They're in a sheltered position."

They walked forward and it was strange, like walking a gangplank toward the edge of the universe. The great, wide bridge stretched out over the Thames as if yearning to fingertip-touch the similarly outstretched section on the other side. Vapor rose from the swollen river, thicker here and hanging heavily.

They looked toward the west and saw the broken shaft of Cleopatra's Needle.

"Oh, no," Dealey moaned, for he was examining the area beyond the snapped monument.

Culver's forehead sank onto the wide balustrade overlooking the Embankment road.

"Steve, what is it?" Kate clutched at his shoulder. He raised his head.

"The railway bridge." He pointed. "Hungerford Bridge."

They saw that it, too, had collapsed into the river. The metal struts had broken in several places and it hung as if by threads, dangling into the river like a sleeping man's fishing rod, still loosely connected to the section on their side. This section had fallen onto the roadway, completely blocking it. The others looked uncomprehendingly at Dealey and Culver.

"There was an enclosure, a compound, beneath the bridge," Culver told them. "A thick brick wall with barbed wire on the top. A mini-fortress, if you like. It's been destroyed by the bridge."

His face set into grim lines and it was Dealey who explained, "The main entrance to the shelter was inside that enclosure."

25

From a distance the wreckage had looked simple, just a collapsed iron bridge, broken in sections so that one part formed a waterchute into the river, the midstream portions mostly submerged, concrete supports shattered in half. Close up, it was a complicated tangled mess of bent and twisted steel girders, scattered red brickwork, huge chunks of masonry, and riddled with cables and wires.

Culver shuddered. It was as though the souls of the dead were revealing their story to him, their horror still existing in the complex of torn metal. He shook his head, a physical act to dispense the notion.

"I know this place," Kate was saying. "The down-and-outs used to sleep under this bridge. There was a mobile soup kitchen every night. But I was never aware of any compound."

Dealey spoke with some satisfaction. "Nobody was meant to. It's surprising how anonymous and innocuous these enclosures are." He corrected himself. "*Were*. The tramps actually wrapped themselves in cardboard and slept against the very walls of the compound. They presented a perfect camouflage. The bridge overhead was thought to be adequate protection in the event of a nuclear explosion.''

"Looks like someone goofed again," Ellison said bitterly. "Is there any way we can get through to the entrance?"

"You can see for yourself. It's buried beneath hundreds of tons of rubble," Dealey replied.

"But there are other places." Culver was alert once more. "You told me there were other entrances."

"This was the obvious one, the one I planned to use. It was the most protected. The others are mostly inside government buildings, and they, of course, will have been covered by the ruins, just as this has.''

"They must have realized what would happen," Fairbank said. "They had to have other escape routes."

"In the main, the other exits are outside what was considered the danger zones.''

Culver frowned. "Wait a minute. Yesterday you told me there were more, other smaller points of access along the Embankment.''

"Yes, yes, that's true. But I'm not sure that we can get into them, even if they aren't covered by debris. These entrances were meant for maintenance inspection and are really only narrow shafts and tunnels.''

"We're not choosy.''

"I'm not sure we'll find a way into the main complex.''

"It's worth a try," said Culver.

"How the hell do we get past all this?" asked Ellison, indicating the massive debris before them. "I don't have the strength to walk around that lot—I think a couple of my ribs are fractured.''

"We'll work our way through here," said Culver. "It might be dangerous, but it'll save time. Are you up to it, Kate?''

She gave him a nervous smile. "I'll be fine. It's strange, but I feel so exposed out here."

"That's what comes from living underground for so long."

"Yesterday it was different. I felt free, liberated, glad to be out of the shelter. Since this morning, though, since we were attacked . . ." She did not bother to complete the sentence, but they all knew what she meant; they shared her feelings.

Culver took her hand and led her toward the beginnings of the wrecked bridge. The others followed and began to climb, Fairbank giving assistance to Ellison in the more difficult places.

"Keep away from anything that's loose," Culver warned. "Some of this junk doesn't look too solid."

The smell of oil and rusting metal was everywhere, but it was a relief from the other odors they had been aware of that day. Culver chose the easiest route he could find, wary of touching anything unstable. The climb was arduous in the damp heat, but not difficult. Soon they were on a level section overlooking the continuation of the road they had just left. Culver paused, giving Kate a chance to rest and allowing the others to catch up.

Below, the wide roadway curving slightly with the river was jammed with scorched, immobile traffic. Another road, equally as wide, veered off to the right toward Trafalgar Square. The mist was minimal now, but Nelson's Column could not be seen. Victoria Embankment, running alongside the Thames, was relatively free of debris, apart from vehicles, for the offices on the north side had been set back from the thoroughfare, gardens and lawns between. As expected, the buildings were no more than crushed ruins: the Old War Office, the Ministries of Defense and Technology—all were gone. The Admiralty at the beginning of the Mall should have been visible since nothing obscured the view, but of course, that had vanished too. Culver briefly wondered if all the works of art in the National Gallery, which was on the far side of Trafalgar Square, had been destroyed beneath the deluge. What value did they have in the present world, anyway? There would be little time to appreciate anything that was not of intrinsic material use in the years ahead. As he knew they would be, the Houses of Parliament and Westminster Abbey had been totally destroyed. Peculiarly, the lower section of the tower housing Big Ben was still erect, sheered off at a hundred or so feet; the top section containing the clock face protruded from the river like a tilted, rock island. And again, surprisingly, only the southern end of Westminster Bridge had collapsed. It defiantly spanned the river, just failing to reach the opposite bank.

The sun's fierce rays sucked up moisture from the Thames, so that it looked as if the water were boiling. Somehow it appeared to him that here were the intestines of the city's torn body, exposed to the light and still steaming as all life gradually diminished. Masts of sunken, ancient boats, those that had been converted into smart bars and restaurants, jutted through the rolling mist. Pleasure boats, their surfaces and passengers charred black, drifted listlessly with the current, the longboat funeral pyres of a modern age. A stout wall, still unbroken, lined the riverbank, and the waterline was high, lapping over the small quaysides that were situated near the broken bridge. Much of the gardens on the other side of the road from the Embankment wall were buried beneath fallen office buildings, but here and there, a tree stuck through the debris, protected from the worst of the blast by the very buildings shattered around them, leaves washed clean of dust by the constant rain, and flourishing under the humid conditions. Culver's eyes moistened at the sight.

Someone tapped his arm. Dealey pointed into the distance. "Look there, you can just see it as the road curves."

"D'you want to tell me what I'm looking for?"

"Don't you see it? A small, rectangular shape set in the pavement quite near the river wall."

Culver's eyes narrowed. "I've got it. Like a tiny block-house, is that what you mean?"

"That's it. That may get us inside the shelter."

Culver shook his head. So many everyday sights, ignored, not even wondered at, all part of the big secret. He recalled mild curiosity when coming upon the odd ventilation shafts around the city, but always assuming they were for the Underground or for low-level car parks. It was only when viewed subjectively that they obtruded from the general background and took on a special significance—like the stockade over the Kingsway telephone exchange and the one they now stood over, crushed beneath Hungerford Bridge. He supposed the art of concealment was to make something commonplace, unnoticeable.

"Let's get to it," he said, and containing their eagerness, they scrambled down from the wreckage.

The going was easier once they were on the ground, only human remains, carrion for colonies of feverishly crawling things, marring their progress. They had still not become used to the legions of insects, but fortunately their swarming droves were concentrated on less resistant entities.

They were passing over a long grille set in the pavement when Fairbank brought them to a halt. He knelt, peering down through the iron slats.

"Listen!" he said.

The others knelt around him and saw there were thick pipes running horizontally a few feet below ground level.

"What are they?" Kate asked, slightly out of breath.

Dealey told her. "Ventilation pipes, conduits containing cables, wiring. The complex is directly below us."

Fairbank hushed them again. "Listen!"

They held their breath and listened.

It was faint, but definite. A humming vibration.

"Generators!" Ellison proclaimed excitedly.

They looked at one another, a gleaming in their eyes.

"Jesus, they're functioning." Fairbank was triumphant. "There are people down there!"

He and Ellison let out whoops of glee.

"I told you," Dealey said, surprised at their outburst, but smiling nevertheless. "I told you this was the main government headquarters. Didn't I tell you that?"

"You told us that." Kate was laughing.

"Wait!" Culver held up a hand. "Is it me, or is the sound getting louder?"

The group listened more intently, Fairbank putting his ear against the grille. "Seems like the same pitch to me," he commented after a few seconds. He twisted his head to look up at Culver.

But Culver was watching the sky.

The others noticed and followed his gaze.

The humming became a drone, a different sound from the one below them, and the drone grew louder.

"There!" Culver stabbed a finger at the sky.

They saw the plane at once, a dark smudge in the hazy sky, flying low from the west. Slowly, as if sudden movement would disperse the image, they rose to their feet, their faces upturned and with stunned expressions, none of them daring to speak.

It was Dealey who broke the silence, but only with a whisper. "It's following the river."

The aircraft was drawing nearer and Culver saw it was small, light.

"A Beaver," he said, almost to himself.

The others looked at him in puzzlement, then quickly returned their gaze.

"An Air Corps Beaver spotter plane," Culver expanded. "On bloody reconnaissance—it has to be!"

The tiny aircraft was almost over their heads. Fairbank and Ellison began to shout as one, waving their arms to attract the pilot's attention. The others instantly joined in, leaping in the air, running back along the Embankment in a vain attempt to keep up with the machine, calling at the top of their lungs, flapping their arms, desperate to be noticed.

"Can he see us, can he see us?" Kate was clutching at Culver. "Oh, God, make him see us!"

Then it was gone, taking their spirits with it. They watched until it became a smudgy speck. They waited until it could no longer be seen.

"Shit, shit, shit!" Fairbank shouted.

"He couldn't miss us!" Ellison said.

Culver put an arm around Kate's shoulders, hugging her close. "It doesn't matter whether he did or not. We're safe now. Once we're inside the shelter, we'll be okay. And there's a whole tunnel network down there, a way out of London."

"I know, Steve. It's just that for a moment we almost had contact with . . . with . . ." She found difficulty in finding the right word. "I don't know—civilization, if you like. Something beyond all this." She gestured at the ruins.

"We'll have real contact soon, I promise you that."

"Do you suppose the plane will come back?"

"Who knows? The pilot might choose another route; he'd want to cover as much ground as possible."

She nodded and wiped a hand across her nose. "It's my day for crying."

He smiled. "You've pulled through so far. Just a little longer."

They returned to the grille set in the pavement and passed over it, no longer interested in the faint thrumming sound emanating from its depths.

Reaching the gray-stone block, they studied its rough surface, walking all around, bemused at first and, soon, worried.

"Terrific," Fairbank said, wiping sweat from the back

of his head. "No opening. How the fuck do we get inside, Dealey?"

The object, massive and dark, a strange monolith, remained impassive and seemingly impregnable. At least twelve feet long and five or six feet wide, it resembled a huge tombstone. Or a huge sacrificial altar, thought Kate.

"There's a hole in the top," Dealey announced simply.

The others looked at one another and Fairbank grinned. The stone blockade was six feet high, perhaps more, and the technician had scrambled up before anyone else could move.

"He's right," Fairbank called down. "There's a part at the end here that isn't covered. It's cunning, you'd never know. And there's a door." He pulled the ax free of his belt. "It looks as if it's locked, but I think I can handle that." White teeth split his grime-covered face in a grin as he surveyed them from his lofty perch. "Care to join me?"

Culver stood below helping up the others, Fairbank pulling from above. He scrambled up after them and looked down into the opening.

"What is this thing, Dealey? It can't be newly built."

"It was an air-raid shelter during the war," Dealey told them, brushing away a buzzing fly and wiping his face with a discolored handkerchief. "At least, it led down to an air-raid shelter. I explained to Culver yesterday that the original underground chambers, built many, *many* years ago, have been expanded through the decades."

"Well, we can see how much for ourselves," said Ellison, growing impatient. "For God's sake, let's get inside."

"Right," Fairbank agreed. He slipped down into the opening and examined the lock. "Don't you have a key?" he called back to Dealey, who shook his head.

"Not for this place," he said.

"Okay, it shouldn't be too much of a problem anyway." He swung the ax.

It took no more than four solid blows to open the door.

It swung inward and a chilling coldness sprang out like an escaping ghost.

Culver shivered. The dank coldness seemed more than just released air. It brought with it a sense of foreboding.

26

The coolness inside was a relief from the humid atmosphere aboveground. They descended the stone steps, Fairbank in the lead, ax tucked back into his belt. The air was musty, the smell of disuse, and the concrete walls were rough to the touch.

Fairbank paused. "There's no light down here." He rummaged in his pockets and passed back two small bright tubes. "Picked these up yesterday," he told them. "Figured they might come in handy for lighting fires." He flicked on the cheap throwaway lighter he had kept for himself. The flame, weak though it was, gave some comfort.

Culver passed his over his shoulder to Ellison, who was bringing up the rear.

"I've got one," the technician said. "Maybe you'd better pass it down to the front, though, and let me have one of those midgets." He handed the lighter to Culver, who passed it on. "It's the one I found yesterday," Ellison explained. "The flame's stronger."

They continued, the lighter casing growing hot in Fairbank's hand. Their footsteps were hollow-sounding and loud. It was a long climb down, and inexplicably, Culver's unease increased with every step. He wondered if the others felt the same. Just below him, Kate let both hands slide against the close walls, as if afraid she might stumble and fall. Her hair was tangled, dark in the feeble lighter glow, and her shirt was torn and still covered in dust. He squeezed her shoulder and she briefly touched his hand with her fingertips, but did not turn around.

Fairbank eventually stopped and brushed away cobwebs from the opening before him.

"There's a big room here." His words had a slight echo. He waved the light ahead of him. "Seems to be empty."

They crowded in behind him, each one branching out so that their lights covered more of an area. Other rooms led off from the first chamber.

"They're all empty," said Dealey, walking to the far end. "This is just part of the old air-raid-shelter system. As you can see, it hasn't been used since the last war." He reached an opening and called back to them. "This way."

They quickly hurried to him and he led them through what seemed a labyrinth of corridors with empty rooms leading off. He finally stopped beside a square doorway set into the wall two feet from the floor.

"We'll need your ax again to force it," he said to Fairbank.

The technician slid the sharp end of the tool into the crack, close by the lock. He exerted pressure and the door easily snapped open. Inside, they could see thick piping, some at least a foot in diameter, and heavy cables. The thrumming was louder, more distinct than when they had listened at the grille aboveground.

"Maintenance entry," Dealey said by way of explanation as he stepped through.

Inside, the narrow corridor, with its wall of pipes and

cables, extended in both directions. Dealey took them to the right.

"You sure you know where you're going, Dealey?" came Ellison's voice from the rear.

"Not a hundred percent, but I think this way should take us close to the new complex."

Dealey had stopped once more and was kneeling, holding the small flame toward a two-by-two-foot grid in the floor. He inserted his fingers between the meshwork and pulled; it swung open like a trapdoor. They saw metal ladder rungs disappearing downward.

"It should take us down to shelter level." The warm glow from the tiny flames softened Dealey's features, but to Culver, the man looked ten years older than when he had first laid eyes on him. Odd that he'd only just noticed.

Culver squeezed past Fairbank and knelt on the opposite side of the opening to Dealey. "How far down does the shaft go?"

"I'm not sure. We must be fairly near."

"Is it safe?"

Dealey looked at him sharply.

"Vermin, I mean," Culver said.

They all tensed in the silence that followed.

Finally, Dealey said, "There's no way of knowing. But what other choice do we have?"

"The usual. None at all."

Culver went in first, exchanging his weaker lighter for Fairbank's and wincing at the hot metal. He climbed down, holding the lighter between thumb and index finger, his other fingers curled around the upright support so that both hands were used. The shaft was circular and metallic, and the hum of machinery grew louder the lower he went, although it was still muted. He heard the others climbing into the shaft after him. It seemed a long time before he touched down in another passageway, this one wider than the one he had just left. Some of the piping and cables ran along its ceiling. There was water on the floor.

Dealey reached him, then Fairbank, followed by Kate. Ellison arrived clutching his side and breathing heavily. "Christ!" he uttered when his feet became soaked.

"Maybe this place was flooded, too," said Fairbank.

"I doubt it," Dealey replied, touching the walls. "They're not damp. Very cold and I suppose dankish, but you'd expect that at this temperature. Not soaked, though. I think the water on the floor is just seepage, nothing to worry about."

"Nowadays, when a government man tells me not to worry, I worry," Fairbank retorted without rancor.

Culver held his light to the left, then to the right. "Which way?"

"It probably doesn't matter. These maintenance corridors skirt the headquarters; they're part of a larger system that protects the main shelter. Either way should lead us somewhere useful."

"Okay, let's take the left."

They went on, splashing water, all of them becoming chilled with the cold. The flames the men carried slowly faded.

Fairbank's was the first to shrink to nothing. He tossed it away and they heard the *plop* as it struck water.

Dealey's was next.

Soon they were groping their way along, barely able to see, hands against the walls for guidance. The idea of trying to find their way in total darkness terrified them all. Culver heard the trickling of water just ahead, but there was not enough light to see where the sound came from. He discovered its source when the ground felt different beneath him. He crouched.

"There's a drain here." He felt with his fingers; cold air was rising from the slats. "Looks like quite a big one."

"It'll lead down to the sewers," said Dealey. "Being so near the river, there must be a constant seepage into the tunnels."

"Steve, let's keep moving while we still have light," Kate urged.

He straightened and they moved on.

Ellison stared miserably at his sinking flame and drew in a sharp breath when it finally went out. A little farther on, Culver stopped again and cupped a hand around his lighter, the only light they had left.

Ellison bumped into Dealey. "What the hell are you doing?"

"Shut up." Culver was peering ahead into the darkness. "I think I can see a glow."

They crowded around him. "You're right, Steve," said Kate. "I see it, too."

"Thank God for that," Ellison breathed.

Their pace quickened and soon the faint glow in the distance grew stronger, became a long sliver of pale light. As they approached, they were able to distinguish a door. It was slightly ajar, the light coming from inside. The corridor ended there.

The door was solid, made of thick metal, painted green. There were flanges around its sides, like the doorway of the Kingsway exchange, to provide a tight seal when closed. Culver pushed against it, cautious for some reason. Beyond, he could see dimly lit gray walls, another passageway. The heavy door resisted his push. There was something behind it.

He shoved a little harder and something moved inside.

Culver looked around at the others, then snapped the lighter shut. He put it in his pocket. Using both hands, palms flat against the smooth surface, he eased the door wider. The light illuminated their faces. When there was enough room, he slipped through.

The body—what was left of it—was slumped against the door, one hand, much of the flesh gone, still gripped tight around the six-inch bar that was the door's handle. Culver felt himself sway a little, even though he should have become accustomed to such atrocities by now. It could once have been a man, although it was hard to tell. The corpse had been fed upon. The head was missing.

One hand holding the door open—the corpse seemed determined to push it closed—Culver quietly called the others in. "You first, Dealey. You next, Kate, and don't look, just keep your eyes straight ahead."

Of course, she looked and immediately moved away, her chest heaving.

"Oh, shit," said Fairbank when he saw the headless body.

Ellison visibly sagged and Culver thought for a moment the man would crumple. Ellison leaned weakly against the wall and said, "They're down here."

Nobody disagreed.

He staggered back toward the open door.

"We'd better get out. We can't stay down here."

Culver caught him by the shoulder and allowed the door to close. It did not shut completely, but stayed ajar, just as they had found it. The corpse's hand released its death grip, the arm slumping to the floor.

"We can't go back," Culver said steadily. "We don't have the light. And besides, the rats may be out there."

"You think this"—Dealey averted his gaze—"this person was trying to keep them out?"

"I don't know," Culver admitted. "Either that, or he was trying to escape." He had decided that the body was that of a man, for the tattered remnants of what looked like olive-green overalls or a uniform of some kind still clung to it.

Fairbank seemed fascinated by the spectacle. "The head," he said. "Why's the head gone?" The stench was there, but it was not powerful, not cloying. The man had been dead some time, the worst of the smell long since dispersed. "It's like the Underground station. Remember the bodies we found? Many of the heads were gone."

"But why?" asked Dealey. "I don't understand."

"Maybe the rats shrink 'em." Nobody appreciated Fairbank's macabre humor this time.

"Can't *you* tell us why?" Culver was looking directly at Dealey.

"I swear I know nothing more than I've already told you. You must believe me."

"Must I?"

"There's no point in my lying. There would be absolutely nothing to gain from it."

Culver conceded. He looked along the corridor, noticing for the first time the blood smears that stained its length. "I guess that answers one question," he said, pointing. "He was trying to escape from the inside. They had him before he even reached the door. He must have crawled along as they tore him apart."

Kate had covered her face, her head against the wall. "It's never going to end. We're not going to live through this."

Culver went to her. "We're not inside yet. The rats may have attacked and been beaten off. This place can hold hundreds of people, Kate, more than enough to defend themselves. And they have the military to protect them, too."

"Then why him, why this one body?"

"Maybe they didn't know he was out here. It's just a corridor, probably one of many. They may not have even known he'd been killed." An overwhelming sense of dread was building up inside him as he spoke. It had been growing since first they had smashed open the door aboveground, and now it was sinking through every nerve cord, through every organ in his body, turning them to lead, filling his lower stomach with its draining heaviness.

"There's another door here!" Fairbank was standing farther down the passageway, pointing to a recess on his right.

Culver gently eased Kate away from the wall and took her with him, the others already making toward Fairbank.

The door was similar to the one they had just left, only wider and higher. It was open.

With increasing trepidation, they stared into the interior of the government headquarters shelter.

She stirred, restless, perceiving a faraway danger.

Her obese body tried to shift in her nest of filth and powdered bones. The sound of running water was lost to her, for she did not possess ears, yet something inside could receive the high-frequency mewlings of her subject creatures. There was no light in the underground chamber, but her eyes had no optic nerves anyway. Yet she was always aware of movement around her.

The huge, swollen hump of her body moved in a deep breathing motion, swelling even more so that dark veins protruded from the whitish skin, skin so fine it seemed the network of ridges must burst through. Her jaws parted slightly as air exhaled with a high wheezing sound; the breath also came from another source, another misshapen mouth in a stump by the side of her pointed head. There were no teeth inside this mouth and no eyes above it. A few white hairs grew from the snout that enabled her to smell, but the protuberance had little other use. Her limbs no longer supported the gross weight, and her claws—there were five on each paw—were brittle and cracked, grown long and curled from lack of use. Her tail was stunted, merely a scaly prominence, no more than that. The Mother Creature resembled a giant, pulsating eyeball.

A mewling sibilation escaped both snouts and she tried to thrash around in her bed of slime, but her weight was too much, her limbs too feeble. Only dust stirred, the bones ground to white powder by her soldier rats, the sleek black vermin who guarded and protected her with their own lives. Whom she now called to her.

There were other movements in the dark, cavernous chamber. They were the twitching, writhing motions of her fellow beasts, those who resembled her in appearance, different from the servant and soldier vermin. Many had been produced from her own womb. And many had mated with her.

Like the Mother Creature, most were captive of their own malforma-

tion, debilitated by their own grotesquesness. And some were dead, others were dying.

She screeched, the sound of a screaming child. She was terribly afraid.

But she sensed her black legions were coming to her, winding their way through the flowing corridors, bringing food, the skulls into which her twisted tusks would bore holes so that the spongy flesh inside could be sucked out, swallowed.

She waited impatiently, in the darkness, obscenely gross, body quivering, while her offspring, six of them and each one peculiarly shaped, like her yet unlike her, suckled at her breasts.

27

They walked through the carnage, their stomachs sickened, yet their minds somehow numbed. Perhaps their
personas, in Jung's terms, had already begun to adapt to
such mayhem, such staggering destruction. Horror and
revulsion touched, felt, insinuated itself into their consciousness, but some inner defense of the psyche, a natural yet mysterious barrier against insanity, prevented
those feelings from penetrating their innermost essence.

The people of this mammoth sanctum, fugitives from
the holocaust above, had been caught by surprise, unaware that another and just as deadly enemy lay within.

The first chamber that Culver and the small group of
survivors found themselves in was low-ceilinged but capa-
cious, its concrete interior dimly, though adequately lit. It
housed eighteen government vehicles, many of which
were tanks and scout cars. Their color, uniformly, was
gray, none bearing markings of any kind. They stood in
neat crammed rows, dead things, granite statues that
seemed incapable of motion.

All the vehicles appeared to be empty.

At the end of the long bay were two massive iron doors, both shut.

Dealey explained that there were curving ramps leading up to ground level behind the doors; there were two more sets along the way, the final pair of doors opening out into a secluded and protected courtyard. Ellison suggested that they leave the shelter there and then, using the ramp and possibly taking one of the vehicles, for by that time they had discovered other bodies, corpses so savagely mutilated that they were barely recognizable as human. The group passed between the vehicles, carefully avoiding featureless cadavers that sprawled in the gangways, making for the exit. Controls for opening the huge doors were set inside a small glass cubicle, and the panes were smeared with dried blood. Ignoring the two bodies, Fairbank tried the switches set in the wall, assuming they would open the exit doors. Nothing happened; the mechanism was inoperative.

They went through an area marked DECONTAM UNIT, not lingering to examine the racks of silver-gray, one-piece suits, the machines that resembled metal-detecting doorways, or the gruesome things that lay on the shower floors.

It was beyond the decontamination area that Culver, Fairbank, Ellison, and Kate began to get some idea of the immense size and complexity of the government's war headquarters. Dealey kept quiet while they expressed surprise, the horror of what lay around them momentarily lost in their astonishment.

They found themselves in a long, sixteen-foot-wide corridor with many other passageways branching off from it. Straight colored lines swept along its length, here and there a particular shade veering off into another corridor; they were directional color codes, and on the wall was a list of sections, all in groups and each group assigned a particular color.

They quickly scanned the list, which ranged from CLINIC to LIBRARY, from GYMNASIUM to THEATER, from PRINT ROOM to FIRE DEPT. There appeared to be a television and radio center, offices with a secretarial pool, a work area, dormitories, and even a station. The latter sign puzzled them and Dealey explained it was the terminal for the railway line that connected the shelter with Heathrow Airport.

"It's a whole bloody city down here," Ellison said in awestruck tones.

They took the central corridor, and as they progressed, there were more corpses in evidence. And with each section the group passed through, their apprehension grew, hysteria beginning to rise and bore through that self-protecting emotional barrier.

The carnage was everywhere, no area, no passageway, no room unblemished. It was a journey through a nightmare, a pilgrimage into Hades. And with each step, each turn of the corridor, the atrocity grew worse, for the dead became legion.

At one stage, Kate moaned, "Why? Why weren't they protected? There must have been weapons. There must have been a guard force, an army of sorts."

The question was soon answered, for they had come to the inner core of the enormous complex.

They were at a T-junction, the corridor extending left and right, disappearing into a curve, suggesting that the shelter's center was circular. The door directly ahead was set at least five feet back into the wall and they wondered if this was an indication of the wall's thickness. In front of the broad metal door was a small desk, mounted into the floor itself, an elaborate but compact console on its surface. There were two cameras set in the corners of the alcove and a range of various colored push buttons set on one side. The sliding door had been jammed open by two bodies, and from what was left of their clothing, it was obvious they had been army personnel.

"What is this place?" Fairbank asked, looking through the jammed door.

Dealey was pressing the buttons of the small desk console, glancing at the door as he did so. "Nothing seems to be operating," he remarked, "apart from the lighting and ventilation. The systems have either been shut down or destroyed."

"Answer the question," Culver told him.

"This place? This is the operations center for the shelter. If you like, it contains the vital organs of the whole complex. The generator and boiler rooms, communications and cypher, living quarters for, er, certain persons, the war room itself. A refuge within a refuge, if you like."

"You said living quarters. You mean there's an elite among the elite?" Culver had asked the question.

"Of course. I don't think I need tell you who would be among that special group."

Culver shook his head.

Kate clutched at him. "I think we should leave, and I think we should leave *now.*"

"There will be weapons inside," Dealey said quickly. "And there may be other survivors."

"As well as the vermin that did all this?"

"They've gone, I'm sure of it. We've had no sight of them since we entered the shelter. I think we can assume they did their worst here, then moved on . . ."

"To fresh pastures," Fairbank finished for him.

"That may be exactly the case."

"But how did they get into here in the first place?" Culver was perplexed. "How could they possibly have infiltrated such an installation? It makes no sense."

"Perhaps we'll find the answer inside." Dealey went to the gap between door and wall. He disappeared through it, not waiting for a reply.

The others looked at one another and it was Fairbank who shrugged, then followed. "What've we got to lose?" he said.

Kate reluctantly allowed herself to be helped through by Culver, gingerly stepping over the torn bodies that had prevented the door from closing. Inside, the smell of death was almost choking, even though it was old and had lost much of its pungency.

And it was inside, among the human corpses with missing limbs, many headless, organs gouged out, that they found the dead rats.

Now they sat in the vast, circular war room, exhausted both mentally and physically, each of them trembling, their eyes shifting constantly, never relaxing their vigilance. They all clutched weapons in their laps, wrested from fingers that seemed unwilling to release their grip, even though the guns had not managed to save them. Two of the group held Ingrams, snub-nosed machine guns, the standard arms for military personnel inside the shelter, while Kate and Dealey had pistols, 9-mm Brownings; Ellison had managed to find a Sterling sub-machine gun from the armory.

They were on a balcony overlooking row upon row of mat black benches, each containing six or seven separate working units, all of which were complete with television monitors, computers, telephones, teleprinters, and switching consoles. Giant screens in the curving walls dominated, even though they were blank. One had been punctured by bullet holes. Dealey had told them that when live, the screens would have shown different areas of the world, indicating nuclear strikes and strategic deployment of military task forces. A particular screen was kept solely for visual contact with allied heads of state and their executives, the pictures to have been beamed from satellites, unless atmospheric conditions interfered, in which case contact would be maintained through cable. The ceiling lamps were recessed and subdued, each section of the benches having individual built-in lighting. Around the walls and below the screens were various other pieces of machinery, including a bank of computers and television screens. A coffee machine, dated by comparison to the hardware around it, lent the only touch of humanity. Just off the war room was a tiny television studio containing the bare essentials for broadcasting. The studio, they assumed, was for broadcasting to the nation, for quite near them on the balcony was another camera, angled toward the long control table they now sat at; this was obviously used for televised conversations with the allies. Next to the television studio was a conference room, its walls and ceiling soundproofed. This was probably where the more "delicate" decisions concerning the future of the human race would have been discussed and made. There were many other rooms and corridors leading off from the main concourse, the war room itself the hub of a concrete-walled wheel, but as yet they had not investigated any of these, nor did they feel inclined to. They had seen enough.

The early Christians may well have suffered such similar massacres in their own Roman arenas—mauled, then torn apart by animals for the blood-lust gratification of their masters—but could even those occasions have been on such a grand scale? This modern arena below was almost overflowing with human remains, as though a large number of the holocaust survivors had fled here when the rodent invasion had begun, perhaps still believing that their leaders would now save them from this new, unforeseen disaster. They had been wrong. Nothing could save them from the fury of these mutant beasts, not even the rapid-fire weapons of the soldiers. How could it be so? How many, *just how many* rats could have caused such massive slaughter? And how could they have got inside the top-security shelter?

It was Alex Dealey, looking weary and dispirited, all trace of pomposity gone, outweighed by adversity, who attempted to supply the answers. He was slumped in a swivel chair, leaning forward over the long table before them, one hand on his forehead, shielding his closed eyes.

"The rats were already inside the shelter," he said quietly. "They were inside, waiting. Don't you see? There are sewers below here, miles of underground tunnels, weirs that control the flow of rainwater and effluence. The rats must have roamed the network for years, scavenging where they could, feeding off the city's waste. Oh, dear God." His other hand slowly went to his forehead and he seemed to sink within himself, his shoulders shrinking. "Food is kept below the main shelter level, a huge cold-storage chamber. It was rarely exchanged, only added to. Hardly any of it was perishable, you see? Any that was, was kept nearer to hand, where it could be easily replenished. For years the rats have had an ample food supply."

"Surely it was checked from time to time?" Culver asked incredulously.

"There was no need; it was considered safe from harm. I suppose it was given a cursory examination at regular intervals, but you would have to see the vastness of the store itself to realize how much was left unseen. All foodstuffs were tightly sealed, as was the storeroom itself; the thought of entry by vermin was hardly considered."

"Not considered at all, it appears," ventured Ellison, shifting in his seat to ease the stiffness of his ribs.

"Poisons were laid and traps were set. Nobody would have realized the unique cunning of the scavenger they were dealing with."

Culver was still puzzled. "There had to be some evidence of these creatures. Somebody must have noticed something."

Dealey looked up and shrugged. "Why? These headquarters have never been occupied. Certainly maintenance work has been carried out, new, more advanced technology installed as the years have gone by, and inspections have always been made at regular intervals; but it's obvious that this breed of rat has kept well-hidden. Its own instincts would have warned it of the treatment it would receive from its old enemy. Remember, too, the extermination of these mutant creatures over the past decade has been carried out ruthlessly and on a grand scale. There have been pogroms against them, if you like.''

Fairbank swept the gun around the room below. ''They got over their shyness fast.''

''After the bombs dropped, yes. It could be they sensed they had the upper hand. Perhaps their numbers had grown to encourage that belief, also. Another point: they may have considered the mass evacuation into the shelter as an invasion of *their* territory. My theory is that all these elements were involved.''

''They were threatened, so they attacked.'' Kate's statement was flat, toneless.

''It's all we can assume.''

''They went up against firepower,'' said Fairbank. ''And against an awful lot of people. They must have felt pretty confident.''

''Or they had a stronger motive.''

Once again, all eyes turned to Culver.

He shook his head. ''I don't know, it's just a feeling I've got. There's something more, something we don't know about.''

Ellison was impatient. ''I still don't understand how it was possible for them to overwhelm them. Doors could have been sealed, the rats could have been contained, or closed out of any number of different sections.''

''Remember the doors where all those vehicles were housed? The big metal doors to the ramps? They didn't function. Like most things around here, apart from the lighting and ventilation, they were inoperative. I'm sure if we examined the main power-switching area we'd find machinery or wiring destroyed, either by the trapped survivors when they used guns to protect themselves, or by the rats gnawing through vital cables. It's not unusual: it's a specialty even of normal vermin. There are all kinds of safeguards in this complex that need power to function.''

"Why the lights and ventilation, then?''

"They're on completely different systems, which obviously haven't been harmed. The headquarters has four generators, each designed to take over should the others malfunction.'' Dealey slumped back in his chair, wiping both hands down his face, the Browning placed in front of him on the table. "It's my belief that the survivors were attacked very soon after the first bombs had dropped, when the people were in mortal fear and disorganized. Can you imagine the scenes inside this shelter at the time? Panic, remorse, total disorientation. Even the trained military personnel would have been traumatized. The survivors were confused and almost defenseless.''

"How many . . . how many would have been here?'' Kate's gun was held rigid in her lap, as though she were afraid to release it even for a moment. She wanted to leave immediately, but like the others, she was totally drained of strength. And they needed answers before they ventured elsewhere in the shelter.

"It's impossible to say,'' Dealey told her. "Hundreds, possibly. We've seen enough dead to know there were a large number of people. Not everybody who had access would have reached the shelter by the time the bombs exploded, and of course, many may have escaped when the rats attacked.''

Culver was hesitant. "The, er, apartments we passed in this part of the complex—you said they were meant for certain persons.''

Dealey nodded. "That was why I was so relieved that they appeared to have been unoccupied. I'm sure the royal family was evacuated from London long before the crisis finally erupted.''

"And the prime minister?''

"Knowing her, she would have remained here in the

capital, inside these headquarters, from where she could direct operations.''

''Do you think there's a chance she and her war cabinet got out?''

There was a long silence from Dealey. He lifted his hands from his lap and let them drop again, making a muffled slapping sound of despair. ''Who knows?'' he said. ''It's possible. It depends on how much they were taken by surprise, or how well they were protected. I have no intention of examining all these bodies to find the answer.''

Culver found the irony of the situation incredible. A fail-safe refuge had been constructed for a select few, the rest of the country's population, apart from those designated to other shelters, left to suffer the full onslaught of the nuclear strike; but the plan had gone terribly wrong, a freak of nature—literally—destroying those escapees just as surely as the nuclear blitz itself. The stupid bastards had built their fortress over the nest, the lair—whatever the fuck it was called—of the mutant black rats, the very spawn of earlier nuclear destruction.

Fairbank had risen from his seat and was staring down at the ghastly scene below. Among the human remnants were inanimate black-furred shapes. He rested his hands on the balustrade. ''I don't understand. They managed to kill a lot of rats down there before they were overwhelmed. But take a close look at some of those animal carcasses. They're unmarked, and they're not in such an advanced stage of decomposition as the others. A lot of these fuckers died more recently.''

Culver joined Fairbank, interested in the technician's observation. ''Hell, you're right,'' he said.

Kate and Ellison barely showed concern, but Dealey rose to his feet. ''Perhaps we should take a closer look,'' he suggested.

They descended the short staircase into the main concourse, repulsed by the strong odors that assaulted them, and wary of what might skulk among the ruins.

"Here." Culver pointed.

They approached with caution, for the rat looked as though it had merely fallen asleep while feeding. Only when they drew close did they notice that its eyes were half-open and had the flat, glazed stare of the dead. Culver and Dealey leaned toward it while Fairbank kept a cautious vigilance on their surroundings.

"There's dried blood around its jaws," Culver remarked.

"It was eating flesh when it died."

"There's no marks, no injuries." He prodded the stiff-haired carcass with the gun barrel, using considerable effort to turn the animal over onto its back. There were no hidden wounds.

"What the hell did it die of?" Culver asked, puzzled.

"There's another over there," Fairbank said.

They went to it, carefully avoiding the moldering decay scattered across the floor. There were few insects so far below ground, and that was at least something to be thankful for. Culver knelt beside the sprawled carcass and repeated the same operation. Bullet holes punctured the creature's underbelly and they realized its outer shell was a mere husk; underneath, it was rotted almost completely away.

"Could they have been poisoned?" Culver stood, his eyes ranging over other carcasses. There had been more in the other sections and passageways, but the group had not stopped to inspect them closely, assuming they had been killed by the humans they were attacking; it was possible that many of these had also died from causes other than mortal wounds.

"It's possible," said Dealey, "but I don't see how. Why would they take bait when they had all the food they needed? It makes no sense."

He was deep in thought for a few moments and was about to comment further when Kate called from the balcony. "Please, let's go! It isn't safe here!" One arm was clasped around a shoulder as though she were cold; the other held the gun.

"She's right," Culver said. "It's not over. There's something more in this hellhole. I can feel it like I can feel an icy draft. The dead haven't settled."

It was an odd thing to say, but the others sensed its meaning, for they shared the same intuitive awareness. They climbed back up the steps, their pace now quickened, urgency beginning to return, renewed fear overcoming weariness. The discovery of the dead, unmarred rats had rekindled their apprehension, its mystery instigating further, unnerving dread. The vast underground bunker had become an enigma, perhaps a death trap for them all. It was as if its concrete walls were closing in, the tons of earth above bearing down, pressing close, a huge oppressiveness weighing on their shoulders.

Striving to crush them into whatever lay beneath the underground citadel.

28

The condition of the power plant explained much to them, for it had been reduced to nothing more than a blackened shell, its complex machinery just charred, useless husks. They averted their eyes from dark mounds on the floor, shapeless forms that had once walked and talked and been like themselves.

"Now we know," said Dealey. There was the sadness of defeat about him. "They did battle with the rats here. Bullets, an explosion—a chain reaction—devastated this place. All their careful planning, all their ultimate technology destroyed by a simple beast. They finally discovered who the real enemy is." He leaned against a wall and for a moment they thought he would sink down. He steadied himself, but did not look at them.

Ellison was shaking his head. "So that's why there was no communication; everything was knocked out."

"Communications, machinery—even the doors couldn't be opened," said Fairbank. "The first one we found could be opened manually from the inside. And the second was jammed by those two trying to get out. But the others must be sealed tight. Christ, they were all trapped inside their own fortress.''

"Surely all the doors aren't electronically controlled," said Kate.

"I'm afraid they are." Dealey still did not look up. "Don't you see? This was a top-secret establishment, the most critically restricted place in the country; exit and entry had to be centrally controlled.''

Ellison had become even more agitated. "There has to be other doors jammed open. Some of the people down there must have escaped, they couldn't all have been killed.''

"Escape into what? Into the radiation outside?''

Fairbank secured the ax in his belt more tightly. "I think we're wasting time here; let's move on and out." He looked directly at Culver.

"You know the place, Dealey," the pilot said. "Just how *do* we get out?''

"There may be other blocked doors, as Ellison said. If not, we'll have to go back the way we came.''

Kate shriveled inwardly at the idea, for she had no wish to retread those same abhorrent corridors.

"Let's start looking, then," said Fairbank. "This place is troubling my disposition.''

They passed on and suddenly the foul mélange of smells became almost overpowering. Kate actually staggered at the noxious fumes and Culver had to reach out and steady her as he fought down his own nausea. It was Fairbank, grubby handkerchief held to his nose and mouth, who called them forward. He was peering into a wide opening from which came the now-familiar thrumming noise.

"Take a look at this!" he shouted, and there was both fear and excitement in his voice. "It's bloody well unbelievable.''

They approached, Culver taking the unwilling girl with him. He covered his face with a hand, nearly gagging when he drew close to the opening; the others were under-going the same discomfort. He looked inside with consid-erable consternation, he, too, reluctant to witness more horror, and his eyes widened, his mouth dropped. His spine went rigid.

The ceiling of the generator room was high, accommo-dating the four huge machines and the largest diesel oil tank Culver had ever seen, its top disappearing into the roof itself. Overhead was a network of pipes, wiring, and catwalks. The walls were uncovered brickwork with only piping and mounted instrument gauges to break up the monotonous pattern. The lighting here was dim; several areas had their own individual sources of light, most of which were switched off. It was uncomfortably warm in-side there, a factor that added to the putridity of the atmo-sphere.

The spacious floor area was an ocean of stiffened black fur.

Kate reeled away, falling, but instantly scrambling to her feet, ready to run.

''They're dead!'' Culver shouted, and she stopped. Still afraid, she went back to the four men.

It was an eerie and ugly sight. And even though the piled bodies were those of a mortal enemy, a strangely piti-ful one. The rats lay sprawled against and over one an-other, hundreds upon hundreds, many with jaws open, bared yellow incisors glinting dully, others with half-open eyes glaring wickedly, although glazedly, at the human in-truders. Still more had managed to crawl along the raft-ers, the piping that networked the ceiling, and lay there as if ready to leap; but those, too, were lifeless, menacing only in appearance.

''What the shit happened to them?'' said Ellison in a low breath.

The others were too stunned to reply. Slowly Culver walked into the generator room until he was at the very

through the spreading blood of their companions. He fired again, the impact scattering the crawling vermin, and Fairbank joined him, aiming his gun into the mass.

They stopped. Watched.

Still there were shapes moving forward.

"Thank God there's hardly any strength left in them," Culver said.

"Let's thank God from the outside, huh? They may be dying, but they still want to get at us."

They let one more burst rip into the undulating bodies, then hurried through the door.

"I don't want to waste time looking for doors that may not be open," Culver told the others. "So let's just head back the way we came. Agreed?"

The others nodded assent and he took Kate by the wrist. "They can't reach us," he assured her. "They're dying, weak; we can easily outrun them."

She gratefully leaned against him, and the five of them began their journey back through the maze of corridors.

Finally they reached the decontam unit. They sped through and found themselves in the vast vehicle pool.

Culver brought them to a halt. "Flashlights! We'll need flashlights."

"And I know where I can find some." Fairbank dashed off, weaving between the strange-looking parked tanks and vehicles, heading for the small glass cubicle at the far end of the chamber by the doors.

He returned shortly with two heavy-duty flashlights. "Here you go," he said, handing one to Culver. "I spotted them earlier. Guess they kept them handy for emergencies."

The group moved toward the wide door leading to the corridor, which in turn lead to the smaller door to the underground bunker. Culver remembered how sickened they had all been on finding the headless corpse still clinging to the green metal door; the sight barely stirred them now. He allowed Fairbank to go through first, both men switching on the flashlights. The last to enter the dark, concrete corridor, he kept his hand on the door.

"Do I close it, or not?" he said to the others. "If I do, there's no getting back inside."

"If you don't, any rats left alive can follow," Ellison said.

Culver looked at Dealey, Fairbank, and Kate. Dealey gave a small nod of his head and the technician said, "Shut the fucker." Kate remained silent.

Culver closed the door.

The corridor was bright with the flashlights, water on the floor reflecting the beams. The coolness of the atmosphere hit them like an incorporeal wave, turning perspiration into icy droplets; air-conditioning inside the shelter had kept the temperature low, but the difference in the outside tunnels was substantial. Each of them shivered. It was a relief to be away from the grim sight of the human massacre and the dead and dying creatures who were the perpetrators; but the chill darkness that surrounded them created its own sense of ominous menace.

Dealey broke the uneasy silence. "I suggest we use the first upward outlet we come to, rather than find the ladder we came down on."

"We don't need a vote on it," said Fairbank, already leading the way down the corridor. He moved fast and was soon well ahead of the others.

"Don't get too far ahead!" Culver called out. "Let's stick together."

"Don't worry, I'll stop at the first ladder," came the hollow-sounding reply.

Kate kept close to Culver, striving to keep her mind free of the day's terrors, not contemplating what the rest of it might bring. They trudged down the dank corridor, splashing water, the noise they made amplified around them, the tenseness a shared, unified sensation. They heard trickling water and passed over the drain they had discovered on their way into the shelter.

Ellison's breathing was coming in short, sharp pants; with every step it felt like someone was jabbing his ribs with a knife. He needed to rest, but although he was sure the worst was over, he refused to consider the possibility while still in the confines of the damp passageways.

Dealey was last in line, constantly casting his eyes around the pitch blackness behind as though expecting the shelter door to be flung open and hordes of squealing rats to burst through.

Running footsteps ahead, coming toward them. A blinding light, freezing them in its glare like fear-struck rabbits paralyzed by oncoming headlights.

Fairbank almost ran into Culver.

The technician leaned against the wall, shining the light back in the direction he had come. He was gasping for breath. "They're ahead of us," he managed to say. "I heard them squealing, moving around. They're above us, too. Take a listen!"

They waited and the noise grew. Slithering sounds. Scratching. Squealing. Coming from the corridor ahead of them. And then, just faintly, they heard similar noises overhead. They became louder, exaggerated by the acoustics of the passageways.

"Back!" Culver said, pushing at Kate to make her move.

"Back where?" Ellison shouted. "We can't get back into the shelter! We're trapped here!"

Culver and Fairbank, shoulder to shoulder in the narrow confines, pointed the Ingrams and flashlights into the tunnel ahead, waiting for the first sighting. It soon came.

They swarmed from the darkness just beyond the range of the beams, a squealing thronging multitude of black-furred beasts, scurrying forward into the glare, eyes gleaming. The vermin filled the corridor, a flowing stream of darkness.

Culver and Fairbank opened fire at the same time, bringing the rush to a sudden, screeching halt. Rats twisted in the air to land on the backs of others, who were themselves in death throes. Yet more took their place, more advanced, bodies snaking low to the floor, powerful haunches thrusting them forward. Culver stopped firing for a moment to yell at the two men and the girl.

"I told you—*move back!*"

They did, slowly, still watching over Culver and Fairbank's shoulders.

The advance stopped momentarily and the two men rested their weapons. Bloodied creatures wriggled on the floor no more than fifty yards away.

"Steve!" Kate was near to breaking. "There's nowhere to go! It's hopeless!"

"Find the drain," he said to them. "It can't be far behind us. Find it quickly."

"Give us one of the lights!" Ellison was screaming in panic.

Culver handed his flashlight over. Ellison grabbed it and stumbled away, aiming the beam into the puddles at their feet.

"Here they come again," Fairbank warned.

The rats were relentless in their attack, jumping over the backs of their injured companions, only the narrowness of the passageway itself preventing the group of survivors from being overwhelmed. Both Culver and Fairbank had the same question in mind: how much ammunition did they have left?

"It's here, I found it," Ellison called out.

The rats were still huddling together in the full glare of the flashlights, hemmed in by the rough walls, neither retreating nor advancing. Culver told Fairbank to raise the beam above ground level for a moment. The two men drew in sharp breaths when the light traveled over the quivering humped backs, for the black creatures stretched far away into the tunnel, well beyond its curve.

"Oh, Christ, beam me up, Scotty," Fairbank said in hushed awe.

"Culver, we can't get it open. It's stuck!"

The pilot turned and saw Ellison and Dealey struggling with the drain cover, Kate holding the light for them. He reached for the ax tucked into Fairbank's belt and whispered, "Start firing the moment they break."

Fairbank did not risk looking at him; he merely grunted affirmation.

Culver knelt beside the two men and handed the Ingram to Ellison. "Help Fairbank," he said, then examined the edges of the drain. "How far down are the sewers?" he asked Dealey, still in a low voice.

"I've no idea." Dealey's reply was equally as quiet. "I think there are channels below us, running into the main waterways, but I don't know how far down they are, or even if they'll accommodate us."

Culver bent low and listened, but although he could hear the water trickling down the walls, he could not tell whether it was running into a stream. He inserted the sharp side of the ax head into the gap between drain and surround.

Fairbank's whisper was harsh. "They're coming forward again! Taking it slow this time, just creeping along. The bastards are stalking us!"

Culver shoved the blade in as far as it would go. "Dealey," he hissed, "push your fingers through on this side of the drain. Pull when I give you the word."

The light Kate was holding shook madly.

"Okay, *now!*" Culver leaned on the blade with all his weight and Dealey heaved upward. For two dreadfully long seconds nothing happened. Then Culver felt something beginning to shift. The drain cover came up with a squelchy sucking and Culver grabbed at its edge, pulling it wide. The lid clanged against the passage wall, the signal for all hell to break loose again.

He snatched the flashlight from Kate and shone it into the opening. The drain was roughly two foot square, large enough for them to climb into. About ten feet below, he saw sluggishly moving water.

Culver had to shout to make himself heard over the cacophony of muffled bullets and screeching rats, and even then the others could only guess at his meaning. He tugged at Dealey.

"There are no rungs! You'll have to drop down into the water. It shouldn't be too deep! Help Kate when she follows!"

Dealey needed no second bidding. He was horrified at having to jump into such a black, unknown pit, but even more horrified at the idea of being eaten alive. He lowered himself onto the edge, then sank his overweight stomach into the hole, using elbows to hold himself in that position. There was little room to spare, but he managed to scrape through. With an intake of breath, he slid down; hanging on to the edge with his fingertips. Closing his eyes, Dealey dropped.

His belly and chin scraped against rough brickwork and the fall seemed to last an eternity. He cried out as his feet plunged into cold wetness, and he found himself on hands and knees in flowing water, the level just reaching below his hunched shoulders. His figure was bathed in light from above.

"It's all right," he shouted upward, almost laughing with relief. "It's shallow! We can make it through here!"

He thought he heard a shout from above and then another body was blocking out the light. Rising, Dealey realized the roof of the channel was arched, extending to no more than four feet at its apex. Loose chippings and water fell onto his upturned face as Kate slid toward him. He reached up and took her weight, endeavoring to lower her gently.

Above, one of the guns had stopped firing.

Culver looked anxiously at the two men and saw Fairbank throw his Ingram away.

"That's it!" the technician shouted. "Empty!"

"Get back here!" the pilot told him, tucking the small ax into his own belt. "Dealey, here comes the flashlight! For God's sake, don't drop it!" He let the flashlight fall and was relieved when it found safe hands.

Ellison came with Fairbank, still firing along the tunnel. Fairbank dropped to one knee beside Culver and leaned close. "We can't hold them back any longer! One more rush and that's it!"

"Give me the light!" Still pointed toward the vermin, the flashlight was handed to him. The firing had become more sporadic, the rats advancing, then stopping, Ellison having the sense not to waste bullets. "We'll get Ellison down there first, then you," Culver said to Fairbank, keeping his voice low in between bursts of fire. "I want you to stay inside the drain to support me when I come through. I'm going to have to pull this cover shut before I come down."

"That's not going to be easy."

"What the fuck is, these days?"

Fairbank grunted and stood with Culver, who reached around Ellison and took the gun. "Get into the drain," Culver said evenly, and Ellison moved away. The pilot faced the rats, gun in one hand, flashlight in the other. "Is he down yet?" he called quietly over his shoulder.

"Nearly," Fairbank replied.

"You next."

"Okay, but first, back up until you're on this side of the hole. It'll make things easier for you."

Hands reached out and guided Culver around the opening. Fairbank clapped his shoulder and wriggled into the drain.

"Make it quick," he said before dropping from view. "I'll be waiting." He was gone and Culver was alone.

Alone except for the creeping mutants.

He gently eased himself into a sitting position, gun and flashlight held chest-high, then slid his legs over the edge. Now comes the tricky part, he thought.

The rats sensed their prey was escaping. The squeals rose to high-pitched screeches as they surged forward.

With a cry of fear, Culver pushed himself off the edge, his elbows catching his weight before he dropped down completely. His feet scrabbled below him until firm hands grabbed his ankles and guided them. Then he dropped the flashlight, grabbed the drain cover, and ducked.

He felt the support beneath him dropping too, giving him room to maneuver in the confined space. He stayed crouched just beneath the grille, knowing it had not sunk properly into its home.

"Take the gun!" he called down, lowering the weapon as far as he could. Someone, probably Fairbank, took it from him. The drain was brilliantly lit by the flashlights.

Culver lifted the grille just a little, pulling his fingers from the opening immediately when something sharp brushed their tips. Using the flat of his palms, he tried again. The weight above him was tremendous and he knew the vermin were swarming over the cover. He could hear their squeals only inches away from his face. He felt talonlike claws through the slits of the drain cover, tearing into his hands, but he ignored the pain, using all his strength to lift and slide the lid around. Fairbank's shoulders trembled beneath him, but the stocky man held firm, assisting him as much as he could.

The cover closed with a firm, satisfying thud. Culver allowed himself to slowly collapse, and Fairbank, sensing it was all right to do so, gently lowered him. Other hands supported him and he gratefully sank into the running water.

He rested there, head back against the slimy brick wall of the channel, brownish water flowing over his lap, his hands clasped around his knees, breathing in deep lungfuls of stale air, his eyes closed. The others sprawled in similar positions, too exhausted to care about the soaking. They listened to the scrabbling, the frustrated scraping above them; the squeals from the enraged vermin sent shivers through them.

Dealey voiced what they all knew. "They may find other ways into the sewer."

Culver opened his eyes and was relieved to find the flashlight he had dropped had been saved. Fairbank held the Ingram above water level, his face a taut mask, eyes staring and particularly white against the contrast of his dirt-grimed face. Kate's head was against her knees, loose, bedraggled hair falling around her face. He resisted the urge to reach out and touch her, knowing there was precious little time for comfort. Ellison and Dealey held the flashlights, the latter also clutching one of the Browning automatics; there seemed to be barely any strength left in either man.

Culver stretched out a hand. "Let me have the gun."

Dealey hardly had to move to give it to him, so close were the walls of the channel. "It got wet when I fell into the water; I had it in my pocket."

Culver took the gun, praying it would still fire. "Ellison—the flashlight."

Without argument, Elison passed it over.

"Any idea which way we should go?" Culver asked Dealey. The sound of his voice sent the squealing above their heads into a new furor.

"No. I don't have much idea of the sewer network and I'm completely disoriented anyway." He glanced up nervously into the opening above.

"Then we'll move in this direction." Culver indicated with the Browning to his left. "That's the way the water's flowing, so it must lead somewhere." He rose, crouching because of the low ceiling, and climbed over the others. "I'll lead. Kate, you stick close to me. Fairbank, you bring up the rear."

They all scrambled to their feet, desperately tired and limbs aching, but keen to be moving on. They waded after Culver, splashing through the filthy water, the foul smell considerably less unpleasant than the other odors of that day. It was difficult to walk, for the sluggish water leadened their feet and the constant crouching put added stress on their legs. Yet it was a relief when the sounds of the vermin faded behind them.

Soon a new sound reached their ears and they paused to listen.

"It's rushing water," Dealey said. "There must be a main sewer ahead of us."

"And a way out," added Ellison.

Their pace was quickening and the rushing noise quickly became a mild roar. It wasn't long before they entered the bigger center channel.

It was at least twelve feet across, the ceiling curved and high. On either side of the swift-moving stream, its spumescent surface littered with debris, were causeways wide enough to walk on. As they shone the flashlights in either direction, they saw conduits and outlets spilling their contents into the main sewer.

They stepped up onto the causeway on their side, each of them feeling a sudden lift in spirits at this new sight.

"We're lucky," Dealey said over the noise. "This tunnel must have been completely flooded when the rainfall was at its worst."

"I can't see any ladders." Fairbank was shining his flashlight more carefully in one direction, then the other. Culver did the same to add more light.

"There'll be some farther along. I would think there's a storm weir in that direction"—Dealey indicated the water's flow—"so we may find a way out along there."

Culver felt a hand slide around his waist and looked down to see Kate gazing up at him.

"Are we safe now?" she asked, her eyes imploring.

He couldn't lie. "Not yet. Soon, though." He briefly pulled her to his chest and kissed her hair. "Keep your eyes open," he told them all. Then he was moving once again, the others filing closing behind.

"Stop! You missed something! Over there." Fairbank was casting his beam toward the opposite causeway.

Culver aimed his own flashlight in that direction and saw the opening, a passageway beyond. He could just make out stone steps farther back. "Any idea where it could lead?" he asked Dealey.

"Impossible to say. It's not a channel or a drain."

Culver stared down into the spume-flecked water. "We can't risk crossing here. We'll have to go on."

"Not much farther, though," Kate said excitedly. "Look, there's a gangway across."

They hurried toward it and found the structure was made of iron, narrow in width, and with just a spindly handrail on one side.

"It has to be fairly close to that passageway for a reason," commented Ellison. "It's gonna take us out of here, I know it."

Culver led the way across, testing the bridge's safety with every step. The metal surface was rusted but firm, although the handrail itself wobbled uncertainly. They hurried back the way they had come, this time on the opposite bank, and soon reached the opening. The passageway was at least eight feet high and wide enough for two men to walk comfortably along side by side. The glistening-wet stone stairway at the end of the passage was easily visible in the illumination of both flashlights.

It led upward, into the ceiling.

Kate clutched Culver's arm. "It's the way out! It has to be!"

Fairbank whooped with glee and even Dealey managed to smile.

"What the hell are we waiting for?" cried Ellison, and Culver had to restrain him from charging forward.

"There's a whole network of sewers, conduits, and pipes all around us—not to mention passageways such as this. Those rats could be anywhere by now: above, behind, or ahead of us. It's their territory, so let's just take it quiet and easy.''

He moved to the foot of the steps and shone the beam upward. Just beyond ceiling level was another opening, a doorway. He began to mount the stairs, taking them slowly, one at a time. The others, heeding his warning but nevertheless impatient, crowded behind him.

Culver reached the top and saw the door itself was old and rotted, a rusted metal sheet battened to its surface. It was open about two feet. He shone in the beam and saw another long corridor. Like the previous one, puddles covered the floor and its walls were of old, crumbling brickwork. It appeared to stretch a long way.

Culver pushed at the metal and the door ground protestingly against the stone floor, shifting only a few inches. Wary of what could be on the other side, he slipped through.

The others came in after him, shivering anew with the dank cold. Culver examined the lock and found an open bolt, rusty with years of dampness.

''This is an entrance for the sewer workers and inspectors,'' declared Dealey. ''It probably leads to an exit along the Embankment, or somewhere in the vicinity.''

''I'd feel safer if we got it closed,'' Culver said. ''Remember what's chasing us?''

Fairbank lent his weight when Culver put his shoulder to the door. It closed reluctantly; Culver shot the rusty bolt with some satisfaction.

Their footsteps were less hurried as they tramped along the lengthy corridor, not because their fear had left them but because weariness was finally asserting a stronger grip.

Another door greeted them at the far end, and this one was locked. A hefty kick from Culver opened it.

They found themselves in a spacious room with several doorways around the walls.

''Ah, now I think I understand,'' Dealey said.

The others regarded him curiously.

"We've come back to a part of the old World War Two shelter. This must be the second level, just below the section we first entered. I was wrong about the passageway we've come through; it wasn't for sewer workers. It was meant as a means of escape should whoever inhabited this shelter be trapped. The whole region is catacombed with chambers such as this. When you consider how long ag—"

"Take a look!" The coldness in Fairbank's voice startled them all. He was sweeping his flashlight along the floor.

At first they thought the objects lying there were just debris, pieces of mislaid junk left by previous generations of occupiers. When they looked closer, the chill inside them all deepened.

The first object to take on an identity was a severed arm, all but one of the fingers missing. The next was the remains of a head, one empty eye socket bored into and enlarged, as though something had been dragged out. A piece of putrid flesh that may once have been a thigh lay close by. The human parts lay scattered around the floor, white bones reflecting the beams, dried and shriveled meat lumps standing alone like strangely shaped rocks on a desert of dust.

The familiar dread returned, only this time more potently, for they were weakened, exhausted, close to total hysteria. Culver caught Kate as she sagged. She did not faint entirely, but that unconscious state was not far away.

Ellison began to head back toward the door through which they had just arrived, and Culver brought him to a sudden halt.

"No!" The pilot's voice was firm, almost angry. "We're going on. We didn't come across any rats on our way into the old shelter, so I figure it's our safest way out. Nothing's making me go back into the sewers."

The words rebounded off the empty walls, as if to mock him.

He continued determinedly, "We're going to walk straight through this, right to the other end of this room. There's a doorway there and, with any luck, a stairway beyond. Just look straight ahead and don't stop for anything."

Culver set off, supporting Kate. The arm around her shoulder clutched the Browning, its muzzle held erect, ready to swing down into action. He kept the flashlight in his other hand aimed directly at the far doorway. Someone behind stumbled and he looked around to see Dealey on one knee, a skull with the back of its cranium cracked open like a hatched egg, rolling to a stop a few feet away.

"Get up and keep walking," Culver commanded, his voice tight. "Don't stop for anything," he repeated.

But they did stop.

As one.

When they heard the child crying.

29

The group stood as a rigid tableau among a macabre landscape of human remnants, listening to the pitiful crying.
Culver closed his eyes against both the sound and the new
pressure. He wanted to be free of this sinister madhouse,
this vault of atrocities, but there was no clear escape, no
relief from the mental tortures it inflicted upon them. His
only desire was to take Kate's hand and run, never stopping until daylight bathed their faces, until clean air filled
their lungs. Yet he knew it wasn't possible. He would
have to find the child first.

They listened, feeling wretched with the plaintive cry.
The wailing was high-pitched, possibly that of a little girl.

"It's coming from over there," someone said at last.

They looked to the right, toward an opening that had
been boarded up with heavy planks, the bottom section
broken inward. The wood looked as if it had been
gnawed.

The crying continued.

"I don't think it's wise to stay," said Dealey, looking around anxiously at the others.

"Then go to hell," Culver said in a low voice.

He felt a slight resistance from Kate when he moved away; then she was moving with him. The others reluctantly joined them at the boarded doorway. Culver and Fairbank shone their flashlights through the gaps between the planks of wood and peeked in. The far wall was at least forty feet away and the room itself was bare of furniture. Fairbank aimed his beam low and tapped Culver's shoulder.

The stone floor of the room had collapsed inward, leaving a ridge of jagged concrete around its circumference. Below was a pit filled with rubble.

The sad, despairing cries tore at their nerves.

"The kid's somewhere below," Fairbank said.

Culver called out. "Can you hear us? Are you on your own?"

The crying stopped.

"It's all right. We'll come down to get you! You're safe now!"

Silence.

"The poor little sod's terrified out of her mind," said Fairbank.

He and Culver began pulling at the planking. The rotted wood came away easily, breaking into long, damp splinters and creating a hole large enough for a man to climb through. They shone the lights in, the others peering over their shoulders.

"Construction work on the new shelter must have caused the collapse," Dealey said. "With the continuous dampness over the years, the vibration from the new works, it's a wonder the whole bunker hasn't fallen in."

Culver indicated the dark chasm before them. "Maybe the nuclear bombs caused the final collapse."

"Steve, please don't go down there." Kate spoke in a

low whisper, and there was an urgency in her request that disturbed Culver.

"There's a kid inside," he said. "It sounds like a little girl, and she's alone, Kate. Maybe others are with her, too injured to speak, unconscious, maybe dead. We can't just leave her."

"There's something wrong. It . . . it doesn't feel . . . right." The first sound of the crying child had sent a harrowing and uncanny sensation spilling through her. There was something unnatural about the voice.

"You don't really think I can walk away." Culver's statement was flat, his eyes searching hers.

She averted her gaze, not replying.

"How can you get to her?" Ellison was still agitated, hating Culver for wasting so much time in this godforsaken hole. "You'll break your neck trying to get down there."

"There could be a way through the sewers," Dealey suggested. "Underneath here must be the very basement of the old shelter, close to the sewer network."

Culver shook his head. "There's no way I'm going back there. Look." He pointed the flashlight. "There's a broken joist over there sticking up from a pile of rubble. The top end of the joist is leaning against the wall, just below the overhang. I think I can make it back up that way. Getting down is no problem; the ceilings are low in here; it's an easy drop." He turned to Fairbank. "I'd like to borrow the Ingram."

The technician surprised him by shaking his head. "Uh-huh. I'm coming with you. You'll need a hand with the kid."

Culver nodded gratefully and handed the Browning to Dealey. "No point in you three waiting. Take them out of here."

Again he was surprised when Dealey refused. "We'll wait for you," the older man said, taking the gun. "We'll be better off if we all stick together."

"You're crazy!" Ellison erupted. "Look around you!

Those bloody rats have been here, and they can get to this place again! We've got to leave now!''

He made as if to grab the gun from Dealey, but Fairbank's hand clamped around his arm.

''I've had all the shit I'm going to take from you, Ellison.'' The stocky man's eyes blazed angrily. ''You always were trouble, even in peacetime, bitching, whining, never happy unless you were complaining about something. Now if you want to leave, leave! But you go on your own, and with no flashlight and no gun. Just don't go stumbling into any hungry rats in the dark.''

Ellison appeared ready to attack the other technician, but something in Fairbank's glacial smile warned him off. Instead, he shook his head, saying, ''You're all insane. You're all fucking insane.''

Culver gave Kate the flashlight. ''Keep it shining into the floor opening. We're going to need all the light we can get.'' Her quietness disturbed him, but he turned away. ''Ready?'' he said to Fairbank.

Muttering something about ''another fine mess,'' Fairbank eased his way through the gap they had created.

Both men paused on the other side, Fairbank shining the light downward. Apart from rubble, the room looked empty. The light beam reflected off black pools of water in the debris.

''Can you hear me down there?'' Culver called out, aware that it was impossible not to be heard.

''The kid may be too scared to answer,'' Fairbank suggested. ''God knows what the poor little beggar's been through.''

They thought they heard a shifting sound.

''You want the gun or the flashlight?'' Fairbank asked.

Culver would have preferred the Ingram. ''Let me have the light.''

With backs to the wall they eased themselves around the overhang, fearful that it might collapse beneath them. Streams of dust trickled into the darkness below. Kate, standing just inside the gap, one leg still in the other room, helped guide them with her light.

Culver came to a halt. "Okay, this is where we go down." They had reached a corner, the flooring wider and seemingly more solid there. He could just make out the iron beam projecting beneath the overhang.

"Hold the light for a moment," he said, then sat down. He turned onto his stomach and lowered himself, his feet finding the angled beam. He let himself go, boots sliding down the joist, the descent to the heap of rubble not long. Steadying himself, he looked up.

"Throw me the flashlight, then the Ingram."

Fairbank did so and clambered over the edge himself. They were soon standing side by side.

Culver swept the beam around the room. "There's nothing here," he said. "Nothing."

He moved forward, and something gave way beneath him. Fairbank tried to grab him as he fell, but was encumbered by the gun. Culver toppled, rolling in the debris. The sound of sliding masonry echoed around the damp walls. Fairbank went after him, and he too fell, cursing as he went down.

And the crying began once more, high-pitched and fearful, the voice of a terrified child.

Both men looked toward the direction of the cries. They saw a dark doorway, another room. A familiar nauseating stench came from that room.

Dust settled around them as Kate's voice from above called out, "Are you okay?"

"Yeah, we're all right, don't worry."

The two men picked themselves up and noticed that, yet again, the crying had stopped.

"Hey, kid," Fairbank yelled, "where the hell are you?"

They heard what sounded like a whimper.

"She's in there," Culver stated what they both knew.

"That smell . . ." said Fairbank.

"We have to get her."

"I don't know." Fairbank was shaking his head. "Something—"

"We have to."

Culver led the way, sloshing through the puddles, stepping over debris. After a moment's hesitation, Fairbank went after him.

The chamber next door was wide and long, its ceiling, fallen in many places, low. Parts in the walls had collapsed, too, creating deep, impenetrable recesses. In the distance they could hear a faint rushing, gurgling noise, the cadence of the sewers. Long cobwebs, like soot-filled lace, drooped everywhere. Scattered on the broad expanse of floor before them were humped shapes, yellow-gray in the gloom. Smaller white shapes glowed almost phosphorously. Dark, even more indiscernible forms lay between.

Both men took a step backward, Fairbank raising the weapon, Culver reaching for the ax in his belt. The urge to run, to flee from this stinking, horror-strewn cellar was almost irresistible. Yet, it held a peculiar, paralyzing fascination. And the distressed whimpers could not be ignored.

"They're not moving," Culver whispered urgently. "They're dead. Like the others in the shelter, wiped out by the plague. They must have crawled back here, their nest, to die."

"All those skulls. Why all those skulls?"

"Look at them. They've been broken into. Through the eye sockets, between the jaws. Look there—holes bored straight through the top of the cranium. Don't you see? They eat the brains. That's why so many corpses we found were headless. The bastards brought them back here to feed off!"

"Those other things . . ."

Culver singled out one of the bloated yellowish-white shapes. Its form seemed peculiarly blurred, indefinable.

"What the hell is it?"

Culver had no answer to Fairbank's question. He moved closer, fascinated despite himself.

"Oh, sweet Jes—" The words faded on his lips.

The bloated creature barely resembled a rat. Its head was almost sunk into the obese body, long withered tusks emerging from the slack jaw. Under the strong light they saw there was a pinkishness to the fine, stretched skin, a smattering of whispy white hair its only covering. Dark veins streaked its body, blood vessels that had hardened and stood embossed from the skin. The twisted spine rose to a peak over its rear haunches; the tail curved round like a lash, its surface hard with scales. There were other projections about its body, these resembling malformed limbs, superfluous and hideous in shape. The slanted eyes glinted under the flashlight glare, but there was no life in them.

"What is it?" Fairbank repeated breathlessly.

"A mutant rat," Culver said. "Of the same strain as the black, but . . . different." Dealey's words came back to him. He had said there were two breeds, born of the same altered gene. "A grotesque," Dealey had called it. It was an inadequate description. He had implied they were undergoing some genetic transformation. Oh, Christ, so this was the result!

There was a rustling, not far away.

Nerves taut, ready to snap, both men whirled around, the light beam stabbing at the darkness.

"Over there!" Fairbank pointed.

Shapes were moving. A mewling sound to their left made them turn in that direction. Other movements, scuffling in the darker corners.

"It's like before," Fairbank said in dismay. "They're not all dead."

Culver swept the light over the sluggishly heaving forms. "They can't harm us. Listen to them. They're weak, dying. They're frightened of us!"

A black shape disengaged itself from the mass. It tried to crawl toward them, hissing as it approached, but it could hardly move. Fairbank aimed the gun and fired; the creature exploded as would an overfilled balloon. He was about to let loose into the pool of mutants when a squealing scream came from a far corner. The two men looked wide-eyed at each other, then toward its source.

"The kid!" exclaimed Fairbank.

The beam reached the far corner, but too many other objects were in the way for a clear view.

"Let's get her and then get out!" Culver urged. He held the ax ready. "Shoot at anything that moves, try and clear a path!"

They set off, both men determined, keeping panic in check, making for the corner where the piteous crying had resumed. Only now the sound was different, more shrill, less like a child's, more like . . .

The realization struck Culver like an icicle dagger. He almost stumbled, almost fell among the fearful writhing bodies. He tried to reach out and bring Fairbank to a halt, but it was already too late. They were there. They had reached the far corner. They had reached the Mother Creature's nest.

"Oh . . . my . . . God . . . NO!" Fairbank sobbed as they looked down at the throbbing, pulsating flesh and its terrible spawn.

"It can't be," Fairbank moaned. "It just can't be . . ."

In another section not too far away, from a hole in the crumbled brick wall, came the sounds of scuffling, of scampering clawed feet.

30

Kate, Dealey, and Ellison flinched when they heard the shot. Kate stood perilously close to the edge of the collapsed floor, attempting to shine the flashlight into the doorway through which Culver and Fairbank had disappeared.

"Steve!" she called, but heard only more gunfire and an awful ululation, a strident, piercing screeching. She turned to the others. "We must help them!"

"There's nothing we can do," Dealey told her. His throat was dry, he could barely speak; the hand gripping the Browning would not keep still. "Keep . . . keep the light on the doorway as a . . . as a . . . guide for them," he stammered.

Ellison remained on the other side of the broken boards, inside the darkened room, listening to the dreadful sounds, the trembling in his legs making it difficult for them to support his body. His hands were clawed against his face, his eyes staring and seeing nothing but blackness. We are crazy, crazy to stay here, crazy not to run, to get out while we have the chance, crazy to think we can defend ourselves against so many. Culver and Fairbank were finished. Nothing could save them! The rats would rip them to pieces and then come searching for the girl, Dealey, and himself! Why hadn't they listened to him? The stupid, bloody fools!

He looked toward the source of light, seeing Dealey's silhouette, the man leaning forward into the opening, clutching the gun. The gun! He had to take the gun! And the flashlight—he would need the flashlight!

Ellison moved quickly.

Dealey turned as the Browning was snatched away; he tried to protest, but was pushed back against the doorway, shards of splintered wood digging into his back.

Gun held forward, Ellison made a grab for the flashlight. "Give it to me!" he screamed as Kate tried to pull away.

He caught her arm, yanking her inward. She fell, tried to kick out at him, but a hand smacked her viciously across the face. She cried out, falling backward. The flashlight was taken from her.

Dealey tried to intervene and Ellison pushed him away once more. He leveled the gun at him. "I'm leaving!" His words were spat out. "You can come with me or you can stay. But I'm getting out now!"

"The others—" Dealey began to say.

"We can't help them! They've had it!"

Ellison began to back away, keeping the weapon pointed at the two figures. Then he turned and began to run, heading for the door at the other end of the room, away from the mayhem below, away from his companions. And, he foolishly thought, away from the vermin.

31

Fairbank shouted his fury, screamed his fear as he fired at the huge swollen mass before them. The creature screeched, the sound of a hurt, terrified child, and attempted to lift her obese body, tried to protect herself, her two jaws snapping ineffectively, her useless limbs thrashing the ground, trampling and scattering the tiny offspring that had suckled at her breasts.

Bullets ripped into her, explosions of blood spurting out in dark jets. In a paroxym of agony, she rose up, exposing her sickening, fleshy underbelly, several of her brood still clinging to her. A frenzied hail of bullets tore her open, but still she moved, incredibly shuffling her way toward the two men.

The pointed head, its incisors like curled tusks, the eyes white, sightless, weaved in front of them; a strange stump protruded from her shoulder next to the head, an opening within it that could have been only another mouth, spitting blood-specked drool.

Culver sank to his knees, strength draining from his

legs. He stared at the heinous deformity, the misbegotten grotesque, horrified, his muscles numbed. But as her foul breath and her spittle touched his cheek, the shock was punctured.

The flashlight at his knees, he raised the short ax with both hands and, with a screaming roar, brought it down with all his force.

The pointed skull before him split cleanly in two. The piercing screech came from the stump next to the cloven head, the toothless jaws wide with the creature's pain, her scaly purple tongue stabbing frenziedly at the air.

Culver struck again, cutting through this other skull, the ax head sinking into the shoulder, into the body itself.

The squirming abomination suddenly went rigid, became frozen just for a few moments. Then agonizingly slowly, it began to slump, nerve ends twitching, torn, bloated body quivering.

But Culver was not finished. His eyes were blurred and his face dampened by tears as he attacked the litter, the smaller, more obscene creatures the monster had given birth to. He hacked their pink bodies, ignoring their faint cries, striking, pummeling, crushing their tiny bones, making sure each was dead.

A hand tugged at his shoulder, the grip hard, violent.

He looked up to see Fairbank grimacing down at him.

"The other rats are down here," the technician said through tight-clenched teeth.

Culver was hauled to his feet, his mind still confused, still dazed by the slaughter. And by what he had slaughtered. He quickly became aware of the darting black shapes in the rubble of the damp underground chamber.

The rats were in turmoil, leaping from an opening in the brick wall, scampering down the slope of debris, squealing and hissing. They poured through, more and more, filling the room, somehow oblivious to the two men. The mutant black rats fought one another, groups turning on one for no apparent reason, tearing it apart and gnawing at the body.

Culver and Fairbank could not understand why they were ignored as the animals swilled around the chamber, biting at the other gross forms that lay dying or dead on the floor, high-pitched squeals intensifying, rising to a crescendo, climbing to a thunderous pitch.

Then they stopped.

They lay in the darkness, black-furred bodies quivering, a trembling, silent mass. Occasionally one would hiss and rear up, but would become passive almost immediately, sinking back among its brethren. The shaking motion seemed to reverberate in the atmosphere itself.

Bathed in blood, grimed with filth, and barely recognizable, the two men held their breath.

Nothing stirred.

Slowly, wordlessly, Fairbank touched Culver's sleeve. With a slight jerk of his head he indicated the doorway they had entered by. Keeping the light beam on the floor before them, the two men began to gently, quietly make their way through the gathered vermin, careful not to disturb any, skirting around when a pack was too thick to step over.

A rodent lashed out with its incisors, hissing at them when they trod too close. The teeth grazed Culver's ankle through his jeans, but the animal did not attack.

At one point, Fairbank tripped and stumbled into a tight group, going down on his knees among them. Inexplicably, they merely scattered, snarling at the air as they did so.

They were just thirty yards from the doorway, both men wondering why they could not see Kate's flashlight, when an eerie keening began.

It started as a single, faint, low whine; then other rats joined in, the keening growing, swelling. The sound ended in a startling unified screech and the vermin broke loose again. But they darted toward the bloody, shapeless carcass of the gross monster the two men had destroyed, the miscreant beast who had nurtured the even more hideous newborn, pouncing on the remains, fighting one another over the scraps, covering the nest completely with their own frantic bodies.

And when there was nothing left of the malformity and her brood, they turned on their kindred, the bloated beasts who were of the same breed but perversely different, savaging them until they, too, were nothing but bloody shreds.

The two men ran, heading for the doorway, kicking aside those vermin still standing in their path. Culver swung the ax as a rat sprang at him, catching it beneath the throat. It squealed and dropped in a limp bundle to the floor. Another leapt and caught his arm, but the leather jacket ripped and the animal fell away. Fairbank scattered four or five others that had grouped in the doorway itself.

They were through and there was still no light from above, but they heard Kate cry out Culver's name.

Fairbank whirled in the doorway, pressing a shoulder hard against the frame, the Ingram pointed back into the chamber they had just left. "Culver, give me light!" he shouted.

Culver did so, shining the beam into the next room. The rats were swarming after them.

Fairbank fired. The advancing rats danced and jerked as though on marionette strings. "Start climbing," he called over his shoulder. "I can hold them without the light for a couple of seconds!"

Culver quickly climbed the heap of rubble leading to the fallen joist. His flashlight lit up Kate standing on the ledge above.

With no time to even wonder what had happened to her flashlight, he yelled, "Catch!" and lobbed his light toward her. She only just managed to hold it; she turned the beam back down into the pit.

Then the thing they had dreaded most happened. The Ingram clicked empty. With an alarmed shout, Fairbank turned to follow Culver, dropping the useless weapon into the dust.

Culver ran two steps up the angled joist, throwing the ax onto the ledge above him and grabbing at the edge just before his boots began to slip down again. Pieces of masonry fell away, but he quickly had both elbows on the overhang. His feet scrabbled for purchase.

He heard screaming from behind.

Kate was kneeling on the ledge, pulling at his clothes, trying to lift him. Dealey, too, had ventured out and had a hand beneath Culver's shoulder. The pilot's boots found a grip, enough to push upward. He scrambled over the edge, instantly rising to his knees, grasping the flashlight from the girl.

Fairbank was halfway up the slope, his lower body engulfed by biting, scratching vermin. One darted up his back, sinking its teeth into the back of his neck. The technician rolled over in an effort to dislodge the animal; his mouth was open in a scream, his eyes tightly closed against the pain. The rat fell away and Fairbank started to crawl again, his hands clawing into the rubble. He rose to a kneeling position, the rats clinging to his lower regions. He tried to push them away and his hands came away bloody, fingers missing.

"Help me!" he screamed.

Culver tensed and Kate threw herself at him, knocking him back against the wall.

"You can't, you can't," she kept saying over and over again.

He tried to free himself, but she held him there, Dealey

using his weight to assist her. And in reality, he knew that Fairbank was beyond help.

"Give me the other gun!" he shouted, and could not understand why they did not comply, why they merely held him tight.

Fairbank was dragging the giant rats with him. They covered him now, making him a creature of black, stiff fur, a monster of their own kind. His screaming had turned into a raspy choking as they tore into his neck. He tried to raise his arms as if still reaching for the ledge, but they could hardly move.

Fairbank fell stiffly backward, crashing down into the rubble, the black pools of water. His blood spread out as the vermin pushed and snapped at one another in their struggle to devour the most succulent parts.

Others were aware of the three people on the overhang above and darted up the slope, springing onto the metal beam and attempting to scramble onto the ledge.

32

The thing that would eventually kill Ellison was lying in the darkness. It did not move, not even breath. It made no sounds, nor could it. It had been dead for some time. But still it would kill Ellison.

The corpse was that of a sewer worker, a senior repairs foreman who had chosen this shadowy place to die. Others in his small work crew, on the day of the bombs, had elected to return to the surface, to find their families, to put their faith in the authorities. This man had had no such faith. He was old, ready for retirement, not just from the job he had worked at for forty-two years but with existence itself. He may have been considered perverse in his belief that life was somehow cleaner beneath the streets than above. What he meant, but what he never told anybody, was that there was a wonderful absence of people in this permanently nocturnal underworld. And everything was more distinct down there, more defined, unlike the murky upperworld where there were shades for everything, color, opinions, and race. He had considered himself a simple man with a penchant for absolutes. The tunnels gave him absolutes.

And the falling bombs had provided the ultimate one. There was no more living, only dying.

He had let his workers go, not even offering advice. In fact, he was pleased to be released from them. Then he had found this place in the dark corridor of the old air-raid shelter.

The old man lost track of time, so had no idea of when the hallucinations began. The scurrying noise had provoked the worst visions, for, inexplicably, they seemed to draw him back to a dreamy reality. The padding, scuffling of small bodies was very close, coming from a grating that ran the length of the corridor in which he lay. He never dared look, for that would mean testing the truthfulness of the dream, and that truth might bind him longer to the existence he was trying to escape.

The old man's delirium was timeless, the slide into peace, not oblivion, easy and gliding, with almost no line drawn between the two opposites, life and death. The body had straightened before the final but slurred moments, legs sprawling outward, arms at his sides, and head slumped onto his chest. It was the way he had chosen and it had not been too unkind to him.

He had thought, mistakenly, that at least his way out was of no consequence and no bother to anyone else; but in that, he was wrong.

Had not the sewer worker chosen that particular spot in which to wither away, and had his legs not sprawled outward, feet pointing east-west, then Ellison would not have stumbled over him, tripped, and lost his flashlight, gun, and a little later on, his life.

Ellison burst through the door, his only desire to be as far away as possible from the commotion back there. He knew the others had no chance: there would be nothing left of Culver and Fairbank by now, and Dealey and the girl would not last long on their own. He did not consider that the latter two had even less of a chance without the flashlight and gun he had taken from them. They were fools and the world was no longer fit for such; only the clearheaded and ruthless would survive. He meant to survive; he had already gone through too much not to.

Beyond the room where Kate and Dealey lay stunned was yet another room, this one smaller and square-shaped. The flashlight soon picked out another door directly opposite. He prayed it would not be locked as he hurried over, and his prayer was answered. So unnerved at what lay behind and so intent on what lay ahead, Ellison failed to notice the sprawled legs, the opposite-angled feet, just inside the door. Both flashlight and gun were thrown from his outstretched hands and he landed heavily. His surprised cry changed instantly to one of pain, then anguish, when something shattered and there was no more light.

Panic sent him fumbling around the hard concrete floor in search of the precious light. He recoiled from the sticklike leg he touched, moving rapidly away, coming up against a wall and feeling some kind of grille beneath him. The slats were wide enough for his hand to go through, and for a moment, his fingers dangled in space. He hastily withdrew them, not liking the cool draft of air that embraced his skin.

He found the flashlight close by, cutting his hand on the shattered glass. He pressed the switch, praying once again, but this time the invocation went unheeded: the light failed to respond.

Ellison began to whimper, occasionally a self-pitying sob breaking loose. The gun. He had to find the gun. It was his only protection. But somebody up there had closed shop: his implorations were ignored. He searched as much of the corridor as he could before giving up, knowing madness or vermin would claim him if he remained in that place one minute longer. He moved to the wall on his right, feeling the grating beneath his feet.

Touching the wall, he moved forward, sure that he was aimed in the right direction, his fingertips never leaving the coarse surface.

A corner. And then a doorway. The one he had seen from the other end just before he had tripped. He found the handle, opened the door, and passed through. He had no way of knowing what kind of room he was now in. He kept to the wall, moving to his right, not stopping until he found another opening. He entered this one, traveling farther into the labyrinth, unaware that if he had chosen the left-hand path, he would have come upon a staircase leading upward.

33

Fairbank's screams resounded in their ears long after he was dead. As they fled from the room, the two men and the girl could not close out those horrifying shrieks from their minds. Dealey and Kate had had to drag Culver from the room. For a few seconds he had stood in the doorway, ax still clasped in one hand, staring down at the heaving mass covered in Fairbank's blood. A rat had appeared nearby, its long, pointed snout sniffing the air as its claws had struggled for purchase. Another had arrived at its side and Culver had used his boot to send them reeling back down.

As they hastened across the chamber, Culver only half-hearing Kate's explanation of the missing flashlight and gun, the vermin were steadily surmounting the overhang, ignoring the shrill combat of others who fought over the remaining human fragments. Still more found other routes from the basement chamber, their senses keen, blood lust roused and still not sated from weeks of plenty.

Strong emotions other than fear were coursing through

Culver: the deep grief for Fairbank, the rending sense of having failed him, the loathing for the beasts themselves, coupled with a wild anger at them.

Kate pointed Culver's flashlight at the doorway Ellison had disappeared through, almost as if the beam would provide a straight, safe path. They reached the doorway, passed through without pause, conscious of the squealing sounds close behind. They traversed the smaller, square-shaped room they found themselves in, heading for an open door opposite. The first of the chasing rats was no more than twenty feet behind.

Culver pushed Kate and Dealey inside, and then followed, quickly turning to slam the door shut. Bodies crashed into it on the other side, rocking the wood in its frame, as the giant rats leapt at the barrier. Culver could see the wood bend in with each thump. He stiffened when he heard scratching. Then came the determined gnawing.

"Get down to the other end!" he shouted. "I'll hold them for as long as possible, then I'll make a break for it!" He kept his foot and shoulder to the door, feeling it move judderingly against the frame.

Kate backed away, keeping the light on Culver, on the door he struggled to keep closed against the hell's demons outside, almost falling over something. She moved away so that the circle of light grew, took in all the doorway, the beginnings of the corridor walls, Dealey, white-faced and shaking like a man with ague, the similarly white-faced corpse that smiled down into his chest.

She screamed, backed away, sent something behind her scudding across the floor. She turned and saw the other flashlight lying there, its glass smashed. It was next to a long grating beneath which were pipes with valves, stopcocks of some kind. And there was the Browning lying in the shallow trench, propped up against the piping. The gun and flashlight were there in the corridor, but where was Ellison?

Her scream had caused Culver and Dealey to turn and

see the starved body of a man wearing overalls, a helmet with a fitted lamp by his side. His emaciated expression seemed oddly pleased with his demise.

"Steve, the gun," Kate said, pointing the flashlight through the grating. "Ellison must have dropped it down there."

"Can you reach it?"

"I think so. I think my hand can go through." She knelt beside the opening and, keeping the light on the Browning, slid her fingers through the slats. Her whole hand sank in and she pushed farther until her wrist was inside too. Her fingertips could just touch the gun butt.

"Hurry!" Culver urged.

Kate was careful not to topple the weapon, knowing it would never be reached if she did so. Her fingers slid down on either side and she closed them firmly like pincers, making sure she had a good grip before slowly drawing her hand up.

The black creature darted forward and bit into her hand before she was even aware of its skulking presence.

Kate's screams jolted the two men like rapid blows from a hammer. They could see only her crouched silhouette, the flashlight lying on its side, shining toward the far door. Her shoulders were jerking as though she were being pulled, her head thrown back in resistance. They guessed instantly what held her there.

A rat, so big it filled the gap between the piping and the floor of the shallow cavity, had locked its jaws into Kate's hand and was tugging at it, its head moving in a swift shaking motion. Other rats were filling the trench, squirming beneath the piping, approaching Kate from the other direction. The concrete trench resembled a long, narrow cage filled with squealing, hissing creatures, their thin heads protruding through the bars, teeth snapping at the air, eager to reach the girl.

Culver beat at the heads nearest to her kneeling body

with the ax as they tried to bite into her. They screeched as their snouts burst open.

"Steve, helpmehelpme!" Kate shrieked. "OhGod-they'rehurtingme!

Culver grabbed her wrist and wrenched it upward. The rat came up with the hand, its eyes protruding, its skull pressed against the bars. He tried to hit at it, but the grille was too narrow, the angle too awkward for the blow to be effective. The beast's razor teeth were locked tight into the bones of Kate's hand.

Over the deafening uproar of squealing vermin and Kate's screams, Culver vaguely heard Dealey shouting.

"They're breaking through the door, Culver!"

He turned, shining the flashlight in that direction. The lower portion of the door was beginning to give way, the wood bulging inward. He saw slivers fall away, a black protuberance poking through, yellow teeth gnashing at the rough edges.

"Get over here and hold the light!" Culver yelled at Dealey.

The older man blanched when he saw the creatures eating into Kate's mangled hand. Even as he watched, a rat snipped off two fingers, retreating with its prize as another took its place. Blood flowed from the wounds, covering the rats' heads, smearing their evil yellow eyes, while Kate writhed, her screaming descending to shocked agonized moans. Culver thrust the flashlight at Dealey, then grabbed Kate's wrist with both hands. He pulled with all the strength he possessed, hoping the sudden jolt would dislodge the clinging rats.

It was no use. He tried to batter the first creature's head against the struts, but the rat still clung. Culver realized the teeth were bound into the bones of the hand—*what was left of the hand*—and nothing would loosen that grip, possibly not even death. He searched for the gun, but it was lost beneath wriggling black bodies.

"Culver!" Dealey was pointing the flashlight at the

door once more. Culver glanced over his shoulder, still tugging at the wrist, and saw the rat's head pushing through the hole it had created, only its shoulders restraining it. Splinters fell away in a different section nearby and long talons appeared, scratching at the wood.

He sensed Dealey beginning to rise, making ready to run for the far door. He caught his arm.

Kate was moaning repeatedly, her eyes closed in a half-faint, her head rolling from side to side. Her hand was in shreds, all the fingers gone now, but the rats still pulled, still tugged, still gnawed at the bloody remnants, cracking fragile bones.

Dealey stared pleadingly at Culver.

Kate's body went rigid with further excruciating pain.

Wood split behind him.

Culver swiftly unbuckled his belt, drawing it from the jean's loops. He placed the ax on the floor, then slipped the belt around Kate's arm just below the elbow. He curled the leather over, tied a half-knot, and pulled it tight so that it sank into the flesh. He completed the knot.

And picked up the ax again.

Kate's eyes opened just as he raised it high. She looked at him, momentarily puzzled. Realization pushed its way through the pain; her eyes widened unnaturally and her lips curled back over her teeth as she opened her mouth to howl.

"*Nooooooooo . . .*"

The ax flashed down, striking her arm just above the wrist. Bones shattered, but it took another blow to sever the hand completely.

Mercifully, Kate fainted.

There was turmoil below as the rats fought over what was left of the hand. Culver picked up the limp girl and stood, the white-faced Dealey rising with him. A quick glance told them that the rat at the door was nearly through, only its haunches wedging its struggling body in the opening. It frantically scrabbled at the floor, snarling its frustration, saliva dripping from straining jaws as it tried to force a way in. More wood fractured close by, and where before there had been only a claw, there now appeared another sleek black head.

And all the while, the starved corpse of the man smiled into its chest.

Culver carried Kate to the far doorway, Dealey leading. They hurried through just as the determined rat broke loose into the corridor, another following, then another, a stream of rampaging devils. Dealey slammed the door on them and fell away as their bodies pounded the other side.

They found themselves in a square-shaped room, another doorway opposite, to one side. But as Dealey flashed the light around, they caught sight of a stairway.

"Thank God," breathed Dealey.

They did not linger. Behind them, the door was already cracking, the smell of fresh blood keen in the rats' senses. Although Kate was not heavy, Culver was at exhaustion point. A trail of blood from the stump of her arm followed them to the stairway and formed tiny pools on the steps as they climbed.

They staggered upward and found themselves in a narrow, doorless passageway that extended in both directions.

Squealing, scurrying sounds from below: the rats were in the room they had just left.

The two men chose a direction at random, hurrying along the passage, Culver having to move at an angle to allow room for Kate's inert body. They could hear the mutant animals on the stairs.

So desperate were they that they almost missed the narrow opening. Only a fresh breeze, so different from the stagnant air they had grown used to, halted Culver. He called Dealey back and looked into the opening. He blinked his eyes to make sure. Faint daylight softened the darkness above.

"It's a way out!" Dealey gasped. "Oh, dear God, it's a way out!"

He brushed past Culver and began climbing the stone steps. Culver lowered his burden, supporting Kate in a momentary standing position; he crouched and let her slump over his shoulder. He straightened, an arm clutched around her legs, the other gripping the weapon, and began to climb, the fresh air already beginning to invigorate him, cooling the perspiration that covered his body, the breeze's sweetness a beckoning hand.

The narrow stairway curved around, spiraling up to lead them from the twilight depths into the bright sunlight of another world, a silent shattered landscape that offered little hope, but at least could still give comfort from maleficent darkness.

Panting for breath, they reached a strange-shaped enclosure, its ceiling high, but its gray slab walls close, a heavy wooden door set in one side. The door had a small, metal-strutted opening in its top section, and from there, the sunlight poured in.

Dealey rushed at it and pulled the handle. "It's locked!" he cried in dismay. He grabbed the struts and rattled the door in its frame.

Culver laid Kate on the stone floor and stepped toward the door, unceremoniously thrusting the other man aside. He smashed at the lock with the flat end of the ax. The lock was old, its mechanism stiff with lack of use; the wood around it chipped away and the lock itself soon clattered to the floor. But still the door would not open. It gave a fraction of an inch, but no more. Culver saw a wide but thin bar on the other side.

He stepped back and kicked, and kicked, and kicked. The gap widened, the metal bar bending outward. A short, sharp blow from the ax loosened it completely from its mounting. The door burst open just as they heard scrabbling on the stairway.

"Get her out!" Culver shouted as he positioned himself

at the top of the stairs. He allowed the first rat to reach the top step before he kicked at the open jaws, sending the animal slithering back down again, colliding with those who were just rounding the final bend. The next had its eyes slashed as the blade swept across its thin skull. It reared in the air, falling back with a helpful kick from Culver into those below. It lashed out, squealing its pain, flailing the other rodents with claws and teeth, causing confusion, itself coming under attack from the creatures, blocking the narrow stairway in a melee of furious bodies. Giving Culver time to run through the door and slam it shut.

He foot struck the padlock that had held it closed and sunlight stung his eyes as he desperately looked around for another method of keeping the door shut. He was on a wide stone stairway, the steps rising beyond the small structure he now pressed against. Behind him was the walkway along the Embankment and in the near distance stood the rectangular blockhouse they had used to enter the shelter. Rain-battered litter lay scattered around the steps and walkway, scarves, hats, bags—items discarded by tourists at the first sound of sirens so many weeks before. There was nothing among them that would hold the door closed.

"Culver!" Dealey called from the Embankment wall. "There's a small boat down here. We'll be safe on the river!"

It was a chance. The only chance they had.

"Get Kate onto it," he shouted back. "I'll hold them as long as I can." He could still hear the rats tearing their fellow creatures to pieces inside the small building. Dealey struggled with Kate down the ramp leading to the pleasure-boat jetty, water lapping over onto the landing stage. Culver waited a few moments, giving them time to get aboard the craft there, then pushed himself away from the door, leaping down the steps two at a time. He raced to the ramp and looked back in time to see the door swing open and the rats come surging out.

He ran down to the jetty and looked in dismay at the large, empty pleasure boat still moored there, moving listlessly on the swollen river.

"Over here!" came the shout, and he saw Dealey standing in a smaller boat farther down toward Westminster Bridge. He made for it.

"Cast off!" he called out, aware that the vermin were scampering down the ramp, several leaping through the railings to get at him.

The boat would have accommodated no more than fifteen to twenty people on the benches set around its interior. A tiny white-topped cabin covered the bow, protection against the spray or foul weather for those tourists lucky or quick enough to find a place inside. The boat was already a few feet away from the quayside, drifting lazily out into the current, and Culver had to take a running leap to reach it.

He landed on the small area of deck, sprawling over the engine box and quickly turning to face whatever followed. Two rats leapt at the same time. One just reached the side and tried to clamber over. Culver dislodged it easily with a slashing stroke of the ax. The other had scuffled over onto the bench, jumping from there onto the engine covering. It skidded around to face Culver, hissing venomously.

Culver struck and missed as the quivering animal ran to one side. It came at him as a bundle of powerful, squirming fury, knocking him back onto the bench, renting his face with needlelike claws.

Culver sank down, the weapon falling to the deck. He pushed up and over, using the animal's own momentum. The rat flew over the side, splashing into the muddy water.

Culver was on his feet immediately and at the rudder and gear stick in two quick strides. Kate lay huddled on the deck, her eyes closed, her face white with shock. He knew she would not yet be in pain—the nerve ends had been cut away and shock was its own analgesic—and was relieved to see her arm was now only seeping small amounts of blood.

From the quayside, the vermin plunged into the water and glided toward the drifting craft.

"How do we start it?" Dealey was close to weeping. "There's no key, there's no damned key!"

Culver groaned, his shoulders sagging. There was hardly any mist on the water, although the sun was hazy-bright above, and he could clearly see the sleek black shapes smoothly moving toward them. Given time, he might have been able to open up the engine and bypass the ignition; but there was no time—the lead rats were already sinking their claws into the boat's hull.

He stooped to pick up the ax and spotted the docking pole lying beneath the bench. "Dealey, use that to keep them off. We may get away yet!"

Leaning over the side, Culver swiped at a body in the water. The distance to the water level was frighteningly short, but at least the current was taking them away from the quayside. Red liquid stained the river as the ax found its mark. Dealey had picked up the long, stout pole and was just in time to push back a rat that was clambering over the side. Another appeared in its place and snapped at the pole, sinking its teeth into the wood and refusing to let go. Dealey had to use all his depleted strength to shake the rat off, shoving it under the water.

Meanwhile, other vermin had taken advantage of the struggle. They scrambled up the side of the boat, using their powerful haunches to thrust themselves from the river.

Culver moved backward and forward, never stopping, knowing if he battled with one rat for too long, then others would quickly steal aboard. He thrust, cut, and hacked, his face grim and a part of his mind cold, almost remote from the action. Dealey helped him, his movements more clumsy, less swift.

The river bank grew farther away, but still they came, a skimming black tide of them. The boat was drifting upstream, moving toward the bridge with its missing span on the opposite side of Thames. Beyond, he could see, rising from the river, the peculiar clock face that was the fallen section of the ancient clock tower.

Culver realized that if the current took them fast enough, they might just outdistance the swimming vermin. If only they could keep them off the boat, if only . . .

He froze.

He had looked up, just for a moment, a quick glance at the bridge itself. Black shapes were darting along its balustrade and the pavement below. Many were peering through the ornate moldings. They were lining up above him, bustling, jostling one another for position, readying themselves to drop down on the boat as it passed under the bridge.

34

It was hopeless. They had no control over the small craft as the current lazily carried it toward the bridge. Still warding off boarding vermin, Dealey caught sight of Culver and wondered why the man was not moving, why he was staring ahead of them, oblivious of the danger they were in. He followed the pilot's gaze and he, too, became still.

He could not speak, he could not curse, he could not even weep. Dealey had become too numbed by it all. To survive the holocaust, to struggle through the terrible aftermath, to thwart disaster at every turn—and now this. To be destroyed by creatures that skulked in filth. A bitterly ironic death.

Culver turned, as if to warn him, and saw that he already knew. Something passed between them. A recognition of shared, impending death? That, and something more. A sudden, cognizant touching of spirits, a startling and rare *knowing* of each other. For Dealey, who was and always had been a pragmatist, it was a spontaneous and staggering insight into not just another's psyche, but also into his own, giving an acute awareness of his own being.

Culver sensed the huge bulk of the bridge looming over them, looked up, saw the first of the rats beginning to drop, landing with a splash in the water just ahead. The boat drifted closer. He saw their quivering, excited shapes above, crawling over the buttress near the Embankment, across the supports, poking their bodies through the thick ornamental balustrade and balancing on its broad top.

Impatient, another leapt outward and managed to land slitheringly on top of the pleasure boat's tiny cabin. It glared down at the two men, but did not attack.

Culver raised the ax, holding it across his chest in both hands, ready for the final onslaught. Once the boat was under the bridge, the vermin would fall on them in an avalanche. He prayed the end would be swift.

An eerie silence fell. Their squealing stopped, so did their trembling. It was as before, in the basement chamber, the lair in which the grotesque creature had suckled her young; the vermin had fallen silent then, just before they had gone mad with blood lust. It was about to happen again.

Dealey offered up an unspoken but fervent prayer, and Kate softly moaned, still unconscious.

The rat on the cabin roof watched Culver. Its haunches began to quiver, the unsightly pointed hump above them tensing. It bared its teeth and hissed.

The roaring, whirring sounds came fast, breaking the unnatural quietness with a swiftness that stunned both men and beasts. Over the deafening noise came gunfire and Culver and Dealey watched open-mouthed as chippings sprayed off the old bridge. The vermin scattered. Many were thrown screeching into the water below, bodies rent by bullets. Others leapt into the river for safety, but still the gunfire followed them, spewing tiny, violent fountains, many of those fountains a deep red.

Confused, deafened by the noise, Culver and Dealey

crouched in the boat as it drifted beneath the bridge. Rats fell onto them and once more they were beating them off, the squealing audible now they were beneath the bridge, the roaring above muted. But this time, the vermin were terrified, demented by the sudden turmoil, scuttling around the boat in disarray, those in the river disoriented, swimming in circles.

Daylight dazzled Culver as the boat passed from beneath the bridge. Yet something still blotted out much of the clear blue sky and he could not understand why, could not understand the thunderous roaring.

Dealey was near him, pointing, shouting something, but the other sounds were too great. A rush of wind, a gale-force breeze, rocked the little boat. Culver dragged himself to his feet and staggered, gripping the side of the boat to steady himself. He looked up once more.

"Pumas," he said, the word lost in the whirlwind. He suddenly understood why they had not seen or heard the helicopters before that moment: the tilted hulk of the Big Ben tower had hidden their approach from upriver.

The three helicopters hovered over the river, one close to the boat below, their wheels retracted, their huge blades creating the maelstrom. Two of them hailed down bullets from specially mounted 7.62-mm. general-purpose machine guns onto the bridge and into the river, while the third maneuvered its draft to push the boat with its three human occupants away from the bridge.

The same word kept forming on Dealey's lips: "Incredibleincredibleincredible!"

Culver stumbled over him and grabbed his shoulder. "It's not over yet!" he shouted close to Dealey's ear. "They're still coming aboard! We've got to keep fighting them off!"

As if to prove the point, two rats appeared just in front of them, sliding over the side. The two men acted as one, kicking out at the beasts and sending them toppling back into the water. But more leapt onto the boat, using it as a place of refuge from the rainstorm of lead. Culver and Dealey attacked them before the bedraggled vermin had a chance to recover. There were still too many, though. More and more clambered over onto the benches and deck.

"It's no good, we can't hold them!" Dealey shouted, panic-stricken.

"Get onto the cabin roof!" Culver told him over the roar. The older man awkwardly climbed onto the small roof while Culver picked up the unconscious girl. It was difficult, but Culver managed to pass her up to Dealey, who dragged her to momentary safety. The pilot kicked at three rats as he mounted the box, one managing to grip his jeans and tear off a shred as it fell back into the well of the deck. Culver swung up onto the cabin roof and knelt there, ready to swing at anything that followed.

Dealey, half-sitting because standing would have been too precarious on the rocking boat, tapped Culver's shoulder and pointed.

Culver looked up at the giant shadow that filled the sky above them. A man was being lowered down to them.

Culver thanked God that the Puma helicopters had been fitted with both machine guns and winches. Feet dangled just above their heads, and then the man was down, Culver and Dealey helping to steady him.

"Not a great time for a pleasure-boat ride," the winchman yelled, and saw the two men were too weary to speak. "I can only take one . . ." He noted the rats below, the man with the ax still striking at those trying to reach the cabin roof. "Okay, I can stretch it to two, but we'll have trouble up top! Let's get the girl into the harness!"

They could hardly hear his words, but guessed his meaning. Together they lifted Kate and secured her in the harness loop, the helicopter maintaining a steady hover above them, skillfully following the motion of the boat. "All right, one of you get behind and put your arms around my shoulders! You'll have to hold tight, but we'll soon get you up there!''

Culver indicated for Dealey to do just that. Dealey shook his head.

"You go!" he yelled.

"Don't be bloody stup—'' Culver began to say.

"I don't have the strength to hold on! I'd never make it!''

"Come on, either one of you,'' the winchman shouted impatiently. "One of the other choppers will pick up whoever's left. I'm signaling for lift now before those bloody monsters start chewing my toes!''

Dealey slapped Culver's shoulder and took the ax from him. He even managed a weary smile.

Culver barely had his arms gripped over the winchman's shoulders before a thumb was offered skyward and their feet left the cabin roof. They soared up, moving rapidly and steadily away from the boat. He looked down anxiously and held his breath when he saw the black shapes swarming onto the white roof. Dealey was standing, swinging the short ax with both hands, knocking the vermin aside, sweeping them overboard or back down onto the deck. But for every one ejected, another took its place. He saw Dealey's ever-diminishing figure go rigid with pain as his thigh was bitten into. Another rat scurried up his back, forcing him to reach behind to dislodge it, the weapon falling from his grasp.

"Dealey!" Culver shouted uselessly.

The second Puma swooped in, a winchman already swinging at the end of the wire. His feet never touched the cabin roof; he scooped up the blood-soaked man and pulled the rat from his back all in one movement. They swung away from the craft, two black forms still clinging to Dealey's legs. Their own weight sent the rats crashing back into the river, flesh and material stretching, then parting under the pressure. Culver closed his eyes as the two figures were winched upward. The third helicopter hovered low, using up its ammunition on the vermin. Gunfire ravaged the boat and the mutant rats that filled it, and when the bullets burst through its fragile hull, reaching the fuel tank, the little craft exploded into a thousand pieces. Culver opened his eyes in time to see the pall of black smoke billow up into the air, a miniature replica of the explosions that had destroyed the city so long, so very long ago.

Reaching hands helped them into the helicopter, Culver hauled in first, then the girl, the winchman climbing in last.

Culver was quickly guided to a seat and he sank down gratefully into the cool shade. The big door slid shut, the interior of the helicopter still noisy but less than before. He watched as Kate was carefully lifted into a fixed cot stretcher and another officer, a medic, he assumed, examined the stump of her arm. The man did not even flinch; he had obviously treated worse injuries during the past few weeks. From a case, he swiftly took out a small vial, which he broke open to extract a Syrette. Expertly and without cutting away her jeans, he plunged the needle into a muscle in Kate's thigh, holding the Syrette there for a few seconds while its fluid drained. He noticed Culver watching.

"Morphia," he explained. "She's lucky we got to her before she came out of shock. Don't worry, she's going to be okay—it looks like a clean severance. I'll dress it and release the tourniquet for a while. Does she have any other wounds?"

Culver shook his head, tiredness beginning to overtake him. "Cuts, scrapes, that's all. Oh, yeah"—he remembered—"we've been exposed to pneumonic plague."

The medic raised his eyebrows in surprise. "Okay, I'll give her a quick once-over. How about you? Need some sedation?"

Again Culver shook his head. He gazed at Kate's wan

face, its lines softened already as the drug began to take effect; he wanted to go to her, comfort her, beg her forgiveness for what he had had to do, but she would not hear. There would be time later. He knew there would be much more time for both of them. He turned away, looking at the tiny windows in the door, the hazy blue beyond. Another face appeared before him: the winchman.

"Flight Sergeant MacAdam," he introduced himself.

Culver found it difficult to speak. "Thanks," he finally said.

"Pleasure," came the reply.

"How . . . ?"

"You were spotted early this morning."

"The plane?"

The winchman nodded. "We thought you might have been from government HQ. Were you?"

"No . . . no, we were trying to get into . . . into it."

The man looked keenly interested. "Did you manage to? Christ, we've had no word from headquarters since this whole bloody mess started. What the hell happened down there?"

"Didn't . . . didn't anyone get out?"

"Not a bloody soul. And nobody could get to the HQ from the outside—all the main tunnels are down. Those bastards hit us harder than anyone expected. Some of the survivors may have got out of the city. Who knows? We haven't been able to search, first because of fallout, and then the freak rainstorms. We've been patroling this stretch of river ever since word got back that your party had been seen. But there was supposed to be more of you. Where're the others?"

"Dead," Culver said flatly, thinking of those who had escaped the Kingsway shelter as well. He suddenly remembered Ellison. In the dark, weaponless. Inside the shelter. "All dead," he reaffirmed.

"But what did you find down there? What was inside?"

The medical officer intervened. "Let him rest, Sergeant. He can be questioned when we get him back to Cheltenham.''

The winchman still looked questioningly at him.

"Rats," Culver said. "Nothing but big bloody rats."

MacAdam's face was grim. "We've heard stories—"

"People managed to get out of London?"

"Oh, yeah, plenty got out."

Culver sank farther back into the seat. "But where to? What to?"

The winchman's face was still grim, but it held a humorless smile. "It isn't quite as bad as you obviously think. The lunacy was stopped, you see, stopped before everything was destroyed. Sure, the main capitals are gone, the industrial cities, many of the military bases; but total destruction was brought to an abrupt halt when the separate powers realized the mistake—"

"Sergeant," the medic warned.

"What mistake?" Culver asked.

"You rest now; you need it. We'll soon have you back at base, where you'll be taken care of. You'll find it's still chaotic, but some order is beginning to return under military rule. And they say a new coalition government's about to be formed any time." The sergeant stood, patting Culver's shoulder. "You take it easy." He turned to go.

"Who started it?" Culver shouted after him. "Who started the fucking war? America or Russia?"

He wasn't sure if he heard right, the noise of the rotor blades almost drowning the reply. It sounded like "China."

The winchman was standing at the cockpit opening, the same humorless smile on his face. Culver thought he heard him say, "Of course, there isn't much left of it anymore."

Culver returned his gaze to the small windows, eager for their light, surprised, but too weary to be further shocked. The gloom of the Puma's interior depressed him; there had been too many sunless days. His mind roamed back, seeing images, scenes he would never be free of.

And he thought of the final irony. The slaying of those who had long before plotted out their own survival while others would perish, choiceless and without influence. The slaying of a weakened master species by a centuries-repressed creature that could only inhabit the dark under-world; mankind's natural, sneaking enemy, who had always possessed cunning, but now that cunning—and their power—enhanced by an unnatural cause. He thought of the giant, black-furred rats with their deadly weapons—their teeth, their claws, their strength. And again, their cunning. He thought of the even more loath-some bloated, sluglike creatures, brethren to and leaders of the black, monsters of the same hideous spawn. And he thought of the Mother Creature—and of her tiny off-spring.

The medic, intent on treating the girl's wound, glanced around in surprise when he heard the man laughing. He began to quickly prepare a sedative when he noticed tears flowing down Culver's face.

The government headquarters had been attacked so fe-rociously because the black rats had believed their queen to be under threat. The poor fools had been wiped out as soon as the shelter became occupied, the mutant vermin disturbed by the terrible sounds of bombs, alarmed at the sudden invasion. The onslaught had been instant and merciless. It was all too ironic. And the greatest irony of all was the Mother Creature's children. The little crea-tures who fed at her breasts.

He wiped a shivering hand across his eyes as if to wipe out the vision. He and Fairbank had been distraught with the discovery. Through their shock, the possibilities had assailed them, the implications had terrified them.

For the small, newborn creatures had resembled human—*human!*—embryos. They had claws, the beginnings of scaly tails, the same wicked, slanting eyes and the humped backs. But their skulls were more like the skulls of man, their features were those of grotesque, freakish humans. Their arms and their legs were not those of animals. And their brains, seen clearly through their tissue-thin craniums and transparent skin, were too large to belong to a rat.

Culver's shoulders shuddered with the laughing. Had mankind been created in the same way, through an explosion of radiation, genes changed in a way that caused them to evolve into walking, thinking, upright creatures? Another dreadfully funny notion: had mankind not evolved from the ape, as the theorists thought, but instead from these other foul creatures? And had that same course of evolvement been unleashed once again?

He wanted to stop laughing, but he could not. And neither could he control the tears. It drained him; it nauseated him. And presently someone was leaning over him, aiming a needle, anxious to release him from the hysteria.

The rats went back.

They swam to the Embankment and leapt from the water, black skins glistening in the bright sunlight. Others, those on the bridge, ran squealing from the thunderous, death-dealing creature in the sky. They gathered in the open, trembling, confused by the violence against them and by the loss of the beasts below who had ruled them. And something else was gone. The Mother Creature and her strange litter, the new alien breed that the black rats had yearned to destroy, for they were not of their kind, no longer existed. The difference of these newborn was beyond understanding and had sent fear coursing through the black mutants.

But they had not been allowed to kill them. The Mother Creature was all-powerful, controlling their will, ruling them and allowing no dissent. Her own special guard had dealt with those who rebelled. And the guard had been felled by the sickness.

Still the rats had protected their matriarch, governed and conditioned by her thoughts. Now those thoughts were no longer in their heads. And their numbers had grown small.

They returned to the gloomy underworld, safe there below the ground, away from the sun. They soon found the human who hid among them in the darkness, his burbling anguish—his smell of pungent fear—drawing them to him. They scratched on the door he hid behind. Then began to gnaw at the wood. They took pleasure in his screams.

When there was nothing left of him, they roamed the dark tunnels, content to stay, to rest, to procreate.

When they were hungry, they left the dank, ever-nocturnal underworld, silently creeping into the open where the night sky and fresh breezes soothed them. They slithered among the rubble of the old city, seeking sustenance and easily finding it.

And only when the first haze of dawn broke did they slink back into the holes, back into the tunnels below, reluctant to leave this new, free territory. This new world that was to become their domain.

ABOUT THE AUTHOR

James Herbert was born in London's East End on April 8, 1943, the son of Petticoat Lane Street traders. A former art director of a leading London advertising agency, Mr. Herbert is now a full-time writer. He is the author of THE RATS, THE FOG, THE SURVIVOR, FLUKE, LAIR, THE SPEAR, THE DARK, THE JONAH, and SHRINE, all available in Signet editions.

Mr. Herbert now lives in the United Kingdom with his wife and two young daughters.